SONGS OF THE
LOST ISLANDS

SONGS
OF THE
LOST ISLANDS

Part One

AN ACT OF FAITH

SACD Catalogue record: 000178361 – 28/04/2016

Book's cover and portraits:
Virginie Carquin - Brussels, Belgium

Heraldry, genealogy and maps:
Sylvain Sauvage - La Tour-de-Peilz, Switzerland

Editorial correction:
Thomas Bailey - Oxford, UK

Editorial review:
Laurent Chasseau - Bristol, UK

Songs of the Lost Islands existing publications

- An Act of Faith - May 2019

- The Lonely Seeker - June 2019

- The Valley of Nargrond - July 2019

Forthcoming publication

- Two Winged Lions (2021)

Biography

C. A. Oliver was born in 1971 and spent his youth between Oxford and Bordeaux. From an early age, he was an avid reader of both the English and French canons, and it was J.R.R. Tolkien and Maurice Druon who would come to influence his writing above all others.

In his teenage years, Oliver and four friends began a tabletop role-playing game. Fifteen years later, after 3,500 hours of discussion, imagination and strategy, what began as a game had developed into an entire universe. As gamemaster, Oliver documented the gargantuan campaign's progress.

This fantasy world lay dormant for several years. Then, in 2014, after witnessing uncanny parallels with real-world politics, Oliver began to forge *Songs of the Lost Islands*, a 12-part fantasy series that draws heavily on the fifteen-year campaign. He started writing the first trilogy at Sandfield Road in Oxford, the very street on which Tolkien once lived. It was concluded at Rue Alexandre Dumas in Saint-Germain-en-Laye, where Dumas composed *The Three Musketeers*.

C. A. Oliver now lives between Paris and Rio de Janeiro, having married a Brazilian academic. *Songs of the Lost Islands* has been above all inspired by what Oliver knows best: the ever-changing winds of global politics, the depth and scope of English fantasy; and the fragile, incomprehensible beauty of his wife's homeland.

ISBN: 9781072132578
Legal deposit: May 2019

Acknowledgements

It has taken me five years to write the first three instalments of *Songs of the Lost Islands*. But developing the world that is the basis for these books was an even longer process.

It is now thirty years since I first joined forces with four of my closest friends to devise the world of the series. It began in the summer of 1989 with the creation of an RPG wargame campaign, in which different Elvin civilizations fought for the control of a distant archipelago. The arrival of Curwë and his companions in Llafal, an Elvin port on the island of Nyn Llyvary, marked the starting point of a story that would go on to last decades.

For the first twenty-three years, we had no intention of sharing these myths, legends and adventures with anyone outside our tight-knit group. It was a secret garden, or perhaps rather a dragon's lair, rich with treasures built up over 3,500 hours of gameplay. No intruder ever broke their way into our various dungeons: the garage of 37 Domaine de Hontane, near Bordeaux; a cramped bedroom in Oxford; and a flat in Arcachon, with a beautiful sea view we never found time to enjoy.

After the campaign had drawn to a close, the years went by and I found that I was missing the thrill of those night-time gatherings: the smell of smoke, the taste of wine and, above all, the noise of the rolling dice.

I therefore eventually gathered the material accumulated over all those years of frenetic creativity, and soon realized that I possessed enough content for twelve books. The distinctive nature of this story lies in its genesis: characters, embodied by players, interacting with plots and settings developed by the game master. Outcomes were decided by applying a set of specific wargame rules, the authority of which was unquestionable.

The result was quite stunning: a fifteen-year long campaign made up of dozens of characters, whose destinies were determined by both the roll of the multifaceted dice and the choices made by the players.

Much to my surprise, the first readers of *An Act of Faith* were very enthusiastic in their responses, and eager to discover what would follow. Some were fascinated by Roquen or Curwë, others resonated naturally with the more reckless Irawenti, while the more aesthetically minded readers were attracted to the Llewenti.

My mind was made up. I embarked on a quest to complete the twelve-book series.

When I started, I had no idea how complex it would be to forge *Songs of the Lost Islands* from all the material I had before me. I now look in utter fascination at the copies of *An Act of Faith*, *The Lonely Seeker* and *The Valley of Nargrond* sitting on my desk and feel relatively confident that the remaining tomes will follow. The debts of gratitude that I owe are therefore very significant.

Firstly, I must thank my beloved family: Mathilde, Marion and Agatha, who probably think me mad, but who nevertheless continue to provide their unwavering support.

I am enormously grateful to the scholars who have helped me negotiate the pitfalls of writing fantasy: Eric Train and Laurent Chasseau read the first drafts of the *Songs* and provided me with their insightful responses and suggestions. Their feedback was invaluable, not least because their passion for the Lost Islands dates all the way back to 1989.

The series could not have been written without Thomas Bailey, a gifted poet who studied at Oxford University, whose expertise and enthusiasm turned a manuscript into the finished article.

I am also extremely grateful to Virginie Carquin and Sylvain Sauvage for wonderfully designing and illustrating the Lost Islands, that last refuge of the Elves. Their prodigious efforts gave me the strength to push ahead, at a time when I was finally waking up to the full scale of the challenge before me.

Virginie is illustrating all twelve books of *Songs of the Lost Islands*. She has produced a series of twenty-three portraits of characters in the novels. Her work also features on the covers of the collectors' editions.

Sylvain has served as chief concept designer for the Lost Islands' world. His achievements include creating the maps of Oron, the genealogy of the clans and houses, and all their emblems and insignia. His overall contribution to the project is even more far-reaching; it includes, among many other things, designing the series' website.

Lastly, I must thank the readers of *Songs of the Lost Islands*, for already making it through more than a thousand pages of stories and legends about the Elves. As Feïwal dyn puts it:

"The quest for the Lost Islands is a journey that cannot offer any hope of return. It is a leap in the unknown. It is an act of faith."

TABLE OF CONTENTS

CHAPTER 1: dyn Filweni

'I am sinking... The tide is too strong. I will be cast upon the rocks.'

'Hold my hand!'

'A cry in the water! Where is his hand?'

'Hold my hand Filwen!'

'Ah! I can't grasp it! We came so close! All that effort, just to die on the cliffs of the Lost Islands!'

'Hold my hand Filwen!'

'Too late! Farewell my friend! I am sinking... but... why did you call me Filwen? Filwen is not my name! Filwen is my ancestor! I am Feïwal dyn Filweni...'

"Feïwal, Wake up! Feïwal!"

A familiar voice called insistently.

"Wake up! You had a bad dream! Wake up! Of course, you are Feïwal! Just as I am Nelwiri!"

Feïwal opened his eyes, gasping for breath. The lively face of his younger brother emerged gradually in front of him.

"There is news! Excellent news! We have finally left the Sea of Cyclones behind us! I believe we made it! We achieved what Father could not," Nelwiri rejoiced.

Feïwal remained unresponsive at the news.

"Now there lie two fates before us. Either we shall make history, or we shall die, swallowed by the Austral Ocean, without a single witness to sing our glorious feat," declared Nelwiri, his voice trembling with joyful excitement.

"May Gweïwal Uleydon[1] protect us!" was the only answer Feïwal could muster, as he struggled to wake up and recover from the trauma of his recurring nightmare.

The two Elves set off walking, side by side, along the railing. They preferred the soaked ship's deck, even though it was relentlessly pitching and yawing in the sea, to their small cabins. It was as if the dawn would never come. They looked with fear and weariness to the rows of black waves, topped with crests of foam, rolling endlessly toward the south.

The enthusiasm of their departure had waned, consumed by the monotony of days aboard that had elapsed in an endless routine, where any sailor's activity was but another link in the chain of perpetual repetition. Wandering this vast ocean knew no end. Their existence marched on, slowly, through sapphire sky and emerald water.

Their words were scattered by the wind into the darkness of early dawn.

Feïwal muttered, "What have I done, Nelwiri?"

"What do you mean?" inquired his brother, with a tone of imperceptible worry.

"What have I done? How did it come to this?"

"The crossing to the Lost Islands is a relentless ordeal. This is what the ancient writings tell us," Nelwiri assured.

---

1 Gweïwal Uleydon: Greater God of oceans, divinity of seas, rivers and waters

"We will never return. I feel it in the wind. A mighty force is now at work, draing us inescapably towards the south. Gone are the days of Essawylor[2], blown away by the ocean wind like clouds in the sky. We will never return, I know it now and it fills me with dread," Feïwal declared.

"Why would we care to go back? Filwen and his sons never returned. We will cross the ocean. Such was our vow. It has always been our clan's high purpose to discover that haven of the Llewenti [3]beyond the Austral Ocean."

"A cursed fate for those doomed to sail the ocean endlessly. Now we shall witness whether Feïwal dyn Filweni is the great navigator that he pretends to be."

"Feïwal, you are the most experienced sailor amongst us. You led us beyond the Sea of Cyclones. No one has achieved such a feat in centuries, not even our father."

"Father was reckless and unthinking. He was impervious to doubt and heedless to our responsibility for others. His only obsession was to honour our vow and cross the ocean, whatever the cost. How many times did he embark upon that extraordinary journey to reach those islands from which no Elf has ever returned? What do you suppose he felt when his ship disappeared at sea, to the atolls Fadalwy wide? What do you suppose he was thinking as he saw his companions die before they were swallowed by the Austral Ocean? I know the guilt he felt in that moment, for it remains heavy in my thoughts as well," Feïwal replied.

Nelwiri became insistent. "Father pushed our dangerous quest to new bounds. He left us a considerable legacy. He bequeathed to us the most comprehensive maps and the most accomplished crews to conquer the ocean. That I know. He would be proud to see us sail in the wake of our ancestors."

Feïwal was hesitant. "His inheritance is a difficult burden to bear. I was bestowed with an honour that demands great responsibility. The quest to discover the Lost Islands is no common ordeal. It is consuming my strength."

Nelwiri reminded his elder brother. "I was so proud that day you were proclaimed Guide of our clan and entrusted with the sacred book of the Llewenti queen."

---

2 Essawylor: 'Woods of the five rivers' in lingua Irawenti. This vast Elvin kingdom is in the northern hemisphere of the Mainland by the tropical shores of the Austral Ocean.

3 Llewenti: 'The Green Elves' in all Elvin tongues

"Son of Filwen, the Ancient and the First," Feïwal muttered barely audibly, as he recalled the last words of the ritual.

"You have no responsibility for what will come to pass. Each of us chose our fate. We are making history, no less," answered Nelwiri.

The conversation was interrupted by the sound of a bell chiming eight times, heralding the end of another shift. Soon the fuss made by those preparing to relieve their companions could be heard. There was no lack of vigilance on this vessel. Night and day, sailors took the watch. Two equal groups of Elves formed the crew. They were called lines, as the two equipages slept on opposite sides of the ship. Every eight hours, they took turns on the deck. One full line was required to manoeuvre the vessel. Only Feïwal, the captain, had the authority to summon both lines together for particularly difficult manoeuvres.

A few weeks had passed since their departure from the kingdom of Essawylor. As they had crossed over that invisible boundary separating the world's two hemispheres, the crew had celebrated the ritual of the Nen[4], in hope and in joy. That night, the songs had been beautiful. They had gathered between the foremast and mainmast to celebrate the beauty of Cil, the Elvin star of the West and the symbol of hope for all Elves that shines so brightly upon those crossing the Nen. Since then, they had wandered the oceanic desert, fruitlessly trying to circumvent the Sea of Cyclones. Many moons had passed; weariness had succeeded joy, doubt and apprehension had followed.

Elves crossed the deck in silence. The ship's crew was composed exclusively of experimented sailors. Each one had been selected with care. They knew the tropical seas surrounding Essawylor well. They had chosen to abandon their homes, to search for new territories, despite the peril, or perhaps because of it.

Some were too exhausted to express their joy at the prospect of some hard-earned rest; others were already focused on the tasks awaiting them. Joyful effusions usually formed an integral part of their culture; that day, however, few were light of heart, though many exchanged ritual signs to ward off sea spirits and protect their companions. A new bond seemed woven between the members of the crew since they had crossed the Sea of

---

4 Nen: 'Imaginary line marking the equator' in lingua Irawenti

Cyclones. During the journey, they had endured the scorching heat, torrential rain and lashing wind. They had managed to overcome their fear and coordinate manoeuvres, even when faced with inevitable prospect of being swallowed by black mountainous waterspouts. Only then had they realized the full extent of the warning that Feïwal had given to the youngest amongst them before they had departed.

"No Irawenti[5] can claim to be a sailor before he has wandered the Sea of Cyclones."

Irawenti meant 'Blue Elves' in their language. While their skin was dull, their eyes were the colour of tropical seas, and azure reflections emanated from their black hair. These Elves descended from clans who had first wandered freely the East of the world, before settling in the tropical forests by the shores of the Austral Ocean. Their domain was Essawylor, at the centre of the Mainland, along the banks of the five rivers.

These sailors belonged for the clear majority to the clan of Filweni. It was not the most influential, nor the richest in the kingdom, but from that line descended ingenious shipwrights and triumphant navigators. Fierce characters they were, who always remained independent, mainly known for their great devotion to Gweïwal Uleydon, the God of the Seas and Lord of the Waters.

Long ago, the clan founder, Filwen the Ancient, along with his sons, had built the greatest ships ever seen on those waters, to sail south and cross the ocean. No news of that lost fleet had ever reached the shores of Essawylor, but the Filweni had ever since perpetuated a love of the ocean. Each of them shared a bond that other Elves could never understand. They all heard, in their youth, the call of the sea, and made the irreversible choice to pursue their greatest dream. The wave-tossed surface of the ocean pulled relentlessly at their heartstrings. They shared with their ancestors an attraction to mystery and exploration. The challenges, the hardships and the possibility of death represented, in their eyes, the ultimate victory, the triumph of faith over fear. The Filweni were not conquerors motivated by

5 Irawenti: 'Blue Elves' in lingua Irawenti

greed and power but explorers who were eager to defeat the vastness of the ocean. In their veins flowed the blood of the most capable sailors a navigator could ever hope command.

Feïwal dyn Filweni was their captain. He was a dyn[6], a noble among his clan who descended from the warlords who had conquered Essawylor and were granted a land to rule and a shore from which to worship Gweïwal Uleydon. The clan of Filweni's guide shared the instinct of those rare sailors who knew how to make sense of the tiniest changes in the colour of water, the sudden acceleration of currents, the migration of certain species of fish or the flight of migratory birds. Life on the ship largely depended upon him. His crew repaired the damage caused by bad weather, refitted spars and rigging. He also commanded the various crafts represented on the ship: carpenters, blacksmiths, weavers and ropers. Feïwal was also the shipwright who had designed the Alwïryan[7], the largest ship of the Essawylor fleet. This achievement was a tribute to the legendary vessel of his ancestor, Filwen, of whom Feïwal was a worthy heir. It was the result of years of study and research.

The Alwïryan now traced its way through the Austral Ocean, heading south. Strong marine currents were drawing it irresistibly towards the infinite south. Never in recent history had a ship from the kingdom of Essawylor strayed so far from its shores.
Almost three hundred Elves were aboard the Alwïryan. Artisans or sailors, all of them possessed that dual obsession for freedom and for exploration.
The vessel was their only kingdom and ultimate refuge. They worshipped it as a deity and cherished it like a precious steed. Beautiful, elegant and powerful, the Alwïryan was one hundred and thirty-foot-long and twenty-foot-wide. Most of its power stemmed from its eighty oars, yet two masts supplemented the great ship's speed and manoeuvrability. Its triangular sails could navigate the high seas, and, when faced with heavy storms and headwinds, its rowers could take to the deck. Its two collapsible masts reduced its air resistance during storms. From the top of the masts, the sailors could look out over the sea from a height

---

6 dyn: 'Descendant of' in lingua Irawenti. The word is used to identify a Blue Elf of noble blood.

7 Alwïryan: 'Bird of the seas' in lingua Irawenti

of one hundred feet. They had built this marine animal with the exotic wood from the silver trees found on the shores of Essawylor. Its rigging weighed more than the royal forge, and its lanyards, laid end-to-end, stretched out for more than half a mile. Thanks to the hull's shallow draught and the great height of its keel, this magnificent vessel could face the open sea sure of its ability to overcome most dangers.

Feïwal had chosen the most direct and the most dangerous course towards the Fadalwy Atolls, those desolate islands at the heart of the Sea of Cyclones which had been named after his father. He was following the flight of migratory birds, retracing the path taken by his ancestors.

The route through the East would have meant confronting the vastness of the Sunrise Ocean, the dwelling of Gweïwal Uleydon, God of the Seas. That crossing would have been much longer and there was always danger for a ship in unknown waters. The ancient texts prohibited navigation through the domain of the almighty sea god. None among the Blue Elves would dare to defy the word of their most revered divinity. The few sailors who had taken this route and returned had reported strange tales of enchanting mist and bewitching songs that intoxicated the mind and induced a lethal stupor.

The western way would have meant a long, dangerous coasting along the rugged shore of the endless equatorial steppe of the Anroch Desert. In those inhospitable regions, there was no hope of replenishing food or water, and the threat of barbarian warships was omnipresent. No explorer had ever returned from those maritime kingdoms, a vast mosaic of human tribes equally disparate and warlike.

But that night, Feïwal was beset with terrifying dreams, nightmares, and, despite the good news that his brother had delivered, Feïwal knew these dreams to be bad omens. His mood was dark, his gaze full of worry and concern. Checking the position of every single sailor in his crew, he crossed the deck in silence. He noticed that no one was talking, no one was singing. Only the northern breeze blowing into the sails could be heard that morning.

"Today is the 290th day of 2542, by Essawylor's reckoning, or year 2200 of the Second Age, as the High Elves would call it," proclaimed Nelwiri decisively, with his usual good humour as he turned to a fresh page of the ship's log.

"It is the 98th day of our navigation. Let us hope there will be many more to come," he added sardonically, to cheer his brother.

"You should not mock the gods, son of Fadalwy! You should know better after all the deaths we've had to mourn!" harshly replied the captain of the ship.

"Siw[8]! I would not dare have such a thought, but you will permit me, I hope, to enjoy this north-westerly breeze, which is gently pushing the Alwïryan towards our glorious future. Let me note down our position and speed. Do you see how powerful the ocean's current is today? It's certainly unusual; almost unnatural, I'd say."

Nelwiri stood on the elegant aftcastle of the ship, on a slightly elevated walkway, which allowed him to look over the lower deck and stand just beside his brother. He held the helm with a firm hand as they headed south. From time to time, he glanced at the wind rune, one of the clan's most sacred relics, which was placed in front of him to help him stay on course. But his attention was mainly focused on monitoring the wind and the sails. Too swollen, they could tear, and even break the yards. If they deflated and beat against the mast, the ship would lose pace.

Nelwiri had a connection with the Alwïryan, as if he were the only link between the hull and the rigging. This was a hard task, and one which he rarely abandoned. Only Gyenwë, another renowned marine pilot, replaced him for a few hours each night. Nelwiri was a true Filweni who, amid the boundless space of the ocean, lived fully, marvelling endlessly at the glorious days, the exquisite nights and spectacular sunsets. He was revered by all for his knowledge of the ocean and famous for his numerous heroic feats onboard. He inspired the rest of the crew with his bold deeds and unflinching bravery. Tall and thin for a Blue Elf, he was an incomparable ship master, despite his apparent playful recklessness.

★

---

8 Siw: Interjection meaning 'Holy star' in lingua Irawenti

Nelwiri noticed that the clan's two other dyn were about to join them on the aftcastle.

"Today, we will have our council earlier than usual; Luwir and Arwela are joining us. They look concerned too. I trust they could not get much rest and they are eager to discuss our options."

A beautiful, elegant Irawenti lady climbed the stairs first, dressed in light blue robes, her long dark hair flowing in the wind. Her name was Arwela dyn Filweni. She was the elder sister of Feïwal and Nelwiri, considered by many to be the wisest of her people, skilled in healing and in the reading of the stars. She was a rare and precious figure onboard, for few practitioners of her art ventured on the open seas. Love for her brothers and her commitment to the clan's quest had driven her on this long and perilous voyage. She made use of her considerable learning, and her deep understanding of the sailors' souls, to ward off bad fortune and to inspire hope.

Luwir dyn Filweni followed her. A robust Elf with a severe expression, he was considered one of the ancients among the clan. The arms of Essawylor, on his silver helmet, were a reminder of his prestige as commander in the army of the kingdom. Luwir was the most experienced fighter but onboard he was known as the oars master. Rowing a ship with a multitude of oarlocks required a great deal of skill and coordination and his crew was composed of highly trained specialists. He knew how to inspire his rowers to work harder and longer without pushing them beyond their limits. That morning, however, his mood was dark. Concern was etched into his face.

"May Gweïwal Uleydon protect us today and in all days to come," Luwir began with the Irawenti ritual salutations as he moved to grasp each of his kin with affection.

The Blue Elves called this warm-hearted form of greetings 'Abriwa[9]' and it illustrated the genuine cordial relationships among them.

---

9 Abriwa: 'Hug' in lingua Irawenti

"I brought the inventory with me. We have important matters to discuss," he declared.

"Abriwa! Luwir, and good day to you too," replied Nelwiri ironically, his look showing that he had already anticipated what the discussion would be about.

Luwir ignored him and drew the book from his bag awkwardly. He always dressed for war no matter the circumstances, wearing a brass breastplate and an iron helm. The old Elf opened the book where lists of all the ship's furniture, supplies and materials were kept.

"I estimate that we have no more than thirty days of supplies and water left," he stressed in a deep voice, pausing emphatically. "Today is probably our last opportunity to turn back and return to Essawylor."

Feïwal did not respond, his gaze fixed on the horizon. Arwela intervened.

"It would be wise, Feïwal. The crew's morale is very low. Our sailors are weary and exhausted, and I fear that they will soon start to despair. They have been at sea for almost a hundred days. Let us go back and restore hope among them," she insisted.

Still Feïwal did not respond.

"Every day, when tending to the wounded, I am bombarded with desperate questions that I do not know how to answer. I try to find words of hope. I struggle with all my strength against the pernicious influence of those cursed sea spirits which plague us. This trip is one long embrace with waves and hail. Small wonder that Irawenti ships have not ventured this far south before," she continued.

Seeing that Feïwal remained indifferent to their case, Luwir made a last attempt to convince his captain.

"Returning home is not a defeat. It is honourable, Feïwal. Siw! We have learnt a great deal. We can come back next year with more experience and better preparation. We now have maps to cross the rocky isles in the Sea of Cyclones. We have lost many days trying to circumnavigate them. Our next attempt will be considerably easier. I say we go back; we can make it in less than sixty days.

Cil Cim Cir[10]!!! We can return home if we start to ration out the crew today. This is our last chance, Feïwal."

To his astonishment, the ship's captain replied in an unusually harsh tone.

"It is not so. The dyn Filweni are no merchants. They do not succumb to sickness of the mind or fatigue of the body after a few days at sea. The dyn Filweni demonstrate incredible bravery and resolve. They can endure hardships and perils for months when they are onboard the Alwïryan.

Do you know why?"

None of them dared to answer; they all understood that the decision had already been made in Feïwal's mind. They would sail until the end of the voyage.

"We, dyn Filweni, have a greater purpose. We have a responsibility to others for we are the keepers of the book of Queen Llyoriane. We are the legatees of her message. Before it is too late, we must find the Lost Islands of the Llewenti, that last haven of the Elves. Only the greatness of our ideal can match our intransigence," concluded the guide of the clan, his voice trembling with uncontained emotion.

To the ears of Arwela and Luwir, this prophetic plea sounded like a condemnation. A long silence followed.

"I suppose this long tirade closes the debate... and we now have the time to address other issues. There are a number of tasks that require our attention," Nelwiri finally offered, to reduce the tension.

_____

10 Cil Cim Cir: 'With the stars' favour', oral expression in lingua Irawenti

Their attention, however, was suddenly caught by the deck's trap door opening. From the bowels of the ship emerged a group of Hawenti[11], as they were called in the language of the Blue Elves.

Fair to behold, this group of High Elves were heavily armoured with plates, shields and long swords. Pale skinned with fine and beautiful features, tall and proud in their bearings, they stood a whole head taller than the common Blue Elves. Despite their slim build, they looked as strong and robust as they appeared agile and quick.

The oldest and greatest of all civilisations, the High Elves were extremely graceful and noble, for they were counted among the greatest and most powerful race in the whole world and their actions had shaped history wherever they dwelt. Considered immortal, they did not die of old age for time had no effect on them. Only violent death was offered to them to depart from life.

A tall knight led them, his head shaven, his chainmail as dark as his eyes. Four of his guards followed him, with a cold and haughty air. Two of his companions, his bard and his councillor brought up the rear.

Every day at dawn, the same ritual sparring matches would begin: a storm of blows, shouts and wounds to entertain the eyes of the sailors. It lasted the full morning. The knight would participate in this exercise to the point of exhaustion, combating four guards at the same time. The bard was playing the same fighting tune with his harp, repeatedly, obsessively, as though he was trying to exorcise a sick curse from the past. The duty of the High Elves aboard this ship was not to navigate, but to fight.

The knight was of high lineage, a Dol[12] lord from Essawylor, heir to one of the most powerful houses of the Kingdom of the Five Rivers. Roquen Dol Lewin was his name: a great Elf, strong, robust and righteous, an imposing figure with a severe-looking face. It was difficult to determine his age, as he was young for the force that he could muster and yet his natural authority gave him the command of an elder.

---

11   Hawenti: 'High Elves' in lingua Irawenti
12   Dol: 'Most noble scion of' in lingua Hawenti

Around fifty High Elves formed the rest of his retinue, prepared to deal with any onslaught from a hostile ship. They were part of the inner circle of the House Dol Lewin's followers, and all were formidable fighters who had survived countless battles defending the kingdom of Essawylor's northern border. They now formed the Unicorn Guard, attached exclusively to the service of Roquen Dol Lewin. Although they were certainly not accomplished sailors, their fanatical devotion to their lord had driven them to set out upon this journey, beset as it was with all manner of dangers. A commander named Maetor led them.

★

Feïwal considered this group for a while, his gaze fixed on their lord. Memories came flooding back to him.

"I do not like them," declared his sister Arwela aggressively as she stepped forward. She was not accustomed to displaying her emotions in such a manner, but she had decided to seize this opportunity to challenge her brother's authority and blame him for his stubbornness.

"I know," Feïwal replied coolly.

"I do not like their arrogance," she went on, "The bard Curwë acts like a flamboyant figure. He dresses in the finest silk even whilst onboard the ship, to mark his difference."

"Curwë is loyal. He is filled with passion for exploration. He will be a valuable friend. I asked him to record a reliable account of our journey. It will be a significant contribution to our quest," defended her brother.

"Siw! All of them behave contemptuously towards our kin. They shirk away from their fair share of the workload. They drink our water and eat our supplies. I cannot understand why we have troubled ourselves with them. They are a burden which will prove increasingly cumbersome," added Luwir, who shared Arwela's feelings towards the High Elves.

"The House of Dol Lewin is a most honourable family and a formidable force in battle. They paid for the peace of Essawylor with their blood. They defended the northern border from the incursions of the desert hordes. They protected our clan over many centuries. We owe them our help," Feïwal replied.

"Yet, at the height of their splendour, there were rumours of conspiracy against the Queen Aranaele, whisperings that that they wanted to increase their growing power even further," Arwela retorted.

"Since when does my beloved sister pay attention to rumours from the royal court, from that serpents' nest?" Feïwal asked, still defensive.

"I do not. But how do you consider the young lord's counsellor, that Aewöl? He is no common High Elf. He does not belong to the House of Dol Lewin. I was told that his servant is counted among the Night Elves, those who prefer the shadows to the shining light."

"I have known Aewöl for a long time. He always demonstrated support for our clan and for all our expeditions. He has studied the ancient writings of the Llewenti Queen Llyoriane and believes in the existence of the lost archipelago. It is Aewöl who convinced Roquen Dol Lewin and his retainers to join us. We can trust him. We will need his lore."

Arwela was unconvinced.

"Trust them if you will. I do not like the thirst for revenge that I see in the eyes of Roquen Dol Lewin. I do not like the attitude I observe in the bard Curwë. I dislike the silence of the lunar Aewöl. They are, altogether, a threat to our endeavours," she claimed.

"Siw! Do not judge them so harshly and so quickly," interrupted Feïwal with authority. "I was in the queen's halls, Arwela, the day Roquen Dol Lewin burst in with pride, despite his despair. There, in front of the entirety of the assembled royal court, with profound anger in his voice, he told of the defeat of his army. He described with poignant veracity the burning of his city and the plight of his people. I still remember the strong emotion I felt when Roquen evoked the massacre of his family. The words fell hard, and together they formed a direct insult to the face of the lordly Dol and the noble dyn who sat in the hall of the diamond throne, gathered around our sovereign.
I heard, and I believed his story. Cornered into an act of hopeless resistance, the army of the House of Dol Lewin had been decimated because the queen deliberately withheld reinforcements. It was this betrayal which caused the fall of a glorious lineage whose nobility dated back to the dawn of time."

Arwela was incredulous.

"Queen Aranaele, whatever her faults, is not one to regret her actions, still less to apologize. He should have known that. Our sovereign is ruthless. I cannot believe that you would deny us a safe return for the sake of these High Elves who we barely know," she complained.

"Undoubtedly, the queen spared him no contempt. I was there when she rose from her throne. I can still hear her cruel words of banishment. I saw with my own eyes how that affront paralyzed the last Dol Lewin with shame. Then, I heard from the back of the hall, the clear voice of the bard Curwë, intoning the song of Lewin. I saw Roquen rising. Galvanized by the impetuous verses, he left the halls of the diamond's throne honourably. Irreparable words had been exchanged. I knew exile and death were the only two options left for him.

It was in that very moment that I decided we should leave the kingdom and sail south; I proposed to Roquen that he joins us in our quest across the ocean. We had waited for too long!

So, do not pronounce any ill words against our guests, Siw! They are our friends.

Be patient, as one day they will honour us. Roquen Dol Lewin's word is not to be taken lightly," concluded Feïwal.

Gradually, the sea turned blue as the sun climbed the sky. The white sails of the ship billowed in the light wind. After the hail and storms of the Sea of Cyclones, their enemy was now the calms of these warm tropical seas that paralyzed the ship. The sailors had a name for these waters; the 'shade islands', large stains below the surface, darker than the surrounding waves, spreading several miles across. Marine spirits haunted these still waters and absorbed all air currents, ensnaring vessels in the calms. Only the toil of rowers could free ships from such traps. Everyone's attention was now fixed on this danger, and whenever the sails began to wave, a profound shudder rippled through the crew. The long journey had exhausted the sailors. All onboard were acutely aware of the diminishing food and water supplies. Speed was now the major preoccupation.

*

When noon had passed, the breeze picked up significantly, driving the last thin clouds from the sky. The ocean flow, like the unseen hand of the God of the Seas, drew the ship southwards at a high speed. Feïwal set about taking several measurements, with an hourglass and a long rope that strung together runes at regular intervals. He was amazed at the sheer power of this driving force, which neither sail nor oar could fight. The Alwïryan and the elements were not so much opponents as partners in a dance. Feiwal again calculated their position by examining the horizon through an azure gemstone, which he claimed could make the stars visible even in radiant sunlight.

For most of the time during the day, Feïwal stood on the aftcastle, next to Nelwiri who was at the helm. He had set up a table and secured to its surface a large map which he annotated with comments and precious details as they journeyed onwards.

When the evening came, a dark cloud rose from the southeast. Feïwal frowned. Crossing the Sea of Cyclones had damaged the ship, and he did not feel equipped to deal with another new storm, or the hits and knocks that would accompany it. He gave a few brief orders. Mounting the rigging, some sailors carefully checked the long ropes that ran along the yards which allowed for movement. Additional efforts were required. They lowered the thin and flexible sails designed for fair weather, and hoisted instead a thicker, more resistant material that was etched with silver runes. Ropes were stretched across the deck for support and safety. Hatches were covered, and a large piece of cloth was secured around the helm to protect the pilot from the waves.

All night long, the wind struck in short, capricious jerks. Several times, the great ship listed to the point where the water began to brush the leeward rail. Nelwiri took the first watch. All was quiet on board, except for the hissing water at the ship's stem. The sail-bearing masts cast their lunar shadows across the deck. A silvery glow emanated from the wind runes, illuminating the face of the pilot and adorning him with a flickering mask. Taking his position by the few stars still visible, Nelwiri confirmed their course with his precious instrument, whose curved rune tended towards an elusive point, the object of all their hopes: the infinite South.

He heard febrile incantations a few steps behind him. Turning around, he saw, on the edge of the aftcastle, Feïwal's silhouette which looked like a fleeting shadow against a threatening sky. Solitary, taking refuge in his invocations, he seemed more alone than ever, preferring to suffer in silence out of his companions' sight, knowing that their friendship and support could not alleviate the doubts that haunted him.

★

The next day, when morning came, the sea breeze was still rising, and the crew lowered the yard of the mainmast to half-height. Nelwiri was managing to escape the tight lows of the swell and to ride on the shifting domes of the high waves. The southeast wind was now hot and cutting, the main sail so rounded that it unbalanced the ship. Water whistled along the hull. The large, heavy vessel jumped from wave to wave, thrusting its bow into the watery blue blades, throwing up flakes of foam. The rain now flowed like silver hair.

Feïwal was afraid, as he always was before major storms. The fear chilled his back and gripped his heart. He was filled with doubt. He was too experienced, though, not to recognize that it was Gweïwal Uleydon alone who held their lives in his hands. But the most difficult task was to conceal his apprehension from those around him. What they needed to see in their captain was that wintry blankness, even as his blood boiled in his veins and his heart pounded with suffering. That sacrifice, that aching loneliness, was what he owed to his crew. If they ever were to doubt him, the battle that was about to take place would be doomed to failure. He stood alone at the stern, motionless, frozen like the statue of an ancient guide of the clan. From his elevated position, he surveyed the entire ship, offering his silhouette to the eyes of all his sailors. The wind lifted his light robes and his long hair of dark sapphire. His gaze was fixed on the horizon. He appeared absent.

A murmur was heard among the High Elves who were at work on deck. All were astonished that no order had been given, and they began to wonder about the dangerous passivity of the captain.

The Irawenti sailors around them were long-accustomed to their master's ways. They curtly reminded them simply to follow orders if they wanted to survive what was coming. The tension was palpable.

Suddenly, Feïwal's voice could be heard, clear and thunderous from the stern. Usually so calm and melodious, it suddenly seemed authoritarian and implacable. Orders came rapidly and without pause. The sailors ran in every direction, each fully aware of what task they had to perform. The ship changed its course, making a quick and masterful jibe. Skilfully working with the currents and gusts of wind, it adjusted to a more favourable position that allowed it to reach its maximum speed. It bowed graciously, amplifying the circle of foam that its hull was pushing forward, like a racehorse suddenly feeling the spur of its master. Instead of trying to flee the danger, Feïwal chose to challenge it.

"Hoist the mainsail, stay the course!" shouted Nelwiri, standing beside his brother. His voice, affected by anxiety, froze the crew.

Nervousness spread to all those aboard as if by contagion.

"There's a problem attaching the main sail's yard!" shouted Gyenwë, the boatswain.

Sailors hurried to his side to help solve the issue. Feïwal left the aftcastle to join the deck. He did not seem affected by the eyes that stared anxiously at him. Arwela came and stood by him.

"All is dark and stormy. Gweïwal Uleydon wildly works up chaos," she murmured. Anxiety marked her face that was usually so smooth. Her intense azure eyes were fixed upon the waves.

"The Lost Islands are somewhere in front of us. It cannot be otherwise. I can feel it. The breath of the wind, growing stronger by the hour, is speaking to me," replied Feïwal, excitedly.

"The mast moves and the hull groans with each new fall. Will the sails hold? Will our pentacles resist the forces attempting to crush us?" Arwela exclaimed.

But the sea's mysteries could not allow Feïwal to reassure her. Suddenly, a roll came from behind, lifting the ship up high before rushing it downwards. The vessel then struck a wave with the same violence as a crash into a hard embankment. The hull shook, vibrated and crashed again. A wave swept across the deck, throwing a sailor overboard; several others avoided the same fate just in time by grasping hold of the rope running along the rail. A cry of panic, a call in the wind, rang out from the back of the ship.

"Sailor... Sailor overboard!"

No reaction followed, no order was given. The victim's companions looked on with horror at the empty space where the missing rope should have been hooked. All eyes turned to Feïwal, who remained motionless, his clothes soaked and his hands frozen blue, not making a single gesture. All understood that nothing could be done, nor would be done, to save him. Amid huge, twenty-foot waves, with a deck flooded by rushing salt water, and sails beginning to tear under the force of the wind, Feïwal would not risk the lives of other sailors to save the lone Elf about to be engulfed.

A huge dark shadow, mottled with pale specks, stretched out across the marine horizon. Long, thin clouds, like torn-up strips of paper, preceded it, foretelling heavy showers. Already the vessel struggled. It plunged into the collapsing sea, its long yard occasionally making contact with the water. Then, it was lifted so high that the oars and ropes were detached from their anchor. The rain began again.

The Alwïryan continued its wild journey. Such was the law of the ocean. Such was the ruthless trial of Gweïwal Uleydon.

★

For several hours, they sailed in a thick dark veil, with a strong breeze throughout, under a warm rain that soaked their clothes and dripped from their faces. For some time, they stopped manoeuvring, frozen as if petrified by the ordeal which awaited them. Feïwal was leaning on the railing, his thoughts lost in the vastness of the ocean when a distinct clatter caught his attention. It was a threatening sound, rising above the murmur of the sea, the groaning of the hull and the creaking of the sails.

"Siw! Did you hear that? Is there something hidden in the rain?" asked Arwela, standing beside Feïwal.

Both concentrated for a while. The mysterious sound echoed again, this time very clearly and from the same direction as before: directly in front of them. It resounded again and again until it became overwhelming. The whole crew had now gathered on the ship's deck. The horrible noise in the dark intensified. A wall of rain surrounded them completely. They could not bear the melancholy howl which invaded their ears. Feïwal shook his head and uttered sacred incantations. He grasped at the small piece of rope tied around his neck, marked with runes, from which hung a silver pendant. He kissed and kissed it again, continuing to do so obsessively, until the horrible sound finally exploded to an end.

"I never heard such a thing... We have entered... something," Feïwal managed to say after the shock had waned.

Panic had spread across the great ship's deck; those fierce Elves who feared neither deadly enemy nor ravaging storm began to shake with terror as their imaginations were driven into the shadows. They looked around them, with pallid faces and haggard eyes, as though a terrifying event was beginning.
A violent gust of wind suddenly cleared the clouds and the rain appeared to stop. For a moment, the vast ocean revealed itself. Towards the south, they could decipher the towering foam of enormous waves, which appeared higher than vessels. These waves formed a formidable fleet driving forward at great speed. A bright halo in the air preceded them. This mighty vision lasted but a few moments before the terrifying view vanished. The crew had been shaken to their core. There was a moment of silence. It soon ended with cries, desperate prayers and panicked shouts.

Feïwal's orders could no longer be heard by the crew. Commands were also being given by the other dyn of the Filweni to restore discipline, but none would obey. Finally, Luwir's horn sounded several times; the sailors began to regain their composure and focus on the instructions given by their captain. Feïwal's voice could be heard once again, loud and clear, as though the guide of the Filweni had been delivered from all anxiety now that the end was imminent. Sailors rushed across the deck to obey his commands. Anchors were brought back and tied around the main mast with thick, heavy ropes, four fathoms long. The task was dangerous and required twenty sailors to execute it. Another dozen Elves, agile as squirrels, clambered onto the rigging, using ropes, halyards and shrouds to maintain their balance whilst adjusting the ship's yaw. Nelwiri was roaring orders from the deck. His howling was scattered by the wind. The sails soon came down. It then did not take long to remove the foremast; the sailors worked in decisive and instinctive gestures.

"We need to maintain our speed! Luwir! Gather the rowers and make haste! We need power to steer the Alwïryan! Urgently!" ordered Feïwal.

In the meantime, Nelwiri was screaming instructions to the crew masters.

"Myem! Lenpi! Osso! Nety! Clear these fools from the deck and take your positions."

He urged all others to find some shelter.

"Cil Cim Cir! Get out of here, all of you! This is no place for you! Get out!" Nelwiri roared.

The crew hastened into the holds of the vessel until the deck was finally cleared. Luwir was the last to reach the deck hatch. He closed it behind him. His deep voice reverberated as he yelled orders at the crew to organize the rowers' benches. Soon, the beating of the drums resounded, coordinating their efforts.

Meanwhile, Roquen hoisted the colours of House Dol Lewin to the top of the main mast. No one offered so much as a word or gesture to dissuade him from putting himself in such a dangerous position. His expression was as hard as ivory. This cold, reckless resolve made Roquen completely unreachable. His piercing eyes had the coldness of steel blades. The white war unicorn against a field of purple, now fully unfurled, proudly faced the air like a sublime challenge to the elements. The Alwïryan, sails and rods down, was naked but for this proud standard. It was ready for battle.

Nelwiri went back to the aftcastle and clung firmly to the helm. He was working with a heavily reduced sail to control the Alwïryan in the wind. The shell, bilge and keel creaked ominously. The Alwïryan was now bouncing between mountains of water. Waterspouts corkscrewed down from a cascading sky ripped apart by lightning. It was pitching and rolling like a frail piece of bark adrift. Nelwiri kept adjusting the ship's course in a continuous effort to escape doom. But the exercise was becoming increasingly difficult; the pilot of the ship was blinded by the growing darkness, surging rain and flashes of lightning. He struggled desperately against the raging ocean. Feïwal was quick to join him. He applied five and then ten degrees of starboard helm to stay on their chosen course. The helm shook violently. Every time a wave came rushing against the ship and buried it under a mass of foam, he trembled with pain, his own flesh suffering from the blows that were hitting the Alwïryan. The two brothers kept only four of their best sailors on deck to help handle the ship. Suddenly, a monstrous swirling water column rose up on the horizon. It advanced at the speed of a galloping horse towards the vessel.

"Siw! It is heading towards us! We are lost," shouted Nelwiri, terrified.

Desperately, he made a full about-turn to port, trying to avoid the huge whirlwind that was now digging a chasm into the ocean surface. Screaming in anger at his helplessness, he failed to avoid the impact. A frightful mountain of water broke onto the Alwïryan, sweeping across the deck, spraying rope attachments in all directions and ripping everything else up into the air. The mainmast could not hold. Already almost broken at its base, this latest onslaught completely broke the wood, and the mast fell to port with a horrendous crash, very nearly crushing Roquen. The standard of the Dol Lewin, that white war unicorn against the field of purple, disappeared into the sea. The helpless Roquen was catapulted against the gunwale. The Alwïryan careered about dangerously due to the broken rigging, still attached by ropes, pulling downwards at the side of the ship and acting like an anchor in the swirling sea. It was taking on huge amounts of water. Roquen escaped drowning and managed to stay aboard thanks to the side ropes. Galvanized by terror, with an intense determination, he summoned all his strength to reach the shelter of the deck by pulling himself along the fallen mast.

The whirlwind disappeared a few hundred feet astern of the vessel, whirling up into the mass of cloud above. Spiralling deeper and deeper in ever narrowing circles, the Alwïryan heeled more perilously than ever. An imposing silence followed, as though a mysterious force had muzzled the storm, paralyzing its monstrous pack of waves before the next assault. This unexpected lull surprised Feïwal; it was as if the wrath of the elements had suddenly been diverted by an occult power, now that all was lost. He seized the opportunity and breathed more freely, surveying the scene for a few moments. Nelwiri, just at his side, was still strapped to the helm, unconscious, apparently stunned by the shock. Feïwal made sure he was still alive by quickly checking his pulse. Below, the deck of the ship was in chaos. His best sailors, his friends, were all lost. They had been blown away by the storm and swallowed by the Austral Ocean. Their cords were still hooked to the railing, but irremediably cut further down. No immediate help could be expected from those who had taken refuge in the hold. The hatch was blocked by an array of debris.

Only Roquen remained to be of any assistance. He was standing on the deck, wounded. Like some mythical image, the tall Elf knelt, motionless. His sword, struck into the wood, maintained his balance though he looked vulnerable to the ravages of the ocean and the ship's dangerous pitching. Powerlessly tied to the plight of the vessel, he was out of reach.

In the blink of an eye, Feïwal decided to act. A strong gust of wind suddenly swept the ship's deck from stern to bow. The navigator extended his arms to spread out his robes in full. The savage wind forcefully buffeted the folds of his cloak, propelling him from the aftcastle to the deck. Feïwal landed with great dexterity and rolled a few yards from the broken mast. With a rapid movement, he tied himself to the ropes, thus preventing any further downfall. He now stood beside Roquen.

"What can we do?" yelled Roquen through the storm.

"Cut the mast! We need to cut the mast loose!" shouted Feïwal as the ship was about to fully tip over onto the sea.

In an instant, with the sort of strength and courage that inspires renewed hope, Roquen stood. His sword sprang from its sheath. Feïwal started shouting words of power in the ancient language of the Irawenti guides. His face was severe, strained by the energy he was unleashing.

"Yagliw wary[13]!!!"

The words he pronounced suddenly began to drown out the noise made by the elements. Reverberating from those incantations, the long gleaming blade of Roquen's sword began to glow, as if possessed by some unnatural fire. The valiant lord struck a first blow at the mast with all the force of his despair, causing a crash. A second strike, then a third, followed the first. The wood was pulverized. Yards, stays, cables, indeed everything, was pulled into the sea by the weight of the sinking mainmast. The Alwïryan rose up, carried by a mighty wave, before its own weight and the violence of the storm sent it crashing back down. The vessel then rose again, finding its balance on the sea. The force of those impacts had shattered the railing of the aftcastle. A crash rent the air. Roquen, senseless, was thrown to the ground with extraordinary violence. The railing of the aftcastle now lay contorted on the deck.

His face swollen, his body bruised, Feïwal remained conscious. Screams of pain could be heard from the hold of the ship. The crew was trapped. The storm, as if temporarily overcome by their valour, seemed to retreat. The lull was brief. Feïwal tried to clear the deck of the mainmast debris to open an access to the hold and release his companions. But the hurricane was unleashed once again.

---

13 Yagliw wary: 'Sparkle of Fire' in lingua Irawenti

Within moments, the darkness of the sky had burst into a demonic dance of foam. The Alwïryan was plunged into a twenty-foot-deep abyss, and then up the side of another wave, before resuming its mad race between the liquid walls.

"To the stern!" screamed Feïwal to Roquen.

But the tall Elf did not stir, nor did he respond. He lay unconscious, his hands still leashed in the deck's cords. The rest of Feïwal's words were lost in a roar of thunder. The ship groaned under the combined onslaught of the ocean and the hurricane, as it was on the point of being pulled apart. It teetered between port and starboard before diving downwards again. The sluices no longer drained the water that washed over the deck. The vessel was dying. Its slow death had already begun. Sea spirits circled around its bruised carcass, yelling wildly. Feïwal maintained his statue-like composure, riveted to the remains of the great mast, ready to disappear with it into the abyss. Impervious to the chaos of the elements, his posture remained defensive as his eyes searched the spray. He finally managed to reach the helm while waves, fifteen feet high, jostled and crashed against the Alwïryan, rolling across the deck like beasts. Cascading water crashed down upon the aftcastle before pouring in torrents down the steps to the deck. There he found Nelwiri, firmly bonded to the helm by ropes. He was still unconscious. His head was bloody. He was no longer master of the ship, whose mad, blind race was steered only by the chaotic winds. Feïwal clung to the helm, trying to regain power. Now confused, his senses were betraying him, and the navigator lost control. He uttered a cry of terror as his mind was swallowed into nightmare. But it was not the storm's redoubled violence that filled Feïwal with terror.

A winged shape, hidden by the spray, flew around the ship. Feïwal could not distinguish its contours exactly, although he recognized the silhouette of a large Elf amongst the swirls around him. However, his eyes were fixed on the two pale wings of the creature. Spread wide, they were beating with tremendous power, taking full advantage of the wind. In an instant, the winged creature was upon the aftcastle. It carried the breath of the entire storm. A flash of lightning set the horizon ablaze. The wind stopped suddenly. An aura of splendour emanated from the divine creature. Long sapphire hair covered the deity's naked and ethereal body, as though shaped in the wind. He held in his right hand a silver trident, the symbol of his sovereign power over these waters. Feïwal stared around him, awestruck, completely motionless and utterly incapacitated. The creature moved forward and he could not resist it. Covering his face, Feïwal knelt in front of it. But his supplications and imploring words soon died on his lips, like a gentle breeze caught up in a whirlwind. In a final effort of will, he held up the sacred relic of his clan, that little piece of rope inlaid with unknown runes. The deity stopped, towering over him spreading its wings and brandishing its trident. Feïwal fainted at the blast of its power.

★

How long it lasted, he would not know, but the moment came when Feïwal finally awoke from unconsciousness. In his dizziness, he attempted to understand the hallucination he had been through. His gaze swept the space around him and scanned his surroundings in search of his companions. Nelwiri was still tied to the helm in a macabre dance. The rest of the aftcastle was empty. He moved towards the devastated railing. He could see Roquen below on the deck. The tall Elf knelt and suffered in silence, his right arm severely injured.

In this twilight of doom, other concerns began to nag at his mind. But he could not do more. He let go. He gave up and started to murmur a song of old, the song of the Irawenti seafarers. With his last drop of energy, he sang beautiful verses about the ultimate refuge of the Elves, the Lost Islands.

Nonetheless, though badly battered, his ship fearlessly continued its course between the towering peaks, plunging into deep ravines only to be reborn at the top of fresh hills of foam. His song's lyrics seemed to preserve the vessel from its ultimate destruction by conjuring protective marine spirits, dissuading the formidable force of nature from striking the final blow. The dance of death between the hungry and ferocious sea and its frail but agile prey continued.

Feïwal's senses had failed him; he resolved to search through the darkness of the night to find his way. He prayed to the wild deity that he and his companions be spared, and that he be granted his soul and his destiny. His eyes burned with salt; his body was broken.

Suffocated by the wind, buried under a deluge of rain, battered by the downpour, Feïwal surrendered to the storm that had made him feel invaded and overpowered. He now chose to give up fighting, yielding to the power of the elements, to their superior forces, completely overcome by the magnificent cataclysm. He lost control, defeated, yet somehow, he was communing with the chaos. His confused mind was wandering into the unknown, haunted by only Griffins and Storm Eagles. Feïwal smiled briefly, thinking of his brother's warning to stop bearing the fate of others on his shoulders. He then lost consciousness.

The ship sped southward, as if sucked into an abyss, unaware of the day or the night, with no one watching over its destiny any longer. It was carried by the monstrous whirlpool, that vast column joining the darkness of the sky to the darkness of the ocean. There was no sign of hope or salvation.

But, eventually, unexpectedly, the Alwïryan met an invisible wall, bursting in an explosion of sand and water on a deserted beach. The whole isle was shaken with the furious vibration, a shuddering convulsion that felt like the final scream of the unleashed elements.

*

Although unlikely, the dawn finally came. The dim morning stillness was torn by a shrill sound, an awkward noise in the majestic symphony that had been played by the sea and the wind since time began. A pelican, chased by the wind, came to perch on the ship's railing, seeking shelter from the fury of the elements. Its repeated cries finally released Feïwal from his torpor. A shouting in the wind brought him back to reality. He recognized, through the surrounding tumult, the powerful voice of Roquen.

"How am I to help him in this chaos?" Feïwal despaired.

Soon the fury of the hurricane began to decline. Feïwal brushed the debris around him aside, got up, and began to call, hailing his sailors and shouting for his kin, but the wind carried his voice away into nothingness. He wandered on the deck, tripping amongst the wreckage and over ropes and debris. Finally, he stumbled over Roquen, who stood motionless and silent; gazing with rage at his own battered body. Feïwal knelt beside him, overcome with emotion.

"Cil Cim Cir! We are safe. We were spared."

Roquen could not answer him. A vicious blow had struck him down; acute pain immobilized him. He endured this suffering without complaint, without a groan, as befitted a lord of the High Elves. Feïwal set about tending to his injuries, but he quickly realized that the great Elf was suffering from more than just physical pain. A mystical force was at work.

It was only at that point that Feïwal noticed a faint star, shining through the veil of darkness which enveloped them. This distant speck of glimmering light was the first of many others that appeared gradually. Soon, the beach where they had run aground was bathed in a soft, silver light. Feïwal took advantage of this calm to rescue his companions. Nelwiri regained consciousness but remained weak and lost. He suffered from severe bruising, but his first words upon waking were to inquire about the fate of his companions. They then set about freeing up access to the ship's hold.

Finally, the first survivors could emerge from the shipwreck. All were oblivious to their surroundings. They wandered around the deck, stumbling over debris, as if looking for some clue. Only the sound of the sea reached their ears. The rest of the crew progressively emerged from the hold, with eyes half closed, like owls coming out of a long night. Arwela scoured through the ranks, providing care and inviting everyone to prayer and piety. Feïwal began to gather his two watch units. While he himself was haggard, he roundly jeered his sailors, urging them to quick mental recovery. The count began.

Many were injured with bruises and fractures. But there was also one fatal casualty, a young sailor from the clan of Gnalweni. It was his first trip out to sea, and he had won over the entire crew with his fearlessness manoeuvring the sails, and his unfaltering hard work. He was found with a shattered skull, his chest crushed under an oar which had escaped its hinges. Many were the sailors who came to bow before his body before it was returned to Gweïwal Uleydon, as was dictated by the marine rites of the Blue Elves. Arwela uttered sacred words and read the ancient scriptures. Overwhelmed, she added a prayer.

"Eïwal Ffeyn[14]! Deity of storms! Eïwal Ffeyn saved us from a deadly force. However, in exchange for his leniency, he claimed the life of the youngest among us. May his soul return to the sea and the wind! The lord of tempests sends us a warning. He demands our humility. This will remain in our minds."

The Alwïryan had emerged from hell. It was battered but still alive; its vital parts were not affected though it was stripped of its masts and spars. The figurehead remained unwavering, despite the last remnants of an aggressive wind. It lay on the beach motionless, like the remains of a warrior fallen in battle. At regular intervals, knocks from the powerful ocean waves served as a reminder of the danger it had escaped.

★

The next day, the sun shone with all its brilliance, rising in a sky flecked with distant clouds. The ocean was still agitated, but its wrath seemed to have been largely appeased. The castaways could now gauge the full extent of the disaster. The Alwïryan, dismantled, its keel deeply buried in the sand, lay down like a flightless bird. The deck was heavily damaged, repeatedly punctured with gaping cracks like multiple bloody wounds. Water was flooding in through breaches in the hull. Pieces of the mainmast sunk through the collapsed ruins of the deck into the sodden depths of the hold. The door leading to the aftcastle had come off its hinges. To the rear, the rising tide began to flood into the stained-glass lords' cabins, but the aftcastle, though covered in debris, was largely intact. The rudder also

---

14 Eïwal Ffeyn: Deity of Winds, divinity of freedom, rebellion and anger

appeared to have been spared. To the front, the foremast, which fortunately had been removed before the onslaught of the storm, was broken off at its hinges. Stripped of its sails, dethroned of its silver gull, the foremast was suspended in an unlikely position over the railing, jutting out like some ominous black gallows.

The ship was laying on the beach of an isle which appeared to be little more than a heap of rock and sand deposited amid the immense and magnificent sea. At high water, the wreckage was submerged, but, when the tide went out, the tips of the rocks were exposed, and it was possible to walk out towards the beach. Fortunately, the Alwïryan had run aground on sandy soil; there was hope that the crew could repair and refloat it.

Some of those who had suffered the least set about exploring alongside the dyn Filweni. They climbed the slopes of the isle towards its southern shore, eventually reaching the other side. Feïwal, leading the small group, was the first to make out the land on the western horizon. Close by he could distinguish on the water multiple islands and islets, with their sandy beaches and steep hills. But, along the horizon itself, laid a faraway strip of white that had to be the rocky heights of a vast land. Feïwal and his companions stood there for a moment in absolute silence, breathing in the earthy wind that carried the scents of wood and the aromas of plants: potent fragrances indeed for those who, for many moons, had enjoyed only the incense of the ocean. Moved to tears, they looked out, craving and hoping for this land, the object of their desire.

They had suffered countless hardships, wounds, and losses, on their journey to finally reach these Promised Islands, the archipelago of the Llewenti. The small group, now quiet and recollected, set off down the path leading back to the beach, joining the rest of the castaways. Without a word uttered or an instruction given, all the Irawenti knelt around the dyn Filweni, forming a crescent around them.

Slowly, almost mystically, Feïwal walked out into the water, submerging his body up to the waist. A moment later, Arwela, the seer, followed him, symbolizing the respect of the entire clan for its guide. Nelwiri the sailor and Luwir the oars master also joined them; together, they displayed the colours of the clan of Filweni: a silver feather against an azure field. The voices of the dyn Filweni rose in unison over the murmur of the wind, proclaiming their ritual verses.

"We are dyn Filweni,
By the grace of Gweïwal Uleydon, we descend from Filwen.
For the glory of Gweïwal Uleydon, we sail from East to West.
The silver feather, Gweïwal Uleydon entrusted us, to adorn our crest.
We are dyn Filweni. We shall cross the ocean as did Filwen."

Feïwal turned to his clan, his long black hair, flecked with strands of azure, fluttering in the wind.

"I am Feïwal dyn Filweni, the Guide who protects the clan.
I am Feïwal dyn, the shipwright and the navigator who braves the ocean.
I am Feïwal, disciple of Eïwal Ffeyn. I am the cleric of the angry deity.
I am the servant of the prisoner. This passage was granted to me."

By late afternoon, the light breath of the ocean breeze had died away completely, and a cloudless sky stretched out above a smooth sea. Obscured by a distant, rocky island, the sun lingered just below the horizon, setting the whole of the western sky ablaze as it set. In the midst of this immense beauty and natural peace, two small white sails emerged from the east. Their silhouettes ascended and descended slowly, with the tide that was slowly retreating from the bay.

CHAPTER 2: dyl Llyvary

2708 of the Llewenti Calendar, Season of Eïwele Llya, 116th day, Llafal

Nyriele dyl Llyvary murmured the last verses of a prayer to Eïwal Ffeyn, her voice still audibly weary. Her hair was wet. A strong autumnal rain just swept the coast.

The beautiful Elvin priestess listened to the sounds that were drifting from the coast, her eyes not quite closed. A multitude of different noises could be heard intermingling on the shores of Nyn Llyvary[15]. Never had she heard so many of them at once. Thousands of birds were greeting the sunrise which marked the end of the most important storm that the Austral Ocean had ever produced in Llewenti memory. Nightingales, hummingbirds, swallows, seagulls, herons and pelicans all sang at dawn.

As Nyriele breathed it all in and listened to the vast but invisible multitude, a seabird swooped down to land on her shoulder, and let out a long, guttural screech. She looked out at the blue morning sky, clear as mountain water, and saw other birds heading towards the hilltop Temple of Eïwal Ffeyn where she stood. They swept quickly through the air, dense as a swarm of insects. When they neared the top of the hill, which looked out across that vast expanse of water, the birds veered upwards, tracing concentric circles high above her head and around the

---

15   Nyn Llyvary: 'The island of Llyvary' in lingua Llewenti

temple's colonnades, before they plunged downwards towards the young lady who stood exposed in the open, her silhouette stark against the temple steps. Encircling her frenetically, like a whirlwind, they seemed, for a moment, to absorb her entirely, before they scattered away in all directions.

Nyriele then turned to the inner circle of the temple, addressing another priestess.

"Our swanships have crossed the passes of the Halwyfal[16]. They have now returned to Llafal[17]. They found the wrecked ship and surrounded those who sailed it. We will soon have news."

"Then they did well. It is quite a distance to the isle of Pyenty[18]," replied Lyrine dyl Llyvary.

She was the mother to the young Nyriele. Nature had endowed her with an aquiline nose, a firm yet sensitive mouth, high-arched brows and beautiful eyes that gleamed like sapphires. She was the most respected matriarch of their clan, expert in the ways of the deities and a scholar of arcane knowledge.

Suddenly, almost with certain violence, she rose from her stately chair and snapped an order at the guards stationed beneath the temple. One of them hastened up to her, somewhat disturbed by her authoritative tone.

"Find me Tyar dyl! He has returned to Llafal. Let him come to the temple immediately. The swanships are back from the peninsula isles. I am eager to hear what news they bring."

The guard nodded and was about to take his leave when she added.

"Yet be discreet! Make it known to Tyar dyl that I do not want this news to spread."

Her eyes then landed upon the heart of the temple, her gaze embracing the beauty of the edifice. Six high, fluted columns, sky-blue in colour, formed a perfect circle around the altar to

---

16 Halwyfal: 'The basin of birds' in lingua Llewenti
17 Llafal: 'The basin port' in lingua Llewenti
18 Pyenty: 'Sand isle' in lingua Llewenti

the deity. The shrine to Eïwal Ffeyn had neither wall nor roof, which allowed for the powerful winds of the hilltop to flow freely through the sacred place.

The temple's wood was an ethereal garden, full of a multitude of plants and protected by tall pine trees. The mild air carried the scents of many flowers, and the wind could not entirely muffle the joyful birdsong. It was a peaceful sanctuary, dedicated to prayer and worship. But it was also a place from which one could hail the powerful energy of the Islands' Flow, that mighty field of magic.

Lyrine loved this place. She had been born in Llafal, the city located on the lower slopes of the hill which led down to the Halwyfal, the magnificent basin that was home to so many species of bird. Her bloodline was noble; she descended from Queen Llyoriane, so was counted among the 'dyl' of the clan Llyvary.

Like all matriarchs of the Llewenti, Lyrine had been trained in the lore of all the Archipelago's deities, but Eïwal Ffeyn was especially important to her. Her dedication to the Deity of Winds and Freedom, to the protector of those islands, was profound. It meant that she loved this place of power, this towering shrine from which the world could be surveyed, from the white shores of the peninsula bordering the Austral Ocean to the north, to the blue waters of the Halwyfal in the east and the green Forest of Llymar[19] to the southwest.

Lyrine surveyed her surroundings for a long time, her thoughts lost in the morning breeze before she finally joined Nyriele.

"Never in my lifetime have I experienced such frantic violence, such an eruption of the elements as in the tales of old," Lyrine said, her voice distant and weary.

She met her daughter's gaze making no attempt to hide her disdain. The secretive Nyriele seemed gentle and naïve, staying silent whenever she could, only ever revealing her thoughts after lengthy observation. Lyrine considered her a weak priestess whose thoroughly frail nature was expertly concealed behind a compassionate and tranquil façade.

---

19 Llymar: 'Green sea' in lingua Llewenti

"We should rest," proposed Nyriele in her calm, soft voice. "This long struggle has depleted so much of our energy. I am sure that our efforts will not have been in vain. But soon our attention will be demanded elsewhere. The hurricane has devastated the coast. There will be many Elves looking to us for help and guidance."

"What of the wrecked ship found by our seabirds?" Lyrine reminded her, "What fool would sail into our waters at this time of year?"

"They must have faced the gravest dangers," Nyriele replied, "though the ship seems to have been spared from destruction. It could be a sign. I felt something during the storm, an intuition of what might come to pass. I would even say that what I foresaw has already begun."

The darkness in Nyriele's eyes dissipated, and a smile broke across her face. Lyrine grimaced at her daughter's words. She showed little love for her daughter but had great respect for her divinations. Nyriele, unique among her people, was the lone inheritor of special powers of foresight. After all, the noble blood of two Llewenti clans flowed through her veins.
Nyriele's had been a late birth; she arrived when Lyrine's union with Gal dyl, warlord of the clan Avrony, was already coming to an end.
The common Elves saw Nyriele as an incredible beauty. She reminded them of the time of Queen Llyoriane, in the early days of the archipelago when the deities themselves could be seen wandering the Islands. In her mother's eyes, her daughter's calm and quiet nature was a sign of weakness, a legacy of her own companionship with Gal dyl whose kinship the Avrony, was considered the lowest of the six clans.

The Llewenti lived according to ancient traditions and customs which dated back before their long exodus to the archipelago.
It was the mothers who assumed the task of mentoring the children. This was particularly true for those of noble blood, and even more so for those daughters whose bloodline promised a future full of potential. Lyrine had imposed a strict and demanding education on the young Nyriele; the ambition she harboured for her only heir was great. Lyrine had especially resolved to cut her daughter off from the influence of her father and his clan. This had proven difficult.

As the young matriarch had developed her own personality, everyone could see that she naturally tended towards the ways of the clan Avrony. She favoured the cult of Eïwele Llyi[20], divinity of Love and of Beauty, enjoyed and promoted the arts, and had an instinct for protecting the weak. This evolution was an intense disappointment for her mother. Lyrine was used to seize every opportunity to make her daughter feel as insignificant as possible.

Once Nyriele had spoken of her divination, there followed a long silence between the two matriarchs. For hours, they rested quietly on their chairs, their eyes half-closed, their breathing deep and steady, their minds finally at peace. Their auras were enveloped in the sanctity of the shrine.

But such peace could not last long. The sun was still high in the sky when, suddenly, a commotion could be heard coming from outside of the temple. Tyar dyl Llyvary, a commander and warlord of the city of Llafal, had come forth at the matriarchs' bidding. Several fighters marched in alongside him. They were all dressed for war, clad in green. The white swan, their clan sigil, could be seen on their cloaks.

"Noble Matriarchs, the swanships found the wreck..." he declared, breathless.

"Indeed! So, my seabirds were right. Is it a barbarian long ship from the Mainland?" inquired Lyrine.

"No, noble Matriarch, it is a large boat, thrown upon the shores of Pyenty by the hurricane. The vessel has run aground. It has suffered considerable damage."

"Then it must be a galley of the Westerners. What madness drove them to sail into our waters?" asked Lyrine.

"Noble Matriarch, the vessel is Elvin-made: it is a big ship, two-masted, like none that was ever seen on our waters," replied Tyar dyl.

"What fool would dare sail the Austral Ocean just before the arrival of Eïwele Llyo's season[21]? And why? This is sheer madness. How close did you get? Did you see its colours, or its coat of arms?" Lyrine demanded hurriedly.

---

20 Eïwele Llyi: Deity of fountains, divinity of love, beauty and arts

21 Eïwele Llyo's season: Four months corresponding to the period November-February in the Llewenti calendar

"I took advantage of the darkness, slipping aboard while the survivors rested," Tyar dyl revealed.

The elder matriarch was growing impatient. "Be brief! Who or what did you find?"

"The sailors are Blue Elves, Matriarch Lyrine! Irawenti! Their hairs are azure...their eyes shining like sapphires! They bear a silver feather on their clothes."

"What fiction is this? To my knowledge, no one has hoisted the silver feather since the days of the sons of Filwen. Few can even remember it, Tyar dyl. You must have been mistaken."

"There is more, Matriarch Lyrine."

"More?"

"A number of High Elves are with them. They look like powerful warriors, clad in plate armour and talking in the Hawenti language of old."

"What can this mean?" Lyrine was incredulous.

"Their banner is a white unicorn against a field of purple." Realising, Lyrine replied, "Would Dol Lewin fighters dare to defy us by sailing into forbidden waters?"

"It is a white war unicorn, Matriarch Lyrine, not the racing unicorn we are familiar with! I know the heraldic lore of the High Elf houses. It is without doubt the sigil of Dol Lewin, but these colours, I am sure, are those of the elder branch."

"The realm of the elder branch of Dol Lewin is beyond the ocean, Tyar dyl. They dwell in Essawylor, in the Kingdom of the Five Rivers. We are far beyond each other's reach. It has been so for twenty-two centuries. You speak nonsense," Lyrine dismissed.

"I swear it. These Elves come from Essawylor beyond the Nen. You have my word. The hurricane must have brought them to our shores. Somehow, the passage was granted to them."

It was then that Nyriele, interrupted. "Mother, Tyar dyl is right. This is what I felt during the storm. This is what I saw in the waters of Halwyfal. They could pass through."

"This simply cannot be... Tyar dyl, you will go back to the ship and bring me its captain," Lyrine commanded.

Tyar dyl was an experienced warlord among the clan Llyvary, and perhaps its most seasoned fighter. He knew that a command such as this, uttered by the eldest of the matriarchs, was not to be questioned. Whatever their titles or accomplishments, male members of the clan Llyvary had no involvement in strategy. This had been the prerogative of the matriarchs, servants of the deities since the days of Queen Llyoriane.

He bowed respectfully and was soon on his way to the city of Llafal, his warriors hard on his heels. Tyar dyl was well known for his fiercely independent nature. He had always steered clear of any clan decision-making, instead focusing solely on his duties as commander of the Llafal guards. He was shorter and less imposing than other noble Elves of his kin, but he was very thin, flexible and renowned for his agility and endurance. His tanned skin and dark eyes contrasted with his long, snow-coloured hair. He was dressed in light leather and his helmet was adorned with a long swan plume.

As he strode quickly down the path from the shrine of Eïwal Ffeyn, his mind raced. He was trying to determine the best course of action to capture the captain of the wrecked ship. As he saw it, he faced several options: brute force, intimidation, treachery or, perhaps, honesty.

He carefully considered each of these possibilities and what they would involve in terms of resources and planning. Keeping his thoughts to himself, he did not share a single word with his companions. Tyar dyl could feel the excitement building within him, a thrill that was becoming overwhelming. He could feel it driving away his ennui; he would keep this precious sensation to himself. For far too long he had endured a life of passive contemplation. He was aware that his days as an Elf would soon come to an end. He knew that sorrow, weariness and disillusion had corrupted his spirit irredeemably. Now he was drawn to silence, isolation and communion with nature. This was a clear sign that it would soon be time for him to join the trees. He had seen others before him follow that very path. And yet, today, this task had been entrusted to him. He interpreted this undertaking as an opportunity to prove himself, to show his younger brethren that the "Old Bird", as some ironically called him, was still warlord of Llafal.

Marching in single file behind him, his retinue hastened down the path from the temple. The high winds gradually diminished as the shelter of the hill began to protect them. The gates of the city were then opened before them. Below, the lower expanses of the city, on the side which surrounded the harbour, were hidden in the shadow of the hill. In the moving mists, Llafal could be glimpsed fleetingly, like an amorphous mosaic of green and pearl. The city was built among pines and cedars, sheltered by that high hill which protected it from the storms of the Austral Ocean and the Llewenti's elegant white houses were scattered amid the colourful, abundant vegetation.

Tyar dyl and his band descended the hill along a wide street lined with tall wooden houses and slender pines. All was calm and quiet. It was as though the inhabitants had locked themselves in their homes in anticipation of a new disaster. As they continued their descent, a sunbeam tore down through the foliage above, illuminating a secluded flower garden.

They reached the top of the wide, stone steps that led down from the main road to the heights of Llafal, to Temple Square which looked out over the Halwyfal basin. Here stood the ancient stronghold of the clan Llyvary, the dominating edifice of the esplanade. It was a striking building made of wood, glass and stone, its architecture fine and delicate. Its white lime walls gleamed in the golden light of the sun. Thick green vines, interspersed with blue and yellow flowers, painted a floral decoration across its front. One could see the entire city from the esplanade. Layers of terraces had been built into the slopes above the shores of the great basin below, and from afar they resembled a crescent moon caressing the vast green water. This vista of symmetrical terraces, walled gardens and natural greenery was perfectly serene, surrounded by the afternoon's golden mist.

After continuing down through several different neighbourhoods, the group finally reached a vast square. In it a fountain stood, with a statue of a great swan in its centre. Clear water flowed from the spring in the middle of the marble pool. Tyar dyl paused, taking a moment to embrace the entire scene with his gaze.

In an hour, the sun's orb would disappear completely behind the treetops but, for now, the Elves of the clan Llyvary were busy. Every afternoon, many gathered at Daly Nièn[22], the name of the great fountain square of the city, to exchange goods,

22   Daly Nièn: 'The fountain square' in lingua Llewenti

services and news. This was the very heart of Llafal where all the guilds were located, and growers and artisans alike all ran stalls. Gold, silver, coins, indeed currency of any kind, were all prohibited according to the ancient laws of the Llewenti. Instead, each guild was responsible for producing what was required by the community. Every day, food, drink and raw materials, but also furniture, tools, weapons, and all sorts of other goods, were available at Daly Nièn. The guilds conducted their business freely, relying on the Council of the Matriarchs to find resolutions to disputes.

Tyar dyl decided to sit at the top of the steps to the Armourer's Guild. From there, he could enjoy the excitement that swept across Daly Nièn in the last hours of daylight when everyone was eager to close their deals. Not wanting to draw any attention to himself, he dismissed his guards, keeping only his second-in-command with him, a young noble Llewenti of the clan Llyvary called Nerin dyl.

A smile played on Tyar dyl's lips; life was ironic. He believed that the arrival of this ship from beyond the Austral Ocean would change the course of history. A mission of the utmost importance had been entrusted to him, an old Elf who nobody cared for, who spent most of his time alone, and who was already contemplating the prospect of his passage. He had no heirs, no companions, and indeed no compassion. All he had left were the memories of an ageing warrior. He checked himself: no, not an ageing warrior, a great champion and an exalted servant of the clan. Despite his high rank, he knew that he had been merely a servant for all his life. He had dedicated his entire existence to others, neglecting his own needs and desires. This used to make him proud and even now he did not regret it. He simply no longer cared. Everything had become meaningless; a void had absorbed all trace of lust, ambition, greed and even life within him. He now knew the tree that had chosen him.
How many times had he climbed it?
How many happy hours had he spent sitting on that branch near the top, looking out across the coast?
How good it had been to feel the wind envelop him! He knew that one day a wind like that would take his spirit away to the forest and he wished for that day to come. A priestess of Eïwele

Llyo[23] had already prepared him. The deity of Fate's cleric had stayed up for many nights with him, under the starlight, explaining how to interpret his dreams and absent musings.

"How shall we operate, Tyar dyl?" asked the young Nerin dyl.

Tyar dyl took some time to answer, as this question from his second-in-command slowly brought him back to the world of Elves, to Llafal.

"I will go," he replied slowly.
"Alone?"
"Alone. This is the best course of action. I will need a swanship, as I intend to bring the travellers food, water and wine, as welcome gifts."
"But they are not welcome here," Nerin dyl protested. "I doubt that the matriarchs will..."
"What Matriarch Lyrine wants is to talk to their captain. I will bring him to Llafal. Alone."
"I will do as you command, Tyar dyl."
The 'Old Bird' then added, "It's extraordinary what wine can achieve. I'd wager that it's far more effective than intimidation. But we must act quickly; Blue Elves are, of course, incredible swimmers. I recall from ancient tales that they are also masterful dolphin-tamers. We do not want them to start spreading around the Gloren peninsula searching for food. Nerin dyl, you will command the rest of the swanships' fleet, forming a ring-fence around the isle of Pyenty. But do so at a distance. Whatever happens to me, you are not to attack without a direct order from the Council of the Matriarchs. Have no fear; I will return safely."

And then, Tyar dyl thought, "From her secret halls in the depths of Nyn Llyvary, Eïwele Llyo has already made her plan for me."

He turned back to Nerin dyl. "Now go to the guilds and load a boat with water, wine, bread, fruit and meat for more than a hundred Elves. Make no effort to explain just yet. Use the clan's

---

23   Eïwele Llyo: Deity of starlight, divinity of dreams, fate, death and reincarnation

seal. We must sail before sunset and need to reach the passes of Halwyfal by nightfall, so that we can cross to the bay early tomorrow with the morning tide... The forest will need to wait for me a little longer," he concluded enigmatically.

The swanship that Tyar dyl sailed was the last to leave the port of Llafal. The clan Llyvary's most important city was also the largest harbour on the northern shores of the archipelago. It could host many vessels, protecting them from the tumult of the Austral Ocean.

All those ships were currently out at sea, on an errand to deliver supplies and aid the many settlements along the coast that had been badly damaged by the wrath of Eïwal Ffeyn during the hurricane. As his boat was heading east into the Halwyfal waters, to circumvent the headland around Llafal, Tyar dyl looked back to admire the amazing scenery of the seashore. Towards the west, in the fading light of the evening, a tumultuous sky charged with threatening clouds towered the high tops of the Mountains. As in a colourful painting of Eïwele Llyi's temple, shades of azure filled the relief on the horizon while taints of forest green marked the Arob Salwy[24] hills in the background. The white houses of the Llewenti sparkled amid the vivid seashore plants, like crystalline stars in a naturally emerald sea.

Suddenly, a few yards from the boat's wake, a great white swan sprang from the blue waters of the vast basin, taking off into the air. Tyar dyl watched this elegant bird, symbol of the clan Llyvary, flying high into the sky. He stayed in this contemplative stance for a moment, his eyes full of admiration for the beauty of the scenery.

*

From the top of the hill, from the heights of Temple Square, Lyrine watched the last swanship depart, with close attention and not without a certain degree of anxiety. She noticed that Tyar dyl had chosen to go alone. It was a dangerous decision, but she was unsurprised. She had given her orders; it was now up to Tyar dyl to set up a strategy to complete his mission. It was

---

24 Arob Salwy: 'The grass hills' in lingua Llewenti

so, now as it had always been among the clan Llyvary. Watching the ship sail out of the harbour, Lyrine reflected upon Tyar dyl's past service.

"The Old Bird' can be trusted. He has never failed me or our clan. He is the most experienced and cunning warlord of the forest. He fought with glory during the last invasion and survived the Century of War, commanding troops and leading the army of Llafal into battle. Nevertheless, he is still a far lesser Elf than Father was. But then, no one in the clan ever would, or could, replace Father. Tyar dyl has no charisma. He seldom even talks. Although a skilled fighter, he is no commander. He inspires respect, but not devotion nor worship.'

She wondered if he would accept the sacred Spear of Aonyn, should war be waged upon them. The legendary weapon was the ultimate symbol of authority over the Llewenti clans' armies. Wielding it implied important responsibility and duty. She concluded that it would be a burden too great for Tyar dyl to bear. A tremor of fear swept over her as she realised.

"Who, then, will lead the fighters if the barbarians return? Or, rather, when the barbarians return?"

Her fear and unease increased and was growing ever stronger. She closed her eyes, despite the soft glow of sunset. She suddenly felt alone, very alone, and it was frightening. Most Llewenti of Llymar lived in the forest, far from the city and hence from any hope of outside help. Lyrine realized then that she had sent the other matriarchs of Llafal away to bring them help after the cyclone for a specific reason. This time, she needed her fellow high priestesses to be out of the way so that she might handle the situation herself. She wanted to control this moment. While she had difficulty admitting it, Lyrine knew that this ship's arrival could, or indeed would, trigger events of immense importance.

The elder matriarch then reproached herself: 'You are no better than any Hawenti tyrant whose authority was passed down his bloodline. This despotism of yours flies in the face of two thousand years' worth of Llewenti tradition. You believe that it is you alone who can command and care for this clan, simply because of your lineage, because of your great powers over the Islands' Flow.'

In her mind's eye, she could see her father again, as she did in her worst nightmares. She could see him dying in her arms from his numerous wounds, handing her his spear, entrusting her with the most sacred weapon of the Llewenti clans. She could see, around him, the corpses of the many barbarians that had fallen at the fury of his blade. Almost a hundred years had passed, but the wounds had not healed, and the pain had not subsided: nothing could compensate for that loss. Her hatred, however, endured: abhorrence for the race of men, for their vile deeds and endless thirst for conquest.

> *'Your hatred must be watched as carefully as a campfire. If it burns too ferociously, it threatens the existence of the whole forest; but if you let it die, you will be left cold and defenceless.'*

She remembered her father's words and kept her emotions in check.
Lyrine concentrated on regaining her composure. She could not allow anyone or anything to obscure her mind or shadow her thoughts. The matriarch knew that one day her decisions would influence the fate of all the Llewenti. In this, she was alone. She would therefore act on her own. The Lady of Llafal breathed deeply, taking in the evening breeze that carried the scents of the Halwyfal. Lyrine turned around and faced Temple Square, its lanterns defiant in the falling night. She strode towards the guards who were always stationed close to her, awaiting her command.

"Send for the priestesses of Eïwele Llyo and have them open the Grey Temple.
Station yourselves at its entrance. Let no one trouble me until Tyar dyl returns. The full moon will soon rise; make haste," ordered Lyrine decisively.

The shrine of Eïwele Llyo was in the southern half of Temple Square, at a distance from the trees so that, when the moon was full, it was bathed in a blue light, its open ceilings revealing the night sky above. It was adorned with silver moonstones and surrounded by a garden of night-blooming flowers. The deity held a prominent place in the clan's pantheon. The divinity of dreams, fate, death and reincarnation, Eïwele Llyo was said to reside in the heart of Nyn Llyvary Island, in a great, underground hall. From inside this vast cave, she would rely upon her evocative power to spread out dreams across the archipelago, as she watched over the destinies of all Llewenti. She was represented as an ancient, withered Elvin creature, personifying the keeper of the souls and the weaver of prophecies. Eïwele Llyo alone could read the patterns of time from stones carved with lava markings which she found deep in the underground. Ravens were her messengers and when they soared across the Islands, the wise among the Llewenti were eager to interpret these signs, for it was believed that Eïwele Llyo knew the fate of all who dwelt in the Islands.

The clergy of Eïwele Llyo did not take long to gather within the temple. The six priestesses were dressed in silvery-grey, diaphanous gowns. With these, they wore silver diadems on their heads, simple sandals, and silver lace sashes around their waists.

As shrouded in mystery as their deity herself, little was known of the clergy's secretive hierarchy. The rest of the clan saw them as mystics and seers, spiritual counsellors to the Elves before their souls began that mystical journey to the undying forest, in search of transcendence. The cult viewed life as a series of mysteries, shrouded by the deity herself, which the spirits of the Elves could only discover through dreams and visions after they had transcended their mortal existences. Worshippers of Eïwele Llyo revered the moon; it governed their souls just as it controlled the ocean's tides. The temple's priestesses also celebrated funerals and guarded the material remains of the dead. Their power to weave illusions and practise divination was deeply respected by all.

Tonight, however, the clerics of Eïwele Llyo had been summoned by the most powerful of the clan's matriarchs. The moon was full and the high priestess, no doubt, would call on their prayers and spells. They prepared themselves to devote several days to playing the harp, immersing themselves in vivid waking dreams, and communing with their deity across the two worlds.

When the elder matriarch entered the temple, which had been prepared, they began the joyous, freeform dance that would precede their communal trance and meditation, but Lyrine stopped them to make her objectives clear.

"We must join with Eïwele Llyo! I intend to call upon the Oracle of Llafal. I wish to look into the waters of Halwyfal."

Terror struck the six priestesses. The matriarch was ready to use the Islands' Flow, to look into the unknown, and to extract some hint of things to come. No one had dared attempt this since the beginning of the Century of War.
The temple doors closed so the ritual could begin.

*

Four days later, Lyrine was told of the warlord of Llafal's return. Tyar dyl had completed his mission and was returning home with a prisoner. The shipwrecked Elves had not put up any kind of struggle before letting their captain go. On the contrary, their joy had been great and their hopes high. The envoy of the Llewenti had been welcomed like a hero and thanked warmly for his gifts. The Blue Elves had improvised an exotic dance, with loud percussion and wild music, to celebrate his coming. The Irawenti were an extraordinary people when it came to celebration and feasting. Their innate empathy and joyful salutations had made a strong impression upon Tyar dyl. He had thus paid the utmost respect to their captain, who in return had voiced no objection to submitting to the matriarchs' bidding.

In the interlude, Lyrine had enough time to recover from the exhaustion which had followed the summoning of the Islands' Flow. Upon Tyar dyl's arrival, she immediately called for his prisoner. Many precautions were taken to hide his presence in the city of the clan Llyvary.

The shipwreck's envoy was admitted to the great hall of the clan's stronghold after nightfall, with even greater secrecy.

The hall was a large reception room occupying the entire top floor. Its walls were fashioned out of stone, but wood was pervasive throughout. Many intricately carved pillars were arranged symmetrically throughout the room creating the impression of an engineered forest. Lush plants gave the place a vital glow. The tops of some reached as far as the beautiful, glass, domed ceiling which covered the hall and revealed the night sky. This intermingling of the wild and the artistic gave the hall an aura of mysticism and wonder. To the east and west, large windows overlooked the sleeping city. Stained glass coloured the light as it filtered through. It created an atmosphere which combined the most delicate art with the highest spirituality. On its southern side, the room opened out onto a terrace which overlooked the Halwyfal. While the north wall was covered with a huge wooden panel, into this had been carved several illustrious chairs decorated with figures from Llewenti mythology. The clan's noble dyl sat on these seats during ceremonies and clan councils.

Down in front of this impressive row of seats, a stage dominated the rest of the hall. Three large chairs, made of wood and foliage, were arranged in an arc. They were the symbol of the Matriarchs of Llafal's power.

Only Lyrine was present that night. The most powerful dignitary of the clan Llyvary sat in the central chair like a queen on her throne. Her long, shimmering, silky hair seemed to create a mysterious aura around her. She wore a green cloak with the hood thrown back. With her eyes half-closed and her head slightly inclined; she was muttering incantations when the castaways' envoy was introduced into the great hall.

The Lady of Llafal scrutinised her guest. She immediately noted that he was dressed with great care, which demonstrated respect for his host and perhaps even some kind of effort to seduce her. A diadem of pearls adorned his head. His long hair, strewn with silvery feathers, was combed delicately and hung down to his waist. The light, silk robe he had chosen to wear was of an unknown origin and design, its shimmering white and azure tones seeming exotic and mystical. But the matriarch's gaze was mainly captured by the tattooed motif which adorned the left half of the navigator's face. Lyrine examined it carefully before concluding that it must have been a protective pentagram. She also noted that her guest had paid little attention to the hostile, watchful attitude of the guards. She was somewhat unnerved by his calm face and inquisitive eyes, azure like a tropical sea.

The shadows of night had encroached upon the palace; the corners of the great hall sunk away into the darkness. The flickering red light emanating from a fireplace played upon the navigator's face, dancing like wildfire. He stood in the centre of the room motionless, silent and staring, fully aware of the solemnity of the moment. The castaways' representative seemed calm and assured. He sat down quietly, resting his hands on his knees, his eyes shining like stars. His long, dark-azure hair reflected the glow of the fire; his serene gaze fixed upon the Llewenti lady.

It was the matriarch who broke the silence first. She chose to express herself in the tongue of the High Elves, in lingua Hawenti, as Tyar dyl had reported that the intruders practiced it. She uttered her first words very slowly, taking care to articulate each syllable, as though calling upon knowledge buried deep within her memory.

"I have been told that your ship ran aground on the beach of a small isle called Pyenty, off the Gloren peninsula. There are very few Elves or men that would dare sail north of Llymar's shores. It is Eïwal Ffeyn's domain, and the devastating potential of his anger is well known. A wise sailor would also know that, were he to escape the wrath of the deity, he would not be met with a benevolent welcome from the forest's inhabitants. The woods of Llymar belong to the Llewenti clans; foreigners are not welcome here."

Lyrine paused, her eyes fixed intensely upon her guest, as she tested the effect of her threatening words. She then continued.

"I see that I was not deceived. You are of Irawenti ancestry. I was unaware that any Blue Elves, pure-blood descendants of those legendary navigators from the dawn of this Age, remained on the archipelago.

Our songs tell us that their blood mingled with our own distant relatives from the clan Llorely who dwell in the city of Urmilla[25]. I was also told that you do not understand our language and speak in authentic Irawenti, an exotic and incomprehensible dialect to our ears. Until recently, you relied on lingua Hawenti to communicate. There are only few of us left who can understand it. It is a dead language. Even the High Elves use it solely for writing manuscripts. The archaic tongue cannot even be heard in the royal court of Gwarystan.

I look forward to hearing your story; your arrival here amongst us is shrouded in mystery. Our vessels travel the seas of the archipelago. Before now, I have never heard a tale of an authentic Irawenti sailing the high seas."

The castaways' envoy let these last words echo throughout the great hall. He then stepped forward, bowed respectfully, and began to answer the questions that had been posed to him. He too spoke in Ancient Hawenti, but quite fluently, as it was common practice in the kingdom of Essawylor. Hence, his delivery was faster, and peppered with various exotic pronunciations of Irawenti origin, which added flavour to the ancient rhetoric of the High Elves.

"I will explain, Noble Matriarch," he began solemnly.

"Our ship does not come from the archipelago; I do not know these islands. We have no affiliation with the clan Llorely of the Llewenti. I regret not to be in a position to speak your language, which sounds elegant and attractive to my ears. I have not yet mastered its subtleties. We are castaways from the Austral Ocean. We come from the distant shores of Essawylor, where Queen Aranaele rules."

At this revelation, the matriarch could not help but shudder. She was silent for a moment, lost in thought, fear etched onto her face. She continued.

"Very, very few sailors have managed to reach these shores from the other side of the Austral Ocean. The dangers are immense. Your errand must be of great importance, foreigner from distant lands."

---

25 Urmilla: 'The harbour of Urmil' in lingua Llewenti

"It is not so, Noble Matriarch. No mission has been entrusted to us. Only the ambition of reaching a friendly Elvin refuge has guided us so far," the castaways' envoy confessed.

He then introduced himself in a more formal manner.

"I am Feïwal dyn Filweni, navigator and explorer. I am not here to represent any king or queen. I am not the ambassador of any worldly power or cause. Others from my kin came with me. We were also accompanied by High Elves who belong to the House of Dol Lewin, once a powerful force in the kingdom of Essawylor.
We chose to flee the tyranny of Queen Aranaele and cross the ocean. I come from the land of the Five Rivers; I hail from beyond the Austral Ocean, where Llewenti songs of old are sung only as fictions which the Irawenti no longer believe to have any truth. Long ago, Queen Aranaele convinced our clans that traversing the Austral Ocean would only lead to the abyss. No Elf who braved it had ever returned.
But we, of the clan Filweni, did not forget the ancient knowledge of our fathers, and we saved it from oblivion. My people discovered the legacy left by the Llewenti after we re-conquered Essawylor. Unlike the other Irawenti clans, we, have kept our old beliefs alive, and we continue to celebrate the fabled legends of the archipelago. We are the keepers of the ancient writings of the Llewenti Queen Llyoriane. The legend of your people kindles the fire in the songs and tales of our bards. The story of the Llewenti lies at the very heart of our identity however unknown we may be to you."

Lyrine admitted, "So it is true. My daughter was right and Tyar dyl too. Despite all the evidence brought to me, I was unwilling and refused to admit it. You have come from far way, Feïwal dyn Filweni, and I do not doubt that you have braved incredible dangers and suffered many losses."

"We have, noble Matriarch! But my clan bears a responsibility. It is we who must lead the way when the dusk finally comes. And that time is approaching. 'We will cross the ocean'; those are our words. We inherited this vow from our ancestor Filwen, the first who heard in his dreams the songs of the Lost Islands."

The Lady of Llafal interrupted him impatiently.

"Tell me more about the fabled Essawylor. Tell me what threat drove you to undertake such a dangerous journey," she ordered.

"Noble Matriarch, I will tell all.

It began several decades ago.

My father, Fadalwy, plagued by a deep, nagging urge, dragged the Filweni on a journey.

He called upon every ounce of the clan's energy and devotion. New maps were drawn. New techniques were developed to better arm our ships. My father was a brilliant shipwright himself, but he was also surrounded by many steadfast followers, who all shared his devotion to Gweïwal Uleydon. The other Irawenti clan leaders saw him as one possessed, bewitched by the God of the Oceans. But we dyn of the clan Filweni never doubted him or the vision he set out for us.

My father cannot witness our success; his ship was engulfed by the sea just off the Atolls which now bear his name. The surviving ships from that expedition were the first to ever return to our shores from so far away. My father's exploits represented a monumental conquest. The great distance travelled by his fleet and the discovery of hidden islands led to the destruction of a deeply ingrained belief. Throughout the centuries, the wisest among the Elves of Essawylor had always asserted that navigation beyond the passage of the Nen was impossible, that any sailor venturing beyond this limit would suffer the worst torments imaginable. Our history books did not deny this theory, nor did even the most resolute of our sailors set out to challenge it.

Cil, Cim, Cir! My father's successful expeditions disproved this unfounded belief. We became bolder as a clan, and a new generation of fearless young sailors emerged, spurred on by an unwavering resolution to test the limits imposed by the clerics' antiquated beliefs. For two decades, we roamed the ocean, searching in vain for the lost archipelago. Our exploratory voyages began to stretch to the edges of the Sea of Cyclones.

Our mission was to save our own kind, to open a pathway to exile should we meet ruin. But during all these attempts, we had to keep the return voyage in mind. We were therefore condemned to failure. The quest for the Lost Islands is a journey that cannot offer any hope of return. It is a leap into the unknown. It is an act of faith."

Feïwal paused, his voice distorted and choked by emotion. He took a deep breath before continuing.

"For a long time now, fear has plagued the Elves of Essawylor. Our borders are consistently threatened by the devastating raids of bloodthirsty men who come from beyond the equatorial steppes, from a dark land cursed by the Gods. The enemy is assembling, in ever-greater numbers, at our borders. Last spring, war came upon us. Men of the Desert Horde invaded from the northern front in the province of Ystanlewin, where the standard of the War Unicorn had flown proudly for so long. The land was utterly devastated; the gates to that city of Dol Lewin were closed. The city's army had long served as a bulwark, ensuring peace and freedom to the rest of the Kingdom. Yet it was defeated, destroyed, before any rescue came.
Dark smoke now rises from the ruins of that once-glorious city and I fear that its fall is but the prelude to many further tragedies.
This is the reason why we come here to you with a message of peace with our hearts filled with hope."

At the matriarch's bidding, a servant interrupted Feïwal's story to bring her wine and fruits. Lyrine forced a smile as she reached over and seized a fine crystal glass from the table. She concentrated hard on pouring the golden liquor into the precious cup, her focus on this simple action masking the turmoil within her.

"Your words are true, Feïwal dyn Filweni, as true as your dedication to this quest. I can see that you believe in what you say. This faith gives you considerable strength... and it makes you dangerous. I understand what you have fought for. I comprehend your noble quest. What you have achieved is without doubt the greatest deed of any navigator in recent history. This is no exaggeration." She nodded once these words had left her mouth, still struck with incredulity, before continuing.
"Even your ancestor Filwen could not survive that voyage, according to tales of old. His ruined ship washed up on the shores of the peninsula. Indeed, he is said to have drowned just

a few leagues from his promised land," she nodded again, her mind racing to measure the implications of such a feat. However, other sailors in that fleet, sons and followers of Filwen, did indeed reach our shores," she added, her voice trembling as she struggled to contain her emotion. "They were not alone... nor were they defenceless."

Her gaze, veiled by a stirring, long-forgotten memory, focused on Feïwal's eyes.

"What are you telling me, Noble Matriarch?" asked the navigator, holding his breath.

A silence ensued. The matriarch seemed to hesitate over which course of action to take. She tried to suppress a deeply rooted suffering, re-emerging from the past. But it proved overwhelming.

"I speak of disastrous events from a long time ago. Some of those ships that you speak of succeeded in their quest. Members of your kin survived, as did the Hawenti princes and their Dol vassals who travelled with them. Their survival marked our doom," she replied severely.

Feïwal did not question her further after this change in attitude, but from the few words that the matriarch had already uttered, he deduced that certain members of his own clan must have made it across the ocean before they settled on some other island. They may have had some connection with the Llewenti clan that she had accused him of being associated with earlier. Feïwal was relieved and found this news reassuring, hence he was blind to what was about to come.

The matriarch rose from her seat; he admired her tall, thin and gracious stature. But an element of fear was growing within him, as he gradually realized that he was under threat. A coil of cold, intense hatred was wound up within the Lady of the clan Llyvary, waiting for an opportunity to spring. She moved towards him suddenly, confronting him with a malevolent look in her eyes.

"Fools! All of them were fools. Utter wretched fools. Fools were the Irawenti who came looking for their promised land. They carried with them, aboard their ships, their own annihilation: the pride and the thirst for power of their companions, the High Elves.

Fools were the Hawenti who believed that power stemmed from war and from gold: those Elves who fought for a forgotten world, a world sentenced to doom by oaths from another age.

Fools were the six clans of the Llewenti that failed to unite to preserve their realm.

The gentle Llorely clan rallied the High Elves before the first arrow was shot.

The naïve clan Avrony sought shelter and protection in the depths of their ancient forests, ignorant of their fate.

The fierce clan Ernaly fought valiantly but alone, refusing to trust their kin.

The cold clan Llyandy remained hidden in their desert of snow, caring nothing for the plight of others.

The evil clan Myortilys saw their power consumed in treachery and deceit, believing that, through betrayal and duplicity, they could rule the Islands.

The Llyvary, my own clan, also failed. We, too, made many mistakes, and failed to follow the right path," she admitted.

Her breath was shallow, yet she resumed her story.

"What these fools all failed to see was that power has always resided with the Islands' deities. The archipelago had long been protected from the turmoil of the wider world.

Chaos only reached our shores when your kin, the Irawenti sailors of the fabled-clan Filweni, appeared in hundreds of ships upon the horizon. These ships bore the banners of the Hawenti houses. But Eïwal Ffeyn could not allow this to happen; he conjured all his might, challenging the power of that fleet, as it sailed the Austral Ocean towards our shores. He summoned to his side Griffons, Hippogriffs and Storm Eagles to fight the invaders, but he was defeated. Eïwal Ffeyn was overcome.

The power of the High Elves had prevailed. The deity of storms was cast out of the archipelago to his doom, incarcerated in the largest jail imaginable: the vast expansive Sea of Cyclones."

Lyrine paused, her eyes empty, as though she was still considering what power could have accomplished such a feat.

"Even the wisest of Llewenti could not ever have foreseen how that lust for power would consume the newcomers as the following years, decades and centuries passed. They became utterly possessed by their accursed ambition. No matter how deep in the forest you hide, no matter how cunning you are in diplomacy, no matter how ferocious you are in warfare, the High Elves are always to be feared.

After every trade agreement, every treaty, every battle, every war, one by one the realms of the Llewenti clans, the six islands of the archipelago, fell to the dominion of the new ruler: Lormelin the Conqueror, self-proclaimed king. Oaths were taken, submissions were sworn, power abandoned and faith in the Islands' deities forgotten. Most of the Llewenti were subdued, falling in line behind the new order by joining one of the Hawenti noble houses. After centuries of conflict, little was left for us.

The Llewenti are hopeful and brave; these virtues make them dedicated servants. The High Elves lead, they lie, and they deceive, and these vices make them highly adept at seizing and retaining control.

Despite the infighting and quarrelling, the Islands' deities had always collectively been the protectors of the Llewenti, the children of the beloved Queen Llyoriane. But the power of the High Elves drove them away to all corners of the lands: far out across the ocean, down into the depths of the earth and deep into the distant mountains. The matriarchs saw their powers diminish as the high towers of Gwarystan rose, where the high mages of the Ruby College were harvesting the Islands' Flow for the new king's benefit."

A silence followed, as if Lyrine needed some time to catch her breath and to reconstruct the events. At last, she continued her tale.

"But there was another force that had always coveted the archipelago, an ever-present threat from the Mainland's distant southern shores. This danger had been kept at bay by the storms of Eïwal Ffeyn, contained by the power of the Islands' deities since the earliest days of the world.

In the thick of the vast tribal grasslands, the human barbarians multiplied for centuries, until the time came when they understood they were strong enough. A new power had risen, the Men of the West, amongst them great craftsmen, led by powerful Sea Hierarchs. They manipulated the barbarian tribes of the Mainland and unleashed all their power upon the Elves of the archipelago.

It began one fateful night in Nyn Ernaly[26], a night of sorrow and death, when the great galleys of the Westerners unleashed a horde of barbarians, who burnt to the ground Mentolewin[27], the great fortress protecting the strait of Oymal[28].

Many centuries have passed since that first raid, and war has been raging ever since, save for few periods of ominous peace. Year on year, battle by battle, Elves gradually lost control of the western islands, their inhabitants fleeing the terrifying raids and relinquishing their lands. The High Elves, clinging to what remained of their former glory, fought bravely, but they were ultimately subdued and withdrew to their fortress cities at the centre of the archipelago, preserving the heart of their realm. They signed a peace treaty with the Men of the West and the Barbarians. They called it 'The Pact'.

Nowadays, most of the Llewenti serve the King of Gwarystan, choosing to live in the safety of his domains and fortresses, obedient to the Hawenti Dol houses. But others chose to remain as the six clans of old, living according to our tradition and remaining free. We struggle every day to preserve the ruins of our ancient realms.

The remaining free Llewenti are scattered and weak, with little hope left after centuries resisting inevitable destruction. Whatever our allegiances, all of us are subject to the Pact, for it has now guaranteed peace on the Islands for almost a century.

The promised islands that you sought is not what you dreamt them to be; the sky burns red with a thousand dreadful warnings."

Lyrine added, with a closed expression on her face. "Where will you look for hope now, Feïwal dyn Filweni?"

---

26 Nyn Ernaly: 'The island of Ernaly' in lingua Llewenti
27 Mentolewin: 'The fortress of Lewin' in lingua Llewenti
28 Strait of Oymal: 'Strait of froth' in lingua Llewenti

The navigator was astonished by Lyrine's story. He took a moment to reply, but, when he did, his voice was still firm and quiet.

"Our quest remains unchanged: it is in the Llewenti, my Lady, and in your clan, that we wish to place our hope. We are lost and can never return home."

"It cannot be; you cannot stay here. The King's eyes are concentrated upon the forest of Llymar, awaiting the Llewenti clans' first challenge to his authority. I will not risk it."

She paused for a while before finally deciding to continue.

"Your kin, it seems, preferred to forget the dark events that led to the formation of the Kingdom of Essawylor. The same is not true for the High Elves of our islands. They will forever remember their oath to King Lormelin. The Conqueror never forgave how his people were chased from Essawylor, how his relative, your queen, seized the throne. He did not forgive neither the vile crimes perpetrated in her name. All those sworn to King Lormelin's service took an oath of revenge against Queen Aranaele's followers. I know from Hawenti scholars that, before launching his fleet across the Austral Ocean, he made all those who rallied behind him commit to this vow. Long after, when Lormelin was murdered, this oath of revenge was passed down, along with his crown, to his son, King Norelin."

Lyrine paused again for a moment and then went on to insist.

"Oaths are not taken lightly by High Elves, Feïwal dyn! Some dedicate their entire life to the fulfilment of such vows, knowing full well that it may lead them to their doom. The war unicorn of Dol Lewin was seen aboard your ship. It is a cursed banner in these waters: the banner of a divided house, whose members fought fiercely during that war of old. They fought ruthlessly: brother against brother, son against father. The High Elves who came with you are a dangerous burden. Think on it! Unlike us mere Wenti, Hawenti are immortal. While we may willingly abandon our existence, they never grow tired of life. They never give up, for their memory is immortal too. Trust me, Feïwal dyn, forgiveness does not come easily to the High Elves."

The recounting of this ancient tale had created a palpable atmosphere of unease between them. It was as if time itself had stopped once Lyrine finished recounting these evil deeds. The oath of Lormelin created an insurmountable barrier between the two Elves. They both felt dread stirring within them.

"You cannot stay in Llymar. That is my decision. We will help you repair your ship before you sail away. The clan Llyvary will not take you prisoner, as we have no allegiance to the King of Gwarystan. But you will need to leave our territory."

The two had been talking for a long time when Lyrine ended her tale, the moon's slow descent in the starlit sky indicating the coming of dawn. It was as if the moon had been waiting for that very moment, pausing for nature to display the full extent of its beauty, in the moonbeams that streaked across the waters of the Halwyfal.

Lyrine sank into her grand chair, slowly closing her eyes. The blood drained from her face, which became as pale as the light hair that framed it. Overcome with weariness, she looked, for a moment, like the target of some malevolent spell. Her eyes suddenly opened again and, as quickly as it had vanished, the colour returned to her cheeks. A striking radiance emanated from her gaze. She looked out upon the waters of the Halwyfal below, its ripening spectrum of colours heralding the imminent sunrise. Her expression was ethereal, like a deity of the Islands who marched alongside Llyoriane upon the archipelago's untainted beaches so long ago. Her face was one of kindness and grace, though marked with wisdom and gravity.

Lyrine kept her gaze fixed upon the Halwyfal and remained like this for some time, before rising slowly from her seat, as if the great basin's waters were drawing her magnetically towards them. The Halwyfal seemed to pull at her soul. Her expression then changed, straining to contain what might have been nervous laughter. Sweat could be seen on her temples before the fear finally hit her. She broke away from the pull of the scene below her.

A long moment passed, during which she neither spoke nor raised her eyes. That was until her voice, formerly so clear, rang out again, but this time very low and stifled, as though it were coming from afar.

"You and your followers have arrived on our shores bearing dark omens: you are harbingers of envy and strife. You are not welcome here, Feïwal dyn Filweni."

When he heard what sounded like her final sentence, Feïwal rose from his seat, his expression one of disappointment and loss. He took up the pendant that still hung from his neck and raised it before the matriarch's eyes. The rope had become worn, but the magic runes interspersed along it seemed to have prevented its complete disintegration.

"This sacred rope is of the highest importance to my clan; it was bequeathed to us by Filwen the Ancient. It is a gift which bears a message from centuries ago, which tells of the destiny of Elves, bidding us to relinquish our power on the Mainland to cross the ocean and seek out the lost archipelago. It was passed down to me through the line of Filwen. Like my father before me, I have dedicated my entire existence to this task and I am haunted by my duty to complete it.
Do you not understand?
The very winds talk to me, urging me to begin my quest, and warning of the impending dangers that build beyond the horizon.
The winds granted us passage across the ocean. It was these winds that gave me a purpose; they ask me now to kneel in front of you and beg for you to honour us by letting us join your kind."

Feïwal, slowly and silently, then sat back in his chair, his deliberate solemnity emphasizing the significance of his plea. The matriarch was quiet, puzzled by the conviction and faith so clearly manifested by the navigator's words. A long silence ensued. Both sat still. They were acutely aware of the gravity of the moment. Finally, Lyrine rose, her gaze marked by pride and determination.

"Who do you think you are?

How dare you use the name of Eïwal Ffeyn in this way?

His breath is the very air of the archipelago, and so it has been since the dawn of time.

We, the matriarchs of the Llewenti clans, are the custodians of his holy word, as we are for all the deities of the Islands. You will reconsider your position and obey my orders, master sailor. Once again: you cannot stay in the forest of Llymar; that is my final decision...

The Irawenti are no enemy of ours but, long ago, they reached our shores with the High Elves and a multitude of conflicts and wars followed. Today, you appeal again for our protection. But you too, have not come alone.

These are ill omens, Feïwal dyn Filweni; these forebodings are dark indeed.

You will sail east. Do not look to the west, for that way you will find a cruel end in the hands of barbarian tribes.

May the sacred winds of Eïwal Ffeyn remove all traces of your visit to Llafal!

I shall not see you again," concluded Lyrine, with immutable authority.

She clapped her hands and guards entered the reception hall, responding to their matriarch's summons. Feïwal stood up and left with them, defeat etched across his face. Tyar dyl then entered the hall to take his orders from the elder matriarch. His face showed a calm determination.

"Tyar dyl, the prisoner is to return to his vessel. In the meantime, you will go to the shipyards of Penlla. Gather all that is required to repair the castaways' ship. Use my seal in all your dealings and do not say a word."

She paused, suddenly realizing that she was in breach of the clan's rules and traditions. The Council of the Matriarchs was the sovereign power in these matters, and she had no right to act without consulting the other high priestesses of Llymar. But then, Llafal had no right to act without the consent of the other cities of the Forest. Her hesitation did not last long.

"You are ordered to bring them the equipment and supplies required to refloat their ship. I am giving them ten days to sail east."

"What if they do not obey?" the "Old Bird" asked in his typically laconic fashion.

"Make it clear," she replied, with a hard edge to her voice, "that any such defiance would result in their death. I will show no mercy."

"I will prepare the swanships for assault. Their heavy weaponry is ruined. With the combined force of our fleet, we could crush them easily from a safe distance," asserted the old commander.

The Lady of Llafal concluded with a commanding tone.

"Have everything prepared. We need to be ready if we are compelled to gather the Council of the Matriarchs. Select your troops carefully and have them all swear an oath of secrecy. We must prevent, at all costs, the news of the shipwreck reaching the cities of Tios Halabron and Tios Lluin too soon. I do not want our allies interfering with my decision. This ship must be chased from our shores. We will ensure it at all costs."

CHAPTER 3: dyl Ernaly

A few days had passed since the end of the storm which had struck Llymar's shores, and life around the Halwyfal was gradually returning to normal.

After a trek across the hills, two maidens, were heading south to the city of Llafal. The day was bright, and the air felt pure in the light ocean breeze. They strode onwards, their pace quickened by purpose and joy. As the two young Elves passed the Temple of Eïwal Ffeyn, they paused, whispering prayers and performing the ritual offerings required of them. The city of Llafal laid some way down the hill, a few leagues away, hidden by the tall pines of the forest.

"Wonderful! It's going to be wonderful!" exclaimed Mayile, the youngest, her bright sapphire eyes blazing.

"The Festival of the Islands comes around every twenty years. You will live to experience many more," Marwen, the eldest, replied in an effort to restore calm, her gait demonstrating her particular nobility.

"True, but this one is special. For the first time ever, it is taking place in Tios Halabron, and the clan Ernaly are hosting it," the younger replied with conviction. Her blonde hair, tumbling wildly about her head, marked each of her movements with a natural beauty.

"I am unaware of anything that the clan Ernaly can do better!"

"They are the masters of music and dancing. Their festivities are legendary. They will be preparing a marvellous feast, I am sure."

"Is that right? And I suppose that marvellous feasts are the main preoccupation of Eïwele Llyi's apprentices?" Marwen questioned.

"They are indeed. We aren't as boring and serious as those Eïwal Lon[29] priestesses," Mayile cheekily replied.

"How dare you mock Eïwal Lon's Temple? If I am successful, I might one day assist Matriarch Lyrine herself. I have a considerable task ahead of me, and I cannot afford to waste my energy on something as trivial as feasting!"

"I understand your ambitions, but I favour Matriarch Nyriele! She does not forbid us from enjoying this life that the deities have granted us! She teaches us of love and beauty, in accordance with my own principles. Now, why do you seem so distressed?"

"My apologies," Marwen replied, realizing that she had only been chiding her friend in order to hide her own feelings. "You are right. I confess I am worried at the thought of attending the festival alone."

"Why would he not come?"

Marwen confessed. "It's been a few days now since the swanships were sent out north into the ocean. Nobody seems to be expecting them back soon. Something unusual is going on, but I do not know their mission. I have asked everywhere but the matriarchs are maintaining absolute secrecy."

Suddenly, their conversation was interrupted by the strange sound of footsteps coming down the forest path, accompanied by an unnatural wind that felt like the very breath of the forest. The plants around them instantly began to shiver, then convulse in a way that they had never seen before. Their path was disappearing, devoured by the sudden growth of the vegetation around them.

Grasses, bushes, even tree roots, twisted around the two young Elves, ensnaring them so that they were unable to move. Trapped, they saw a creature progressing up the hill towards them.

---

29 Eïwal Lon: Demigod of sunlight, divinity of wisdom

"What could it be? Was it Elf or beast? Animal or Plant?" cried out Marwen.

The creature's thin body was shrouded in a large robe made entirely of green feathers and foliage. Upon her head were antlers, proudly displayed. Her unnatural eyes were an intense, burning emerald. She wielded in her right hand a long whip of bough, whilst her left gripped a great wooden staff, shaped like a halberd, which she leant upon as she marched forward.

Quickly climbing the hill, the creature ignored the surrounding chaos with sovereign disdain, as though nature's act of homage and obeisance was owed to her.

Soon she was upon them, and the two young maidens recognized her as a female of their own breed, though inhabited by some mystic power.

"Nase gnally! Nase gnally!" [30] the creature growled aggressively when she discovered their presence.

The two young Elves, struck equally by fear and wonder, struggled against their entanglement but still tried to turn away, in an attempt to show that they would not impede her passage. By the time they regained control of their emotions, the vision had disappeared; the path and woods around them had reverted to their original state.

"Who was she?" Mayile asked, breathless.

"I do not know, and yet... she resembled a character from the tales of old... the Daughter of the Islands..." replied Marwen, as stunned by the encounter as her friend. "Lore was her name," she continued, "a matriarch of clan Ernaly who was granted an unnaturally long life."

"Let's follow her!"

"No! This could prove dangerous! We have no idea how she might react!"

"Do as you wish, I shall go," the younger maiden obstinately replied.

---

30 Nase Gnally: 'Out of my way' in lingua Llewenti

"Stop! The power of the Daughter of the Islands is drawn from the earth; Eïwele Llya[31] herself is her ally. She is dangerous and powerful. We cannot imagine her wrath if she knew she was being followed!"

But Mayile was too excited to listen to these wise words of caution and respect. She turned back, seizing her chance to track the legendary creature. Marwen had no choice but to follow at a distance. Despite herself, she could not deny the overwhelming excitement that had also taken hold of her.

The two Elves broke into a run, heading back up the hill, stopping and starting as they negotiated the path's twists and turns. But they had been too slow to react, and their efforts were in vain. When they reached the top of the hill, the two friends found the glade surrounding the Temple of Eïwal Ffeyn to be deserted. Only the sounds of the ocean wind could be heard as it frantically rushed among the colonnades. From here, the two young Elves had a direct view of the Halwyfal basin and the dangerous passes to the ocean beyond; the vista was like an unspoiled image of the island in its infancy. They could not help but burst into hushed, excited conversation about what had just happened.

At the noise of their chatter, a great, grey hawk took off out of the shelter of the temple, spiralling upwards into the air. Soon it reached high altitude and beat its wings rapidly, before the momentum launched it on a smooth, graceful glide with the wind. Its large wingspan carried it quickly over the magnificent landscape: the vast ocean, the tiny islands, the rugged coastline, the white shores, the sandy beaches, the golden dunes and the infinite woods of Llymar.

The great forest extended from the northern shores of Nyn Llyvary to the slopes of Arob Nisty[32] in the south, from the ravines of Arob Tiude[33] in the east to the strait of Nyn Llorely in the west. Two hundred square leagues of a variety of conifers

---

31 Eïwele Llya: Deity of nature, divinity of fauna, flora and fertility. She is also known as 'The Mother of the Islands'.

32 Arob Nisty: 'The grey hills' in lingua Llewenti, Rocky Mountains separating Llymar from the south of nyn Llyvary

33 Arob Tiude: 'The evening hills' in lingua Llewenti, mountain chain separating Llymar from the west of nyn Llyvary

and trees made up the 'green sea', as the Llewenti also called it. The dominant species by far in this vast area was the maritime pine.

In the centre of the forest, there laid a smaller, natural area of woodland which had survived even the glacial Early Age. There, pines coexisted with other species of tree, chiefly oak, alder, birch, willow and holly. It was in this direction that the great hawk had chosen to set its course, heading southwest as it left the Halwyfal and the ocean behind it. From high above, it observed with pride how the other birds darted away from it in terror, seeking the forest's protection. The hawk was known by all manner of creatures to be a violent predator. With its sharp vision and calculating mind, it was seen by the Elves as the most intelligent hunter, and the deadliest.

In less than an hour the great hawk had crossed more than ten leagues. Apparently reaching its destination, it plunged out of the sky down to what looked to be a green mountain at the heart of the forest. But this was no common hill: it was a grove of sacred essence known as Tios Halabron. Long ago, the Llewenti had settled within this thicket of holly trees, building huts and shacks upon platforms high in the branches. The gigantic trees here gave their name to their city. Their height could exceed two hundred feet. Their scale was colossal; their roots spread out wide and deep underground, sometimes emerging at the surface like monstrous sea snakes. They were sacred to the Llewenti, who considered them to be servants of Eïwele Llya, 'The Mother of the Islands' and divinity of fertility and nature.

The giant trees transported the pure air above the canopies down into the depths of the Islands, where Eïwele Llya dwelt. They were called Eïwaloni[34], or "divine trees" in the language of the Llewenti, for the power of the archipelago's deities had raised them from the earth a long time ago, before any Elf had ever set foot upon the Islands. The tree city of Tios Halabron was built largely beneath nine of these gigantic conifers: the biggest at the centre, surrounded by eight others. The central trunk diverged into various branches that grew out horizontally to meet the encircling trees. It was on this broad foundation that the main platform of the city had been built.

---

34 Eïwaloni: 'Divine trees' in lingua Llewenti

Spreading its large wings and lifting them upwards, the great hawk quickly decelerated before diving down into the thickness of the sacred grove. It headed first towards a large wooden cistern, full of water, located at the top of the central tree. Pausing for a while, as if wary of some unexpected danger, the hawk carefully surveyed its surroundings. Only the sound of the gravity-fed water system could be heard distinctly. The tank collected rainfall and supplied the fountains further down in the city.

Private dwellings occupied multiple isolated platforms high in the trees. The woven mass of wood and leaves formed natural ceilings and walls, with openings here and there, windows which overlooked the entire Forest of Llymar.

The largest, intermediary level of the city was built on a platform of planking and intertwined boughs, five dozen feet above ground level. Smaller branches and offshoots grew up through the flooring, serving to brace whatever structure lay above, or occasionally forming the corner post of a house or shop. The ceilings of the Llewenti dwellings were made of branches, either woven or shaped into planks, and thatched roofs protected them from above.

The large hawk steered its course with ease, gliding between the branches and through the foliage, skirting around the numerous huts, nets, platforms and rope ladders that formed the magnificent city in the trees. Light was scarce, but the bird of prey knew the place well, and descended towards the ground with speed, raising little attention from the numerous wardens positioned at guard stations. Many Elves were busy hauling up cargo, by the block and tackle winches powered by some invisible means.

Most of the merchants' trading, however, was conducted at ground level. Hidden among the gnarled roots of the tree trunks, were a series of small shops, taverns, inns and artisans' lodges. In these parts, visibility ranged from near darkness to a dim twilight. Just above the ground, ramps, rope walkways and wooden buildings formed an intricate maze. Out beyond the trunks, but still beneath the broad canopy of leaves, were the weavers' and spinners' workshops. It was there that the famous cloth of Tios Halabron was manufactured.

Despite the apparent chaos and disorder of the place, it did not take long for the hawk to find its habitual shelter. It landed half way up the northern tree trunk, near the very heart of the great tree. It explored the thick bark for a while until it found the knot which formed an opening, a hole into which it jumped before flying down through the trunk. The dive was short; soon it extended its wings to slow the fall and come to land.

The giant trees of Tios Halabron guarded, within their trunks, vast, excavations which were used as shelters. The ability of the Eïwaloni to guard against the elements was an indispensable lifeline in extreme conditions. The hawk's nest was in one such haven.

But it was not alone. Other birds rested quietly upon branches high up in the immense cavity, close to its natural ceiling. The arrival of the great hawk instigated a great panic among the other birds, until it reached its resting place on the highest branch, thus marking its dominion over the nest.

The noise of this commotion briefly interrupted the discussion which was taking place below, at the very bottom of the cavity, where a larger area was organized. The room was furnished with tapestries, carpets, precious furniture and refined crockery, giving the place a most hospitable atmosphere. Musical instruments, ranging from a great harp to zithers and flutes, stood upright against a large bookcase crowded with antiquated works of literature.

Three Elves had gathered in the shelter of the Eïwaloni.

The first of the three Elves was a High Elf: pale, old and severe, with thin lips and cold eyes. His hair was combed with the greatest care and was an unusual snowy white. He wore gloves and his azure gown, cut from the finest silk, was almost free from embellishments. Only a coat of arms, depicting a golden arch, was embroidered upon his left shoulder. His name was Curubor and he came from the House of Dol Etrond. He was also known as a scholar of exceptional skills who most Llewenti called the 'Blue Mage'. Even among the immortal High Elves, he was considered ancient.

After his family's territories had fallen under the dominion of the human barbarians, Curubor had chosen to settle in Tios Lluin, an antique city of the Llewenti, whose ruins were at the heart of the Forest of Llymar. The matriarchs of the clan Llyvary, owing him much honour, had accepted his coming. Assisted by numerous enchanters and artisans, the Blue Mage had resolved to restore Tios Lluin to its former might.
Curubor Dol Etrond was at home in Llymar.

The two Elves who sat in front of him were both Llewenti: one robust and upstanding, the other thin and hunched over.

The tall one wore dark beige and brown hunter's clothes. His stockings were splashed from some recent errand in the woods. He had an abundance of blonde hair which looked almost mane-like and a handsome, slightly tanned face, with shining eyes. He held himself in such a way that demonstrated an undeniable force and his haughty bearing clearly exhibited his noble origins. His name was Gal dyl, from the clan Avrony, the sixth and lowest clan in the Llewenti hierarchy. He was the last in his lineage; no other had survived the barbarian invasion which had led to the fall of their island.
Gal dyl was a survivor, a refugee who had found asylum in the Forest of Llymar. Scorned by the noble dyl of the clan Llyvary, he nevertheless held a prominent position in the forest, having won the heart of their most prominent matriarch, Lyrine. And from the union of these two noble lines, Nyriele had been born, the most beautiful lady of her time, revered by all as the worthy descendant of Queen Llyoriane. Gal dyl had experienced many disasters, many defeats and many losses. But fate had thus far spared this witness to a forgotten world.

The final member of this secret council, the smaller of the two Llewenti, had a lustreless complexion, a finely drawn mouth, and hawk-like eyes. Fierce beauty radiated from his features. Three white feathers hung from a dark green cloth tied around his brown hair and his tunic was a beautiful emerald green. His name was Mynar dyl Ernaly. He too was an important figure in the Forest of Llymar, the most powerful dyl of the clan Ernaly, and the true master of Tios Halabron, ruling over more than three thousand Elves in the city of trees. He too was a refugee, as were all of his kin. Long ago, the barbarian tribes had conquered their homeland, the island of Nyn Ernaly. Mynar dyl was a stubborn fighter; he was the last of the Elves to abandon his territory, cross the Strait of Tiude[35] and seek refuge in the Llymar forest. A life of wandering through hostile territory had built his fierce character. He was known throughout the Forest of Llymar as a ruthless, unforgiving chief. The clan Ernaly's struggles during the barbarian wars had been crucial for the survival of the Llewenti. As a result, the clan Llyvary had handed over command of Tios Halabron to them, where they now dwelt and watched over the sacred trees. Mynar dyl was their warlord. No one questioned his authority.

The sun was setting in the west; it was still daylight under the tall trees of Tios Halabron and dappled light streamed down through the forest's foliage. But it was dark within the Eïwaloni; the meeting was illuminated solely by an enchanted mirror. The light reflected off three runes of silver which formed a triangle in the corner of the room.

In front of Gal dyl Avrony laid a jug of cider and an ancient book sat in front of Mynar dyl Ernaly. Chalk, ink, parchment and an array of maps lay before Curubor Dol Etrond.

The ancient High Elf resumed his speech after the unexpected interruption from the hawk's nest.

"You seem unable to comprehend the threat that lies before us. Many times, did I warn you about the dangerousness of this Ka-Bloozayar, and now four years have passed since he reached the western shores of Nyn Llyvary. Allow me to be perfectly plain: this is no ordinary man. He is an authentic Dragon Warrior, a barbarian chieftain from the Mainland who has survived the ritual of fire, ice and darkness. Undoubtedly, he has been entrusted with sacred authority to reawaken the forbidden Cult of the Three Dragons. Since arriving, he has accrued considerable influence among our enemies beyond the hills. He cannot have any other aim but to start another war."

---

35 Strait of Tiude: 'Strait of the evening' in lingua Llewenti, strait separating Nyn Llyvary in the west from Nyn Ernaly. It is a dangerous narrow sea where strong currents from the austral ocean meet the sea of Isyl.

"Curubor, every year for the last two decades you've lectured us about the threat of war," replied Gal dyl, visibly annoyed at the ancient Elf's didactic tone.

"Believe me, Gal dyl, when I say that Dragon Warriors are no small threat. These men are not priests. They are not kings. They have no interest in bolstering their number of followers, or in gaining new territories. They are fanatics who have nothing but scorn for the concept of diplomacy. They are weapons that have been created by the Cult of the Three Dragons for one purpose: mass carnage. My contacts are many across these islands. Friends from afar have given me information pertaining to other Dragon Warriors who have been witnessed on the archipelago. One such barbarian chieftain, named Ka-Blowna, has already gained legendary status among the tribes of the southern island."

Keeping his cool, Curubor, was proving particularly insistent, his cold blue eyes fixed scathingly upon his two Llewenti companions. The ancient High Elf uttered each word with a deep, calm tone, taking care to mark each syllable's importance. While Mynar dyl appeared reluctant to pay much attention to these warnings, Gal dyl did not seem nearly as impervious; Curubor's words and demeanour had left a deep impression upon him.

Gal dyl nervously ran his hand through his long blonde hair before replying.

"I respect your warning, noble Curubor. Your advice is equally wise and cautious, and I thank you for it. Let me assure you that the three clans of Llymar are as ready for war as the House of Dol Etrond. Should the need arise; we will defend this forest with all we have.
But my personal belief is that peace will prevail. Let us be honest with ourselves: we might not like it, but the Pact between King Norelin and the Men of the West is a success. The flourishing trade arrangements between them shall guarantee peace and collaboration with the Westerners, and it is the Westerners who control the barbarian tribes with the promise of their goods and the threat of their war galleys. It is a vicious circle from which we're choosing to be excluded! This has been the case for almost a century. I cannot foresee any of the barbarian

tribes breaching that Pact in the name of this bloodthirsty cult. Besides, the druids are becoming ever more influential among men, and those clerics are servants and disciples of the Mother of the Islands. They would never allow the tribes to fall into darkness again."

"The Cult of the Three Dragons," Curubor insisted, "is not some obscure religion embraced only by humble, lowly men, Gal dyl! This you must always remember. The Cult ruled the lives and beliefs of the barbarians for centuries. I do not deny that the Westerners have ostensibly ensured its destruction. But four generations of men is nothing like enough time to erase such a pernicious influence from the barbarians' sick minds. A threat, no matter how ancient, should never be forgotten..."

"Certainly not! Ancient threats, rather like ancient legends, should always be remembered," Mynar dyl, the third participant at the meeting, interrupted unexpectedly. The light smile on his lips showed that he meant far more than he had said.

Surprised and somewhat puzzled by Mynar dyl's mysterious comment, Curubor replied with a smile.

"I, myself, am like an old dragon: in the darkness of Tios Lluin's ruined palace chambers, I plot and plan... but my only aim is our collective safety. I have brought you updated plans, which include the new fighters we assimilated into our ranks last year. Enclosed too are details of the secret hideouts that I have organized in the west, with lists of the equipment, weapons and supplies which have been prepared there. You will also find information about the one hundred and twelve units of allied soldiers and the fourteen warships that we can summon under our banners. In total, if we were to combine all forces from the three clans and the House of Dol Etrond, we would command more than three thousand fighters.

"I have included details of the movements, supplies, reinforcements, tactics and plans of attack for each clan, army and unit. With these plans at our disposal, the enemy shall not stand a chance against our army. If the barbarians dare to cross the mountains of Arob Tiude, if they dare move to attack us, they will fall directly into our deadly trap."

Gal dyl distractedly leafed through the maps and notes that Curubor had provided him; this cursory glance was enough to confirm that the Blue Mage had clearly laid everything out, leaving nothing to chance. Each commander had a specific role to play, and even contingency measures and alternative back-up plans were described. Gal dyl froze, properly seeing the highly detailed preparations that were laid out in front of him. Was it the thought of what might come to pass? Or was it the reminder of how unprepared his clan had been when it was crushed by the barbarian invasion of Nyn Avrony? Gal dyl was not a cunning or guarded Elf; he chose to speak his mind and express his innermost feelings.

"You talk of war as though it were imminent. There is something frightening about the obsession you have with possible threats. It's as though you believe that we should always live in fear. But now is the time for the sacred hunt! In the depths of Llymar, hunters are sweeping the forest in search of the most glorious prey. Soon we will be celebrating Eïwal Vars[36], our Father, with a glorious feast. There will be dancing and music... wine and spirits! The young female Elves will reveal their beauty to attract the best of the males.
Haven't we had enough pain? Enough sorrow? We've already suffered such destruction and loss. I say we've had enough! I refuse to live wracked by worry for the safety of our kind. Let's enjoy the time that has been granted to us. Let us live freely. Further struggles will be upon us soon enough, to be sure."

Mynar dyl gave an acerbic smile at this outburst but chose not to intervene. He looked from the ancient High Elf to the tall Llewenti warlord with amusement, as if the outcome of the discussion was of no consequence whatsoever. Ignoring Mynar dyl's sarcasm, Curubor replied, adopting a kind and gentle tone.

"Your words are most touching, Gal dyl, and in your raw emotion I recognize the most admirable qualities in Llewenti's nature: your thirst and pleasure for life, and your primal passions, natural urges passed on to you by your deities. Unfortunately, the nature of the evil that threatens us is such that the ways of your deities will not be enjoyed for much longer.

---

36 Eïwal Vars: Deity of hunting, divinity of war and strength, lord of forests and beasts

I am afraid to say that an objective analysis of our situation calls not for peace: it rather demands unhesitating confrontation. While we celebrate Eïwal Vars with sacred hunts, Eïwele Llyi with lascivious dancing, and Eïwele Llyo with spicy wines and colourful smoke displays, men are multiplying in their thousands, and the threat of war grows ever greater.

Think of it this way: as we celebrate each festival on these islands, a new generation of barbarian warriors is born, and they grow up nourished by stories of their ancestors' heroic conquests against the Elves.

For every Llewenti birth, how many humans, do you imagine, come into existence? Three? Four? Perhaps five?

Gal dyl, the reality is very different from what the so-called Pact with our enemies set out to achieve.

We, the Elves of the archipelago, will never know true, lasting peace, until the day that we expel all men from these islands for good. This great responsibility falls to us: the dyl of the Llewenti clans and the Dol of the Hawenti houses."

Despite Curubor's kind manner of speaking, Gal dyl realized that, once again, he had shown weak naivety in debate. Displaying one's true nature would never be advantageous when meeting Elves such as a Dol Etrond sage and a dyl Ernaly warlord. Seeking to divert attention from his own faults, he turned to the other meeting's participant, who had so far remained almost silent.

"What about you, Mynar dyl? I am surprised; for once you're keeping your thoughts to yourself. You aren't seizing the chance to push some agenda of your own. It is most strange. You were the one who summoned this secret council. What is the purpose of this meeting? And what, exactly, is this ancient book, that has seemed to absorb your attention since we arrived?"

Mynar dyl Ernaly was unusually calm and peaceful. In that moment, his composure was one of true serenity. It was clear that his mind was wandering, contemplating some far-off opportunity seen only by him. Alarmingly, his attitude was frighteningly like a predator who knew that its prey had no hope of escape. Carefully arranging the grey hawk feathers that identified him as a noble scion of clan Ernaly, Mynar dyl finally spoke.

"You talk of possibilities. You talk of the future. I prefer to focus on the present."

Gal dyl seemed puzzled, almost stunned, by this. Curubor, stolid as ever, ventured a guess at Mynar dyl's meaning.

"It seems that you know something we do not, and that this little secret of yours is cause for some excitement. I would go so far as to say that you look happy, even though such a trivial emotion never held much value for you. Have I hit upon it?"

"Out with it then!" ordered Gal dyl, making his discontent clear. "Let us hear what you have to say, so I can finally understand what was important enough to interrupt the sacred hunt of Eïwal Vars."

His host's temper did not impress the most influential Elf of the clan Ernaly. Still smiling, visibly enjoying each and every detail of the exchange, Mynar dyl opened the ancient book before him, selected a page with great care, and began to quietly read a passage in lingua Hawenti.

"Before the Dawn of the Second Age, those territories bordering Essawylor belonged to that race known as the Llewenti, and these same Llewenti did dwell along those Shores, and they did repose beneath those Stars, and in time they did prosper; the Llewenti cultivated Language and Custom, feeding themselves from the Bounties of the Seas and the Forests. In the Hearts of these Elves bloomed a profound Love for the Ocean, and ere before long had they mastered the art of navigating the open Seas.

But, in this remote Region, hitherto preserved, presently there arrived the Troubles of the World beyond.

Tha wicked race the Men, that hailed from those vast equatorial Steppes, did mount an Invasion and a most profound Fear spread forthwith amongst the Llewenti. At the sight of that aforesaid Invasion, variously the Elves hid, fled, or resolved to fight. And yet their Skill lay in the Hunt; their Cunning did not know Warfare. Little is known of those early times, but the ancient Chants recount how Llyoriane, She with the Golden Voice, revived the Hope that had expired. Among her Kind, she was the most wise in the ways of the Seas. When Llyoriane's fair Voice rose above the Waves, the Winds are believed to have calmed, the Foam of the Swell is supposed to have turned to a most pleasing Silver.

And Llyoriane did traverse the Lands, to pay visit to those scattered clans of Elves and goad her Brothers in Exile.

Her Words were thus: Woe to us if we remain on these Shores in the hope of escaping an inexorable Fate. Our Destiny will be found southward, across the Austral Ocean, where the Star fell. There, upon certain disparate isles, we shall make our Home, where we shall remain until the World falls and the Reign of the Elves comes to an end.

And her Voice had such Power that those Warlords of the Llewenti, whose Clans had hitherto never bowed to any Sovereign, recognized her as their Queen. The Llewenti prepared for their Voyage, and they did build such a Fleet as will never again be seen in this part of the World. Thousands were the Longships that sailed as they made their Escape, away from the most ominous Clouds, which marked the ruins of War and obscured the Night Sky. That southward Voyage across the Austral Ocean was long and difficult, and many were the Elves that were lost forever to the Waters. But we know of Legends that tell of how the Song of their Queen opened the Gateway to the hidden Islands.

The Shores of Essawylor and their surrounding Forests were too precious to be left to the despicable Men. Other Elvin tribes sought to reconquer that most precious Realm. The Irawenti descended down the Ivory Mountains, sailed along eastern Rivers, and reached its Shores. A most pugnacious kind they were, having survived the Ravages of many Wars. They reclaimed the former Dominions of the Llewenti, repelling the Invaders back to the equatorial Steppes. The Irawenti kept for their new Realm the ancient Llewenti name of Essawylor, the Wood of the Five Rivers, as their distant Kinfolk had so named it. They discovered Relics left by their Predecessors and thus did the old Legends of the Llewenti come to enrich the Songs and Fables of the Irawenti.

Several Centuries then passed, and the Irawenti preserved their new Land, in spite of the many wild and bloody Invasions of Human Tribes who tried supplanting the Elves in those Regions of the World.

Their Civilization flourished and their Art grew; thereupon their Influence extended throughout the Wood of the Five Rivers, and yet their Fascination for the Flight of the Llewenti remained.

A wise Elf among the Irawenti, the noble Filwen, fought with much Determination to preserve these Legends. He chose not to reside among his Kin in the Shadows of the tall Cypress Trees, for in his Heart he did suffer a most perturbing Unrest, and thus did he elect to settle, with all his Family, upon the Beaches of the Bay of Essawylor, where he henceforth lived, delighting in the Heat, the Barrage of the Seas, and the scorching Sun. He avoided other Irawenti Clans and evaded their Struggles and Quarrels, for this Elf instead preferred the Company of marine Birds. It is said that he learned to converse with such Birds, and that they taught him the Secrets of the Seas and the Winds.

As this Friendship grew, between Elf and Birds, he sought to accompany them farther away, to follow their habitual and natural Migration beyond the Austral Ocean, and thereupon did he learn the Art of Navigation and hence did he invent novel Techniques for the Design of his Ships. Filwen was not truly esteemed by his own Kind, and yet History has proven that this he was no simple Fisher, but rather an Elf of significant Powers, whose blue Gaze reached beyond the farthest Horizon.

His Object was thus: to traverse the Austral Ocean and discover the lost Archipelago of the Llewenti."

Taking a breath and marking a pause with all the surety of the excellent reader and speaker that he was, Mynar dyl glanced at his small audience. Gal dyl was listening intently, though he appeared to be having some difficulty understanding the Hawenti language of old which the dyl Ernaly mastered as a distinguished scholar.

Suddenly, Curubor intervened, almost instinctively.

"I wrote this book... I remember... I wrote this book a long time ago, a very, very long time ago..."

"That is correct," answered Mynar dyl, evidently satisfied with the reaction that he had provoked. He went on. "The book dates from the Year 651 according to the Llewenti's reckoning, which corresponds to Year 143 of the Second Age in the High Elf calendar. It was written in Ystanetrond[37]. The title is rather ambitious: A History of Elves."

"But this is more than twenty centuries ago! How did you come into possession of such a relic?" asked Gal dyl in disbelief.

"I gave it as a present," Curubor answered. "I offered it to one of Mynar dyl's forefathers though I cannot remember his name." His fingers stroked his thin and delicate nose, as if such an action could help him unearth that ancient memory. "I am glad it was neither lost nor destroyed, despite all the disasters that the clan Ernaly have suffered since that heroic time."

"The clan Ernaly is known for its bards and its scholars," Mynar dyl explained proudly. "Dedication to the preservation of knowledge is a tradition for us as it is a part of our nature. But, if we may, let us return to the story of Filwen."

"Upon a particularly clear morning, Filwen paced about the Creeks of Essawylor's Shores, and presently he discovered a mighty High Elf, to wit, none other than Gloren, the fabled Prince, lost in a most contemplative Exile. Tall and sturdy was he, as was the Constitution of all his Kin, and his Hair was as dark as the very Night. From his pale Complexion issued a divine Light, and in his grey Stare he appeared to hold the Wisdom of the World. His Appearance was of a lonesome Demigod, wandering the Coast, singing to the Waves of his Pain and his Guilt. Filwen observed him at length, filled with Devotion and with Love, fascinated by the Beauty of that Hawenti Voice which mingled with Songs of the marine Birds. Then, to his Astonishment, he did perceive that the verses declaimed by the great Elf had provoked a mighty Change in the Depths of the Ocean. A powerful Force of Light and Brilliance had come into Being. A Deity had been summoned.

---

37 Ystanetrond: 'The city of Etrond' in lingua Llewenti. It was the former fief of House Dol Etrond in Nyn Avrony, eventually conquered by the Westerners.

He named the invisible Goddess Cim, She who fertilizes and illuminates the Seas. Cim was to the Seas what the Sun is to the Earth, the Source of Life itself. From the Depths of that clear and tropical Sea, She shone most like a Star, absorbing all Light and transforming it into most unusual and luminous tones of Azure. The Bay had become a Fragment of the Greater Gods' creation, a Vision of the World's very Beginning. And Filwen called it: Essaweryl, the Gift to Essawylor.

Stunned as he was by the Power of the great Elf, directly did Filwen run to him and bow at his feet, and he did swear upon all the Stars to convey the Sincerity of his Devotion. But, to the surprise of Filwen, Gloren raised him up, his Eyes full of a certain Sad Bitterness. And thereupon did the Fate of the two Elves become irrevocably bound.

Though the Hawenti Language remained too complex for the Irawenti Sailor, Gloren was quick to adapt to the Dialect of his newfound Companion. He learned much from Filwen, of Essawylor and of Irawenti Legends, but, above all else, was he fascinated by the Ode of the Llewenti, the Song which celebrated their Voyage beyond the Ocean, that Filwen sang with more Skill and Conviction than any other Elf. Neither Gloren's own mournful History, nor the fearful Events in the North that led to his exile, were mentioned at that time, owing to the most profound Grief that did still lay heavily in his Breast.

Rumours of the great Elf's coming, and of the Advent of Cim, were soon spoken widely throughout the woods of Essawylor, and afore long a great Pilgrimage was underway; Elves from far and wide travelled to the Lands of the Clan Filweni to show their Devotion to the Great Elf of Light as they had so named Gloren. But Gloren had been Prince among the High Elves and, more than any other, he knew the Weight of Kingship and the Burden of Oaths once pronounced. One Night when the Moon was fair, he confided to his Irawenti Friend.

"There are no Gods but those that we are willing to accept, Filwen. But if these Clans do solemnly believe that a Goddess dwells in the Depths of the Seas, it is my most heartfelt Hope that *such a Belief will bring Peace and Prosperity and keep Tyranny at bay. My Fate is no longer to worship the divine Light, and I fear that the Curse that haunts me shall affect you in turn. The Wrath of the Gods is much like the head of the Lava of a dormant fiery Mountain: once inflamed, it can never be extinguished. Forthwith I renounced my Heritage, that which made me King among Elves and the Heir to the most glorious among them, for now I seek only Peace and Redemption. And so, if I may have your Accordance, I shall accompany you in your Voyage across the Austral Ocean, I will assist you in your Quest to seek the Archipelago of the Llewenti, where that fateful Star once fell. May my contribution be of some Assistance to you and your Kind," thus pronounced the Hawenti Prince his resolution to Filwen.*

And therefore, one summer Morning, a tropical Breeze carried, the Alwïryan, Bird of the Seas, that same Ship designed by Filwen, the legendary Irawenti shipwright, towards the infinite South. And from the Shore, his Sons, the dyn Filweni, admired the Flight of this Ship which, when the Wind swelled in its vast Sails, rose high above the Waves, surrounded by a bevy of Swans. At the Stern stood Filwen, who, by his Power alone, steered the Course of the Ship. At the Bow of the Alwïryan was Gloren, a Harp in his Hand. Legends do recount that the Power of his Songs ensured a safe Voyage, for the two Companions succeeded in avoiding all the Lures and Snares of the Ocean, including, among other Perils, many devastating Storms and pernicious Currents. Last of all they escaped the evil Mist, whence they finally reached the pristine Waters of the Archipelago where the Star had fallen."

Taking advantage of a pause in Mynar dyl's reading, Curubor interrupted the tale, his voice shuddering with restrained emotion.

"I'm glad we've gathered, Mynar dyl, to recall these memories. The songs that Gloren left to the High Elves are most precious and inspiring. My hope has always been that he would change our fate, undoing the curse of his Father. The path he set for us will shape the destiny of all Elves, or at least those of us who remain true to our destiny on the archipelago."

Gal dyl's interest had also been captured by the tale. He was a true Llewenti, those who lived in the woods and dwelt in forest communities. He was a remarkable archer and an expert maker of bows. Gal dyl was more attuned to nature and the company of birds and animals than to ancient history, where his knowledge was somewhat limited. And yet, tonight, he perceived the ethereal influence that these tales of old, these legends of deities and heroes, had upon his material world, indeed upon the very air that he breathed.

"What became of them? What became of Gloren and Filwen once they reached the archipelago's shores?" he asked, unable to contain his curiosity.

"The Matriarchs of the clan Llyvary tell us that their ship, the Alwïryan, was wrecked off the northern peninsula of Nyn Llyvary. Filwen died; Gloren survived," related Curubor, somewhat drily.

"The wrath of the angry deity!" added Mynar dyl, with a tasteless fascination in his eyes.

"One particular song recounts that, before disappearing into the waters off the cliffs, Filwen pledged his allegiance to Eïwal Ffeyn, in exchange for the safe passage of future sailors," revealed Curubor, deep in thought.

"Well, we can safely say that the Irawenti navigator did indeed complete his quest: he found the archipelago, or at least the seabed surrounding it. I suppose that, in death, he achieved his life's mission..." Mynar dyl added cynically.

"But if Gloren survived, why do we know so little of his destiny?" asked Gal dyl eagerly. Beneath his golden hair, a greenish tinge had overcome his fair complexion, as his curiosity became anxiety.

"That, Gal dyl, is another story entirely, and, if there are any Elves left who could tell it, they have elected to remain silent thus far," replied Curubor.

"Legends have it," ventured Mynar dyl, "that it was the power of Gweïwal Uleydon himself that saved Gloren from the chaos of the winds. The waves of the mighty sea god brought him to our shores, for his destiny had not yet been fulfilled, and he still had much suffering and grief to endure. But let us return to this ancient manuscript, a source of much knowledge and wisdom. We may well find answers to these burning questions of yours," concluded Mynar dyl, with his characteristically cold yet eloquent tone, before he took up the book once more.

"Gloren was not the only High Elf condemned to his Doom by the Curse of the Gods. His House and all his Kind, had likewise left the green northern Plains and taken the Road of Exile. For many Decades did they wander the wide World, descending Rivers, crossing Mountains, traversing Steppes and losing their Way in the Deserts.

The Day came when their diminished Ranks reached the edges of the Forest of Essawylor, whence flows the Estuary of Siàwy Mien. As they set Foot on its Banks to quench their Thirst at the River, they experienced a great Joy, owing to their Success in escaping the Traps of the equatorial Steppes, and in traversing that driest Ocean of Sand and Fire. It had been the greatest Hardship imposed by the Gods that the High Elves had ever overcome.

Soon did they unfurl their red and gold Banners and blow their Trumpets, issuing a fearless Challenge to the World. The western Wind carried their Clamour deep into the Woods of Essawylor, like the Echo of a great Victory, which was heard by the Irawenti far away, whose Hearts did overflow with Awe.

Rumour of their Coming did spread through the Woods and Rivers and presently did the Elves of Essawylor gather along their Borders, with Eyes full of Wonder. For, although the Lives of the Irawenti, like those of the Llewenti, could span many Centuries, the High Elves were immortal, and upon their Brows and within their Eyes the Fire of Eternity could be seen.

Whilst some did possess the sand-coloured Hair and grey Eyes of the Silver Elves, most of the Troupe was formed of Gold Elves in their thousands, with dark Hair and severe Gazes.

Tall and strong they looked, and their Power and Wisdom knew no Comparison.

Beneath their dusty Garments, one could distinguish their most splendid Armour that had withstood the Desert, their Swords set with many Jewels, and their Helmets assembled of many Colours. And thus did these Spectres emerge from the Desert, and did enter the Forest of Essawylor just as Apparitions from the Isle of the Gods.

In front their Princes did ride, surrounded by their packs of Hounds.

Lormelin, Son of King Ilorm, came first, considered the Greatest and Wisest among them.

Princess Aranaele followed him, and the dark Pride of her Father, King Tircanil, whom none lamented, was inherited by her.

Thenceforth, other great Lords of the royal bloodline closed the march of this great Troupe; but fabled were they to have more Interest in the pursuit of Pleasure, than in the honouring of their House.

Behind the Dor princes, the Dol Lords of the noble Houses did command the Columns of High Elves that stretched for a great length behind them. Amongst that Multitude there thronged Attendants and Mages, Warriors and Captains, Artisans and Blacksmiths, Bards and Hunters, and a great Confusion of Carts and Horses.

The Irawenti did welcome this glorious Procession with both Respect and Fear in equal measure. They served as Guides to the High Elves and their Installation in Essawylor was facilitated by them. In exchange, Opals and Crystals and a thousand other Gifts, such as their Eyes had hitherto never beheld, were received to adorn their Homes. And so, in the Land of the Five Rivers, the two Breeds of Elves gathered and the Knowledge and Skills of the Irawenti were much enriched by virtue of their contact with the High Elves who themselves henceforth eagerly discovered new Lands and a Civilization hitherto unknown to them.

After the passage of three years, Prince Lormelin organized a Celebration; the great Occasion had its place in a vast green Meadow that overlooked the ivory Mountains, where the River Siàwy Lenpi[38] had its Source. There henceforward came many Elves: Dor Princes of the four royal Lines, Dol Noble Lords and their Houses and also many Irawenti Guides of the twenty nine Clans of Essawylor. There were Songs, Dances and multiple joyful

---

38 Siàwy Lenpi: 'The Fifth river' in lingua Irawenti

Salutations, for all that were present felt Relief in their Hearts and were well disposed to celebrate. Vows of Friendship were thus exchanged and heartfelt Tributes made.

Many were the High Elves who revelled in this happy Time, thankful that their Efforts were at last rewarded, after the Sufferings that they had endured throughout their long Exile. They had sailed the wide World, from its northern Borders to the tropical Shores of this Hemisphere. They foresaw years of Peace and Prosperity.

But some, still tortured by the Curse that haunted them, interpreted Gloren's progress to Essawylor as a Sign of their Fate: they formulated a Scheme to traverse the Austral Ocean and reach the Archipelago of the Llewenti, their ultimate safe Haven. The Legends of the hidden Islands, whose Vastness, Diversity and Marvels ignited their Imagination and sharpened their Thirst for Conquest, fascinated more of them still.

Prince Lormelin was one such High Elf, and, at this great Gathering, did he seize his Chance to convince other Hawenti Princes, and some Irawenti Clans, of the Worthiness of the Scheme. On the third day of Celebrations, with the Dor Princes, the Dol Lords and the Guides of the dyn assembled in Council, one of Lormelin's Vassals, Dol Oalin, proposed the Argument:

"Let it be known the High Elves did not come in strength from the North to carve new Territories in Essawylor, for the Irawenti are numerous and are themselves capable of preserving these Elvin Lands. Our Destiny is to follow the Path of the fabled Gloren; we must listen to the Words of his Songs and renounce all Ambition for an Existence upon the Main Land. We must endeavour to traverse the Austral Ocean, thus escaping the grasp of the Gods evermore. Doubt it not: we will need the Help of the remarkable Irawenti Shipwrights to build our Fleet, and the Assistance of their glorious Sailors to conquer the Ocean. For this we shall pay handsomely, with Gold and Jewels but also with Arms, Horses and new Territories, at that time when we have reached the Archipelago where the Star fell."

Thus spoke the Vassal Dol Oalin. But Aranaele, Daughter of King Tircanil, the most arrogant and violent Scion of the royal Bloodline, directly retorted in most rude Exclamation.

"Dol Oalin! Who has granted you Permission to speak on Behalf of the High Elves? Is it your Liege, Lormelin? Does he consider himself our King? It cannot be so, for a King must have a Kingdom, and I do not see this Prince ruling any Land. Without doubt, he is of royal Bloodline, but we, the Dor Princes, are one and all Descendants of Kings; the Blood of the mightiest Elf flows equally in our Veins.

I say the High Elves must remain in Essawylor and settle here. Cim, Goddess of the Irawenti, issued forth from the Waters to announce our Arrival. The Deity will give her Blessing to the birth of this, our Kingdom: so great a Realm that even our Cousins in the North will envy us. The foolish Design to traverse the Ocean could only have sprung forth from the Minds of Cowards, weakened by decades of Withdrawals, Evasions and Concessions.

It may be true that Gloren survived the wrath of the Gods, but he did so at the price of abominable Renunciation and great Dishonour.

Shall the High Elves follow such a Path forevermore?

To speak truly, I see this Proposal as the ultimate and most desperate Manifestation of the Curse that haunts us. Prince Lormelin is a mere Instrument of the Gods, and his ruinous Blindness shall lead only to the Oblivion of the last Remnants of our Race in the Depths of the Austral Ocean."

Thus spoke Aranaele, admittedly a great Orator, and forthwith did her Words arouse much Rage and Hatred among those that were present. Lormelin, his Mind obscured by devastating Anger, did leave the Gathering, accompanied by his Vassals. However much the other Princes attempted to exploit this disharmonious Exchange. The Hearts of the Irawenti brimmed full with Fear, as now they had beheld the Madness of the High Elves.

And thus, the great Rupture of the surviving High Elves came to pass. To prevent further risk of Dispute or Confrontation, Prince Lormelin and his Vassals did hurriedly leave. They descended the River of Siàwy Lenpi and reached Essaweryl Bay, near the Territories of the clan of Filweni. None of Lormelin's Lords had failed him.

However, the other royal Houses hesitated, delayed to see which way the Balance would lean, resolving to load the Winner with the full Weight of their Vassals once that Victor was known.

Conversely, Princess Aranaele exhausted no such time, for she was cognizant that only the Irawenti Clans could offer her the Crown of that Kingdom that she aspired to found, and forthwith did she employ all Means at her disposal to rally them. She was the richest among the High Elves, her Father King Tircanil having drawn vast Wealth from his Trade with the Gnomes in the North.

She was quick to distribute her Treasures amongst the Clans to honour their Guides and Priests, and when such Bribery did not have the desired effect, she issued Threats and employed Blackmail, for she was equally treacherous as she was cruel, and her Ambition knew no Bounds.

It was when Aranaele donned the Garments of the High Priestess of Cim that she did make the Irawenti fully submit to her Power, for her wily Insight had shown her the Advantages to be drawn from such an Office. The Irawenti, although cunning and advanced in their own Ways, were nonetheless gullible and superstitious. The Advent of Cim had provoked most profound Changes in the Bay of Essaweryl; its Waters did become much enriched, with Algae, Seaweed and many Plants of unknown Qualities, which brought forth the most unfamiliar Fish, of which new Species arrived with each new Moon. Whales now swam along the Coast, and a new Age of marine Hunting had begun. The Sea seemed to offer all its Richness to the Irawenti and guarantee its lasting Abundance.

In time Aranaele had a vast Temple, on a Cliff overlooking Essaweryl Bay, constructed, and the Light of its highest Tower could always be seen from the Clan Filweni's Territory on the other side of the Bay. Servants of Aranaele roamed Essawylor and did summon Elves from all around to come and pay Homage to the Generosity of the Goddess of the divine marine Light. And, thus, The Cult of Cim was born.

It was not long before the Princess did reap the Rewards of such omnipresent Fervour. It had not yet been three years before a Council of the Irawenti Guides recognized her as Sovereign of Essawylor. She thence did sunder her Domain into Provinces, and did order that the deserting Princes, who she believed had led her Kind into Perdition, be pursued. Aranaele wished to prevent their dangerous Expedition and to rule over all Hawenti Houses and Irawenti Clans. To realize such Ambitions, she was prepared to wage War.

But such dark Designs were most reminiscent of the recent History of the High Elves in the north, and the Wounds sustained in those turbulent years were not yet healed. Moreover, many of them feared the growing Power and Authority of the Queen and the blind Devotion that she inspired in scores of Irawenti. For the High Elves worship neither God nor Star, and they spurn the Teachings of all Cults, leaving such Exaltation to others; verily, ever since they broke their promise to the Gods, their Instinct had been to trust only their own Wisdom and Powers, and to abhor the Unknown and the Tyrannous.

The other Hawenti Princes soon understood that there would be no place for them in this new Kingdom. Having sought to negotiate a compromise in vain, forthwith did they renounce the newly crowned Queen and abscond, followed by their numerous Vassals.

All defected to the side of Prince Lormelin.

Thence did thirteen noble House and three royal Bloodlines unite to recognize Lormelin as King of the Hawenti. This was an unassailable Majority and, in accordance with ancient Laws, it promised him and his Heirs the Crown of the High Elves henceforth.

Among even the Vassals of Aranaele, most fatal Schisms soon began to arise in all Quarters. The House of Dol Lewin tore itself asunder after cruel Disruptions, as the Lord of the House cast out his younger Brother, ignominiously accusing him of Conspiracy and Betrayal. Blood was shed, until part of that noble Family chose the road of Exile, following Lormelin, who they judged to be their lawful King and Suzerain.

Thus, it came to pass that the greater part of the Hawenti rallied to King Lormelin Dor Ilorm.

He most prudently chose not to succumb to the belligerent Impulse of some of his Dol, for he sensed, amid the growing Hostility between his own Hawenti Majority and the Multitude of Irawenti that supported his Rival, the Beginning of a long, bloody War. Indeed, his Purpose was not to conquer Essawylor, but rather it was to rally a Fleet and sail to the lost Archipelago of the Llewenti.

Thereupon did he direct his Efforts to the construction of Ships, in preparation for the great Migration, combining the Expertise of the Shipwrights and Sailors in the clan of Filweni. Ever since their arrival in Essawylor, the Elves of that Clan had gathered Books and Maps. They had become the wisest among the Irawenti in the ways of the sea. Their Reports and Communications had been recorded in the Clan's archives as they organized expeditions in order to perfect the art of Shipbuilding. Ancient Naves that were commanded from the quarterdeck without a bridge, incapable of shipping more than thirty Sailors, had been replaced by high-edged Vessels of more than three hundred tons, able to hold off the Sea in heavy weather whilst remaining the fastest in the Austral Ocean. The clan Scholars had developed their occult powers to become Masters of navigation, literate in reading the Stars, and experts of declensions, calculations and meridian tracings. The sea held the preeminent place in their Songs.

As Lormelin's Armies did defend themselves against the incessant Attacks from Essawylor Troops inland, these Irawenti of the clan of Filweni, great masters of Crafts and Artisans built, in a mere few years, the most formidable Fleet ever witnessed in that part of the World since the very Departure of the Llewenti.

Afterward, with the glorious Dawn of Spring, the majestic Vessels were finally ready to depart and to set sail towards the lost Archipelago where the Star had fallen. Sitting atop the Ships' Masts, flowing in the morning Wind, were the Colours of the noble Houses: the royal Red of the Dor Princes, the dark Green of the House of Dol Nos-Loscin, the midnight Blue of the House of Dol Etrond, along with many other prestigious Insignia, which all signified the Challenge that this Fleet did issue to the Austral Ocean, and their Ambition to conquer a new World. It was in that solemn moment of Departure that, at the front of the great assembled Fleet, King Lormelin, Son of Ilorm and rightful King of the High Elves, resolved to swear an irrevocable Oath. He swore, in the name of Cil, the bright Star of the West, that he, and his future Heirs to the Throne of the High Elves, would never forgive those who betrayed him upon that day, and that they would hence wage War with any of that Ilk if they dared follow him across the Ocean. The Oath that Lormelin issued forth to the Waves was thus.

> Be he Enemy, Rival, Usurper, or Traitor most impure,
> Be he of dark Hawenti blood, or Irawenti blood azure,
> I hereby make a Vow, with lucid Mind and solemn Breast,
> That should he undertake to persevere us in our Quest,
> Neither Shield, Armour, Magic, nor Sword of Beast or Elf,
> Nor Fear, nor Guilt, nor Mercy, nor even Doom itself,
> Shall deliver him from the timeless, terrible Wrath and Scorn,
> Of great King Lormelin or my Descendants yet unborn.
> Death shall we deal to Traitors, whomever they may be,
> Death to all from Essawylor who chase us across the Sea.
> This is our Vow, Cil!
> May you doom us if we fail.
> By your divine Light, Cil,
> I pray we shall prevail!"

Mynar dyl closed the ancient book ceremoniously, allowing the dreadful words of Lormelin's oath to reverberate throughout the great cavity of the Eïwaloni. There was a long silence.

The hawks, up in their nest, seemed as struck by King Lormelin's powerful verses as the noble Elves did beneath them. Finally, the great grey hawk, from his commanding position on high, shivered and shook.

Mynar dyl slowly rose from his seat before leaning across the table towards his audience, making as if to share some great secret with the utmost discretion. Gal dyl and Curubor, intrigued, sat up and moved in towards him. Mynar dyl spoke quietly. What he had to say took some time. The calmness of his voice and the candour in his eyes made the truth of his words undeniable.

His sudden revelation, that an Irawenti ship from Essawylor had crossed the un-navigable ocean and reached the shores of Nyn Llyvary, erupted into the room like a thunderbolt in a cloudless sky.

The secret meeting between the ship's captain and Lyrine in Llafal, followed by her autarchic decision to force the shipwrecked Irawenti to leave, meant that the storm was just about to reveal its full force. Their voices began to rise. Gal dyl shot to his feet violently and began pacing in circles to calm his anxiety. Curubor lay back in his chair, his fingers stroking his chin in an effort to stimulate his mind.

Mynar dyl observed the great confusion and tumult among his guests; this was the moment of opportunity that he had been waiting for. He seized it to mount his attack.

"As we speak, two high priestesses of the clan Ernaly are making their way to Llafal. They will summon the Council of the Matriarchs. They will ask questions and demand explanations regarding the wilful misconduct of Lyrine. Seldom, in the history of the Llewenti clans, has an individual acted with such despotism. The Lady of Llafal will need to account for her secret conduct, and for her personal decision with regards to this group of Irawenti. Now is the time for change!"

"This is beyond belief! This is beyond belief!" Gal dyl repeated, unable to grasp the full implications of Mynar dyl's threats.

Curubor was faster to recover; he moved quickly to challenge the dyl Ernaly.

"What do you mean to do? You cannot be intending to lay blame upon the mightiest of our matriarchs? You would trigger a conflict!"

"Such is not my intent, my Lord Curubor. But the time has come for us to stand tall once again. We, the dyl Ernaly, have not bowed before any queen since the days of Llyoriane. Too long have we endured this state of confusion: let us put an end to the Lady of Llafal's abusive ways. I will summon the Council of the Forest. No longer will I accept any authority but that of the Council! Is that clear?" burst Mynar dyl, losing his calm composure in ambitious, power-driven mania.

"Mynar dyl, the Council of the Forest only gathers under exceptional circumstances... in times of war."

"These are exceptional circumstances, my Lord Curubor," the dyl Ernaly vehemently insisted. "When was the last time that an Irawenti ship reached our shores? These are extraordinary times, Curubor, and extraordinary times require extraordinary measures," he pressed, desperate to gain the advantage.

The Blue Mage seemed to acknowledge Mynar dyl's argument. His mind raced to fathom the implications of such a monumental shift in the forest's governance.

"If you were to follow such a course, the balance of power would shift to the clan warlords and the noble dyl; the nine matriarchs would be outnumbered in the Council of the Forest," Curubor reflected.

But soon another voice interrupted these speculations. This third voice was loud and clear, trembling with justified rage. At last Gal dyl intervened, stomping about the room, unable to stand still, like a cornered, startled deer before the hunter delivers his final blow.

"I am appalled by what you suggest! I am outraged! How could you possibly use these incredible events as an opportunity to plot against the Lady of Llafal? How dare you be so spiteful and ungrateful? Can you not understand that, if the wisest of our matriarchs did act quickly and decisively, she must have had her reasons? Lyrine sees far ahead. Her gaze can discern, in the waters of the Halwyfal, events that will come to pass, things that are beyond your power to comprehend, be you an ancient mage or a scholarly bard. The very deities of the archipelago protect her!"

Gal dyl then paused, breathless. He could prove a formidable orator when confronted by an imminent threat. He sat back down at the table, placing his powerful, strong arms upon the map that lay before him, as if he were an angry, omnipotent deity surveying a miniature battlefield. His gnarled fingers dug down through the parchment and sunk into the antique wood of the table beneath; the noise of his clawing was the only accompaniment to his plea.

Something very like anger was brewing between the three Elves.

Gal dyl took a deep breath, and consciously made the effort to relax his proud, incensed brow. He took his clenched hands away from the map before continuing.

"We should not rush into anything. Our time will come soon enough. Our forces are currently too scattered. Our potential must remain dormant for the time being. These exceptional circumstances, I believe, are nothing more than the events that could precede our downfall."

But Mynar dyl could not contain his wrath for much longer. His smile evaporated. His movement had become convulsive, like a snake before it strikes at its prey. He burst into a long rebuke, full of rage and arrogance.

"What kind of commander do you pretend to be? Is this all that the last remaining dyl Avrony has to offer? Is this all the bravery that a son can muster in the name of his own matriarch mother? I know you held her head in your hands, the same head that had been severed and mutilated by barbarians. Is this really all that this same warlord, betrayed by the High Elves, will do to restore his honour? I am aware of how you fled your realm aboard a beggarly fishing boat, abandoned as you had been by Hawenti warships. Does it not fill you with rage to wander this forest like a shadow of the past, like the very embodiment of the terror that was inflicted upon our people? Gal dyl! The evil resides in our incapacity to act and in our lack of determination to change the course of history. The danger is neither in the direction in which the birds take flight, nor in the oscillations of the Halwyfal's waters."

Mynar dyl's violent outburst left Gal dyl speechless. He muttered a few inaudible words to himself.

"Ah! And you expect these damned dreams to triumph..."

Still growling, he sat back in his seat, his face blank and haggard. The lion had been reduced to a cat. It was then that Curubor decided to intervene.

"Peace! Peace! Such a personal tirade is neither necessary nor helpful and neither is stirring up pains from the past. We will never restore these ancient powers; much less win back our own lost territories, by tearing ourselves apart."

The Blue Mage paused before putting forward what he saw as the real point of contention.

"There is one question, only one that we should be asking ourselves. What shall become of the shipwrecked Irawenti?"

The three Elves sat in silence for a time, observing each other like three competitors before a race.

"If the Matriarch of Llafal intends to extinguish them, if her will is for them to fall into the clutches of King Norelin, then I believe it would be a real waste, for one can surely rely upon the son to fulfil the will of his late father. Lormelin's oath can only be broken by the extinction of his bloodline," reasoned Curubor.

"Leading the castaways into the jails of the King of Gwarystan is precisely what Matriarch Lyrine is doing," Mynar dyl replied. "As we speak, shipwrights from Penlla are helping to repair the Irawenti's formidable vessel, yet the swanships have been deployed all around the Gloren Peninsula to ensure that they can only head east."

"This is not only inappropriate, it is completely unacceptable," Curubor asserted. "These additional troops would have been of great value to our cause. Seasoned Hawenti guards would be invaluable assets in battle. The Irawenti sailors' knowledge of the sea could prove decisive when we face barbarian long ships. Their presence here would also enrich and diversify the Council of the Forest, diluting the dyl of the clan Llyvary's influence. But, most importantly, there can be no reason to doubt the newcomers' lawful intentions. The oath of Lormelin stands between them and our opponents," the ancient Elf concluded.

Mynar dyl immediately saw Curubor's argument as an opportunity to gain the upper hand, though he knew full well that, at heart, he cared very little for the fate of the shipwrecked Elves.

"I am afraid that now there is nothing we can do, as it can only be a matter of days before the Lady of Llafal's plan is completed. We shall suffer greatly from her untimely and autocratic acts."

Gal dyl could not oppose this reasoning. Seeing that he had become passive once again, Mynar dyl decided to pursue his attack.

"As the matriarchs of the clan Ernaly proposed, let us gather the Council of the Forest. Let us meet in Tios Lluin and decide, in that great, ruined city, the future of our governance. The era of the matriarchs' omnipotence is over. The time has come again for the clans to rule supreme, as we once did in the Centuries of the Elvin Wars. These are dark days, fraught with bad omens, and we need to react decisively."

"I disagree. I completely disagree," Gal dyl fought back, but already he felt his resolution beginning to weaken.

But Curubor had made up his mind and decided to put an end to the debate. In the softest of tones and with a bewitching look in his eye, he addressed Gal dyl.

"What Mynar dyl proposes is not so much a change, but rather a return to the Llewenti traditions of old. Matriarch Lyrine will still be the most eminent member of the council, and no doubt her words will still be thoroughly obeyed. The clan Llyvary will retain its large majority, and no course of action will be decided upon without its full support. We need you, my dear Gal dyl; the Elves of Llymar need you: the three Llewenti clans, of course, but also the House of Dol Etrond.

For, if the Council of the Forest is summoned, the Spear of Aonyn will have to be retrieved from the Temple of Eïwal Vars. Such is the tradition; a Protector of the Forest will have to be elected."

"You do not mean to propose me, do you?" Gal dyl asked incredulously, his gaze betraying considerable dread at the very idea. "The Spear, granted to us by Eïwal Vars, is the most sacred weapon of the Llewenti. It was entrusted to the first dyl of the Llyvary by Queen Llyoriane herself, and it has always remained within that clan. It is a weapon of great power that only the mightiest warlord can wield. Lyrine's father was the last to do so. He died heroically, the Spear in his hands. None of us can surely pretend to succeed that glorious warrior," Gal dyl continued.

"Certainly, none of the dyl Llyvary!" added Mynar dyl, thinking about the 'Old Bird' Tyar dyl, the impetuous but inexperienced Nerin dyl, and the wise but puny warlord of Penlla, Leyen dyl Llyvary. This leaves us with only two legitimate contenders for the fabled title of Protector of the Forest," he added, with a wry, cunning smile intended to increase Gal dyl's discomfort. "Will the spear of Aonyn be granted to Gal dyl of the clan Avrony or to Mynar dyl of the Ernaly, to the chief of the peafowl or to the lord of the hawks?"

"Mynar dyl is right, Gal dyl, only one of you two could ever live up to this position, and the honour that accompanies it. Legends pronounce that, in the early days of the archipelago, Eïwal Vars wanted a weapon mighty enough to legitimate command of the Llewenti army; he wanted such a weapon for the most talented of his progeny, and in his time that was Aonyn, the eldest of the dyl Llyvary. But neither song, nor holy lyrics mention that any one clan holds the sole right of inheritance. Both of you have a rightful claim to wield the Spear," Curubor asserted, with the indisputable authority of an Elf born in the First Age.

Faced with such a cruel dilemma, Gal dyl did not know how to react. Mynar dyl seemed to be enjoying the situation, a peculiar, serene smile drawn on his face. After a long silence, disrupted only by a screech from the hawks high up in their nest, Mynar dyl spoke. His smooth voice adapted itself to a flattering, courteous tone, as he attempted to stir Gal dyl.

"Who was the victor of Tios Lluin? Who brought to an end the most decisive of battles with the barbarians, where the noblest failed and the most valiant died? Who is our greatest hunter, our most skilful bowyer and our most accomplished archer? Who is the mightiest with the javelin? Who, indeed, is the hero of the ladies when the festival's contests start? Who commands the attention of the matriarchs? Who..."

Seeing that Mynar dyl might have continued for some time, Curubor intervened, his deep voice's solemn tone concluding the discussion.

"It is in you, Gal dyl, that we must place our hope."

To emphasize these last words, the Blue Mage stood, and he was followed by Mynar dyl. There was silence. Gal dyl slowly stood up, terrified by the decision that had just been made.

"I am as the ocean," he stumbled, "I have my own currents, my own tide... When the tide is low I appear empty and vulnerable, but, in a storm, when the waves rise in tumultuous clamour... I can... I can..."

"I do not doubt," Curubor intervened, "that the matriarchs will decide to entrust you with the sacred Spear. Your leadership shall be the very crest of the ocean waves, Protector of the Forest."

"I have never seen the blade of the Aonyn Spear," murmured Mynar dyl, as though in a dream. "They say that it is more enchanted than life itself, and more beautiful than perfect death..."

Curubor bowed respectfully, as was appropriate for a Dol of his lineage, saluting his two companions. The ancient Elf gathered up his large, dark blue cape, swept it around his shoulders, and then went to take his leave. He paused, adjusting his hood so as to hide his face, and then climbed the stairs towards the exit.

Four impressive guards stood at the opening of the Eïwaloni. They were seasoned fighters, dedicated to the service of their master. It was easy to recognize the clan Ernaly's colours on the fabric woven into their hair. The hawk feathers they wore marked their rank within the unit. They were heavily armed with javelins, short swords, bows and quivers stocked with war arrows, all worn over their fine chainmail. The Ernaly guards had been instructed not to let anyone interrupt the meeting and were expecting their warlord and his secret guests to leave at any moment. This gathering was one of upmost secrecy; Mynar dyl, Gal dyl and Curubor were highly influential Elves, reluctant to be seen speaking together by other dignitaries in the Forest of Llymar. It had been a long while since they had met and although they certainly had a number of common interests, an unavoidable suspicion existed between them.

Seeing that all was in order, the Ernaly guards bowed respectfully, all the while keeping an eye on the surrounding area.

Curubor stood back for a moment, muttering a few unintelligible words. By the time the two Llewenti nobles had exchanged their brief salutes, he had vanished into the night. Gal dyl could just make out his shadow for a moment before it finally disappeared into the foliage of the forest.

Mynar dyl nodded slowly and then suddenly turned towards Gal dyl, with a hard, menacing look in his eyes. He spoke almost inaudibly.

"Remember this, Gal dyl Avrony: I know you, and I am aware of what you have done. Whatever you decide, whichever path you choose, you must keep that in mind."

A flash of murderous anger appeared in Gal dyl's eyes, but he stopped himself, saying nothing. He simply saluted his host according to the ritual of the Llewenti, placing his right hand on Mynar dyl's opposite shoulder. Then, he adjusted his long cloak, and retrieved his weapons from the hands of the Ernaly guards: a magnificent long bow, a quiver full of plumed arrows, and a scabbard of a long sword inlaid with emeralds. Nightfall had arrived; pale, flickering moonlight filtered softly through the thick foliage of Tios Halabron's sacred trees.

The silhouette of Gal dyl was soon lost in the shadows of the forest. His pace quickened until his airy strides barely brushed the soil, soon disappearing into the night and leaving no trace of his passage.

Turning towards his guards, Mynar dyl noticed that his younger brother had joined them. He was a tall, strong Llewenti, whose ugliness was well-known among the clan Ernaly.

"Voryn dyl, we have much work to do! Events are in motion once again!" he repeated several times, carefully considering his next move. "The Council of the Forest will soon gather. The clan Ernaly now needs the support of all its members. We will need Dyoren. Our elder brother enjoys great influence, and he inspires respect in others. The prestige of his name and the fame of his legendary sword will, I am sure, be a formidable asset in our struggles to come. You must seek him out and convince him to defer his quest and return home. He must do so, for the interest of the clan and for the future of the forest."

"The last that I heard, Dyoren was in the Valley of Nargrond[39]. It is a dangerous place and is difficult to access."

"If that be so, you must make haste. Gather the guards and go to Penlla; from there you must set sail in the clan's long ship. Both notice of your coming, and news that the Seeker is recalled to the Forest of Llymar, shall be sent to Gwa Nyn[40]. Wherever he has gone, wherever he is hiding, I do not doubt that rumours of our search will reach him. You shall not find the Seeker: he shall find you."

Mynar dyl saw with satisfaction how Voryn dyl nodded in acknowledgment before taking his leave. Not for the first time, his brother was setting out on a dangerous journey without questioning its purpose, blindly obeying instructions. What Mynar dyl felt in that moment was the thrill of power, real power: the kind of authority that can decide the future and write history.

Mynar dyl's mind was finally at peace; he basked in this delicious haze of success. All his actions, all his efforts, were driven by an innate desire to plan, to act and to rule. His extraordinary, highly developed set of abilities distinguished his clear superiority in such affairs. The clan Ernaly's matriarchs, its noble dyl, the commanders, guild masters and stewards all now appreciated Mynar dyl's unique nature. The time had come for the other clans of the forest to appreciate it too. Much was

---

39 Nargrond: 'Crater' in lingua Hawenti

40 Gwa Nyn: 'The Gran-island' in lingua Llewenti

at stake; he had a great responsibility in the future of this land. The hawk's preferred time for hunting was before nightfall, just as the daylight begins to die away. And, indeed, the clouds were gathering above, and night would soon be upon the Islands. Mynar dyl was the most powerful Elf in the clan of the hawk, the clan Ernaly.

Others were bound to fall short in one way or another. The matriarchs were mere females. Their power was to be reckoned with, but, crucially, they had no experience of bloodshed. The warlords of the clan Llyvary were either brave but very young, or much older, experienced Elves, who were close to joining the spirits of the forest. None had his firm convictions, his iron resolution or his strength in command. Gal dyl was inherently weak and easy to manipulate. He was the worthy heir of the clan Avrony. Curubor was a Hawenti. This High Elf, unfaithful to his king, could certainly not be trusted. At best, he could be used.

Rest and recreation were unfamiliar to Mynar dyl, and before long he was on his way, swiftly moving on to the next task. Whereas daylight was necessary to carry out his responsibilities and exercise his body, the night was a unique opportunity to read, write and compose music.
He appreciated being alone in the shadow of the night. Then, he felt able to capture the true essence of the Elvin world, in both its material and ethereal dimensions. Those were his favourite moments. Lost in his thoughts, he dismissed his guards, returned to the shelter of the Eïwaloni, and went over to his precious musical instruments.

It was then that, to his most alarm, he discovered that he was not alone. For some time, he froze, suspended by sheer dread, before finally catching his breath. He kneeled slowly, in a display of utmost respect.

"Daughter of the Islands! This visit is an immense honour!"
"Mèolpa girith[41]!" the fabled matriarch spat back aggressively, her eyes burning like two shining emeralds. She thrust her antlers into the air like a stag before battle.

---

41 Mèolpa Girith: 'Stand up' in lingua Llewenti.

"I am forever grateful for your assistance. You bring much honour to the clan Ernaly. I have profound respect for you because you have remembered your origins. This is most helpful, and increasingly essential, as the threats against us accumulate."

"The ambitions of the clan Ernaly are nothing to me! Only the Mother of the Islands is of any consequence," said the ancient Elf, her deep voice flooding the room like a torrent cascading down a mountain. Her face showed tension and, even anger.

"I understand, and I respect your duty to the Mother of the Islands. You are the emissary of Eïwele Llya, entrusted to protect the archipelago. Your eyes see far beyond the interests of the clan, but I beg you to consider that we, the dyl Ernaly, are faithful servants of the Mother of the Islands." Mynar dyl bowed to further demonstrate his submission.

The Daughter of the Islands approached the warlord and murmured in his ear the story of her unexpected visit to the matriarchs of Llafal.

"It was no common hurricane that struck the northern shores of Nyn Llyvary. Eïwal Ffeyn attempted to break free from his bonds. The storm deity has now become dangerous. His imprisonment has driven him to madness, and he is becoming uncontrollable. I fear his wrath and his thirst for revenge. His destructive power could severely wound these islands, were he able to escape that vast oceanic prison. I foresee that his vengeance would be blind and furious; he could shock the archipelago and its natural balance forever."

"Eïwal Ffeyn shows no mercy," Mynar dyl replied, his voice charged with devotion.

The Daughter of the Islands then spoke of the matriarchs of Llymar, and in particular of Lyrine's self-assurance and temerity.

"The matriarchs of Llymar are conscious of their rising power, and they are not afraid to use it. The Lady of Llafal consulted the Oracle of the Halwyfal and called upon Eïwele Llyo. Such a demonstration of power has not been seen for a long time, and it shall not go unnoticed... Her daughter, the young Nyriele, has come of age. I know the power that flows in her veins... This is a dangerous time, laden with so many potential perils, and the coming of this ship from Essawylor is but the prelude to many other grave events that will shape the future of these islands. Matriarch Lyrine has foreseen it."

Mynar dyl replied, "I have heard your words, and I will keep the Lady of Llafal's prophecy in my mind. But what am I to do, Daughter of the Islands? What should be the clan Ernaly's role in the events to come?"

"Be on guard. Observe the balance of things. Keep an eye on the young matriarch, for she shall play a great part in what is to come... Gather your forces and be ready to move swiftly. Eïwele Llya may call upon the hawks of the clan Ernaly at any time."

"The Mother of the Islands holds our destiny in her hands," Mynar dyl acknowledged with absolute obedience.

He then stood up proudly, reaching his full height, his glance settled upon an invisible horizon.

"This is it. A ship from Essawylor has reached the shores of the archipelago. The deities have set events in motion once again."

CHAPTER 4: Dol Lewin

The darkness of night frayed away upon the shores of the archipelago, dissolving into blue-grey shadows. In the east, a band of light, thin as a sword's blade, announced the birth of a new day. The Alwïryan was anchored a hundred yards from the southern shore of the isle of Pyenty. Aboard the ship, silence reigned, only occasionally broken by the sound of ropes quivering in the breeze of the dying night. Deep in their reverie, the crew were finally enjoying a restorative night's sleep after what had been another hard day's work.

The Elves of the clan Llyvary had kept their word. They had provided equipment, tools, and materials in abundance to facilitate repairs. During each visit, they had taken the same precautions. Arriving on their long canoes at dawn, they would maintain a strict distance from the castaways. They remained silent but showed no hostility. Occasional stolen glances, however, betrayed their curiosity, as it was not unusual for some of them to linger, admiring the exotic beauty of the Irawenti females.

For six days, two teams of divers worked underneath the vessel, armed with long-bladed daggers and various tools. Graving the ship had been impossible due to a lack of resources and

117

time, but the Irawenti, who were excellent swimmers, had set about repairing the keel and the lower shell while the Alwïryan was still afloat. They would remain underwater durably before surfacing, filling their lungs with air before diving down again. Often, when the tide rose fast in heavy weather, the frailest swimmers would be risking their lives, narrowly missing the rocks. When the tide proved too perilous, the need to stay underwater was all the greater; it was then that the sailors would rely upon their captain's powers. They lined up along the deck to receive his blessing.

Feïwal had mastered the flow of the air to such an extent that he could capture the essence of the wind within his hands. Endlessly generous, he passed on the gift of Eïwal Ffeyn to his followers, allowing them to hold their breath underwater for far longer than natural. From the bottom of the keel to the waterline, the divers removed shells, barnacles and sea moss, the weight of which hindered the ship's speed.

Some were sitting in a circle splicing ropes. Others were carefully caulking the planks of the deck, which had suffered in the humid temperature. Down on the deck, more sailors were busy repairing the sails that had been saved, both the thick, rough canvas for heavy weather sailing, and the lighter ones used in fair climes. All had severely deteriorated. Precision were required to stitch the clan's sacred runes back into the material.

In the hold, the fighters of the Unicorn Guard, supervised by their commander Maetor and assisted by the sailor Gyenwë, were engaged in the long, painstaking work of repairing the hull, which was still split in some places. Using special tools, they widened any ruptures and filled them with straw, which they then densely packed in using the tops of their axes. Bway[42], a resin originating from Essawylor, obtained from the sap of exotic trees, sealed in those areas. Although the ship's vital parts still needed serious repair, the Alwïryan was afloat again and just before the Matriarch of Llafal's period of grace was set to expire.

---

42 Bway: 'Plant resin' in lingua Irawenti

The Irawenti liked to sing on the deck with joy and enthusiasm, expressing their infinite gratitude that they had survived the ocean's crossing. The beat of their drums resounded ceaselessly across the waves.

They venerated neither god nor deity, save for Gweïwal Uleydon, the Great Lord of Waters who had always been their protector. However, they firmly believed in the influence of stars over their destiny. They worshipped three in particular: Cil, Star of the West, high in the sky, divinity of hope and promise; Cim, Star of the Sea Depths, which dwelt deep in Essaweryl[43] bay, revered as the divinity of wisdom and regret; and, finally, Cir, Star of the Earth's Core, divinity of despair and degradation. The wisest Irawenti, the visionaries of the clans, knew how to interpret their positions. The three sacred stars which, according to their beliefs, held their destiny were honoured and praised with ardent singing and fervent prayer.

At night, Cil, their symbol of hope that shone so brightly in the western night's sky, was celebrated with effervescent fireworks. Cim, gleaming light of the sea's depths and dearest in the hearts of Irawenti, was venerated according to their ancient traditions. Enchanted shimmers of light cast from the deck of the Alwïryan illuminated the surrounding waters, drawing the many fish and dolphins of the bight into a wild dance.

The deadly influence of Cir, that divinity of despair and dark light of the earth's core, had been warded off by sacred fires that were lit on the isle of Pyenty, ablaze in the twilight.

The captain's report of his visit to the city of Llafal was noticeably vague but this had not diminished the crew's enthusiasm. Apart from a few historical and geographical details about the archipelago, the only news that Feïwal had shared with his companions was the compelling necessity to leave the wharf and pull away from the shores of the Llymar forest.

These sailors had reached the Llewenti Islands and defeated the ocean; their euphoria would not be affected by the hostile attitude of the clans of Llymar. They had learned that the archipelago was extremely vast, with six main islands and countless smaller isles, and with so many to be explored, the crew's imaginations

---

43 Essaweryl: 'Bay of the Woods' in lingua Irawenti, located at the centre of Essawylor, north of the Austral Ocean

had been ignited. The castaways had so far only glimpsed the magical beauty of the archipelago's landscapes, but they relished the prospect of discovering the Islands' creeks and beaches. The climate was very different from Essawylor's tropical heat, and they could not help but wonder about the new varieties of fruit, plants, trees and animals that they might soon encounter.

Many of the sailors had second callings as naturalists, hunters or artisans. Each knew they were about to discover a world, full of mystery, hidden amongst the archipelago's seas, mountains and volcanoes. Many different Elvin communities also populated the Islands. Descendants of the clan of Filweni lived on the island of Nyn Llorely. The crew's hearts burst with joy at the promise of a reunion with their distant kinfolk. The Llewenti Archipelago they had reached was a far cry from the idealized promised islands described in their ancient book, it was true. Here they would not be protected from the turmoil of the Mainland, or from the threat of future expansionist efforts from men. But the prospect of discovering new Elvin cultures and traditions was still hugely exciting.

They envisioned realizing the dreams of the generations of sailors and explorers who had gone before them. Neither the insurmountable difficulties associated with returning home to Essawylor nor the idea of leaving their homes and families behind, perhaps forever, ever crossed their minds. Such was their abandon that, despite Feïwal's words of warning, they felt invincible, as if no ill fate could ever now befall them.

The morning's mist obscured the view of the sea and dampened the sound of the waves. The chain of the anchor creaked. The shrill cry of a sea bird tore through the air. On deck, in the midst of what was left of the mainmast, stood a formidable Elf of high stature and broad shoulders, shaving his head with great care and attention.
Roquen Dol Lewin would perform this task every morning, alone, never accepting any assistance in the exercise. It was a ritual for him, and a way to unburden his body after the considerable exertions of the day.

The razor blade skimmed his skull with precision, though stubble remained. His eyes, usually piercing and resolute, appeared empty. His large mouth hung open, revealing white teeth that glowed like nacre. The Hawenti lord was lost in his thoughts.

The sound of footsteps behind him did not disturb the rhythm of this meticulous activity.

His councillor, Aewöl, came to stand beside him. The pale Elf moved like a shadow, dressed without ostentation in a black tunic. His silver diadem reflected the silvery light of the moon. Due to his own restless nature, he too was ill at ease aboard the ship. He could often be seen pacing distractedly around the deck. Aewöl was tall and black-haired, with lunar-white skin. Though his eyes were dark, they somehow possessed their own intrinsic brightness. His gaze was sharp and piercing. He was a High Elf like Roquen but of different origin and allegiance. Aewöl was endowed with rare talents and powers. He was especially able to discern what is hidden in consciences and to draw out the truth from its hidden veins.

"Are you well, my Lord Dol Lewin?" he inquired.

"Hmm...." was the only response he could solicit from Roquen, visibly annoyed at the interruption.

"The crew is worried, as are your companions. You seldom talk and barely eat. You torment your body with work and exercise. But, most of all, you never rest. It seems a shadow has fallen upon you."

"Leave me alone. I need to think in peace."

"Did you believe in honour?" asked Aewöl unexpectedly.

"I did," Roquen answered instantly, though surprised by the question. Aewöl had been his occult councillor for a long time, and the tall lord knew better than anyone the futility of trying to hide his feelings from his insight. "It is honour that has dictated my entire existence. I am... I was... I was an honourable knight... heir to a powerful House whose memory stretches back to the very awakening of the Elves. I was strong, proud and tall. I never once failed to honour my word," Roquen said with some difficulty, as if he had to consciously remember who he once had been.

"And did you hail from the Kingdom of the Five Rivers?" Aewöl pressed.

"Yes, I did. It was my home. I was born there. I defended Essawylor. I gave my blood for its salvation."

"Did you love your family and were you true to the House of Dol Lewin?" Aewöl continued.

"I loved my family and I worshipped that name. Ours is among the greatest bloodlines. We are descended from the heroes who served the High King of the Elves, from those who walked alongside the Gods. The founder of our line was Lewin, who rose to power following incredible feats in war, and who perished in the mightiest battle. We formed alliances with all the great houses of the High Elves; we chose our brides from the Houses of Dol Amrol or Dol Morlin..."

Aewöl continued to address Roquen insistently almost demonstratively.

"The purpose of your existence was to preserve what you held dear: your honour, your house, your kingdom. Such was the importance of those unbreakable bonds. And yet they were all taken away from you. You were deceived and betrayed. You lost everything or... almost everything. Most Elves, even the very noblest, would not have survived such trauma. They would have fallen to the ground and died or, worse, they would have resorted to murder and destruction until they met their own bitter death. However, despite your inconsolable despair, you have survived. Why is that?"

"I do not know the answer. My abilities diminish day by day; I no longer live up to my rare bloodline. My failure to preserve our fief fills me with the most profound guilt. I am the last ruler of my house and the one who has lost the homeland that his elders had built, strengthened and preserved. My pain is overwhelming; a void, emptiness fills my soul. I live haunted like a spectre among the living. It is strange, I feel as if I already belong in the halls of the dead, whilst I watch my form walking this ship's deck. I do not know when it will end, or if it will end... indeed, should it end?" questioned Roquen.

"You may well feel like this now, my Lord Dol Lewin. But you have not seen it all. There are many dark paths, paths that I hope you will never have to explore. An ill fate, once endured, can lead you to places of even greater evil, where spirits torture your mind until it loses cognition, clarity and perspective. Despair can turn you against the last loyal friends in your entourage as surely as a fire ravages dry wood. Isolation can transform suffering into murderous madness. So, Roquen, believe me when I say that you are no ghost yet. You have been spared, and now you have the chance to lead a second life." Aewöl's expression had changed as he spoke. A pained grimace was etched upon his face.

"What is this fable?" asked Roquen incredulously, but inside he did sense that his councillor might have experienced such cruel suffering himself, having described it so vividly. Regaining his composure, Aewöl explained.

"I know there can only be a second life once the first has ended. I believe that you cannot see this yet, for it will take you years, decades or maybe even longer for you to free yourself from this foolish pride and your debilitating sense of duty. I fear that, no matter how many times I say this, you will never understand but the day will come when this great opportunity presents itself. But if you believe nothing else, know this: fallen bloodlines can regain their promise through the exceptional deeds of surviving members."

Aewöl emphasised these last words with a fierce brightness in his eyes. It was hard to say whether he was speaking for his lord or for himself.

Roquen replied. "Words, these are the words of a councillor. However wise they may be, they are only words, they cannot fill my sense of emptiness, nor redress my lack of purpose. They cannot extinguish my anger. Think of what I used to be! I was Roquen, son of Roen, heir to the House of Dol Lewin. Considered the strongest and bravest fighter in the northern province, I commanded an entire army. Do you not recall the banners of all those units of fighters that came to honour me before the battles in the north? All the knights in the host came to bow before me! None would dare defy my authority. Remember the splendour of the Ystanlewin balls and contests, where the females would compete to entrust me with their colours. You were there, Aewöl. Even from your dwellings in the dark forges of Ystanlewin, you would have known who I was at that time. I was the very embodiment of glory, of magnificence, of grandeur. Now, after such a heart-breaking demise, how can you say there will be another Roquen?"

"For the time being, the only comfort that you shall find is in the prospect of revenge."

"But I am changed," the defeated lord exclaimed. "Now I am as helpless as any other Elf. I cannot carry out just retribution for the evil done to my kin; it feels as if an unending sea now lies between me and my revenge."

Aewöl pressed on. "Have we not proven to the world that no ocean is endless? Believe me, our immortality means that the chance to wreak vengeance is never lost forever. We are High Elves: eternal as long as we have purpose. Thirst for revenge will give energy and motivation if the powerful urge can be properly controlled. It will ignite your imagination and feed your desire!"

"I have no such patience; I wish that I could kill that despicable queen with my bare hands! I want to watch her die, slowly, in the worst possible agony."

"Beware, Roquen! Your sorrow is changing into a sickness of spirit, a madness which will be difficult to cure. We can all see it in your eyes. Murderous, unshackled thoughts charge wildly round and round your mind, torturing you. Neither your education nor your experience could help you to master such powerful and pernicious impulses. There will be irreparable damage unless you bring it under control, there can be no doubt. Be careful not to follow the path of some of your kin. You must find a way to take away those self-destructive thoughts. The time shall soon come when important decisions will have to be made. Your own fate is at stake, but so is the fate of others. Do you care nothing for those who have faithfully served you?"

This final piece of advice seemed to affect Roquen deeply. He relented at last, turning to his councillor and saying,

"You speak wisely, Aewöl. I will remember your advice. Now you should rest and leave me to finish this night's watch."

"May the coming dawn bring you wisdom and peace, my Lord. I will have Gelros assist you in your task."

"Yes, send for Gelros. At least he will not trouble my thoughts with idle chatter," concluded Roquen as Aewöl took his leave.

Calm was restored. The only noise that could be heard was the sound of two dolphins skimming the waves as they circled the ship curiously. The moonlight illuminated their gleaming fins. Quietly Aewöl's servant, Gelros, took up a high vantage point so he could watch over the ship's deck. He was a Morawenti[44], one of these few High Elves who favoured living in the dark shadows of the forests, preferring night to daylight. Gelros was a quiet but formidable character, and fierce with bow in hand.

Calm had indeed restored but, with that calm, the dark thoughts had returned too, laying siege to Roquen's mind just as they had done every night and day since the fall of Ystanlewin and the death of his family. Once again, Roquen was seized by that great feeling of emptiness. The affliction, the sorrow, the grief, and the pain were all proving overwhelming. His mind, tortured by lament, could not summon the strength to think clearly anymore. He gradually sank into an inescapable madness as dark, tortured thoughts circling round his head. His expression was of a deep, intense despair. When he looked at his hands, panic struck him.

They were cut. He remembered that he had cut his hands in a moment of insanity.

"Wash your hands in water, dear son," his mother had instructed.
"I cannot. I have cut them. My hands do not work anymore," he replied, helpless.
"But your hands are your freedom, my son. What are you to do without your hands? You shall have no power and shall soon fall into darkness. You shall abandon yourself to the worst in you," she proclaimed.

A sudden movement in the water brought Roquen back to consciousness. The two dolphins were still frolicking in the waves. Inhaling deeply, the Dol Lewin lord watched them, in a rare moment of innocent tranquillity.

---

44 Morawenti: 'Night Elf' in lingua Llewenti

From the depths of his soul, a voice urged him to break free from his rage and reclaim his destiny. That was until he thought back to those palace halls, to his humiliation at the hands of the queen, at which point anger seared through him once again. The painful betrayal was still overwhelming. For centuries, the House of Dol Lewin had served the monarchs of the royal House of Tircanil without question. Dol Lewin Elves had given their lives during great battles. Members of the House of Dol Lewin had suffered death, exile and eventually ruin, all in the name of an oath sworn to a cruel king and his evil daughter, even more abusive and quick-tempered than her father. His parents, blinded by their utter deference for feudality, had raised him in the strict respect of the House of Dol Lewin's traditions. Roquen now realized his education, beliefs, values, and even his own identity had all been lies. Pure rage streamed through his veins.

Standing still in the shadow of the mainmast's remains, paralyzed by his mental agony, Roquen suddenly noticed that two shadows had slipped over the railing and climbed onto the aftcastle before climbing swiftly down. After a pause, the silhouettes progressed along the edge of the deck. Their bare, wet feet slipped as they crept across the wooden surface. Their torsos, coated in dark oil, did not reflect the pale light of the white moon that shone down between the shrouds and the yards. Smooth and quiet, like two wild cats on the prowl, the two furtive intruders crossed the deck without attracting attention. Still, without hurrying, they headed silently towards the remains of the mainmast.

In a single, lightning-fast movement, Roquen leapt from the shadows and violently seized the first scout with one hand, whilst his head was crushed by a powerful blow from the other. Grabbing him with both hands, Roquen threw the intruder against the ship's railing several yards away. The propelled body landed with a heavy crash. The spy then struggled to his feet, finally managing to take a few steps forward, before falling headfirst onto the floor. He remained motionless.

Gelros, from his vantage point raised the alarm from above.

"Guards! Guards! Intruders on deck!" he shouted.

The Night Elf shot two arrows, almost simultaneously, at the dolphins, which set them swimming off away from the ship. A brazier was lit on the aftcastle, illuminating the hasty silhouettes of sailors gathering in the dark.

"Siw! Alarm! Alarm!" cried the crew as they arrived.

The second spy, now isolated, was for a split second stunned by the fate of his companion. He then bolted away from Roquen in panic and, before the Dol Lewin lord could seize him, he dived overboard into the sea. His only hope now was to reach the island's shore.

"Gelros! Catch the other one! Get him! Don't let him escape!" Roquen yelled frantically.

Gelros dived into the water from the deck. He swam forcefully towards the shore in pursuit of the spy, before disappearing into the dark of the night. The Alwïryan was shaken awake by a clatter of armour and weapons. Guards assembled on the deck and sailors rallied to their battle stations, armed with bows and crossbows. Orders pierced the silence of the night.

The dyn of the clan Filweni gathered around Roquen who ignored their pleas for wisdom. He also refrained from asking his own household for advice. This intrusion was an opportunity to prove his authority as commander in times of peril. He was determined to track down the fleeing spy and make him talk.

An hour passed before Gelros returned with his prey. Roquen's most trusted scout had not failed him. He returned with a small Elf, tied in ropes, like freshly captured game. But Gelros' prize was very much alive and struggling against his entrapment. The Night Elf presented the prisoner to his lord. Despite his savage appearance, his Llewenti origins were undeniable. Slender, almost frail, with narrow shoulders and an emaciated chest, his face was illuminated by two bright eyes which shone with fear.

"You took a long time, Gelros! Too long! It is now morning and we do not know who may be watching us. No doubt there are spies of the matriarchs all over this isle," Roquen spat harshly.

"I was delayed, my Lord," replied Gelros, calmly. "I had to track him across the bushes. He is skilled in the ways of the wilderness."

"Is he an Elf of the clan Llyvary?"

"No. There are no rune markings about him."

"Who might he be then? Is he friend or foe?" Roquen asked with impatience.

"I do not know, my Lord."

"A dolphin-rider, operating slyly under the darkness of night; he concealed his passage from all of us. He did not escape you however," Roquen noted with admiration. "You did well, Gelros, like in the old days of Essawylor! You were the best tracker in my army, as stealthy as a jaguar."

"I also have this. I took it from him," the scout replied simply.

Gelros took from his cloak a tattered scroll, apparently without a seal, and handed it to Roquen. The lord opened it with great care.

"A map of the bay, with our ship's position and the movements of the Llewenti patrol ships. It is not sealed by any glyph or rune, unmarked so that no one can trace it back to the author. Now, what would this wild Elf want to learn about us that the matriarchs do not already know? And why would he seek to avoid the patrols of the clan Llyvary? Gelros, let us take him to your master. We shall learn more," declared Roquen.

Gelros and his prisoner split the crowd of sailors that had gathered on the deck and moved towards what remained of the cabins. They reached the main one, where the captive could be isolated from the rest of the crew. Roquen followed close behind, explaining what they had discovered to Feïwal, as he walked.

The councillor, Aewöl, was already waiting for them to join him. As they entered the cabin, he stood up to his full height in front of the prisoner, who was on his knees. Aewöl's silky black hair blew lightly in the wind which was whistling through walls. His dark eyes became more intense. Gelros and Roquen turned and left the room. They knew that their presence was no longer required.

Outside, all was quiet. The swanships were nowhere to be seen, even though the matriarchs' deadline was only a day away. Murmurs rippled through the crew; their nervousness was palpable. The dyn Filweni had to shout their orders to restore discipline among the ranks. Their minds were also distracted by what was going on in the main cabin, but they did all they could to hide it.

★

At last, Gelros approached Roquen and Feïwal. Aewöl had finished questioning the prisoner and wanted to share what he had found. The pale Elf still stood in the shadows of the cabin, deep in thought, considering the implications of what he had just learnt. His voice was deep and sounded distant.

"I did not want to break him, for he could still be useful to us. His own resistance did not last long but, when his mind was revealed to me, I felt a power attempting to stop my progress. Someone powerful protects him even though he bears no rune. I first thought of the high priestesses of Llafal, but I would have recognized their magic. The matriarchs draw their power from the deities of the archipelago; they can influence all of nature even Elves, but the resistance I felt was something different. I believe I may have confronted a powerful mage..."

"What did he tell you, Aewöl?" Roquen interrupted in a threatening tone. "Did he talk? There are other methods we can try if need be. Does he want to suffer the same fate as his companion, who even now lies between life and death?"

"He did talk, my Lord; rest assured that my own talents proved useful. Our immediate prospects now look unfavourable in light of his remarks.

If we sail east, following the shores of Llymar, we shall be at the mercy of the three inhospitable Llewenti clans that dwell in the forest under the rule of the matriarchs. The clan Llyvary is the largest and most powerful. It controls most of the forest settlements and the three cities of Llafal, Penlla and Tios Lluin. The other two clans are the Ernaly, who dwell in Tios Halabron, and the remains of the Avrony. Both are allies to the clan Llyvary.

Beyond the strait, at the boundary of Nyn Llyvary's territorial waters, lies the island of Nyn Llorely. It is home to another Llewenti clan, but they live under royal rule. While we could expect some assistance from the clan Llorely, as they have ancient ties with the Irawenti, a prince of the royal House rules the island in the name of King Norelin. There is little chance we could escape his reach. Further away, the infinite vastness of the Austral Ocean awaits and that could only lead to our doom. If we sail west, beyond the Gloren peninsula and the mountains of the Arob Tiude, we shall reach the dominion of the human tribes. Their territory extends from the western part of Nyn Llyvary and beyond to the southern shores of the Mainland. The two islands of Nyn Ernaly and Nyn Avrony, the "jewels of the sunset" as they are called by the Llewenti, are surrounded to the west, south and north by the Sea of Isyl which separates the archipelago from the Mainland. Nyn Ernaly and Nyn Avrony were taken from the Llewenti during the last barbarian invasion, and they now lie under the dominion of the human tribes."

"Siw! But who is this Elf? And where does he come from?" interrupted Feïwal suspiciously.

"His name is Vyrka. Llewenti blood flows in his veins but he claims to be a wild Elf, unprotected by any rune. He, along with his companions, turned away from their clan, defying the authority of their matriarchs and noble dyl. These wild Elves have been cast out by the Llewenti for refusing to accept the King Norelin's peace treaty. They killed their high priestess after she submitted, which he claims sealed the fate of their homeland. They have been banished by their communities. All are forbidden from giving them food or shelter on pain of death. He says that many of his fellow rebels live on the Gloren peninsula, that strip of land stretching across the horizon to the west. They operate in small bands of fighters. Unlike those living under the protection of King Norelin, they are still in rebellion; they have never accepted that end of the last war. Driven from their land west of Nyn Llyvary, they live miserably along the rivers of the peninsula, concealed by the forest from their enemies. They are regularly devastated by the bloody incursions of barbarians seeking Elvin slaves. Nevertheless, they continue their struggle with courage and faith, convinced that the fires of war shall be lit across these lands once again."

"What do they want from us?" asked Roquen, growing impatient.

"News of our arrival has reached them," Aewöl revealed.

"How?" insisted Roquen, asking what Gelros and Feïwal both wanted to know.

"Vyrka says the wild Elves have protectors, spirits that roam the peninsula of Gloren at dawn. They call them 'Blue Bards'. Though they fear to approach them, the wild Elves listen eagerly to their songs, for they carry news from the Islands, warnings of potential threats and even prophecies."

"What is this fable, Aewöl?" interrupted Roquen, more doubtful than ever.

"Vyrka speaks the truth, or at least what he believes to be the truth. Of that I am sure. But there is more."

"What?"

"The ruins of a great tower lie by the sea, at the heart of their territory. It is called Mentollà[45]. Over the last few days, the 'Blue Bards' have gathered in great numbers beneath the ruins of the ancient fortress, to celebrate the coming of new winds from beyond the Austral Ocean," explained Aewöl.

"We are the messengers of Eïwal Ffeyn's winds!" Feïwal interpreted.

"This wild Elf and his brother were sent on an errand by their companions to find us. Word has spread of our coming to the archipelago. Something is at work beyond our control," warned Aewöl.

"It was Eïwal Ffeyn who granted us our passage. Rumours of our coming precede us," Feïwal reminded them. All could see in his gaze the formidable faith that possessed him.

★

With the prospect of an imminent departure, the castaways now hurriedly repaired what they could. Sailors were busy on the deck. Even while working hard, they were passionately engaged in conversation. It was in their open nature to share their feelings, hopes and fears with one another. Most of the High Elves considered such effusive behaviour to be excessive, but it lay at the heart of the Irawenti identity. They spoke mainly of the forest clans. They were eager to familiarize

---

45 Mentollà: 'The haven fortress' in lingua Llewenti

themselves with their erudite language and refined customs. The Llewenti were a myth for the numerous free Elves nations who lived on the Mainland. They were the living descendants of those who had first followed the Falling Star to build their future far away from the turmoil of the world. Art, books and other artefacts that they left behind in Essawylor, had inspired the Irawenti's fascination with the Llewenti culture. There was much impatience to meet them; even the rather cold reception their captain had experienced could not wane their enthusiasm.

These Irawenti had been raised and educated according to the clan Filweni's customs and beliefs. They believed in the legend of the Falling Star, that meteor which struck the archipelago, illuminating their passage to it. For centuries, they sang the same verses and muttered the same prayers during clan ceremonies, celebrating the great meteor's vital importance to their fate. For centuries, this noble aspiration, to elevate the soul and broaden the horizons, had been little more than an eccentric dream. None imagined that the Austral Ocean could be defeated.
Yet here they were: castaways of the Austral Ocean. They were isolated on a small isle of the archipelago but, without doubt, now within range of their spiritual destiny.

A religious fervour had taken hold of them; as the afternoon passed, their chants expressed their zealous devotion. The crew sung of the perils of their life at sea, the longing for the shores of their homeland, and the great hope they felt at the prospect of discovering more islands of the coveted archipelago.

"In Essawylor we dwelt, from Essawylor we hail!
Then we left our home
Through the waves and foam
Now to Nyn Llorely we sail!"

On and on, their songs continued as they improvised verses in a merry competition to come up with the most creative and inspiring rhymes.

In the evening, the dyn Filweni gathered around Feïwal, away from the crew's intense activities and speculative chatter. They sat down in a simple circle on the wooden floor of the aftcastle.

In the commotion, the gathering of the ship's council had not been noticed by the others. The four dyn were soon joined by Roquen, who sat in front of Feïwal, in respect for the Irawenti tradition.

Aewöl and Curwë followed him. The Dol Lewin lord was rarely seen without his two most trusted companions. He relied on Aewöl for his wise council, measured temper and wide knowledge. He loved the bard Curwë for his impertinence, fervour and humour. Roquen liked to compare their dual influence to the rays of the moon and the sun, for each carried a magic of its own.

All the council members had preferred to let the day pass before meeting to consider their decision with clarity.

Roquen was restless and agitated. The turbulence of recent events had affected him, changed him, more than anyone else aboard. The Dol Lewin lord was convinced that his companions must have by now perceived the weakness that he was suffering from. In his eyes, there could be nothing worse; his personal strength was the foundation of his authority over other, lesser Elves. All his life force was now devoted to concealing from others the doubts which tormented him. He was no longer sure of his destiny or purpose.

As if attempting to break the malicious stigma, Roquen spoke first, staring blankly ahead. He was expressionless, his whole demeanour betraying his lack of resolution.

"The proud standard of the war unicorn has disappeared into the depths of the Austral Ocean. It has been taken from me, as was everything else. That standard was a sacred relic, given to Lewin, my ancestor, by his wife Iriagaele of the House of Dol Amrol, to seal their union. It had survived every battlefield of the First Age. It saw our glorious defeats and also... our ignominious victories. It was taken from me... swallowed by the ocean. It is a sign, a sign that I cannot ignore. Its loss announces the end of my house...and it seals my own fall...

From now on, I ask you to know me as Roquendagor, simply Roquendagor, a knight without banner."

The High Elf paused. He was deliberately and freely choosing to renounce his heritage. Abandoning his Dol inheritance relieved him from a burden that was proving too heavy to bear. Roquen continued in solemn voice.

"Dyn Filweni, we owe you our life and our freedom. We remain indebted to you, yet our paths will have to divide. Our presence by your side poses a great danger. It jeopardizes the noble quest you embarked upon and threatens to thwart the great ambition of your kind."

With these few noble words, he removed any responsibility for the Irawenti towards his former household. Standing behind him, the bard Curwë, who had not been consulted, realised the impact of Roquen's declaration. He thought ahead anxiously to what the immediate future might hold for them, lost in that hostile wilderness without the assistance of the Irawenti. At his side, Aewöl remained still, his face blank. But his gaze hardened. He, too, had not been consulted.

The Irawenti remained silent, each processing the consequences. Nelwiri, the youngest of the dyn Filweni, sat slightly apart, twirling a small piece of wood between his nimble fingers. He visibly did not expect to be involved in the debate. He therefore could not mask his surprise when Feïwal asked his opinion.

"Siw!" he exclaimed in surprise. "I have no such opinion. Where the ship goes, I will go ..." He smiled smugly at the ambiguity of his response.

All eyes turned to Luwir who, while the oldest and most respected noble of the clan, was nevertheless second to Feïwal. He hesitated, preparing to mark each of his words with authority.

"The Elves of the House of Dol Lewin have shared the pains and sorrows of our journey. I do not believe that, after all that we have been through, their fate can be separated from our own. Abandoning them would be like abandoning a part of ourselves.

I will stay by their side, but I suggest that others aboard the ship try to sail to Nyn Llorely and to reach the City of Urmilla where some of our distant relatives dwell. They will plead on our behalf, on all of our behalves."

Aewöl intervened, seizing the opportunity to influence the debate. To the surprise of all, he argued the opposite to what could have been expected of him.

"Those are generous words that do you much honour, Luwir. They are worthy of your title, Commander of the clan of Filweni. But, alas, the oath taken by King Lormelin did not disappear with his death. His son inherited it along with the crown of the archipelago. This oath is a fearful thing. Only the death of young King Norelin and the extinction of his line could allow the House of Dol Lewin to hope for some clemency. There can be no bright future before us or before those who choose to join us. You must abandon us. Any other choice would mean taking a perilous path, strewn with many pitfalls."

Heads bowed, and eyes turned away, as each Elf processed these words. Turning towards Roquen to recommend a way out, Aewöl added in a lighter tone.

"I recommend that we and the Unicorn guards head for Mentollà and settle among the wild Elves. There are many ways we could rally them to our cause. They are warriors, numbering in their hundreds, waiting for someone to lead them. Furthermore, that ruined tower is located strategically, beyond the clutches of the king. It is easy to defend and set apart from both the human barbarians and the hostile Llewenti clans: a perfect haven for the outcasts we shall become. Its shelter promises us many possibilities for the future. Let us hope our Irawenti friends find their way on the archipelago, and that one day they can return aboard their vessel."

It seemed as if Roquendagor did not even contemplate replying; his mind was absorbed elsewhere. Feïwal turned to his sister.

"Arwela, I saw how, earlier this night, your gaze was lost in the constellations. What have you read in the stars? Could you unravel the designs of Cil, Cim and Cir?"

Arwela was highly respected among the clan of Filweni; no major decision was made without first obtaining her advice. She was calm, beautiful and serene as she began to speak. Following her instinct, the Seer of the clan of Filweni was eager to help, but she did not want to say too much.

"I did attempt to understand the stars' mysterious influence. Celestial bodies appear strange on this side of the ocean. Their heavenly shapes seem closer, more numerous, more vivid than in our hemisphere, and the fading moonlight only augments this effect. All of Cil's magnificence is on display, but the three stars are far apart. My art is now reaching its limit.
Siw! No one can predict how their influence will affect our fate. The road to the east, to the island of Nyn Llorely, is wiser and safer; I have seen how Cim illuminates its shoreline.
Hope but also danger lies to the west, where the course is uncertain, difficult and unknown. Towards sunset, I see how Cil and Cir fight to control our destiny; none can say which of the two will prevail. Will promise triumph over doom? That, I cannot tell."

There was a long silence. Feïwal, who until now had kept his feelings secret, felt his heart freeze in the solemnity of the moment. He knew that, beyond their own survival, the fate of many others depended on his decision. Feïwal had always buried his inner thoughts and never let anyone influence his emotions or decisions. Not even his own kin could truly sway him. Turning his gaze to his sister, he spoke with surety.

"The elder matriarch of clan Llyvary traced the eastern course for us: that same matriarch who so distrusts us, and who pretends to stay the rising winds of Eïwal Ffeyn. The Lady of Llafal fears us, blinded as she is by the ancient beliefs she has inherited from a fallen world. She saw that our coming announced great changes to her world. But she is afraid of what those changes might be, even as the spirits of the forest sing the news of our coming, even as they gather in the ruined tower to celebrate the breeze that blew us from the ocean! My friends, we cannot trust her.

Cil, Cim, Cir! I will therefore lead you to the west and take the forbidden path. We will challenge the matriarch's command, and the threats that any royal oath poses to us.

We will look to Mentollà.

Siw! I am the Guide of the clan of Filweni. I roam free and no authority in this world will ever decide my fate."

All nodded in agreement.

"My friend Roquendagor! Abriwa! Let us seal today our alliance! We represent new hope for the Elves of the archipelago. Together we shall do great deeds! Come here and let us celebrate!" Feïwal rose to embrace the tall knight, in accordance with the warm-hearted ways of the Irawenti.

The other members of his family did not share his enthusiasm. The strengthening of their ties to the High Elves worried them. Indeed, none of them rose to celebrate this renewed friendship. However, Curwë, who appeared greatly relieved by this decision, joined them and declared.

"This day shall be marked with a stone, Feïwal dyn. Your inspiring leadership has guided us so far and our renewed vows of friendship shall give rise to glorious feats to come, I foresee it now. It is a wonderful thing, when Elves of different origins unite. It deserves a song."

Aewöl rose in celebration, using the opportunity created by the Curwë's declaration.

"Indeed, something inspiring has been born today. We unite today to become the Sari[46], those who will open the way."

And after this ambitious augury, he embraced his friends, one after the other. Aewöl's face was brightened by the pleasure of friendship.

Filled with joy at these warm effusions, Feïwal confirmed their newfound resolution.

---

46 Sar(i): 'Guide(s)' in lingua Morawenti

"We will first sail east, but when night falls we will about-turn and make haste towards the west. Let us pray that Eïwal Ffeyn's winds carry the Alwïryan safely to port."

"In this case," Roquendagor stated, looking weary, "all is well. And I can finally rest."

He stood up and, without a word more, was on his way. The tension that had been building within him over the past few months was gradually vanishing, creating a troubling emptiness. His senses were disturbed, his gait unsettled. Making slow, unsteady progress, he managed to reach the ship's hold without assistance. For more than three months, he had not really rested. Elvin sleep was a deep reverie and Roquendagor had not experienced it for a long time. Aewöl had warned him this could lead to insanity. His councillor had prepared specific potions to assist him through his period of mourning. But pride and stubbornness had prevailed and Roquendagor had refused to absorb the soothing beverages; the vials had been set aside.

As the Dol Lewin heir abandoned the name of his House, rejecting his bloodline and the responsibilities and duties that came with it, he was seized by a profound weakness. He needed the potions. Roquendagor smiled when he finally retrieved them from their hiding place in his cabin. He opened them eagerly, drank them and let the unnatural fluid act through him. He laid down in his hammock and fell into a deep slumber.

★

What Aewöl had used to prepare his potions, Roquendagor did not know. But their effect had been almost immediate; he was plunged into a deep, remedial sleep, which lasted several days. But, after a while, his dark dreams returned, though now they were of a different nature. He would feel his body floating helplessly in the waves. His clothes would be soaked. Sometimes he would have difficulty breathing, as the saltwater fought its way up through his nose. The sensation of drowning would start to fill him with dread, and he was incapable of expelling the horrible feeling from his mind. Horrible noises, like waves crashing against rocks, disrupted his senses. He would hear desperate cries around him from Elves doomed to the same fate. He would then feel other creatures touching him, grabbing him…

"So, this is it, death is trying to seize me," he realized, becoming angry. "Not yet!" he resolved with wrath.

Roquendagor began to awake. The halls of the dead bore a striking resemblance to the Alwïryan's hold. Curwë and Gelros were nearby, trying with difficulty to raise him. The keel was severely damaged and split. The hull had taken on huge quantities of water. The ship was disintegrating, breaking at the seams. At the very moment Roquendagor had realised his desperate situation, a deafening crash rung out as the Alwïryan hit the rocks. A beam broke away, striking him hard on the head. He was once again unconscious.

★

It was still night when Roquendagor awoke, his body wedged into the sand of a beach. He was covered in blankets from the neck down. Tilting his head up, he saw multiple fires illuminating the scene before him. He was at the mouth of a small river, from its bed clusters of rock protruded from the water, creating rapids and pools along its course.
The vessel lay disembowelled. The remains of the Alwïryan were strewn across the beach, It had crashed against the rocks before running aground on the sand. Some of his companions were busy extracting all that could be saved from the ship's remains. Aewöl and Curwë were coordinating the Unicorn guards' efforts to recover the plants from Essawylor that had been stored in the ship's holds.
Most of the crew had gathered around Feïwal to listen to his prayers in a display of great devotion. The guide of the clan of Filweni was standing on a large rock, haranguing the survivors and exhorting them to pray to the angry god, Eïwal Ffeyn.
Arwela approached Roquendagor.

"Cil, Cim, Cir! It is good to see that you are well," she said delicately.

She was relieved that her efforts to cure him had been successful. As a seer of her clan, Arwela was blessed with rare healing skills. She had inherited ancient powers which enabled her to perform vital acts of healing. With her great abilities, Arwela had managed to save Roquendagor from his injuries and her natural draughts had finally neutralized the effects of Aewöl's vials.

"Eïwal Ffeyn delivered us from the ocean's wrath," Arwela continued, looking up with admiration at her younger brother, who was still in the midst of that moving clan ceremony, hearing now the tributes of his followers.

"What has happened?" Roquendagor muttered, fighting to overcome a deep residual ache in his jaw.

"Siw! As soon as we turned west, breaking our vow to the matriarchs, the Alwïryan became caught in a great struggle between the violence of the waves and the power of the winds. Feïwal, once again, saved our lives. He was able to steer the ship to this shore, west of the Gloren peninsula, though he could not prevent the Alwïryan's ultimate destruction. Now we sing our praises to Eïwal Ffeyn, for it was the angry deity's will that saved us from our doom."

Roquendagor could not help admitting his admiration. "Your brother is inhabited by such unshakable faith. It is the source of the firm resolution and bold bravery he demonstrated. It saved us already twice."

"Feïwal is the Guide of the clan. He was entrusted with the quest for the Llewenti Islands," simply replied the beautiful seer. But in her tone, Roquen could perceive that she meant much more. Intrigued, he asked.

"How is it that this legend inspires such devotion?"

"According to the ancient tales left by the Llewenti queen, Llyoriane, a Stone formed the heart of the meteorite that hit the Islands. It carried within it the knowledge of the free Elves' destiny. It was believed that glyphs and runes were inscribed upon the Stone by the deities of the archipelago.
For us, who, at the beginning of time, had refused the invitation of the Gods, the Stone is our ultimate object of desire." explained Arwela.

"So, this is what Feïwal is after. That alone will be enough to give him my support," Roquen concluded before closing his eyes again.

*

To the east of the bay, ribbons of red cloud announced the birth of the day. The morning fog soon cleared. Flocks of seabirds circled the wreckage of the Alwïryan, diving down from time to time into the river in search of food.

The crew was quick to set to work, and before long they had formed a chain of Elves leading up to their former vessel. The Irawenti were particularly gifted for the loading and unloading of ships. They worked silently in a regular rhythm, obediently following the instructions of Luwir. Bags and crates were passed from hand to hand towards the shore, where a unit of guards, commanded by Maetor, waited to sort and store them.

Feïwal focused on his duties as captain, checking food supplies and ensuring that no valuable equipment suffered further damage. The other dyn of the clan of Filweni were at his side to support him, sensing the grief that afflicted him after the ship's destruction. The Alwïryan was more than just a legendary vessel; it was a symbol of their freedom.

Many birds of all kinds gathered around the shipwreck as if to pay a last homage to the proud ship. The scout Gelros strolled among them, taming a small crow and a white seagull. He had a natural affinity and skill for communicating with animals, most of all birds. They seemed to submit willingly to him.
Towards the end of the morning, the gentle sea refracted a bright silver light in all directions, as the tiny waves of the river spilled slowly up its banks. Their work was complete. Along the shore, in the shade of the pine trees, they finally rested. While they were stunned by the beauty of that wild place, they mourned the loss of their ship, which lay mutilated.

The castaways of the Austral Ocean now needed to reach the southern end of the Gloren peninsula on foot. They had to cross a wild forest, the Sognen Tausy[47]. Located to the northwest of Nyn Llyvary, between the Austral Ocean and the Mountains of Arob Tiude, these dense, wild pine woods clung to the cliffs.

---

47   Sognen Tausy: 'The savage woods' in lingua Llewenti

It was a craggy and hostile territory, with a terrain that made journeys difficult and also provided endless hiding places. This land did not belong to any dominion and was left abandoned so as to separate the Elves of Llymar from their barbarian enemies.

They knew the region was closely watched by Elvin sentries, for they always lived in fear of human invasion. They maintained constant vigilance against incursions from the barbarians coming from beyond the Arob Tiude; those bloodthirsty men were always eager to challenge the power of the Elves.

There was an old, abandoned road that meandered through the woods, where the sea breeze carried the smell of resin. Their track traversed the hills of pines and cedars, weaving its way from north to south across vast, uninhabited lands. The soil was poor but not completely dry.

It was their prisoner, Vyrka, who guided them. The wild Elf estimated that Mentollà was located to the south, no more than ten leagues away. It was quickly agreed that a small group of scouts go ahead with Vyrka to prevent any hostile encounter. The rest of the company was heavily armed and would advance slowly behind them.

Roquendagor volunteered to lead the expedition, and would only allow Gelros, to accompany him and Vyrka. He held the scout's path finding skills in high esteem and could rely upon his enhanced senses and natural alertness. He also felt more confident with his former hunt master's powerful bow backing him up. Gelros carried two birds with him; it was agreed that he would send only one of them back once they reached the ruined fortress. The crow would signal evil tidings while the gull would indicate that the path was clear.

Before departing, Roquendagor reminded the prisoner.

"Your brother is being held hostage. The unfortunate is still alive though severely wounded. Any treachery would result in a sour end for him. You shall be discreet, and you are not to communicate with any of your kin before we all reach the safe haven of Mentollà."

Vyrka could not understand the words of the threatening knight, as Roquendagor spoke the Hawenti language of old, but he knew them to be strict instructions of some kind. Bowing respectfully, he murmured in his own mother tongue, obedient and respectful. It was clear that the lordly manners and commanding presence of Roquendagor had impressed him beyond measure. It could be seen from the look in his eyes that he would submit to his authority.

They took their leave of the main group without ceremony and, by the beginning of the afternoon the three Elves were on their way. Before long, the clouds became tinged with a dark, threatening grey. It started to rain heavily. The weather could change quickly in these lands, close as it was to the ocean. Vyrka frequently looked up to the sky, as if fearing an airborne threat. They had intended to make haste, but the elements did not allow for easy passage. The soil was waterlogged. The track was slippery. The old road had not been used for years and was tangled with boughs, bracken and wild deep-rooted trees. They were often forced to skirt around obstacles, and the wild Elf's assistance was proving vital; even Gelros was surprised by the difficult conditions.

The Sognen Tausy was a wild forest like no other. The streams and rivers which ran through its hills carried a magic of their own. From the cliffs at the edge of the forest to the foothills, where the old trees were small but strong, there existed all around a powerful field of energy. It was a land of pure nature; uninhabited save for those outlaws and refugees who chose to hide in its wild recesses.

They stopped a number of times to catch their breath. Surprisingly, it was always Gelros who requested the breaks. Yet, the scout had his reasons; he knew that his liege would never demand respite, nor wish to admit that he could be outlasted by a mere wild Elf. During these short rests, there was little conversation.

Roquendagor was preoccupied with the desolation that surrounded the ruins of Mentollà. He suddenly asked Vyrka in lingua Irawenti, for its origin was similar to that of the Llewenti tongue.

"Why didn't the wild Elves choose Mentollà as their stronghold?"

The answer was not clear and the difference in language did not facilitate its understanding.

"We, runeless Elves, shunned the place. We chose to live away from Mentollà, but I do not know for sure," vaguely explained Vyrka.

Roquendagor guessed that it was no more than superstition that kept them away and he recalled that Aewöl had mentioned the Blue Bards, spirits of the Sognen Tausy woods whose mysterious ways greatly influenced the wild Elves. His curiosity grew.

He was relieved when their path finally led them to a vast clearing. From the glade, the group could glimpse the tall silhouette of Mentollà's ruins, perched at the top of the coastline's escarpment. They saw a large, round tower: eroded, scarred and falling away in places. The once impressive fortress, built upon a rocky outcrop, looked out over a wide creek that the archipelago's deities must have carved to safeguard it from the ocean's fury.

On the opposite shore, to the southwest, angry waves crashed rhythmically against the cliffs producing a thunderous roar. The rock was hard as marble, yet still along those steep slopes the occasional impressive tree would grow. These trees had been exposed to natural erosion and had weathered many tempests, but their roots still clung desperately to cracks and cavities in the rock. With the beautiful sandy beach below, the spray of the waves and the tempered ocean breeze, the place was a marvel.

To Roquendagor, Mentollà looked like the High Elves might have built it in the early days of the world; it was tall, robust but elegant. Indeed, it was of Hawenti origin, built by King Lormelin's masons and artisans over twenty centuries ago. Decades of hard work and dedication had been required to raise it. The stone markings which adorned its broken doors showed its age.
Roquendagor exclaimed.

"What a formidable construction!"

Vyrka agreed.

"In their songs, the bards of the Islands sing about the great tower of Mentollà. They relate the ancient Elvin wars which resulted in King Lormelin's victory over the Llewenti clans. Mentollà was a key part of the High Elves' triumph. Its powerful armoury, including siege engines and catapults, guarded it against those sea routes to the north that were already made so dangerous by the ocean's wrath and Eïwal Ffeyn's fury. It also protected the creek, the only shelter for many miles along that hostile coastline, marked as it was with reefs and steep cliffs."

"I understand," replied Roquendagor. "From the port's well-protected position, a fleet can be prepared. It could pose a serious threat to the shores of Llymar and the cities of the Llewenti clans," he concluded thoughtful.

"The tower is not as powerful as it used to be. Nowadays, there is no longer any trace of the legendary silver dome, the masterpiece of the Blacksmiths' Guild of Gwarystan that in the ancient times served as the landmark to ships and was feared by all," explained Vyrka.

The three scouts cautiously approached the outer walls. Gelros was on high alert, scanning his surroundings at every step. Firstly, he crossed the ditch before climbing the escarpment. Gelros saw a breach in the ramparts and rushed straight for it. He had made it inside. A colossal external wall surrounded him. It was built with granite from the Arob Tiude Mountains. Inside the great outer wall, there were six ruined stone buildings with collapsing arches, crumbling chimneys and no ceilings. Gelros could see gaping holes that had probably been doorways, through which the remains of stairs climbed upwards towards the sky. Ivy, brambles and wild trees decorated the walls. Now the place only served as shelter for reptiles and nocturnal birds. Above him loomed the keep, a tower of a hundred and fifty feet, its round stone walls broken only by arrow-shaped windows. Its door, an immense iron structure covered in pentacles, lay broken at the foot of a large opening. The top of the keep resembled an open, jagged mouth.

The tower sat atop three huge stone arches, largely intact, that interconnected to form a wide fortified walkway at the base of the tower, where catapults and ballistae could have menaced both the ocean and the forest. From that platform, such heavy projectiles could have comfortably overwhelmed any attackers from land, as well as any vessels seeking refuge in the creek below.

Now convinced that they were safe and alone, Gelros called to his two companions. Roquendagor solemnly entered the fortified compound, demonstrating his respect for such an ancient construction, a place of valour and courage.

The tower had faced many sieges during its long history, and each one had left its mark. Vyrka proved more respectful to his captors than ever and started to provide explanations. He gestured with his hand to the various scars upon the thick walls of the fortress.

"These small marks were caused by Llewenti projectiles during the distant Elvin wars, a very long time ago," he said. "My forefathers were using light stones and fiery projectiles, which failed to harm the fortress. The deep wounds you see above were caused by the barbarians' trebuchets. They came here aboard their long ships many times," Vyrka added with fear in his eye.
The wild Elf continued, "During the Centenary of War, the Westerners' great galleys delivered the fatal blows which partly destroyed this great tower with boulders and flaming missiles. The Men of the West have mastered the art of sieges. The weapons they use are fearful instruments of death, the likes of which had never been seen before. Many cities and fortresses of the archipelago have fallen facing those great galleys. See how the tower has been ripped open on the north side of its base. This was the work of the Westerners' siege engines," stated Vyrka sadly.

Roquendagor could not follow everything the wild Elf was saying, but he added, for Gelros' benefit.

"No doubt that it was this exposure that the attackers exploited to wreak carnage inside."

Indeed, even now, a strong breeze hissed and screamed as it possessed a mind of its own. It seemed to lament that although it had once commanded the winds, those winds now commanded it.

"Eïwal Ffeyn's breath," Feïwal had mentioned. Only now did Roquendagor understand what the Irawenti captain had been referring to.

"It is not by mere chance," Roquendagor thought aloud, "that the clan of Filweni chooses to settle in this desolate place. What better shrine to honour their deity of storms?"

"Vyrka, tell us more of Mentollà's fall," Roquendagor requested, using elementary words in lingua Irawenti.

"It was a great battle, a century ago. All the Elves present were killed. My father and elder brother were among those who perished. The siege lasted three full months before the great galleys of the Westerners came to bombard the tower with their missiles. The barbarians, whose assaults had until then been repelled, finally broke through the defences, reaching the besieged Elves inside," explained the wild Elf.

"Do you fear this place?" asked Roquendagor, curious.

"Yes, so many Elves died in such horrible circumstances. But let us say no more of that."

"I understand. I too have known the trauma of war," admitted the knight. Something close to compassion could be seen in his gaze.

"It was forbidden to stay in Mentollà, until that night when the Blue Bards gathered in great number within the compound to celebrate the extraordinary arrival of a ship from the Sea of Cyclones," recalled Vyrka.

"I sense that you and your kin seek protection," Roquen speculated. "You can trust us. There are not many of us but our strength in battle surpasses all expectations. Tell your wild friends in the woods and the hills that they have nothing to fear. If they seek assistance, they will be welcome in Mentollà. We will offer them our protection. You are weak, but you are brave. Your mind is slow, but your body is nimble. I like you, small Elf."

"I need to explore the inside of the keep," declared Gelros, interrupting Roquendagor. He always was on the lookout for potential dangers. "Vyrka, you will lead the way," the scout added. The heavy rain was returning in force.

The group divided in front of the tower's broken door. Gelros and Vyrka entered the structure, finding cover from the hail.

Roquendagor, however, chose to remain outside. The rolling clouds were so low they seemed to be rising from the ocean rather than falling from the sky. Rain was streaming from the mountains, drenching the ground, and cascading down between the rocks, but Roquendagor decided to continue his exploration, entering the creek below the fortress. He advanced slowly, using his sword to clear a route through the wild grass. The ocean roared in front of him and thunder bellowed above him. He was walking a dangerous and slippery path, but he did not seem to care. Reaching the creek, even the terrifying spectacle before him failed to distract from his thoughts.

The end of the trail led to the ancient natural port of Mentollà. There was a narrow jetty built between the ocean and the creek. Each time a wave struck, the sea broke furiously against the jetty, engulfing it before falling back with a great crash into the cove. The wind and the ocean battled ferociously. It would have been dangerous to linger there any longer. Roquendagor began the climb back to the tower. He had seen enough. The creek of Mentollà, sheltered by this ancient pier, could harbour up to a dozen Elvin naves.

Approaching the tower, Roquendagor suddenly noticed inscriptions on a large boulder that was beside the path. They were Hawenti scriptures which remained unmarked by erosion.

> *"All hail Norelin, of the House of Ilorm,*
> *Son of Lormelin,*
> *Liege of Gwa Nyn,*
> *King of Hawenti,*
> *Protector of Llewenti,*
> *And Overlord of the Isles. Hereby does he warn To all:*
> *If ever you enter Mentollà, and choose to here reside,*
> *Not Wall, nor Gate, nor Fort, nor Arms of any kind,*
> *Shall save you from the Fury of those who have the Pact signed.*
> *Let the Haven Tower remain empty. Let*
> *the Peace of Norelin preside."*

Roquendagor read these words several times. They struck him as deeply as the insults of Queen Aranaele in the halls of Essawylor, which first incited him to rebel. They conjured in his mind a vision of war and ruin. So great a pain did they inflame in his heart that he chose to erase the king's inscription.

Roquendagor was known as the strongest Elf in Essawylor, but he also possessed remarkable agility. He positioned his body so as to lever the formidably heavy stone. With a horrible cry of pain, he managed to push it into the void. The stone crashed down upon the rocks thirty feet below, bouncing before sinking into the haven's waters. The warning of King Norelin sank with it.

Following this prodigious effort, Roquendagor, possessed by the sacred fire of rebellion, turned to the forest and roared, as if appealing to the whole universe.

> *"All hail Roquendagor, son of Roen,*
> *Hereby do I proclaim:*
> *No warrior, mage or king*
> *Shall stand in my path*
> *As I seize the fort of Mentollà!*
> *To assuage my woeful fate,*
> *I entrust this ancient place*
> *To Feïwal dyn Filweni.*
> *'Till the winds cease to blow, 'till these islands' dying day*
> *I declare the Haven Tower shall be a shrine to Eïwal Ffeyn!"*

He was now at peace. The knight sat by the breach in the tower, waiting for his companions to come back from their exploration. The air was heavy with spray. He inhaled deeply, appreciating that place where new life had been granted to him. Mentollà was a place burdened by its past. The fortress had been severely wounded, and its ruins only showed the vestige of their former glory. Yet to him it stood proud and immutable above its surroundings. He wanted to live there and restore the ruined fortress. The care and attention that he would dedicate to this task would help to heal his wounds.

Noises from the tower interrupted his musings. A fleeting sensation of hope had visited him for the first time since the disaster of Ystanlewin.

"My Lord! The tower is empty and secure," Gelros announced.

Like most of the castaways of the ocean, Gelros could not help showing uttermost respect to his former liege. Still unsure of exactly how to address him, the Morawenti scout continued.

"I found markings around the upper levels, and also underground. They indicate that a large group has been here recently. Wild Elves would be my guess. They could well have been here yesterday. They were in a hurry and did not attempt to conceal their passage.
Fresh footsteps indicate they carried heavy loads. I even found a small forge recently installed in the tower's lowest levels. There are also numerous tools, large quantities of metal and various ores stored within."

The news surprised Roquendagor. He placed his hand on his companion's shoulder.

"You did well, and the tidings you bring are reassuring! We may have allies. Send your white gull to our companions. Welcome to our new home, Gelros! For it is in Mentollà that we shall dwell hereafter," he announced.

★★

Although it was autumn and heavy fog dominated the mornings, but the afternoons nonetheless brought warm sun. Large coastal trees bathed the ancestral stones of Mentollà in purple shadows, as the light streamed down through their reddening leaves.

Life was swiftly organized within the fortress; such was the nature of all Elves. They were perfectly able to while away their time simply enjoying the beauty of their environment without ever becoming restless. But when adverse times demanded prodigious effort, their resolution and perseverance could not be matched.

The community had prioritized the restoration of Mentollà's buildings and ramparts. It was first set up as a temporary dwelling. With the sails and wood from the wreck, the settlers constructed large tents to shelter themselves, as the barracks would not be repaired until after winter.

All were adapting to their new climate, not without a certain amount of bewilderment. Some of the High Elves put their masonry skills to use, gradually rebuilding the fortress walls. Loggers provided the carpenters with wood, who in turn made planks and beams for the shipwrights. The Commander of the Unicorn Guard, Maetor, was leading them, and his experience was proving effective. He was in charge of fortifying the compound and installing its defences. The elite fighters under his command gathered stones and heavy wood that could be fired at attackers in the event of a siege. Using their extensive experience of warfare, they developed deadly traps all around the fortress. His troops worked in a kind of frenzy, toiling from sunrise to sunset, always fearing a surprise attack.

In the meantime, others, commanded by Aewöl, rekindled the new forge. In the shadows of the fortress's vaults, they made gongs, spindles, axes, locks, and repaired any damaged metal objects that they had brought with them. Aewöl had been master of the Smith's Guild of Ystanlewin in the days of Essawylor. He was an alchemist of great skill; his natural intelligence and innate gift for handiwork was combined with an insatiable passion for self-improvement. Very few other artisans in the Kingdom of Five Rivers could rival him. Aewöl was taught by his father, a great smith and Enchanter himself. Their skill came from the Gnomes of the north, who were masters of forging deadly weapons. Aewöl knew that now was the time to produce such weapons and many like them. Experimentation and invention would have to wait for better days.

The Irawenti of the clan of Filweni were not outdone by such intense activity. It was less than two weeks before the sailors to launch their first boat into the peninsula's waters. It was a narrow, lightweight boat, carved from a tall pine tree. It moved rapidly, propelled by both its sails and a team of rowers equipped with short, flat blades. It could carry up to six Elves.

Each day they would bring home plenty of supplies for sumptuous meals. The sea was full of shellfish. Oysters, in particular, could be found in abundance around the rocks at the mouth of the creek. They caught pounds and pounds of fish simply by casting their dragnets, so rich were those unspoiled waters. The Irawenti were renowned for their ability to dive to great depths; indeed, they preferred hunting underwater with tridents, as it required both skill and agility. They excelled at catching the abundant bream and bass.

Others, led by Gelros and Curwë, roamed the trails of the Sognen Tausy forest in search of wild fruit and game. Their hunting trips were very successful, and each new day they would marvel at the novel fauna and flora they were discovering. While pines and cedars were more common, but apple trees, wild vines, and oaks could also be found.

They set about introducing the plants of Essawylor that had been saved from the shipwreck into their new environment, beginning with nutmeg and cinnamon before planting date palms and mango trees. It only took a few weeks for the first samples to take root, promising a rich harvest when summer arrived.

Gelros made sure that a team of hunters was permanently on shift, checking on the snares and traps, bringing in whatever had been caught, and replacing the fruit that had served as bait. Before long hares, pheasants, partridges and other wild birds found their way into the meals of the small Mentollà community. The hunters took care, however, not to stray too far from their base, as they were cautious not to trespass into the wild Elves' hunting territory.

One day, when the sky was blue, and the sea displayed a beautiful emerald colour; Arwela invited Roquendagor to a walk, a few leagues north of the fortress, where the Alwïryan had run aground.

The knight was first surprised by the proposal but finally accepted, somehow stiffly.

★

152

When they reached the mouth of the small river, they met with Nelwiri who led a small group of Irawenti artisans busy around the vessel that had once been the glory of Essawylor's fleet. Its great mast which used to proudly dominate the tropical seas now lay spilled across a foreign shore. Only the hull and keel, deeply buried in the sand, bore any resemblance to its former grandeur.

The Irawenti had built a raft equipped with a hoist and improved it by adding a rudder, a small mast, a sail and a plank to prevent flooding. This perfunctory boat proved crucial in retrieving the heavier, bulkier objects from the wrecked ship's bowels. They brought back all kinds of tools and materials, and possessed pieces of fittings, cables and sails aplenty.

Nelwiri, eager to share his enthusiasm, explained to Roquendagor.

"I know these materials are invaluable for restoring Mentollà, but the sea is often perilous and prevent us from working as efficiently as I would like. I ordered that we first extract any equipment which might perish in the coming winter storms: halyards, beams, struts, guy wires, pulleys and even some heavier parts. All the elements that are crucial to rebuilding a ship are now safe, dried and ready to be reused."

"For what purpose do you do that?" Roquendagor asked, somehow surprised.

Nelwiri added. "My ambition is to construct a new long ship that would allow us to explore the archipelago more widely. The task is immense, as few remains of the Alwïryan can be recycled, and we lack all the equipment and infrastructure for a project of that magnitude. We would have to build a dock for careening the new ship, construct medium-sized boats to transport materials, and design strong pulley machines to lift loads."

"Many months of hard work at the Fortress are required before you can think of setting a new vessel afloat. Even then, the tasks ahead require skills that are well beyond you and your followers," said Roquendagor drily.

"I am impatient to return to sea and continue exploring the Islands. We are imprisoned within the walls of Mentollà; it is at sea that we will be safe," tried to advocate the sailor.

There was a long, embarrassed silence, as it was clear that the two Elves would not come to a common view.

Arwela decided to change the subject.

"I met with the wild Elf Vyrka and dedicated a lot of time to learning the language of the archipelago's Elves."

"I noticed your light was often lit at night," noted gently Roquendagor.

"Indeed, I devote my time to creating a complex book of translation and expression. Vyrka contributed greatly to my task, and, to my amazement, we discovered that the roots of our respective Elvin languages are very similar," explained the Lady of the Filweni.

Roquendagor added with the tone of a scholar. "The Irawenti developed their spoken and written skills after conquering Essawylor once they had discovered the cultural legacy of the Llewenti. The two languages originate from the same roots." The knight was not accustomed to entering into this kind of talk.

Arwela understood that it was a way for him to show respect and consideration towards her. She went on, "I am extremely pleased with my progress, and I now can organize classes for our small community."

Roquendagor nodded. "Elves of all origins and abilities should attend your lessons, all should be eager to expand their knowledge."

Nelwiri concurred and encouraged his elder sister. "All of us praise your patience, and grace. The exquisite Llewenti words you will teach us will invite us to travel the Islands, meet the inhabitants, and celebrate the beauty of their language and culture," he insisted with a smile.

At the end of the day, when Arwela and Roquendagor came back to Mentollà, the knight was feeling better. It was with certain regret that he let Arwela go to her duties. The Seer brought out a soothing presence to all. But she was always very active.

Arwela also took special care to record the day-to-day life of the community. Sat in front of her makeshift desk with her parchment, pens and ink, beginning to write in cursive Irawenti script, the crudeness of their situation faded somewhat from her mind. It was a ritual for her to take the clan's book and record, as the night sky resumed its slow rotation, the events of the previous day. In those lands, the constellation of hope, a group of five stars surrounding Cil, the light of the west, gradually disappeared as winter approached. While it would have been fully visible from the northern shores of Nyn Llyvary at summer solstice, each month afterwards one more star would disappear below the western horizon, until the revered western light itself slipped away, marking the beginning of autumn and the coming of long nights. Arwela studied this phenomenon with great interest, eager to understand its implications. She could already sense the effect it had upon the powerful competing deities, and, as the stars shone on, her anxiety only grew.

One day, her brother Feïwal honoured her with a visit after a class and she shared her worries with him.

"I'm very concerned. Autumn has come and Cil has abandoned us, disappearing beyond the horizon. The star of hope will not reappear for several months, I believe. Siw! We should be frightened, for we are now at the mercy of Cir's power, and I can already perceive the dark influence that the star of despair will have upon our destiny. From the depths of the earth, it manipulates the minds of those that despise us. Feïwal, we must follow Nelwiri's suggestion and devote our energy to building another ship, rather than fortifying this cursed tower."

The clan's guide shared his elder sister's concerns, but there was no way to reverse the plan that had already been implemented. It was now too late; decisions about the community's work for the coming months had already been made. It would not be easy to change their course. He attempted to reassure her nonetheless.

"I understand, and I agree. I too am anxious to reach the shores of Nyn Llorely. I too grow impatient to greet the Llewenti of that island and introduce ourselves to our distant relatives."

But this disclosure failed to reassure Arwela. She pressed on.

"It is in the city of Urmilla that we will find protection. I cannot believe that our brethren would surrender us to an unjust power. We must build the boat as quickly as possible or, in the very worst case, seize one from the ports of Llymar. I sense that our need to depart is urgent."

"Arwela, I promise that once Aewöl and Maetor have finished repairing the fortress gates, all of our strength and resources will be dedicated to that objective," replied Feïwal, unable to commit to anything more.

Nevertheless, the black omens perceived by his sister had affected him, and only added to his own misgivings. At first, he had been worried that the community might not be able to survive in such a wild and isolated environment. However, as the days passed, he could not deny how quickly progress was being made. Above all, he was heartened by the synergy of the Hawenti and the Irawenti, united by the same objectives and purpose. Feïwal was now revered by all as the true lord of Mentollà. He assumed his new role with serenity and kindness. Feïwal understood that a new destiny was forming before him and his faithful followers. It was an exciting thought, full of promise, but the guide of the clan of Filweni was both wise and shrewd: he knew that such a destiny could not be realised without a cost, and he feared this sacrifice would be a heavy one.

*

At night, under the beautiful starry sky, when fragrant aromas emanated from the trees, and a fresh breeze rose gently from the sea, the community would gather around Curwë. From the first joyous sound from his harp, they all acknowledged the talent of the minstrel, and the dancers celebrated their spared lives.
Curwë regaled his audience with his cheerful talk and merry tales. He was often accompanied by Arwela, who excelled at the flute. Maetor would also take part, marking the beat with drum. Curwë would sometimes drift off from the dance entirely, becoming carried away by his inspiration and improvising a tune that celebrated the beauty of their new life. In those moments their dancing would stop, and the crowd would listen in silence full of renewed hope, returning home once the long melody

had finished. For a while, their longing for Essawylor was kept at bay. Such was the infectious nature of the Bard; he always looked to the future and celebrated, with endless merriment and laughter, the beauty, joy and absurdity of life.

Yet, despite his playfulness, Curwë was also worried. He noticed that his liege, Roquendagor, deliberately staid away from the life of the community. He never attended any of the wild dances so loved by the Irawenti, shunning the musical joy that Curwë could provide. It seemed that Roquendagor deliberately avoided anything that could heal his mind or alleviate his bereavement. Curwë knew that his pride stopped him from sharing this with his retainers, so he respected his lord's isolation, waiting for the first signs of recovery. Advice from Arwela had strengthened his resolve to remain patient.

Meanwhile, Roquendagor suffered in silence. That fleeting glimmer of hope that he had glimpsed when he first found refuge in Mentollà had been extinguished.
The knight took great care to hide his distress from those around him. He was aware that he was not in full control of his faculties and that a sick curse still pervaded his mind. Realising this made progress, as it helped frame in his mind the evil that he so needed to fight. Roquendagor was a warrior, and he needed an enemy for him to work out how to regroup and gather his forces. After some introspection, he soon noticed that there was a pattern to the sick intensity that affected him. Evenings, and above all starless nights, were the most horrible; his mind would become engulfed in grief and anger. He would struggle against madness; it felt like he was drowning, as if his mind were unable to breathe. His thoughts chased around in endless anxious circles, and he felt entirely unable to escape.

His only alleviation was in extreme exercise, the physical pain he experienced would temporarily dampen his mental agony. Exhausted by his efforts, he could finally find some rest, if only for a few hours. Sunrise would bring him great relief; for the first hours of each day he would enjoy relative peace of mind, a result of his agonizing exertions the night before. During the day, he would summon what little strength he had left after nights of battling his demons and devote himself to designing a siege weapon that could be installed on the remains of the tower's walkway.

Roquendagor was a formidable character, he was one of the most praised young Elves for his perseverance and prowess in combat, but he was also uniquely talented at designing new instruments and sketching out construction plans. He excelled in mental disciplines that had a pragmatic purpose, while he despised all abstract academic subjects, which he left to those he regarded as weak, loquacious scholars.

The task of devising this weapon was no mean feat; the small amount of space available on the remains of the walkway demanded a completely new design that would have to take inspiration from both ballistae and catapults. He had to plan how the weapon could be supplied with ammunition. The challenge was daunting, but its completion could prove crucial, as the main advantage of Mentollà was the platform provided by its tower, which dominated both the sea and the plateau below. Placing a powerful weapon in such a strategic position would make a vital contribution to their defences.

Aewöl visited him regularly to enquire about his progress, giving him useful advice. He brought the tools and materials necessary to begin making the weapon. But Roquendagor was no fool; he knew Aewöl's night visits had another purpose. He could see in his companion's bright eyes the desire to check up on him. Aewöl was closely watching over Roquendagor in his own distant way.

The work progressed well, and Roquendagor's idea to combine the various remains of the Alwïryan's ranged weapons proved fruitful. After a few weeks' work, they began tests. The ballistic device launched heavy projectiles over great distances. Some missiles could even reach the edge of the Sognen Tausy woods, over four hundred yards away from the tower walls. Aewöl looked relieved; he had been impatient to see the siege weapon built. Turning to Roquendagor, he said with satisfaction.

"I was eager to finish this work. You deserve our congratulations and gratitude, Roquendagor, for devising such a deadly device. Our community is safer as a result. Anyone approaching our walls, from the bay or the forest, will now be met with powerful retaliation."

"We need a name for our new ballista," Roquendagor declared succinctly.

"Indeed, and that name should reflect our will to fiercely defend our cause. We should not be naïve. Reaching the archipelago was not the end of our journey. The path before us holds many dangerous pitfalls. There are very few on these islands, be they Elves or men, who will welcome us willingly. Even fewer will extend a hand of friendship in our hour of need."

"That is no surprise. A powerful oath stands between us and the Islands," Roquendagor replied.

Aewöl's eyes were now as cold as a blade, as though he had suddenly been reminded of the threats that they would inevitably face.

"You are right, Roquendagor; we must become strong, powerful and feared. This is the only way we will gain the respect and cooperation of our potential allies. Demonstrating our extraordinary abilities in war is what will gain us influence. Men, like Elves, bow to whoever is strongest, whoever wields the most power. Whatever values they may have learnt in their temples, whatever ethics they may have praised in their songs, they would all, without exception, betray their closest friends to survive, and some will even do so for a taste of more power, glory or influence.

Blind generosity is a sign of weakness and desperation. Naïve honour often equates to no more than idiotic defencelessness. We may smile and bow to the ambassadors of our neighbours only once we have established our reputation and proven our strength. Only then can we enter into diplomacy: responding to their lies and false promises with machinations of our own. This world is no more honest than a vast fair," Aewöl murmured, his voice altered by a cold deep-seated hatred.

"Time will tell... In the meantime, I have thought of a name for our ballista. I have learnt some Llewenti words from that small Elf, Vyrka."

"What do you suggest, Roquendagor?"

"Ganol wallen[48]"

"What does that mean?"

"I am not certain, as my proficiency in the local dialect is limited. But, I think it roughly translates as 'far-reaching death,' or something similar."

"I like it; the name is most fitting for its purpose. May 'Ganol wallen' do us proud when the time for blood and death arrives," Aewöl concluded grimly.

★

One night, when the stars were bright in the sky, and the full moon illuminated the tower's pale radiance, Curwë could not help but pay a visit to his former lord. He had been greatly inspired by the music and dancing that evening, and the joyous uproar from around the bonfire had lightened his heart. He was dressed magnificently, in a tunic of rare silk studded with fine jewels. A precious gold diadem decorated with rubies sat atop his long, chestnut hair. His wardrobe, that had been the cause of so much malicious Irawenti gossip, had nonetheless been saved from the shipwreck. He intended to fully enjoy the last remnants of his former richness, and his clothes were the symbol of the fame and power he had earned in Essawylor. He left spiteful comments to others and had always ignored any malevolent remarks directed towards him. He was excited that night, and it showed in the light in his beautiful eyes. Their colour was a shining green, so unusual among the High Elves that it was thought, among the maidens, that Curwë's emerald eyes possessed a bewitching power, capable of charming any Elvin female according to his will.

But, that night, Curwë was not attempting to conquer the heart or favours of any maidens; he had made the most striking discovery of his life. Sauntering up to his lord and friend as if they had parted just moments before, he addressed him in his characteristically impudent manner.

"My Lord, I must say, I am rather glad you did not completely butcher that first spy that night aboard the deck of the Alwïryan. What mighty blow it was though, and I do not

---

48 Ganol wallen: 'Long-range death' in lingua Llewenti

doubt the miserable spy would have been honoured to have perished under such a glorious hand! It just so happens that his brother, our new friend Vyrka, son of Vyerkyasin, if I remember his ancestry correctly, is extremely grateful."

Curwë made a dramatic pause for effect.

"I now understand why we risked our lives, souls and swords to cross the Austral Ocean. Look at what the generous Vyrka has brought for us... a jug of Llewenti wine!"

Roquendagor gave a quick look, but the weariness of his gaze showed his utter lack of interest in his companion's acclaimed beverage. Even the bard's humour was unable to lift the veil of darkness which imprisoned Roquendagor's soul. Yet Curwë was far from giving up and continued with his theatrical oration.

"This may well be the most delicious beverage one could hope of tasting for miles around; unless, that is, one was to peruse King Norelin's personal reserves. I imagine that Vyrka picked up this example from one of the settlements of the Llymar marches. The wild Elves take what they need when the need for it arises, dangerous though it may be. And, my Lord, I must say, I concur with them entirely, for I would risk my own life in the blink of an eye if it meant I might hold my lips to such a bewitching fluid again."

"I might have a taste of your wine, Curwë, if you promise to stop calling me 'my Lord'. I do believe I was clear on the matter," Roquendagor answered severely.

"It is somewhat difficult to converse with a person without using his name... but pardon me, your lordship, I insist, for the wine of these islands will lighten your heart and clear your thoughts. It is a blessing from the deities of the Llewenti! I, for one, would be more than happy to swear my allegiance to those matriarchs if it meant I could quench my thirst with such delightful drams each day. Yet fear not: I am several jugs away from betraying you entirely."

While the bard continued his flowery speech, Roquendagor decided he might as well honour his side of the bargain. Taking the amphora with both hands, he examined the clear, golden liquid within, and took a moment to inhale its vapours. Then he drank several long gulps, without paying any particular attention to the vast aromatic richness of the exquisite beverage. A symptom of his curse was that he could no longer detect the taste of food or drink, however glorious it might be. Having drained the jug, he paused for a moment, trying to discern what effects the golden wine might have had, if any. Soon enough, a powerful energy flooded through his limbs before finally reaching his heart and his head. The fluid seemed to wash away the impurities from his soul and resurrect his will. In a moment of absolute lucidity, he turned to his companion, his voice lighter from the drink, but still authoritative.

"As sweet as any fine Elvin lady!" Roquendagor declared.
"A fine remark, my liege," approved Curwë, visibly happy at the reaction.

Sensing an opportunity to cheer his companion, the bard decided to elaborate.

"Indeed, there is nothing quite like the flavours of our finest maidens; even this precious wine cannot compare...This morning I spent a fair amount of time contemplating the coming and goings of the beautiful Irawenti females in our community. I could not help but think that our friends of the clan of Filweni have adopted the wisest attitudes towards love. The Irawenti value freedom above all things and enjoy the life that has been granted to them. They forge temporary bonds that are mutually beneficial and can be broken without pain or regret. Love can last a night, a year or even centuries; it does not matter. The promise of everlasting commitment does not interest them, for they are wise enough to understand that, like the tide of the Ocean, love ebbs and flows as it will. It is the Irawenti who have fully grasped the essence of Gweïwal Uleydon's teachings."

Even before Roquendagor began his retort, his angry gaze revealed his disagreement.

"The only Irawenti I pretend to know are Arwela and Feïwal. They are not at all as you describe; they seem to be wise beings, with complex souls that long for the noblest of feelings."

Honour was at the cornerstone of Roquendagor's values; sworn oaths were sacred to him. In truth, he had grown up among the Hawenti aristocracy, breathing in the same stale air, embracing the same arrogant ideas, and always reaching for the same obstinate conclusions. Now, the knight was realizing how divorced he had been from the Irawenti communities, ignorant about their ways and customs. He nevertheless continued.

"Love between two Elves is the most precious gift, for it holds the power to procreate and prolong, through a beloved heir, our immortal life. That irrevocable bond should be protected at all costs, for great evil comes when others try to sever it."

Curwë, sensing that the tension was growing and that his rhetoric was losing its charm, changed the subject.

"Our generous friend Vyrka told me that Elvin ladies are very different in these lands. They are more dominant when it comes to relationships. They have the right to freely select as many companions as they wish, and each companion knows his place: as intimate friend, devoted protector or passionate lover. The Llewenti live in a matriarchal society where the women hold communities together and participate in clan rule."

"A detestable custom!"

"A just condemnation, my suzerain! As for myself, I would never succumb to such tyranny," Curwë replied obsequiously, trying to provoke a reaction by repetitively referring to Roquendagor's former high rank.

The knight smiled, appreciating the humour behind the audacious tactics of his companion.

"You do not need to live in the shadow of my glorious self forever, my friend. You have already paid your debt to my family many times over, with your courage, loyalty and service. Back in Essawylor, your potential was stifled. Whatever deeds you achieved, whatever distinction you earned, whatever virtues you may have been celebrated for, you would never have been rewarded with what you deserved. Your triumphs would have been seen as a challenge to those of higher rank, a reminder of their mediocrity and lack of ambition. You would always have been considered a scion of an unknown bloodline, a Silver Elf with green eyes and fair hair, with neither family nor lineage.

But your time has come, Curwë. The archipelago awaits you. Therefore, step out into the light, and show this new world your merits. I am sure there are many minstrels on these islands ready to sing of your future feats," he claimed.

These generous words filled Curwë with joy; even though he would always consider Roquendagor his lord, mentor and revered master, such a vow of friendship did him much honour. Overwhelmed by happiness and gratitude, Curwë stood and shouted to the stars.

"Elves of Llymar! Elves of the Llewenti clans! I drink to your good health and fortune! May the deities of the archipelago bless you for producing such glorious nectar! I would cross the unfathomable ocean again for another precious sip!

However, beware. Beware! For the mightiest Elvin heroes have reached your shores, and, with their formidable deeds, they shall change your fate forever!"

CHAPTER 5: dyl Avrony

"The bird of prey spiralled upwards into the sky, as if performing its mating ritual. Once it reached a certain altitude, it dived down towards a young Elvin lady, who looked up, saw it and tried to escape, fleeing in terror. Everything seemed lost until a great peacock, with magnificent green plumage, sprang from the bushes and intervened between the lady and her aggressor, in a desperate attempt to protect her. The two birds began to fight; which would triumph was uncertain, for although the bird of prey was more aggressive, the peacock was tough and fiercely defensive.

But then a third winged creature joined the fight; its arrival was unexpected, and its appearance even more so. Its vibrant plumage instantly distinguished it from all other birds, for its feathering was bright red and yellow. Its legs were covered in scales of gold, and its eyes burnt with fierce, striking yellow. It was a phoenix. The legendary creature immediately directed its attacks towards the bird of prey, and a distinctly violent, ruthless confrontation ensued. The struggle was fierce, but the peacock did not seize its chance to withdraw. It seemed determined to defend the Elvin lady at all costs. Joining the bloody melee again, it attacked the mythic bird, wounding it several times before provoking its wrath. The phoenix turned, letting its more dangerous opponent take flight and escape, before striking the peacock with its formidable claws.

"No! No! No!" Nyriele screamed, her eyes filled with tears.

"Nyriele, it is only me. Wake up! The time has come! The ceremony will start in two hours. We must prepare! Wake up!"

The young matriarch opened her eyes, emerging from a terribly intense and disturbing nightmare. She recognized the walls of her house in Tios Lluin. The sun had not yet risen, and her room was bathed in soft moonlight. Gal dyl, her father, was kneeling by her bed. He wore splendid ceremonial robes in the mahogany and beige colours of his clan, cut from the finest silks. In his daughter's eyes, Gal dyl was the embodiment of true nobility, the authentic heir to the bloodline of Eïwal Vars. Sorrow and pain had inflicted their worst upon the last surviving dyl of the clan Avrony, but he had never succumbed to these knockbacks. He still had his tall, proud stature and powerful build, and he remained as fast and agile as any stag of the forest. In that moment, his long blonde hair was as radiant as ever, but could not conceal his concerned gaze. Beneath his evident anxiety, however, the profound love of a father for his daughter was unmistakable.

"Oh Father, you are alright! I thought... oh, I saw horrible things... You are alright... I am so relieved..."

She then recounted her nightmare to Gal dyl, insisting upon each and every detail, her eyes filled with tears. She threw herself into her father's arms, her body still shaking with shock and fear. After a moment, she placed her hands on his shoulders and leant back to look into his eyes, telling him again about the most disturbing part of her nightmare.

"I am sure it was a green peacock. The eyespots upon the feathers were unmistakable. It was similar in size to its two opponents, but less heavily built. It fell after being attacked by the phoenix. I do not know if it survived," she explained, tears rolling down her cheeks. Once again, she sought the comfort of Gal dyl's arms.

"It was just a bad dream, Nyriele. It will have sprung from your worries about the future. Do not allow your emotions to overwhelm you. It would not be fitting for a matriarch of the clan Llyvary. You must remain strong."

"My dreams are not like the dreams of others, Father. You know this. I seldom have any at all but, when I do, they always mean something. I have powers of insight. Even Matriarch Lyrine acknowledges it."

Gal dyl was surprised that his daughter had referred to her mother as 'Matriarch' Lyrine. The formality of the title highlighted the ever-growing distance between mother and daughter.

Gal dyl held Nyriele, doing his best to comfort her. Trying to take her mind off the nightmare, he said.

"Did you know that the peacock helps disperse the seeds of many different species of plants, contributing, in its own way, to the circle of life?"

He paused, thinking about his own life, his destiny, and the legacy he would leave behind in Nyn Llyvary. He continued.

"Peacocks live in forests, in perfect peace and harmony with their environment. They mostly eat fruit from the ground. Their song is hailed as the most beautiful of all birds."

Gal dyl spoke gently, stroking his daughter's shining hair, deep in thought.

"The Elves of my clan really are like the peacock. It was not by mere chance that Avrony, our first Matriarch, chose that bird as our sigil and its light green shades to be our colours. She was the last of Queen Llyoriane's daughters. She was granted the smallest island of the archipelago, though it was also the most beautiful. We are indeed the peacocks of the forest. We have nothing to do with birds of prey and, as your dream rightly showed, we would do well not to mix with them. You said the peacock's second opponent was a phoenix."

"A phoenix is similar in size to an eagle. It has a sun-like halo," explained Nyriele.

"I have never heard of such a creature upon these islands."

"It hails from the fabled Essawylor and is said to be immortal. Once it dies, in a flourish of flames and smoke, it gains new life from the sun, rising from the ashes and taking flight once again. The phoenix was adopted as a symbol by Queen Llyoriane in the early days of our history. According to legend, one such bird protected her from the machinations of the Islands' deities."

This left Gal dyl puzzled. But he warmly embraced his daughter before taking his leave to let her prepare for the day.

Nyriele's room was located at the top of the house, above the main hall. The view of the forest below was beautiful. Light streamed in through a small window that looked out over the tops of the pines. The furnishings in the room were made from dark wood. Wall hangings, originating from Medystan[49], represented the odyssey of the Llewenti and their Queen Llyoriane. The only other objects in the room were an oak altar, a statue of a matriarch carved from pine, a bed enclosed by blue curtains, and a precious carpet from Ystanoalin[50]. There were no mural paintings, nor any ostentatious decorations to adorn the walls. The room was furnished simply, with carved wood and polished iron.

Nyriele wore white robes, with modest golden jewellery. She was finely but simply dressed. Her favourite silk gown greatly enhanced her elegant silhouette. It felt natural for her to display her beauty, and among the Llewenti it was considered neither unusual nor vain. Every morning, the young matriarch started her day with ritual prayers that honoured beauty and love in all their myriad forms. She opened her window and muttered soft, powerful words out into the forest air. The leaves of the trees around her house seemed to sway back, as if the trees themselves were bowing to her grandeur. The faint moon gently lit her face. She could hear water dripping from the rooftop. She uttered a few final words of prayer.

"Eïwele Llyi's beauty is all around me, and for this I give thanks. Its radiance lights up my life and nurtures my soul. I shall find beauty wherever it takes root, and I shall help that

49 Medystan: 'The Great Walled City' in lingua Llewenti
50 Ystanoalin: 'The City of the Dol Oalin' in lingua Llewenti

beauty flourish, so that all may partake in the joy and happiness it brings. I shall always give shelter to Eïwele Llyi's creations, for her teaching guides the course of my life."

Having spoken those words, she felt free and light, and could suddenly sense the power of the Flow of the Islands coursing through her veins.

A few moments later, the father and daughter were leaving their small stone house which stood in the western part of Tios Lluin. The streets were still empty. While the heavy mist that surrounded them foretold the arrival of dawn, in that moment it also obscured the sparkle of the stars above. The city of ruins gradually awoke to darkness.

"What do you make of this unusual gloom?" Nyriele asked her father. "Eïwele Llyo obscures the many splendours of the city with a shadowy web of illusion. The deity of dreams is sending us a message. One way or another, she will have her say in what will be decided today."

They were heading east towards the enchanting vestige of Tios Lluin's Temple of Stones, which lay at the heart of the ruined city.

The site of the Temple was vast; it occupied a circular area of land that spread out for more than five square miles of forest. Thousands of gigantic stone blocks had been erected throughout the forest, amongst which there were also various monuments, graves, wells and great pits. These blocks created a complex series of paths that, together, made up a symbolic network which mirrored astrological constellations. This map corresponded with the positions of the sun, moon, stars and planets in the canopy of heaven and thus imbued this collection of monuments with complex liturgical significance. It was a place where earth, sun and stars converged. The genius architect of the Temple of Stones had demanded that the huge slabs of blue rhyolite be hauled from the Arob Nisty Mountains across a hundred leagues of steep terrain.

The first person that Gal dyl and Nyriele encountered in the deserted alleys was a young Elf, who wore a long silk gown so fine that she appeared to be dressed in a mantle of stardust. Her face had a serene glow.

"Good day to you, and welcome to Eïwal Ffeyn's masterpiece," the Elf said with a warm smile, before disappearing behind a corner of the labyrinth.

Llewenti legends told how, long before any Elf set foot upon the lost islands; Eïwal Ffeyn himself had found refuge on the archipelago. The deity of the wind had fled the wrath of the Gods to join his consort, Eïwele Llya, and their many offspring, including firebirds, hippogriffs and griffons. When he discovered that a storm giant had captured his beloved spouse and held her prisoner, abusing her at will, his fury knew no bounds. A great battle commenced across the Islands, and the struggle lasted for decades. Eïwal Ffeyn finally prevailed against the storm giant and his sons: sons whom the storm giant had forced Eïwele Llya to provide for him. It is said that, to punish his enemy, Eïwal Ffeyn condemned him and his descendants, the giants of the Arob Nisty, to build Tios Lluin's Temple of Stones, and that he cemented the great construction work with their blood and their bones.

Several thousand years had now passed, but the legend, however fantastical, could not have seemed more real to Gal dyl and his beloved daughter, as they walked towards the still-majestic ruins of the ancient shrine.

The father and daughter were united by a deep bond. A relationship as strong as theirs was highly unusual among Llewenti of noble blood, for it was the custom that young children were taken from their parents at a very young age. Gal dyl had been honoured with Lyrine's love until he had fathered her successor. Llewenti custom allowed noble females to choose their companions, and the Lady of Llafal had soon selected other, more obedient lovers. Unexpectedly, Gal dyl's sudden fall from her mother's favour had only increased Nyriele's love for him, and since then he had been her favourite parent and most trusted confidant. The two shared an adoration of beauty, a thirst for freedom, and a love of uncomplicated relationships.

Joy and empathy were their most cherished values. And it was not a rare event for the warlord of clan Avrony to entertain his only daughter with stories worthy of the humblest bard, just for the sake of a smile or giggle from her.

A magical mist drifting up from the earth gently enveloped the streets that they walked through, along with the trees, houses and ancient stones they passed. The humid smell of wet grass and leaves dominated scents of the surrounding flowers.

Almost six thousand Elves lived in Tios Lluin, although it could host ten times as many. The city had been gradually constructed within the perimeter of the Temple of Stones. Large buildings and small wooden constructions completed the map of streets within the gigantic stones. The inhabitants were mostly Llewenti, but there were also many High Elves of the House of Dol Etrond who had settled in Llymar with their lords, Curubor and his nephew Almit. They governed the city, but Llewenti customs were supported by the force of the law and two matriarchs of the clan Llyvary.

Gal dyl had always wondered why the Dol Etrond lords had settled in Tios Lluin. Some Elves in his entourage who disliked the High Elves believed the only reason they dwelt there was so that they could own the Temple of Stones, along with all its ancient secrets. The matriarchs of the Llewenti could only marvel at the power of the Flow of the Islands inside the temple of Tios Lluin. Some believed that Eïwal Ffeyn had used the High Magic there to tear a Star down from heaven, hitting the centre of the main island, Gwa Nyn. The impact had levelled mountains, reshaped rivers, carved out valleys and had even awoken a volcano. Eïwal Ffeyn's incredible feat had confirmed the wind deity's dominion over the archipelago, and his insolent opposition to the Gods.

'If that legend is true,' Gal dyl thought as he approached the ancient shrine, 'then the idea of an Elf attempting to control such immense power is frightening.'

The warlord of the clan Avrony despised the place; it filled him with dread and stirred up painful memories within him. Ninety-nine years had passed since Gal dyl had last set foot in Tios Lluin, when the city had been the bloody setting for the deadliest battle in thirty centuries of Llewenti history. Thousands of Elves, among them dozens of noble dyl and matriarchs, perished in the darkest disaster that the Llewenti of Nyn Llyvary had ever experienced.

Witnessing her father's growing unease, Nyriele gently broached the subject.

"Father, I can see that you are thinking of the battle and that it fills you with dread."

"It was almost a century ago, but I still hear them dying in agony. Even now, I smell their burning flesh and feel the heat of the great fire. I can see them crawling, begging for help. I can still see the flames dancing hypnotically. I cannot stand this horrible feeling."

"But the ultimate victory was yours, Father."

"I arrived late, and none of those besieged in the Temple of Stones were saved. That is the bitter truth of my supposed victory. All those Elves burned to the death, they might as well have been consumed by the fire of an ancient red dragon. Elders of your clan died in that battle too, fighting desperately," Gal dyl replied, regretfully.

"But it was you who ended the siege of Tios Lluin and repelled the enemy. You became the greatest hero in our recent history," Nyriele added in an effort to comfort her father.

"So, stories say...and people were made to believe. But it was the House of Dol Etrond's knights who hunted down the barbarians, and it was your grandfather's desperate charge from within the siege that first broke the deadly circle of enemy warriors. He was the true Protector of the Forest and High Warlord of the Llewenti clans; he was the true wielder of the Spear of Aonyn. Surely Yluin dyl Llyvary was a hateful Elf, and one who I greatly despised for his scorn towards my clan. But he also was the greatest hero of our time. No wonder his daughter, Lyrine, possesses such might and pride. Do not overestimate me, Nyriele! The strength in your veins comes from your mother's side, not mine. You descend from the white swan far more than from the green peacock."

"It is you who I love, Father, and I always will. My prayers go with you, and the rising power of my rune protects you. So be comforted, and do not let the past get the better of the present. Look at the flowers that adorn this garden. Tios Lluin is beginning to breathe again."

Indeed, spring was returning; the trees were budding, grain was sprouting from the earth, and life was beginning again. Llewenti legends told how the cycle of the seasons was originally brought about the deity Eïwele Llya herself.

The tales described her deep love for her sister, Eïwele Llyo, the deity of dreams, who resided deep below the earth at the heart of the island of Nyn Llyvary. Llewenti myths conveyed how, for a few months at the end of each year, Eïwele Llya, or the Mother of the Islands, would visit her sister's great underground halls from which she commanded the dreams and fate of the Llewenti. During the winter, therefore, the Mother of the Islands' power would retreat from the archipelago; life and fertility drained away from the land and the forest alike, and the further away one was from Nyn Llyvary, the harsher and colder the air would become. It was during this period of decay that the two deities would combine their mighty powers to renew the cycle of life upon the Islands. They breathed new vitality into the trees and the plants, and also into the souls of their followers who had fallen. Nothing and no one were overlooked.

And so that cycle of life resumed once again. The generous Flow conjured the fecundity of nature upon the Islands again and again.

*

Gal dyl and Nyriele continued towards the heart of the great city of stones, walking in silence along the streets. Gradually, they saw lights being lit; torches set ablaze and smoke beginning to rise from the rooftops as they passed by. The homely smell of hearths began to flood the streets they navigated. Before long, here and there windows and doors of the city's stone houses were opening. The Elves they met saluted them with the greatest respect. Gal dyl was loved by the city's inhabitants; his hunting feats, festival triumphs and joyful demeanour had earned him a glorious reputation.

The young Nyriele was worshipped like a muse who embodies the hope of the Llewenti clans. Her timeless beauty, benign nature and forgiveness delighted her followers, who in turn rewarded her generously with their unceasing love and affection. Nyriele represented art, beauty and joy. She often acted in secret to protect young miscreants from the harsh justice of the matriarchs.

All of a sudden, the two heard a low rumble, ringing out around them like a muffled groan from the forest. The priests of Eïwele Llya's cult were summoning the power of the Eïwaloni, the sacred trees. The forest was calling, relaying a message to the other cities of the Llewenti: to Tios Halabron in the west, Penlla in the east, Llafal in the north, and even to the most remote settlements of Llymar. The Council of the Forest was about to begin.

This news was relayed by the clans' war horns, sounded to accompany the call of the Eïwaloni. It spread throughout the woods which surrounded Tios Lluin, inviting all to gather around the sacred circle of stones.

The circle was in fact a vast, hexagonal crater, very deep and wide, and was surrounded by eight gigantic blue stones. Steps had been carved into its sides, and the sacred area could host thousands. Nature had escaped the wild gardens of the city and had encroached upon the structure. Trees, plants and roots covered the ancient stones, cobbles and slabs. Within the antique pit, each of the six sides led to a separate underground temple, the doors to which were surrounded by beautiful mural architecture, as if they were gateways to the domains of the Islands' deities. Their creation was more recent; the stone used for their fluted colonnades, steps and reliefs came from the white cliffs of Penlla. The six strong doors had been whittled from the wood of the Eïwaloni, and they were all intricately carved with powerful glyphs and runes.

"It is strange that the matriarchs would choose the southern side of the esplanade to erect this shrine to our three sister deities, while the temples of Eïwal Vars, Eïwal Ffeyn and Eïwal Lon were left with the northern part," said Gal dyl, his eyes marvelling at the splendour of the place.

"Towards the south lies the heart of the archipelago, the source of all life, fertility, beauty and dreams, but also doom. The northern boundaries of the Islands have always been Eïwal Vars and Eïwal Ffeyn' s domain, for it was where their protection was most required," explained Nyriele.

"Look how Eïwele Llya's temple occupies the preeminent position; the Mother of the Islands is surrounded by her two sisters. Eïwele Llyi's shrine is to her right, for it is beauty and love that first gives life, while Eïwele Llyo's sits to her left, as is fitting for the deity of fate, transcendence and doom, which all mark the end of the cycle of life. The other temples were also arranged very deliberately: that of Eïwal Vars, the Father, occupies the centre, and he is surrounded and supported by the chaotic power of Eïwal Ffeyn to his left and the harmonious strength of Eïwal Lon to his right. For, just as death will always follow life, chaos will always prevail over harmony, until a balance is found, and the cycle begins again," continued Nyriele.

"I had never considered it that way before," said Gal dyl, somewhat naively with awe in his eyes at his daughter's wisdom.

Indeed, she had now become a true matriarch and a great scholar.

They looked towards the south-eastern part of the great circle. Hundreds of Elves were already seated, silent and still, waiting for the day to commence. Seeing the gathering crowd reminded them of what important matters would be discussed as the day progressed. Nyriele seized her father's hand.

"Today, there are some who will attempt to lead us into a trap. They will force us into a corner, where our only choice will be between submitting to King Norelin or opting for secession, and therefore ultimately our complete isolation."

"Is this painful dilemma not inevitable? Could the current precarious balance really be maintained for much longer? Has the time not come for us to reclaim our destiny?"

"Reclaim our destiny?" inquired the young lady, surprised and anxious.

Nyriele paused before continuing with a feeble voice.

"Reclaim our destiny? Do you not see how much suffering and destruction lies beyond those noble words?"

★

The clan Ernaly's army was the first to gather on the steps of the sacred circle, occupying the south-eastern part of the ruins. The day before the council, they had taken the road to Tios Lluin. They came from Tios Halabron, and from the hamlets which surrounded the city of sacred trees. At the sound of the war horns, five hundred fighters, organized into twenty units, had assembled and set out on an orderly march into the depths of the forest.

Mynar dyl the Fair, their charismatic warlord, had led them, with his younger brother, Voryn dyl the Ugly, walking by his side.

The Elves of Tios Halabron had brought with them the falcons and hawks of the woods; hundreds of birds which were now perched amongst them in ominous silence.

The clan Ernaly's fighters had been waiting for this moment for a long time. They had arrived in their dark green war clothes proudly displaying their weapons and armour: helmets, breastplates, long brazen shields, short swords, javelins carried in pairs and short bows on their backs. They each wore a certain number of feathers according to their rank: one for the common fighter, two for the captains and three for the noble dyl, whose bloodline could be traced back to Eïwal Vars. The warriors' feathers were plucked from the hawks of the clan, and one could guess which unit a fighter belonged to according to the colours of their feathers.

Mynar dyl saw Gal dyl and Nyriele as they approached the circle and walked over to greet them as they descended the steps. The fair warlord of Tios Halabron was dressed in his resplendent war attire, fitting for an Elf of his reputation and position.

His long cloak, robes and boots, a mixture of brown and green hues embellished with silver markings, all came from the finest workshop of Tios Halabron. A rich ermine fur was wrapped around his neck.

For armour, he wore a leather coat with interweaving straps. Gaiters and gauntlets, covered with runes and markings, supplemented his protective clothing.

He was fully armed, with two fine shining long swords, a pair of daggers, a short bow with a quiver full of lethal arrows on his back and his famous javelin.

Mynar dyl's pace and his striking appearance made his determination to march to war very clear.

"Noble Matriarch, good day. Protector of the Forest, good day to you too," he began. His voice was calm, a faint smile on his lips.

"Good day to you, Mynar dyl," the father and daughter replied somewhat coolly.

"This is a glorious day indeed, and the beauty of the fairest Elves shall illuminate it further," he added, his charismatic gaze fixed upon the young matriarch.

He continued.   "The meeting has been organized according to ancient tradition. The people of Tios Lluin will sit on the upper steps, while the fighters of the army will occupy the lower ones. captains and priests will sit on the front row. Only the noble dyl of the clans, and the Dol of the House of Dol Etrond, will be allowed inside the circle to address the crowd. As for the warlords of the cities, their seats are arranged in an arc at the heart of the esplanade, facing the Temple of Eïwal Vars and the Council of the Matriarchs who shall sit below it. You shall stand in the centre, Gal dyl, as befits the Protector of the Forest. You shall hold the Staff of Emeralds and use it to signal whose turn it is to speak. Therefore, you shall command the discussions. This is a great responsibility; you will undoubtedly influence the outcome of today's council."

"Thank you, Mynar dyl. We ought to start now. The day will be long and there is much to be discussed," replied Gal dyl simply, eager to bring this exchange to a close and wishing to release his daughter from Mynar dyl's insistent gaze.

The Elves exchanged ritual salutations. Nyriele whispered a few words to Gal dyl before hurrying to the Temple of Eïwal Vars.

"Father, remember Matriarch Lyrine's advice. Our very existence is at stake. Do not let them push us into an impasse."

Gal dyl did not reply. Mynar dyl was still lingering close by. Apparently, he had not finished what he wanted to say. Waiting until the young matriarch was away, he turned again to her father.

"I have been watching you, Gal dyl," he said, friendly and compassionate. "I see your confusion and doubt growing every day. I understand how you feel. My brother Dyoren once described to me what it is like to wield an ancient relic like the one which will be yours."

Feeling doubtful, Gal dyl replied: "Have you ever observed geese migrating south in spring? They always follow a guide who knows the secret of the winds. I am no such guide, regardless of the Spear that I will wield. I cannot lead the three clans into an abyss when I have not fathomed its depth. Until now the Islands' deities have protected us, but their favour is as fickle and changeable as the wind."

"But think of it this way, Gal dyl: we do not have a choice. The souls of the dead, which haunt the shores of Nyn Ernaly, talk to me, whispering of their pain. Day by day, little by little, the destructive hand of man weakens the power of Eïwele Llya. With each tree that falls, the Mother of the Islands is slowly dying. Time cannot fix everything, for some damage is irreparable. But time will reveal all: the good and the bad...

The Oracle of Llafal shall indeed be proven true. When we go to war, Llewenti blood will be spilled and Eïwele Llyo will no doubt come knocking at the door of many of our homes, but the reclamation of our rightful home will have begun. Once again, the Llewenti heroes will be celebrated in the songs of the bards. Once again, the warlords of our clans shall write the legend of our holy weapons in letters of blood. If we want to triumph, we must strike fear into the hearts of all. This can only be achieved with the roar of war. Believe me, my friend; our destiny is set in stone. You do not have a choice."

The threatening note of this line concluded Mynar dyl's speech and the warlord of Tios Halabron returned to his seat.

Gal dyl took a moment to reflect, surveying the scene before him. Standing in the middle of the circle, he inhaled deeply, sensing the growing agitation around the place of worship. The steps were filled with fighters from all the clans, all eager to find their place, creating tension. All were fully armed, ready to march at the council's bidding.

He then noticed the arrival of an unexpected group. A unit of sailors from Cumberae, with pale features and snow-white hair, were making their way towards the circle. Their master, wrapped in a cloak of white lion skin, led them. His name was Aertelyr, a renowned merchant. Gal dyl recalled that a large vessel had sailed into Penlla several days ago. Each spring, it brought goods from the distant south; steel, raw materials and furs were exchanged for wine, fruits and cloth.

The Prince of Cumberae ruled the southern regions of the archipelago on his own, and therefore he did not respect the trade blockade that King Norelin had imposed upon the three clans of Llymar. Its representative was an important presence at the meeting. The appearance of the prince's master of trade, and the permission to use a large merchant ship, meant that Cumberae could well become an active ally. A gathering such as this had not taken place in a century; it was therefore unsurprising that it was provoking such excitement and enthusiasm even amongst those who lived beyond the borders of the Forest of Llymar.

Finally, calm was restored amid the apparent chaos, a certain harmony emerged, and Gal dyl could survey the entire army that he commanded, now gathered on the steps of the stone circle in front of him. It was a large force, organised into units and cities, proudly displaying their pennants and banners.

Llymar's army was made up of more than two thousand fighters. They were mobile troops: equipped sparingly with leather or brass plates, their faces protected by helmets, their arms by long shields. They were a formidable force in the face of an enemy in wooded terrain.

The deadly arrows of the clan Llyvary's archers, the lethal javelins of the clan Ernaly's warriors, and the ferocious slings of the clan Avrony's scouts were powerful instruments for that type of warfare. Widely dispersed across the battlefield, Llewenti combatants could also rely on the strength of their fearsome Hawenti rear guard.

The House of Dol Etrond's cavaliers and knights wielded weapons and wore armour of the most elaborate Elvin steel, forged in Tios Lluin by the renowned Smiths' Guild which was led by Almit Dol Etrond. The 'Golden Arch Guard' was a devastating adversary in close combat. They were known to never turn their backs on a battlefield; such was their discipline and morale.

Llymar's army was commanded by the nobility of the forest. All of them were present at the council. Gal dyl counted them carefully, recalling their names. They would be allowed into the circle to have their say in the debates, and he would have to introduce them to the crowd as he passed them the Staff of Emeralds.

He was the last and only scion of the dyl Avrony bloodline and only representative of that clan.

Almit and Curubor would represent the House of Dol Etrond. As warlord of Tios Lluin, Almit would be one of the last orators.

Mynar dyl and Voryn dyl would debate on behalf of the clan Ernaly; Mynar dyl the Fair would sit beside Gal dyl as warlord of Tios Halabron. All of this was simple enough.

It would become more complicated when dealing with the clan Llyvary. There were nineteen dyl, most of them young, who had never participated in the affairs of the forest before. He did not know them personally, except for the dubious Leyen dyl, warlord of Penlla, and Nerin dyl, his impulsive grandson, who was second to the warlord of Llafal, the 'Old Bird' Tyar dyl. The most ancient warrior of the forest would sit on his other side. He was the only Elf of any importance from the clan Llyvary, as Gal dyl knew that he would be the spokesperson for Lyrine, and her words were not to be taken lightly.

Gal dyl expected that the Lady of Llafal would reign unchallenged over the council of the Matriarchs; there were nine of them in total, and the clan Llyvary's seven dignitaries clearly outnumbered the two high priestesses from the clan Ernaly.

Nevertheless, none of the nine holy clerics would be entitled to speak at the Council of the Forest, for tradition dictated that the forum was exclusively reserved for those who fight and command in war. The role of the matriarchs was to consult the Islands' deities and eventually approve whatever decision had been proposed by the Council of the Forest. Only once, a very long time ago, had the matriarchs chosen to reject the assembly's verdict but this was still a sore memory for some present that day.

Gal dyl was still lost in his thoughts when the drums of Eïwal Vars' temple suddenly sounded, drowning out the murmur of conversation and the whisperings of the trees.

"The time has come," Gal dyl thought. He could not suppress a shiver.

Eïwal Vars was the Llewenti deity of war, hunting and strength. In the Islands' legend, he was revered as the 'Father' as he had saved Queen Llyoriane from the grasp of the dubious deity Eïwal Myos[51]. In turn, she granted him her love and gave birth to the matriarchs, who went on to bear the dyl of the clans. Eïwal Vars was worshipped as Lord of both forests and beasts. All Llewenti hunters venerated him deeply, for it was he who was meant to watch and protect them in the wild. No one worshipped him more devotedly than Gal dyl, who had always taken care not to offend him, for he knew that the deity's retaliation could be swift and brutal. Eïwal Vars had taught the Llewenti that, in order for there to be life, there must also be death; in order for some to feed, there must be others who are hunted; and, in order to have peace, there must also be war. These teachings dictated Gal dyl's conduct in the wild; while he was accustomed to slaying ferocious beasts, he only ever hunted just enough game to eat. Eïwal Vars message was now at the forefront of Gal

---

51 Eïwal Myos: Deity of illusions and shadows, divinity of art, poetry and pleasure

dyl's mind; unlike certain other warlords, Gal dyl had always attempted to balance the deity's destructive side with the other values that he represented.

Inhaling the fresh morning air, fragrant with the odours of the forest, Gal dyl walked slowly towards the Temple of War, his mind focused on controlling his emotions. He felt the gaze of thousands of Elves, and it weighed upon his shoulders more heavily than any chainmail. He climbed the six majestic steps up to the empty seats of the matriarchs, and then knocked heavily on the temple door. The noise of his knuckles pounding against the hard wood echoed for some time.

"Who comes here?" nine female voices solemnly asked in unison.

"Gal dyl Avrony, son of Matriarch Vyre," he replied loudly so that the full assembly could hear. After a pause, he continued:

"I am Gal dyl Avrony, last warlord of his bloodline and Protector of the Forest."

"And what is your purpose, Gal dyl Avrony?"

"I come to retrieve the Spear of Aonyn and the Staff of Emeralds, for the Council of the Forest has gathered."

The heavy doors opened slowly. The nine matriarchs of Llymar appeared on the threshold. All of them were shrouded in long green gowns. On top of their traditional ceremonial garb, they each wore a single piece of jewellery: a silver necklace from which hung their respective rune. Their faces were shadowed by large hoods, so that each could not be distinguished from the other.

Bowing his head respectfully, Gal dyl entered the underground temple. He followed the matriarchs down one staircase, then a second, before finally pausing at the top of a third and looking out into the heart of the temple.

Motionless, with bowed head, Gal dyl looked down upon the priest of Eïwal Vars.

The cleric was kneeling in the crypt, his burning eyes fixed upon the approaching procession. Long beaded braids fell from his temples down onto a brown hood that protected his neck. Bright green stones were woven into the material across his chest. His sleeveless tunic of brown cloth left his arms exposed.

They were adorned with silver bracelets. A large cloak, the colour of chestnut and cut from the finest fabric, dragged along the ground behind him, rippling forward with reluctance with each step that he took.

Flanking him on either side stood two apprentices, servants of the deity of war and hunting. They were tall, strong Elves, dressed in brown robes with copper trim. Their long hair was dyed green and mystical runes covered their faces. In their hands, glittering with silver rings beset with emeralds, they held two ornate lyres. They played as they sang a warlike hymn to their divinity in deep and solemn voice.

After a silent prayer, the matriarchs moved into the heart of the temple, Gal dyl following close behind. They stepped down into an aisle and progressed along it slowly, between the lines of sacrificial altars on either side. The darkness lifted as they walked, as if the shadowy spirits who inhabited the temple were withdrawing to watch them as they passed. The matriarchs looked tall with their large hoods draped over their heads.

Reaching the main altar at the centre of the temple, one of them stepped forward. As she lifted her hood, Gal dyl recognized his daughter, Nyriele. She was as pale as moonlight. Her gaze was fixed on some faraway point. She began murmuring ritual prayers to the deity of war. Her narrow nostrils quivered, and her eyes welled up with tears. Managing the oppressive force which was trying to overcome her, she began to sing hymns dedicated to the bloodthirsty divinity that she so despised. Nyriele was a matriarch, and all matriarchs had to devote themselves completely to the six of the archipelago's deities. She sang of the tales of Eïwal Vars: a long litany of victories and heroic feats that floated through her imagination like clouds in the sky.

The priests behind her trembled and from time to time they plucked a mournful chord from their lyres. They were all experiencing an overwhelmingly powerful, mystical fear and they knew that their deity was close by.

Gal dyl approached the central altar; a resplendent masterpiece carved from the marble of the Arob Nisty Mountains. He stopped just a few yards away from it. As the priests' chanting grew more intense, reaching notes of unnatural pitch and timbre, Gal dyl knelt in front of the altar.

Six banners were illuminated by candlelight around him. He briefly glimpsed at the emblems of the archipelago's clans: the dark buzzard of the Myortilys, the white swan of the Llyvary, the snowy owl of the Llyandy, the grey hawk of the Ernaly, the azure seagull of the Llorely, and the green peacock of the Avrony.

Dried flowers smouldered nearby, releasing a thick perfume. Names of former masters of the Spear were glorified: Aonyn, Bane of Giants; Adarsy, the Owl Slayer; Aecaly, the Hound Hunter and several others. Yluin the Tall's name concluded the list of legendary heroes. This initiation ritual was being followed with great precision, in all its detail, according to ancient tradition that had begun with the offering of the relics by Eïwal Vars himself. The priests, still chanting, celebrated those gifts bestowed by the deity of war. And so, their song said.

> "For the Protector of the Islands, he did make
> A shield that was broad and strong
> Armour brighter than fire which shone
> A helmet beset with an emerald crest
> A spear which obeyed its master best."

The first three of those artefacts were now lost, with the many heroes who had fallen in battle. But the legendary weapon had proven to be as loyal as the deity had promised. The Llewenti clans still possessed the powerful spear.

Gal dyl, kneeling in the crypt, raised his hands up and laid them down in front of him on the cold marble of the sacred altar. In his deep and fervent meditation, he began to glean the final sacraments that would make him the High Warlord of the army and the bearer of the holy weapon. His unease grew stronger and stronger as the ceremony progressed. Becoming overwhelmed by doubt, vulnerability and guilt; his anxiety became uncontrollable and obvious to those around him. The chanting culminated to a violent climax, he felt the force of an explosion before him and he could not help falling onto his back and crying in shock and pain.

Soon, he stood and tried to regain control of his senses. He turned to see the holy weapon, the gift of Eïwal Vars, the Spear of Aonyn, in front of him on the sacred altar.

Gal dyl was stunned. For a moment, he did not move at all, frozen by the apparition of the relic and astonished at the demonstration of the clerics' powers. His anxiety became fear; his guilt became torturous. Standing shivering, he did not say a word.

"Speak the words of requisition, Protector of the Forest, speak the words of requisition and seize the power you seek," the overbearing voice of Lyrine commanded impatience and anger in her voice.

Gal dyl returned to his senses, his pride hurt by Lyrine's order. He felt like a child, frozen by fear, diving into the ocean for the first time. Opening his left hand, he finally pronounced the incantation, shouting it hastily in an effort to overcome his fright.

"Aonyn ekméo na miha cami!"[52]

Suddenly, the spear was in his hand. He was struck by a powerful blast which sent a sharp pain from the tips of his fingers right up to his shoulder. His sight was obscured by a sudden bright light and then, horrible visions appeared before him: screams, battles and fire, which grew in intensity and violence until he felt a severe and sudden pain in his back. Gal dyl almost fell back to his knees. Drowning, he struggled to escape the power that had engulfed him but was unable to surface. He feebly stumbled around the crypt, wandering without purpose.

"Please hand me the Spear of Aonyn, Protector of the Forest," Nyriele gently intervened. "It is time to fit your armour," she added, her comforting hand gripping his forearm.

---

52 Aonyn ekméo na miha cami: 'May the Spear of Aonyn come to my hand' in ancient Llewenti

He released the weapon and the visions ceased. The priests had already gathered around him with the rest of his trappings. Although not the original gifts from the deity of war, which had been lost long ago, they were nonetheless of fine craftsmanship, and they were imbued with the powerful protective magic of the forest. A cuirass, leggings, a helmet and shield were layered on top of his precious silk tunic, while the nine matriarchs came to surround him chanting prayers of blessing and protection.

Once this was over, Nyriele approached him again, the Spear of Aonyn in her left hand and a fine silver goblet in her right.

"Protector of the Forest! Drink the wine of the deities, the blood of the Mother of the Islands. It shall give you the strength and vigour that you shall undoubtedly need for the tasks ahead."

Accepting the ceremonial chalice with both hands, Gal dyl slowly drank the precious liquid in long gulps, savouring the full essence of the sweet nectar. The wine refreshed and invigorated him. A strong power flowed through his veins, chasing away all traces of doubt.

The short ceremony was now over and Gal dyl reclaimed the Spear of Aonyn from the young matriarch. The coveted object was lighter than he had anticipated, given its tremendous size.

Nyriele wrapped a voile of rare silk around his neck, embroidered with her own magical rune.

He stood there proud and tall. His blazing eyes met his daughter's gaze, and for a moment he remained motionless and silent, looking at her but with glazed eyes.

She could see in his soul that the fire of war now consumed him from within. She could not help but step back.

Gal dyl heard the creaking of the temple doors being opened by the priests. He buried his face into the immaculate silk voile and decided to attach it to his brass breastplate. He rushed towards the opening, escaping the confinement of the temple and the site of his momentary weakness.

Outside the temple, sunlight had pierced the early morning darkness. A warm, humid wind from the north was pushing the low clouds across the sky. The entire population of Tios Lluin had gathered around the circle to hear the debate of the council and behold its army.

The soldiers were still gathered on the steps of the holy crater, organized into orderly units, each with their own pennant and sigil. The army sat in wait around the temples, watching intently for the spear-bearer to appear. When the doors of Eïwal Vars' shrine opened, and the blade of the holy lance was revealed to all, a shiver ran through the assembled crowd. Then, a moment later, they greeted their lord with a loud cheer as he stepped back out onto the stone steps.

A group of six fighters hastened towards Gal dyl. When they heard the Protector of the Forest's first commands, snapping like the rapid strikes of a whip, they quickly formed two orderly lines around him. The army roared three times, celebrating the esteemed combatants who would form the Protector's Guard. The six elite warriors surrounding Gal dyl answered the crowd in unison, with three loud cries. The force of their cheers revealed their determination.

Then, the band began their ceremonial descent down the steps from the temple door. Their footsteps echoed around the carved crater while the nine matriarchs, their faces now exposed, emerged from the temple and gathered around Gal dyl.

Lyrine stepped forward. With silver lace she attached the green flag of Llymar to the holy lance: a golden arch with an Eïwaloni tree beneath it, surrounded by a white swan, a grey hawk and a green peacock. The ultimate symbol of the Protector's authority over the forest was now in Gal dyl's hands. Boosted by the crowd's cheering and the flag's radiance, the warlord continued forward proud and tall, towards the circle's centre.

The oldest matriarch, Yere dyl Ernaly, daughter, lover and mother of fighters who were killed in the wars with the barbarians, walked towards the centre. She was a noble figure, short and thin, with hard features and haughty black eyes.

Her snow-white hair and her back, bent over with years, marked her seniority. She inspired fear in those around her, for she was born a very long time ago. While the decline of her body showed her unnatural age, her spirit had not yet resigned to join the trees. The Llewenti almost always entrusted their soul to Eïwele Llyo's care before the signs of age spoiled their appearance and diminished their ability to enjoy life; beauty was their obsession; such was the curse Eïwele Llyi had bestowed upon them.

Yet, Yere was different and drew an unnaturally strong life force from her determination to seek revenge. Her purpose on the archipelago was not yet fulfilled.

Her thoughts and memories went back as far as the toughest and bloodiest time in Nyn Ernaly's history when the barbarian hordes had conquered her homeland over a thousand years earlier. She viewed the Forest of Llymar as a declining realm, where the pains of the past were forgotten, and the threats of the future overlooked.

She despised the way things had become, with the growing power of the guilds, the renewed prosperity of the clan Llyvary, and the weakness and frivolity that seemed to dominate contemporary life upon the Islands. The entire forest knew all too well the dread inspired by the sight of her ugly yet proud face, and the sound of the oak staff which she used to support her aging limbs. Although Yere dyl Ernaly was feared, she was also respected. In a culture where books were scarce, and where Elves who could read them were even scarcer, her long memory and wide knowledge were of great value. The young noble dyl would never have heard the stories of their warring forefathers, nor would the young matriarchs have ever learned the secrets of the forests, the waters and the winds, were it not for her.

Descending the porch steps, the matriarch of the clan Ernaly advanced slowly towards the centre of the circle, where Gal dyl stood. Suddenly all was silent. The Staff of Emeralds was in her hand. Complying precisely with the ancient rites, she chanted a long incantation to each of the six deities of the archipelago. A gust of wind blew over the assembly. She ended with an invocation.

"O deities of the archipelago, O mighty Eïwali! O protective Eïwely! Hear the complaint of your children, for the Llewenti call upon you!"

Her voice had grown to a kind of wild cry. Her energy was almost spent, and she was close to fainting. Gal dyl, who was standing next to her, made a move to support her. She ignored him and summoned yet more strength. The ancient matriarch handed the staff to the High Warlord. She completed the ritual with very little ceremony, marking her disdain for the new Protector. Slowly returning to her grand seat, set into the steps up to the

Temple of Eïwal Vars, she joined her peers at last. From where they sat, the nine matriarchs commanded the vast assembly, and the entire crowd could see them in their full, ancient majesty.

The debates could now commence.

Gal dyl stood alone in front of the silent crowd. His heartbeat quickened. He paused for a long moment, as if to catch his breath. Just as he was about to begin, a voice sounded unexpectedly behind him, from the row of matriarchs.

Lyrine stood on the temple steps. Without asking anyone for permission, without even deigning to descend into the circle to request the Staff of Emeralds, she addressed the whole assembly, her voice loud and distinct. The First of the matriarchs was asserting her superiority over all others. All could see that her decision to speak was made very deliberately.

"The western winds bring rumours of a storm. The human barbarians are preparing for war. As we begin our council today, their first detachments gather at the bottom of the Arob Tiude pass. Their aim is to besiege the ruins of the ancient tower of Mentollà and to seize its strategic harbour. They intend to hunt down and destroy a small community of Irawenti, castaways of the Austral Ocean, who have dwelled there since the season of Eïwele Llyo. Controlling Mentollà is a violation of the Pact; it would pose a great threat to the Forest of Llymar. The enemy would be at our borders. If the barbarians took Mentollà, they would hold the vital port of the north coast, and would no doubt use it as a base for a future attack on our lands."

She allowed the severity of the threat to linger in the air for a moment before continuing.

"Backed by the fell priests of the cursed Cult, a Dragon Warrior is leading the barbarian army. He sees the attack on Mentollà as a unique chance to become leader of all the human tribes across the Islands. If Mentollà is conquered, he will be the hero who broke the Pact, the man capable of uniting the barbarian tribes again. He will claim his rights over the Risen Throne and put an end to the continual disputes over succession. No doubt this young Dragon Warrior is ambitious and impatient. We have been watching his rise to power for several years and have observed with horror how he has rid his people of the Druids' influence, and perverted their hearts towards that evil, ancient religion: The Cult of the Three Dragons."

The Lady of Llafal's words reverberated around the circle.

"We are faced with bloodthirsty human tribes, and the prospect of an attempt to conquer our lands that shall be more determined than ever. Many of us are resigned to a long campaign of resistance. But a course of action must be decided. Will we march to war? Will we face the barbarians alone? Will we break the Pact?
Or will we instead seek an escape, preserving only that which is essential to us? Will we denounce the aggression and respect the Pact? Will we call upon King Norelin for protection? Our destiny upon the archipelago shall depend upon the decision that we make today," she concluded, before sitting back majestically on the central seat of the Council of the Matriarchs.

The troops of the clan Llyvary were positioned in the centre of the assembly, in the preeminent position as befitted to the main body of Llymar's army. Most of them originated from Llafal and Tios Lluin, and sadly could still remember the grief and pain caused by the last war. But there were also a few units from Penlla, the oceanic port in the east. Gal dyl turned to their representative, thus honouring him.

"You have travelled a long way, Leyen dyl Llyvary of Penlla, and you have arrived on time. You should hold the Staff of Emeralds first," he said loudly so that the many thousands gathered around him could hear.

The warlord of the city of dolphins stepped forward. He had a reputation for being cautious. A popular song in Tios Halabron implied that his legendary moderation was, in fact, a disguise for cowardice, and that he had survived so many long conflicts because he chose to fight nothing but the fish in the ocean. He was noticeable among that great martial assembly because he was not dressed for war. Instead, he was wrapped in a long azure cloak, his fingers covered with many precious rings. His round and jovial figure, along with his rhetorical skill, gave the impression of deception, which provoked immediate distrust.

His units were assembled in an orderly manner on the steps behind him. In their eyes, there was no gleam of the warrior. Penlla had never been forced to defend its high walls. However, it had often seen its sons depart to fight in the wars of other Llewenti cities, and there were many who had never returned. Penlla's inhabitants were sailors, fish hunters and dolphin riders. They worshipped the deities of the archipelago and expected peace and prosperity in return. Their representatives whether noble dyl or holy matriarchs, were expected to deliver words of wisdom and prudence at the Council of the Forest.

Leyen dyl moved forward to seize the Staff of Emeralds, ceremoniously positioning himself in the centre of the circle. For him, the temples' esplanade was a stage upon which he could flaunt his oratory flair while also expressing his views.

'How can one so foolish and extravagant behave with such narcissism, as though he were only here to flatter his own ego in his self-appointed role as a wise advisor?" Gal dyl wondered. "Why do I doubt myself so much, despite my renown and fame, when such a self-serving coward can parade so shamelessly?'

Leyen dyl started speaking with his usual condescension, arguing that the Council of the Forest's operations must be transparent.

"Elves of Llymar! More than ever before in Llewenti history, recent events, which concern us all, have been shrouded in secrecy. The Matriarchs of Llafal deliberately concealed from us the arrival of this ship from Essawylor. Independently, they decided what should become of these migrants from beyond the Ocean. We now discover that they dwell in the forbidden tower of Mentollà. What do we know of these newcomers? Why has information of their comings and goings been kept from us? The Elves of Llymar deserve to know."

Surprise rippled through the ranks of the high priestesses, for none expected the warlord of Penlla, known to be neither warlike nor lordly, to commence the council so aggressively.

Seeing that her mother would never deign to answer such a misplaced inquiry, and that the other matriarchs were enjoying the moment far too much to react, Nyriele stood up and replied, her voice pitched in a beautiful calmness. She chose to ignore the question and the disguised reprimand, concentrating rather on Mentollà and its new inhabitants.

"Noble Warlord of Penlla, I concur with you. It is critical that we focus on the fate of the castaways. There are no more than three hundred of them, mainly of Irawenti birth. They lost everything following their shipwreck, but we know that they have since been receiving the support of the wild Elves of Sognen Tausy. Throughout the entire season of Eïwele Llyo, they worked diligently, and they are currently finalizing the restoration of the tower's defences. It is as though they foresaw a forthcoming threat. A climate of tension now sweeps across the Arob Tiude hillsides.

We believe that their small army could put up a strong resistance from behind the security of Mentollà's walls, for they are well armed and benefit from the leadership of experienced Hawenti fighters. Furthermore, it now appears that their community is favoured by Eïwal Ffeyn, and that their Guide commands the essence of the wind."

Leyen dyl Llyvary seemed pleased with the attention his question had received. He continued, confirming that his naves were already preparing to set sail from his port city. Due to its isolated location upon a cliff top, Penlla had been chosen to host the arsenal and reserves of the fleet. The city was perched on an escarpment which was only accessible from the harbour via a fortified narrow road. Throughout its history, Penlla had never feared danger from sea or forest.

"Our fleet is a force to be reckoned with, numbering no less than fifteen swanships and thirty units. As we speak, work is going on in the docks. Sailors busy themselves around hoists and cranes, loading provisions and weapons aboard the naves for the long expedition that could soon be upon us," the warlord of Penlla revealed. "We can rely on our fleet. Let us use its force to protect Mentollà from the sea. There is an unprotected area of terrain right in front of the gate of the fortress. A barbarian assault seeking to exploit it would be overcome if we covered the area with the projectile weapons of our swanships. If they do not seize the ruins of Mentollà, the barbarians shall be forced to fall back to their homeland.

We will simply have to wait for King Norelin's judgement. The young sovereign has not so far proven himself. He has never been in a position to show his power. He will seize this opportunity and inflict swift justice."

The assembly would have liked to believe the old Elf's words and embrace his optimistic strategy. But his pacifist appearance, graceless movements and the faltering hesitation in his voice did not inspire trust.

Gal dyl had been cunning to let the warlord of Penlla speak first. His clumsy intervention at the end of the debate would have been hazardous, given the unease it had created. With a quick glance to his daughter on the temple doorsteps, he knew that she was silently complimenting his astute opening move. The Protector of the Forest could still feel the effects of the divine nectar in his veins and, proud of his manoeuvre, he assuredly took back the Staff that commanded the debate. In clear, commanding voice, he said.

"Curubor Dol Etrond desires to address the assembly. Let us hear him with attention and respect, for he is the wisest and most literate among us."

The Blue Mage was most elegantly dressed. Although, he was wrapped in a comfortable azure-coloured robe, he did not show any other sign of ostentation or wealth. His white silvery hair had been combed carefully. It was his custom to adopt a simple guise and to tint his hair with a light colour, to mask his origins. All that were present recognised his natural goodness and gentle temper: remarkable qualities for a High Elf that had seen the end of the First Age and had suffered the long exodus to the archipelago.

Curubor began his speech with a fragment of Hawenti poetry.

"An Elvin King with a crown, adorned with rubies,
  Four Dor princes with gold and silver diadems,
Eleven Dol lords with bronze medals of their cities..."

After a pause, Curubor continued thoughtfully.

"The first lines of this old poem celebrate the triumph of Hawenti nobility over the inhabitants of the archipelago. Today, sixteen High Elves rule the Islands from the top of their red towers in Gwarystan. Sixteen Lords receive the homage of tens of thousands of Elves. Their influence is so great, that even our deities fear them.

Do you know why?" He asked before providing an answer to his question.

"Because these Elves are power incarnate. That is the sole reason they control the destiny of the vast majority of the Islands' inhabitants.

Common Elves and men are the royal army's fighters; they are the artisans of the guilds, the hunters and harvesters and the obedient retainers who bend the knee and sacrifice their share of the magic Flow.

But in actual facts, it is the common Elves who really control the destiny of these islands. The decision to submit is theirs; therefore, the power is theirs...

Now, if power lies with the common Elves of the archipelago, how is it that the young King Norelin and his vassals can rule so many?

A Hawenti knight would reply, 'The blood in his veins is the blood of the mightiest bloodline. He is legitimate.'

A Morawenti merchant might say, 'The King controls coin minting. He possesses gold and wealth.'

A Llewenti scholar may argue that 'The King closed the temples and banished the matriarchs, seizing sole command of the Flow of the Islands.'

All three could be correct, each in their own way. Yet I explain King Norelin's dominance in another way...

Commoners will always pledge their loyalty and support to the ruler who will offer them the most protection, the most prosperity and, ultimately, the most hope.

I see the confusion on your faces. I see astonishment in your eyes. 'What is this game of riddles that Curubor will have us play?' you may ask yourself.

I will answer you, Elves of Llymar.

What the matriarchs' rule guarantees us is freedom, the chance to live according to the Islands' traditions, and the favour of our six deities. Besides, the guilds of the forest, through their devotion and hard work, bring us the fruits of their artistry and craft. We already possess hope and prosperity.

We need only demonstrate that we can protect our cities. And then we will show that we can rule and protect.

The Council of the Forest dates back to the dawn of the archipelago itself, when the deities walked the Islands, long before the reign of any Hawenti sovereign.

But the council still lacks the sort of power wielded by King Norelin, precisely because it is not seen as powerful in the eyes of many.

What we need is a conflict. We need a war, and we need a victory. Those who have been left haggard and terrified by the many disasters of our past shall seek our support. Those Llewenti, who live under the shadows of the high towers of Gwarystan, shall be desperate to return to the clan rule of old. Even certain Hawenti houses shall perceive the change in the winds of time, and they too shall seek to break free from royal rule. Do not judge the High Elves so harshly. We must look to them with compassion, for many of them have heard the call of our deities and are seeking their guidance.

It is our duty to show the strength of Llymar and the weakness of Gwarystan. It is our duty to show them the way and welcome them into our noble assembly.

The ancient stones around this circle were already here when the first Council of the Forest gathered to honour Aonyn, the first wielder of the Sacred Spear. This was twenty-three centuries ago."

Ending on a poignant and sonorous note, Curubor Dol Etrond handed the Staff of Emeralds back to the Protector before enfolding him in a lengthy embrace, marking his deep affection and uttermost confidence in the last warlord of Avrony.

Such a demonstration of support and friendship, coming from such a respected character filled Gal dyl with joy.

Still affected by the warmth of the divine beverage he had drunk in the temple, he looked around, seeking a new orator. Such was the crowd's enthrallment with Curubor that, unsurprisingly, none dared follow the Blue Mage.

Using his authority as master of the assembly, Gal dyl finally decided to let the youngest noble of clan Llyvary make his debut. It was a difficult task, and the young Elf did not prove very convincing; he failed to put forward a clear proposal, but rather gave away all his own doubts and uncertainties.

The Staff was then passed from speaker to speaker for many hours. Gal dyl paid little attention to their arguments and meagre oratory talents, as he knew that the key performances would come later in the day. He did notice, however, that opinions of the clan's Llyvary's young dyl were already very diverse and inconclusive.

*

The sun was already beginning its descent when a pain in Gal dyl's back forced him to move from his previously comfortable position. He could not suppress a shiver when the clan Ernaly's most dreaded commander decided to end the insignificant prattle of a young dyl of clan Llyvary. Regaining full control of his senses, Gal dyl allowed him to step forth.

And so, Voryn dyl of the clan Ernaly, the younger brother of Mynar dyl, stepped forward. The entire assembly knew him as the most feared of all the noble dyl present that day. His silhouette was long and emaciated. Haggard and contorted, he had sharp, severe features that, far from reflecting any divine light, told only of despicable war, the only world he knew. An aggressive and restless grey hawk was perched on his dark leather glove.

A shudder ran through the crowd as he seized the Staff of Emeralds from Gal dyl's hands and suddenly shouted:

"The population of men grows day by day, while our own numbers can only progress slowly. The destinies of men and Elves are antithetical; there can never be lasting peace. Our doubts and our denials only condemn us to be destroyed by our enemies. We are doomed to exchange these vast forests, which we have rightly inherited from the Islands' deities, for a few meagre groves surrounded by vast withered pastures used to rear the slave animals of our enemies. Look at what has happened to Nyn Ernaly over recent decades! Some of our kin still live there, under the supposed protection of the Pact, beset and indeed besieged by the unceasing expansion of humanity. Small settlements become hamlets, hamlets become villages and villages become cities. Each expansive step taken by men is always marked by some new aggression against the Elves. Forests are demolished to provide wood, glades are obliterated to become crop fields, hills are toppled to become quarries and, worse still, hunting territory is supplanted by enclosures for livestock.

It is not easy to predict how far their devastating madness will go. They are mortal creatures; none of them care about the world that they shall leave behind, for they will eventually be returned to the nothingness from whence they came," Voryn dyl concluded disdainfully.

With these last words, he just expressed the superiority that the Elves felt over the mutable humans. The lives of the Llewenti did end, one day or another, but they considered themselves to be immortal, like the Hawenti, for Eïwele Llyo granted them eternal life through reincarnation in the forest.

The crowd marked its concurrence with a long, deep murmur.

Voryn dyl's speech had come late in the day because he had chosen to ignore the less influential speakers of the clan Llyvary, waiting until they had spoken before emphatically putting forward the case for war.

He had immediately seized his audience with the violence of his words and the strength of his argument. He continued, alternating between denunciation and invocation.

"Remember our history! Examine closely the tragic events we went through!

We were not defeated by the barbarians. In truth, a few High Elves deceived our valiant army and betrayed the glory that was earned at the price of its fighters' blood.

These were the same High Elves who agreed to the Pact with the invaders."

He then moved to condemn the new collusion between King Norelin and men.

"Our human enemies, whether they are barbarians or Westerners, are visible, vulnerable and mortal. They can be found, they can be attacked, and they can be defeated.
But the Elvin traitors," he continued with scorn, "Slip by invisible, hiding their wickedness from the eyes of the very Elves that they pretend to protect. They attempt to inspire trust in the depths of our souls with their kind words and peace offerings. They plant their pernicious advice, and even now it spreads its roots ever deeper into our lives, until one day we shall no longer have the power to resist. They ask for another little concession, then a little more, always a little more."

Voryn dyl let his audience consider these last words by leaving a long pause, during which he looked around to ascertain the reaction that he had provoked. He knew how to play upon the troops' exasperation; hence he finished by concentrating his attack on King Norelin, who sat upon his Ruby throne in Gwarystan. He denounced in a few scathing sentences.

"This young tyrant has, for over a century, travelled through the archipelago promoting the expansion of his capital city. He has spent his life trading with our enemies.
But he has always cowered from the points of our javelins. Yet does he not still pretend to command these islands? Does he not, even now, chain our hawks to the ground?" Voryn dyl demanded of the crowd, arousing reactions of resentment and hatred.

"No, brave combatants of the forest, no. We do not have to fear his army. It is not in the nature of this King to conquer! He always avoids open conflict. I do not doubt that he shall seek some compromise; he will want an agreement which would allow him to tighten his grip upon us a little more still."

Voryn dyl's speech was proving fruitful. Many assembled fighters from all of the clans began to openly express their agreement. With every invective, with every reference to the past, the crowd erupted in cries of hatred and calls for war.

Nerin dyl Llyvary felt the need to intervene. Praised for his empathy and pragmatism, the young captain of Llafal was viewed as the rising hope of his clan; for many, he embodied strength and wisdom. He felt it was his responsibility to stop this great speaker's momentum before the entirety of Llymar stumbled into war. He stood up and, holding out his hand commandingly, requested the Staff of Emeralds from Gal dyl. The Protector accepted his request and, with the greatest authority, took the Staff from Voryn dyl's hands and passed it to the noble young Elf from Llafal.

"We are all aware that Voryn dyl knows the art of rhetoric, but before we allow ourselves to be carried away by his words, let us first draw our attention to what he did not say. Not so long ago, a number of proud warlords ignored signs sent by the deities and chose to fight against the sands of time. The burned bodies of their dead, buried under the ruins of Tios Lluin, are all that we need to remind us of their deeds. If we, too, try to swim against the current, we too will end up drowning," said Nerin dyl, his hands waving, as if gesturing to the spirits of the victims who had been slaughtered in that very place.

For a moment, Voryn dyl was disconcerted. He heard a murmur of anxiety from the assembled army. But he quickly recovered and, without asking the Protector of the Forest's permission, mounted a brutal counter attack.

"We are here to decide on our future. Let us not be turned away from our destiny by this unwanted diversion, sprung upon us by a weak, superstitious Elf who claims to be a captain of his clan. His only great deed to date was being delivered by his matriarch mother!"

This arrogant insult went far beyond what was generally allowed within the assembly. Everyone could see the mockery and contempt in Voryn dyl's malicious eyes. Furthermore, the dyn Ernaly had replied without the Staff of Emeralds in his hand.

On the steps of Eïwal Vars Temple, one of the matriarchs stood up. Lyrine held up her right hand, her palm facing the crowd, signalling both her disagreement and that she wished for him to be removed from the debate. She stood there for some time, alone and in silence. The tension throughout the assembly was palpable. Before long, Nyriele stood up with her, soon followed by the five other dignitaries of the clan Llyvary. They represented a clear majority, and Voryn dyl did not dare argue any further. He left the circle to join the anonymous ranks of his troops. He knew that he had made a strategic error. When he passed Mynar dyl's seat, his brother refused to look at him, making his profound discontent and justified anger clear. It would now be extremely difficult for the clan Ernaly to win the debate.

"The House of Dol Etrond calls for the Staff of Emeralds," said Almit, as he rose from his seat.

The elegant High Elf was dressed in a royal blue toga and carried a golden helmet under his left arm. Almit seldom spoke but, when he did, it was purposeful. He was renowned as a smith and alchemist of great skill. Almit was rarely seen in public, instead preferring the discreet company of enchanters and artisans. He was, in fact, a warlord by inheritance only; he left the tasks of conducting the affairs of the city and leading the House of Dol Etrond to his great uncle, Curubor. Still, he wore the helmet of his ancestors, and the ancient relic distinguished his rank as the first of his bloodline.

"I must say: I am surprised. No one has so far addressed the matter of the castaways," he started, looking around like a guild master addressing his apprentices. "Have we lost all sympathy? Do we not have any concern for these unfortunate refugees?"

A wave of guilt washed through the assembly.

"They deserve our time. They too have risked their lives to reach our shores. They achieved this incredible feat with the very same hope, the very same ambition that our ancestors possessed when they crossed the seas a long time ago. I say they join our community. I say they are to be considered Elves of the archipelago.

Why would we not rescue them? Why not use this opportunity to inflict a severe blow to our enemies and gain new allies? Are we so strong and immutable that we deny that their support would be of help? Are the eighty units of our army strong enough to defend us from our enemies? Would we not benefit from controlling Mentollà and its strategic harbour, by adding a province to the Forest of Llymar, by improving our fleet with ships of unknown capacities, and by inviting an additional clan to join this noble assembly? I say that it is a unique opportunity, and one that we must not waste. Let us march to war. Let us destroy the barbarian invaders. Let us eradicate the priests of that cursed cult. Let us decapitate the Dragon Warrior and put his head on a pike. The enemy is surging blindly straight into the merciless trap that we have spent decades designing. He does not stand a chance, for we shall surround him and slowly put him to death, like a stag cornered by hounds. We will gain new allies and send a message to the rest of the Islands: the power of Llymar is great. The archipelago does not need the King of Gwarystan to administer justice."

Almit delivered these terrifying words and bloodthirsty proposals in a calm, monotone voice, its undertones making his suggested course of action seem like the most reasonable and appropriate. Looking almost remorseful that he had needed to speak again, he added.

"What I find even more surprising is that I have not so far heard a single word about our post-conflict plans. This is no longer the time for our armies to march to war for the sake of defending the greater good or avenging their honour. We cannot afford such noble deeds anymore. War is not a guaranteed escape route, nor should it be a stalemate. It is the pursuance of a just policy once diplomacy has exhausted all other options. Our hope for the future is clear in my eyes. No matter how thorough our victory on the battlefield, we cannot kill all the men that live on Nyn Llyvary. We cannot push their women and their children into the sea. I say that our greater goal should be to influence who rules the barbarians in the future. I say we should favour the Druids, for only their influence can thwart the Cult of the Three Dragons' powerful rule over the men. Let us inflict a historical defeat upon our enemy. Let us decapitate the evil warrior who drives these weak people back along the path of death, so that we can impose new rulers with peaceful beliefs."

Visibly satisfied with his inspiring oration, the Dol Etrond lord finally sat down, handing the Staff back to the Protector.

Gal dyl was impressed by Almit's confident argument and concurred with its rational logic. Nevertheless, he felt uncomfortable with his cold reasoning, for he could perceive the obsession for power and domination which lay behind it.

Seeing the disorder that this intervention had provoked among the army's ranks, another of the four warlords of Llymar Forest decided that the time had come for him to speak. Mynar dyl the Fair stepped forward. There was a moment of hesitation; Gal dyl did not hand the Staff of Emeralds to him straight away. The Protector seemed somehow paralyzed and his tensed facial features showed he was suffering greatly. The restorative effect of the golden wine was waning and the ache in his back was becoming unbearable. The more the warlord of the clan Avrony leaned on his spear to stay upright, the worse the pain became, like a dagger piercing deeper into his flesh. His vision was disturbed from time to time by horrific images of war flashing before his eyes.
Finally, he focussed his mind upon the debate, and Gal dyl realized that the representative of Tios Halabron was standing by his side, waiting to be handed the Staff of Emeralds.

Showing the utmost respect as he received it, Mynar dyl began his speech very softly, as if he were affected by the solemnity of the moment. Much of the crowd was unable to hear and had to lean forward and strain their ears. Silence descended like a rapid gust of wind across the assembly ranks. The crowd's attention had reached its peak.

"The Llewenti were born under the stars by the banks of the Inner Sea. When they were offered wealth and submission, they chose independence and vulnerability," he stated quietly, raising his voice gradually as he continued.

"Their resolution was so firm that they inspired the rebellious deities who had challenged the authority of the Gods to devise a refuge at the other end of the world. Our ancestors crossed the ocean and paid the price of many lives to escape tyranny and war before they reached this haven. The archipelago's deities dedicated their power and influence to protect us for centuries, until the High Elves seized our islands for themselves. But we did not bow when the Hawenti conqueror forged his kingdom. Nor did we bend the knee when the human barbarians and their allies, the Westerners, surged and stole what was left of our domains.

Do you know why? Do you know why we have proven so resistant, so enduring, so brave?

It is because... above all else... we value liberty. It is the most profound part of our nature to identify and overcome anything that threatens to confine us. But this freedom we have earned means that we have the right to choose, the right to decide our own destiny.

Over the centuries, many exercised this right, this gift inherited from the triumphant battles of our ancestors. Tens of thousands of Llewenti decided to leave the matriarchs' rule and serve the King of Gwarystan. I believe that today there are twice as many Elves living under the protection of the king's banners than there are living among the six Llewenti clans. We cannot blame them for turning their back on their brethren, for abandoning the old faith, for deciding to lay their share of the magic Flow of the Islands at the feet of the Hawenti sovereign, and in so doing weakening the matriarchs' power and the influence of the archipelago's deities. We cannot blame them because they were free to do so.

Indeed, today, we are free to choose to join them. We could choose to ask for King Norelin's protection. We could decide to kiss the ruby on his royal finger. It would be easy; it might even be wise. We would not have to risk our lives and territories. We would be welcomed as many before us have been welcomed. We would be given coins, stamped with the King's face and the royal sigil, in exchange for our goods and labour. We would be given parchments decorated with authentic royal seals to prove that we own the lands that we have always possessed. And with that gold and paper, there are many things that we could do. We would be allowed in Gwarystan, that many-towered city of incomparable splendour. We could attend their magnificent spectacles of music and fireworks. We could buy small stone houses in the maze of their streets, and we could finally trade with all the archipelago's islands. Our merchant ships would have access to the other Hawenti cities and even to the tribes of men. For they too dwell in Gwarystan, haunting its alleyways. What an opportunity! What a chance before us to accumulate gold!

We would, however, be obliged to abandon our traditions, our laws and our obedience to the matriarchs and warlords. We would have to serve under the command of a Hawenti lord, and above all we would have to respect men and their ever-growing presence across these islands. Do not be deceived. This is the choice that we are being offered today."

Mynar dyl's voice had true musicality. The rhythm of his words syncopated like notes on a musical score, captivating and charming his audience. The warlord of Tios Halabron was the master of subjugating the minds of common Elves. Indeed, his cunning argument and crafty rhetoric were proving very convincing, not only to the clear majority of the troops, but also to the numerous noble dyl of the clan Llyvary, who were his real target. As opposed to the other speakers, Mynar dyl did not express his personal opinions or ideas. He was developing a speech specifically to win the support of those who could make the difference.

"As for me," he concluded, "I choose fidelity and faith. I choose to honour my word to our matriarchs for they are the most precious treasure we here possess... they are the object of my whole-hearted devotion."

The orator inspired genuine feeling in all who listened. The crowd watched as he walked with dignity towards the stairs of Eïwal Vars Temple and dropped a single white flower at the feet of the youngest matriarch, Nyriele. A sense of heroic poetry was in every sentence he uttered, but also in his manner, his eyes, and his very voice. The assembly, deeply moved by the noble gesture, could not resist applauding, and many rose from their seats in a standing ovation.

Feeling that he just managed to overturn the course of the day's argument, Mynar dyl moved to exploit his advantage further.

"Gal dyl, I know you well...very well. Do you not concur? Will you not lead us towards certain victory? It is now your turn to give us your thoughts, Protector of the Forest."

And with this invitation, Mynar dyl obediently returned the Staff of Emeralds. As he did so, he looked at Gal dyl sharply, a last threatening injunction to submit to his proposal. He saw how the Protector of the Forest was unsettled.

Grabbing the Staff, Gal dyl rubbed at his eyes and stared at a fixed point on the ground in an effort to overcome his disorientation. Cold sweat trickled down his back, contrasting with the day's warm atmosphere. A voice screamed inside his head like a wild animal. An unfortunate foreboding haunted him. Horrible memories came flooding back to him.

'A small boat of the clan Avrony was anchored in a wild creek in the high seas of Gwa Nyn. Gal dyl was the last survivor of his family onboard. Alone, he had managed to flee the island of Nyn Avrony, now conquered by the barbarians. He could not sleep; his heart was swollen with remorse, tortured by the calls of others of his kind who had been butchered. But, all of a sudden, the anchor slipped as the ship keeled over in the waves, it drifted rapidly and crashed against the reefs in an apocalyptic howl. There was water everywhere and he could hear that voice, that voice...'

The crowd observed Gal dyl, and a murmur permeated the ranks as he failed to react to Mynar dyl's invitation.

To everyone's surprise, Tyar dyl suddenly sprang from his seat. The warlord of Llafal had remained silent and motionless until then. Stepping forward was a great effort for him because he had to struggle against his own nature to do so. Although he was deeply respected by everyone, no one really considered him, for his temperament was quiet and humble, and he seldom spoke or expressed his opinion. As the eldest noble dyl of the clan Llyvary, he did not seek the title of the Protector of the Forest, although his bloodline and experience gave him the right to claim the Spear of Aonyn. Since he had been overlooked as

Protector, his influence had waned, and it was clear to all that his time to join the trees was close. Nevertheless, the 'Old Bird' was undertaking one last flight.

"There is another solution," he declared.

"We can call upon the Druids. The servants of the Mother of the Islands designed the Pact and convinced all parties to respect it. There are both men and Elves in their assembly. They undoubtedly possess the potential to control the barbarians and eliminate the threat of the Cult of the Three Dragons.
I say we simply defend our own borders and let the Druids administer justice beyond them. War is altogether a disproportionate reaction, a calamity; it is my duty as the most ancient warrior of the forest to avoid it, for the sake of my kin."

The 'Old Bird' was finished. As calmly as he had assumed the position of the speaker, he returned to his seat. Tyar dyl's brief and unexpected speech had once again shifted the tide of opinion. The clan Llyvary's many noble dyl looked hesitant again. He was the bravest fighter in the forest, famous for countless feats of arms; none would dare accuse him of cowardice or inexperience. Besides, everyone present knew that if the unassuming warlord of Llafal had spoken, he must have been given instructions by Lyrine to do so, as he had always been her faithful servant. Growing apprehension overwhelmed the noble commanders and their troops.

Now standing alone in the circle, all eyes fixed upon him, Gal dyl's position could not have been more difficult. The increasing pain in his back disrupted his thinking. The burning sensation in the hand which was holding the Spear of Aonyn reminded him that he had never sought this high position in the first place. In a desperate attempt to find the support of his beloved daughter, his eyes searched for where the matriarchs were sat. But his gaze was captured by Lyrine's spell, and in the depths of his soul, he could sense her implacable determination. He could see her doubting his abilities and disdainfully looking down upon his weaknesses.

Hurt by such an insulting judgment, Gal dyl straightened, forgetting the pain in his back and his burning hand. Strong-willed, he pushed the disturbing vision from his mind and focused on the crowd around him. Sounding like a hero of yore and brandishing the Spear of Aonyn, he proclaimed.

"I have been guided by duty and honour my entire life. I would rather die than beg favours of King Norelin. I cannot look towards the western part of Nyn Llyvary without seeing forests and valleys that were owned by the Llewenti since the dawn of time. Those territories were stolen from us by the shameful compromise accepted by the young King of Gwarystan, self-proclaimed sovereign of the archipelago.
How many Hawenti noble houses safeguarded their wealth and possessions by selling ours? But we saved the rest of our heritage by refusing to succumb to King Norelin's rule. So, let the enemy come. And let us confront it with the Spear of Aonyn! What is your response to that?" Gal dyl roared at the crowd.

Nobody had ever heard him speak with such authority and, if some had doubted their high warlord's determination, they were now fully convinced that he possessed the strength to wield the Spear of Aonyn. A long pause followed. The crowd became threatening.

Suddenly, an Elf who until then had been unobserved fought his way down the crater steps through the assembled fighters and commanders. He easily reached the circle, as everyone moved out his way to create a path. His face was hidden by a large, dark green hood, but the bare sword on his back left no doubt about his identity.

His name was Dyoren, the elder brother of Mynar dyl and Voryn dyl. But he was widely known as the 'Lonely Seeker', a solitary traveller whose songs and music had earned him the reputation of the greatest bard that was ever known to have walked the paths of the archipelago. Its shining blade was adorned with the brightest emeralds. He carried it bare upon his back, as no sheath could contain it. This legendary broad sword distinguished him as the envoy of a secret order, to which all owed their respect.

Without pausing, Dyoren crossed the esplanade, passed Gal dyl without even looking at him, and reached the stone steps of Eïwal Vars Temple. He grasped the broad sword, swinging it round from his back, and brandished the bare blade.

He suddenly threw the weapon at the dark ancestral doors with incredible strength. The shining glaive flew into the heavy panels with a resounding crash and stuck the wood. A distant, painful groan could be heard, like the rumble of Eïwal Vars himself.

Turning to the crowd, the Lonely Seeker exclaimed.

"If the matriarchs decide, the Blade of the West shall go to war, alongside the Spear of Aonyn."

"I hear your call, Dyoren, and I will gladly march at your side," replied Gal dyl, taking up the gauntlet, he, in turn, launched the sacred lance against the temple door.

More were moving forward. Mynar dyl threw his javelin into the temple doors, and was soon followed by his brother Voryn dyl, and then many other noble dyl of the clan Llyvary, save for a few who were still loyal to the warlords of Llafal and Penlla. The army ignored this small faction of peace seekers and unleashed its fury. Voices crying out for war could be heard everywhere, from all clans and factions. The choice was clear: Llymar Forest demanded war.

The matriarchs rose, slowly forming a procession behind the eldest as they crossed the circle and entered the Temple of Eïwele Llyo to consult the omens. Once inside the holy shrine, Lyrine isolated herself. Ignoring her peers, who were busy preparing for the ceremony, she crossed the vast underground hall and slipped between two carved pillars, arriving before the imposing altar to the deity. A few yards behind it, a frame of black wood containing an engraving was positioned within one of the numerous alcoves. Candles bathed it in subdued light.

Hidden from the other high priestesses, the Lady of Llafal knelt in front of the artwork, her heart swollen but her eyes dry. She stared devotedly at the inanimate, inexpressive figure, as if the noble image might come to life and answer her prayer. The artist had represented a fallen clan warlord, half-naked on a bed of leaves, with drops of blood spilling down his side. His right hand was mutilated, hanging limply from his arm, yet it was still holding a spear. His eyes were closed, like those of a dying Elf. Pallor and suffering imbued his countenance with a divine aura that the face of a Llewenti will only express when passing from one life to the next.

The engraving bared one inscription, written in runes of blood:

Yluin dyl Llyvary, Protector of the Forest

The lady extended her arms toward the image and spoke to it, exactly as if she were praying to one of the deities.

"On your deathbed, father, I begged you to wait, I begged you not to leave me to face the clan Llyvary's fate alone... Still crying over your bloody corpse, I took an oath, an oath of vengeance and death, to have the human barbarians pay for your blood with theirs. But in doing so, I imposed upon our clan a dreadful burden, even as it submitted to me, and called me its most trusted matriarch. Through the words of some, and through the actions of others, Eïwele Llyo came to remind me of this oath. And as all the dead Llewenti see her influence, you must have observed, Father, as I have, that dark omens are gathering. I have no doubt that your restless soul is still filled with anger and the thirst for revenge. I have no doubt that you expect your heir to impose the only just punishment imaginable. Well rejoice, my father, for I am about to take many of our clan into the care of Eïwele Llyo, to honour the oath sworn upon your body."

Lyrine got up onto one knee and kissed the hand that seemed to hang outside the frame. She was crying. Now that the council decision was made, and the entire assembly was calling for war, she had no other choice but to fulfil her oath. Reluctant as ever, she now reckoned that she had no escape.

"In the early history of the Islands when the Llewenti walked by the deities' sides, they looked up at the same black sky sparkling with stars, and they shared their divine hope.
But we shall never see their indulgent dream of an eternal sanctuary, preserved from the world, become a reality. Fear, guilt and remorse: such are the disfigurements that defile our

souls, like the burned flesh of a sacrificed warrior of yore. Forgive me, Father, forgive my bitterness. My eyes dried up after weeping for you, those eyes that you loved so much."

The Lady of Llafal had made her decision: she would have the clan Llyvary march to war. She would be true to that oath she had once uttered. Though her conscience forbade any other choice, her wisdom allowed her to foresee the dangers of the slippery slope that they had created. She returned to the other matriarchs around the altar, her mind finally clear.

★

Since his intervention that morning, Curubor had stood, among the nobles of Llymar, almost motionless, his eyes half-closed, listening with great attention to each speech as though they were barely audible, despite the proximity.

Observing the matriarchs exiting the temple of the deity of fate, he turned towards the commander of his personal guard, who was standing by his side, and with a smile said.

"Duluin, you may gather the knights and prepare to depart. I expect we will leave for Llymvranone[53] at the first light of day. I am afraid that the Council of the Matriarchs will ask me to carry news of war to the envoy of King Norelin. It would be wise for a unit of the Golden Arch Guard to accompany us. There will be turbulent times ahead."

---

53 Llymvranone: 'strategic site' in lingua Llewenti

CHAPTER 6: DOL ETROND

2709 of the Llewenti Calendar, Season of Eïwele Llyi, 1rst day, Forest of Llymar

The two Elves had been walking for a few hours when they finally decided to stop at the summit of a steep hill. The sun was gradually warming the air around them and, as its golden rays crept above the peaks of the grey mountains, the dew coating the leaves of the bushes was slowly melting away.

Without making a sound, the first scout sniffed the air, and turned his gaze towards the towering heights of the Arob Nisty Mountains, to the southwest. Spring was on its way; the snow was retreating further and further up the peaks. He pointed out the northern slopes to his companion. A forest of tall pine trees obscured their route to the pass through the mountains. The forest was dark, dense and full of mystery; it reminded the two Elves of the evil, wild woods described in the ancient songs of their clan.

Their expressions were grave, as if haunted by faded memories of a troubling dream. The encroaching darkness of the forest reminded them of the challenge they would soon have to face. They exchanged glances; both knew that they could not turn back from the mission that lord Curubor had entrusted to them.

It took them an hour to reach the edge of the forest. A great wind from the north sent dark clouds in their direction and the leaves upon the thick, shadowy trees shuddered. Then the rain began. For the following two hours it fell heavily as they trekked up the mountain, soaking the clay soil and streaming along the path. It was as if nothing could live under the shade of the trees, like in the evil woods of the fables. The lack of life in their surroundings was increasingly unsettling. The path was completely deserted. No creature ran through the meadows, fluttered from branch to branch nor skittered on the forest floor. It was like the world before the coming of the Elves.

Uneasy, the two scouts of the House of Dol Etrond questioned this lifelessness, interrogating the threatening trees, the dark clouds, even the very air around them, for answers. They were not alone, as a unit of guards followed a short distance behind them, but the two scouts could not help feeling like they were the only living things for miles around. The sun had not yet set, but already a cold, dark night was making its presence felt. The northwest wind whistled through the air, filling the ears of the isolated Elves with a sound more menacing than silence.

The smaller Elf, who seemed to be of higher rank, stopped his companion, placing a hand on his shoulder.

"You know full well that, in battle, I would never step back to save my own life. And yet, tonight, I feel affected by some strange force which overwhelms my senses and forbids me to go any further. Call it what you will: superstition, or even... fear. Yes, maybe it is fear."

His companion turned, terrified by these threatening omens. Yet they had spotted nothing, heard nothing, and seen nothing.

"You believe we're being followed?" he asked.

"Oh, no, I'm not thinking of wild Elves or even the prowling Arob Nisty giants. No! The danger that I feel is different. It's instinctive. Something is approaching us and... threatening us. I cannot tell what it is which is why I am so scared."

The smaller Elf's emphatic and persuasive voice barely contained his emotion and his remarks soon began to affect his companion. For several hours, the taller Elf had walked like a brave ranger in the footsteps of his chief, even though his mind had been constantly tortured by his growing fear. But now, he could no longer control his emotions. His expression was furious and unyielding. He did not have the heart to question his companion anymore. Gathering his equipment and checking his weapons, he examined their surroundings and then turned, retreating down the steep path southwards, towards the protection that the Dol Etrond unit would provide.

He had just started running down the path when he saw a movement out of the corner of his eye. Three, maybe four figures pursued him along either side of the path, pushing aside foliage and slaloming between the pine trunks. He screamed, calling for help. Running as fast as he could, he could not clearly see where he was going, and fell several times. But suddenly, he stopped his gaze fixed ahead of him. A roar of panic ripped through the air. He saw before him many mutilated corpses, savagely crucified upon the branches of the trees. They were his companions, his friends, the guards and the knights of the Golden Arch. Sensing danger behind him, he turned back to look up the hill; it was then that he saw them approaching. Numerous dark Elves, more than he could count, were progressing slowly down the path, heavily armed, carrying ropes. His gaze went from the crucified corpses before him to the approaching murderers behind him. He darted to the side, off the path, running faster and faster through the trees, only to fall from the top of a ravine into a deep precipice. His body crashed down onto the rocks far below.

The smaller scout, who so far had not moved an inch from his position further up the path, raised his hands towards the sky in helpless terror. He had not seen what had happened, but the agonised cry of his companion echoed with horrific vividness in his head. He looked around, knowing how hopeless his chances of survival were; he could already see the sinister halls to which Llewenti souls go after death. He let out a shriek: the shriek of an Elf who could see his own death.

"He's been murdered. He is dead!" he whispered desperately, leaning on a tree for support.

His heightened senses perceived the shrill sound of an arrow shooting through the air. A deep shudder ran through his whole body. He forced himself to listen again. Silence, all he could hear was the pounding of his own heart. Suddenly he could hear footsteps rapidly progressing along the path. Then, in the depths of the woods, a dark shape appeared. He let out a terrifying roar and charged through the thicket to meet his enemy. He ran blindly and recklessly. He hit something hard and fell to the ground. Someone was grabbing him, shouting in his ear. Someone was instructing him to... calm himself.

His body was still shaking violently. His legs were barely able to support him. Yet, around him, the world had suddenly become brighter, less gloomy, and the sky turned a deep, rich blue. His limbs slowly began to relax, more and more with each shaky breath.

"You no longer have anything to fear. You are now under the protection of my rings," said a calm, deep voice.

The scout recognized his liege Curubor Dol Etrond, bending over him with hands wide open, displaying the colourful gems of his four rings.

"A shadow can be cast from behind or in front of you, but never from above. Therefore, look to the sky; you shall soon escape the murderous spell," said Curubor mysteriously.

He explained, reassuringly as ever, "Your mind was obscured by a wicked illusion: the work of ghost killers wishing to push you to your death. Their power comes from underground, from the realm of Gweïwal Agadeon[54]," and, to emphasise what he was saying, the dark amethyst of his fourth ring glowed with a pale radiance. Curubor turned to the unit which escorted him and emphatically ordered.

"Fall in behind me. Under no circumstances are you to leave the track. Stay close to your companions and let us progress swiftly. We must cross the mountain pass before nightfall. These woods are full of evil. A dark, powerful magic inhabits them. I can hear an insidious music which distorts the Flow of the Islands, like the song of a cursed bard."

The guards obeyed without question. They were highly disciplined, with unending confidence in their lord. To ward off evil spirits, they unveiled the House of Dol Etrond banner, the Golden Arch upon an azure field.

---

54 Gweïwal Agadeon: Greater God of Earth, the Halls of the dead King and Lord of the underworld

Duluin the Tall, commander of the unit, marched towards the head of the party to join his lord.

"This is most unexpected. We had anticipated threats from renegades and smugglers in these mountainous parts, but such potent sorcery..."

Curubor concurred. "It is most unexpected indeed. Tios Lleny and the lands around it looked very different when I last crossed this mountain pass. I remember an isolated city at the end of the road, with very little to distinguish it beyond its vineyards and nectar gardens. Its population was very diverse, with many lowborn Elves, but also artisans and merchants, who were prized for their alchemical skill and considered the best winemakers of the island. The city had also become a haven for petty thieves and smugglers, beyond the reach of the royal stewards. But it was certainly not a place where one could witness the forces of the amethyst. Someone has come here recently, someone whose music must be powerful enough to summon the shadows which pervade these woods so that they might guard the region from the ignorant and the weak.

Can you not hear that music being carried through the leaves by the breeze?

Can you not hear those deep voices communing under the ground?

This evil, powerful chant is the cause of that spell.

Time is of the essence; our army will soon meet the enemy in the west. We cannot turn back now, but I do find myself wondering if crossing the Arob Nisty was a judicious decision."

After leaving Tios Lluin, Curubor had chosen to head south of Nyn Llyvary through one of the few paths which crossed the Arob Nisty Mountains. He had judged that the pass, though harsher, would be much shorter and faster than the sea route. The Blue Mage had only resorted to this radical option because the first battalions of the barbarians were already marching eastwards.

Soon after the Council of the Forest had ended, Curubor had decided to send an albatross to the Royal Court in Gwarystan. The great sea bird carried news of the impending threat of war and brought a request for an immediate conference with a royal envoy in Llymvranone. He calculated that his unit would take six days to reach the main port of the west coast of Nyn Llyvary. This plan assumed many long, forced marches, with very short nights of rest. They had indeed made quick progress south of Tios Lluin and into the deep forest of Llymar. But their momentum had slowed as they followed the banks of the Sian Llewa[55], the green river, a difficult terrain, and the stamping ground of hunters. The heart of Nyn Llyvary was particularly wild; few Elves dared to venture into those parts, fearing the smugglers and the renegades banished by the King.

Now a few leagues from the border of the royal domain, the Blue Mage of Tios Lluin was drawing upon all his talent and experience to hasten his unit and encourage its passage. He could frequently be seen at the front of the band, boosting the moral of his troops with his commanding voice, devoting all his energy to the success of their mission.

★

A few hours later, just after nightfall, the group finally emerged from the woods on the southern slopes of the Arob Nisty. It was weak moon, smaller and dimmer than Cil, the Star of the West, which had finally pierced the clouds. As they walked on, the moon gradually grew in size and strength. Its mystical halo expanded, flooding the southern stretches of Nyn Llyvary in vivid silver light. In the dissolving heat of the spring night, Curubor and his armed entourage stood for a moment, motionless, at the entrance to the valley of the Sian Kanny[56]. They rested on the edge of the woods, enjoying the gentle breeze of the pines. Hidden night birds sang out. The very heartbeat of Eïwele Llya seemed suspended in the night. The rays of the setting moon contrasted with the shadows of the wild branches. Far away, towards the east and along the horizon, they saw the shimmering blue of the Llyoriane Sea: the heart of the archipelago. The path leading down from the Arob Nisty heights was a tortuous track which meandered through the hills. In this part of the island, with its high altitude, chestnut, walnut and birch trees had replaced the pines and cypresses of the coastline.

---

55 Sian Llewa: 'Green River' in lingua Llewenti
56 Sian Kanny: 'Red River' in lingua Llewenti

For the next few hours they progressed south through the foothills of the mountain range, unsure of their exact location or where precisely they were heading, distantly hoping to avoid the Valley of Giants, a landlocked territory hallowed by the Llewenti. Elves never ventured into that place, for it was feared that Eïwele Llya's bastard sons, the giants of the Arob Nisty, still resided there, and none would dare provoke their wrath.

Morning came. Their exhausting journey had almost ended. To the north, a huge black cloud was rising, overwhelming the sky. Soon a heavy shower was pattering down upon the leaves of the trees. Two knights of the Golden Arch were sent to search for shelter, while Curubor remained with the rest of his unit, progressing more slowly. After another full day of walking, when the two pathfinders returned with their good tidings, the moon had already appeared between the streaks of clouds. After a long and tiring march, Curubor and his small entourage eventually reached the shelter of a refuge.

The wooden building was rectangular, low and wide, built between three pine trees. On either side of the door, two torches were lit to welcome travellers. Light from the main room was shining through the gaps between the ill-joined beams of the front wall. It was likely that wardens of the frontier were inside. Curubor hesitated. Perhaps this was not the wisest time to seek refuge in a remote frontier shelter. If cautious, he would suggest they continue further along the track, finding some wild area suitable for a camp. But his hungry and exhausted troops were already making their way towards the entrance of the building, eager for a hard-earned rest.

Curubor did not dare stop them; instead, he cautiously lingered behind. As the door opened, he heard the newcomers greeted with loud cheers, merry laughter and warm invitations and Curubor soon reproached himself for faltering. He realised with a smile that the gold and blue colours of the House of Dol Etrond were still held dear on this side of the Arob Nisty. Inside, the room looked like a stable. Its low ceiling, blackened by smoke, was pierced by several windows. There were no fittings beyond a long shelf which held up some old pottery, and a few chairs, with legs which sunk into the soft clay floor. Torches provided a weak, flickering light and filled the room with the thick smell of resin. There were two Llewenti inside, wardens of the frontier bearing the emblem of Tios Lleny: a red grape upon a field of grass. Their faces were sunburnt, and their helmets were adorned with the red feather of the King's Hunters. Their keen eyes and their quick movements mimicked the wild beasts that lived alongside them. But they were not alone; a third character joined them in their drinking. Despite his modest attire and average size, all that were present could tell he was a High Elf. But his skin was a bluish grey, his hair was jet black, and his small eyes seemed more accustomed to shadows than to sunlight. He was a Night Elf.

Once Curubor had entered the room, he cut short the usual ceremonial greetings and ordered that the refuge be guarded for the rest of the night. Visibly tired and worried, he did not linger in the main room for long but claimed the upper level of the building for himself, the most protected area of the refuge. Curubor was weary; the journey had been long and eventful. His mind was still haunted by unsolved riddles. An unknown power had worked some fearsome witchcraft, Amethyst High Magic, to distort the Flow of the Islands and block access to the mountain pass. Bringing his attention back to the tasks to come, he abruptly turned to the two wardens of the frontier.

"You are to immediately depart for Tios Lleny and inform its steward of the arrival of Curubor, of the House of Dol Etrond, along with his cortege. Tell him to ready a boat for us. King Norelin is gathering the royal army in Llymvranone. We will have to move off quickly, for we plan to descend the Sian Kanny tomorrow. Be gone and make haste. We shall keep your Morawenti friend with us." He then asked the third drinker in the outpost.
"What is your name?"
"Nuriol is how I am known. I come from Menstoro[57] in the hills."
"Well, Nuriol of Menstoro. Come and talk upstairs with me."

Curubor's commanding tone forbid the Night Elf's protest. He followed the Blue Mage obediently. On entering the upper room, Curubor began methodically inspecting it. He looked up towards the small window in the ceiling, suddenly beholding the

---

57 Menstoro: 'Underground fortress' in lingua Llewenti

night-blue sky beyond, which seemed studded with diamonds. He was struck by the beauty of the vision, in all its ephemeral intensity. It comforted him and gave him strength.

Now fully focused on the task at hand, he turned to his guest.

The Morawenti, despite being an offshoot of the High Elves, had never truly been considered to be Hawenti, for they did not mingle with Gold or Silver Elves. Curubor had always felt that they had an enigmatic, dark quality to them. Spite, revenge and betrayal were to be expected from them. Nuriol appeared a primitive character, a creature, guided only by his own base appetite, not by reason.

"Whom do you serve, Nuriol?" suddenly interrogated Curubor.

The attack came as a surprise. "What do you mean, my Lord?" Nuriol responded nervously, his face tense, realising that he was trapped.

"Who is your master? Which rune protects you?"

"I serve no one, my lord. I belong to the wine guild of Tios Lleny."

"That is a lie, winemaker. I can read it in your mind! Do not provoke me to unnecessary violence... I see in your eyes that you are from the bloodline of the Night Elves. I see that you swore the oath of shadows, and it is this that makes you so grim and weary. You are now bound to a long, bitter duty. I see it in the pallor of your face," said Curubor.

Nuriol defensively responded, sensing that the Blue Mage had intrusively read his mind.

"I was indeed in the valley of Nargrond when it was invaded by the clan Myortilys. I did swear the Oath of Shadows to take revenge against those evil Elves. But you ought to have seen how they sank our city beneath the lake, how they slaughtered our kin and massacred our children. Such malice cannot be forgiven, even after centuries."

Curubor replied softly, with empathy. "I know what you have been through. You belong to those ill-fated Elves who fought in the blood-soaked wars. In those battles, no mercy was ever sought nor offered. There are scholars who say that your quest for revenge continues unabated to this day. Some even say it is still secretly commanded from the shadows. What do you say of this?"

"I cannot answer you." Nuriol was determined not to yield to any trick or threat.

Curubor grew angry. "This is most unfortunate for you, miserable insect. Do you think you can resist the will of Curubor Dol Etrond?" The Blue Mage approached Nuriol, his powerful gaze fixed upon him.

Already an imposing Elf, he seemed to grow taller. He put forward his right hand and opened up his palm, displaying the gems which adorned his four rings: the red ruby, the blue aquamarine, the dark amethyst and the azure sapphire. Nuriol, speechless and stunned, was suddenly thrust to the wall by an invisible, overwhelming force, his body two feet above the floor. His expression was panic-stricken; he tried to cry, but no sound could be heard. He remained desperately mute while the psychic claws of his aggressor penetrated his mind: searching, investigating, and tormenting him. Finally, Curubor ceased, and the Night Elf fell heavily onto the ground. Nuriol remained motionless, his body curled up, as though completely broken.

"It is as I suspected, Nuriol of Menstoro. You are a liar, a stubborn liar who will not yield. You know that you are protected by a powerful rune and that failing to keep your oath would cost your soul."

Curubor violently tore off Nuriol's coat and ripped at his clothes until he could grasp his exposed shoulder. Nuriol could not fight back, as if he were a puppet cut loose from its strings. Curubor covered the bare flesh with a silver powder, pressing it down into the skin as he murmured incantations. After a few moments, a triangular rune appeared on Nuriol's shoulder.

"So, this is it... most unexpected. The Guild of Sana has survived..."

For a moment the Blue Mage was lost in his thoughts, contemplating what his discovery meant. Nuriol used this time to regain his composure. He tried to stand, but only managed to sit up with considerable difficulty.

"You may go, Nuriol. Leave this place and go back to where you belong. I have a message for your new master, for I know that he is not far away. Tell him Curubor of the House of Dol Etrond sends his regards and expresses his sympathy. I felt such pity and sorrow for the previous guild master's misfortune. Tell him that a new age is upon us. Everywhere, Elves are rising, renouncing King Norelin's protection, denying his sovereignty. There are opportunities for everyone in the new world just beyond the horizon. Now, be on your way. Go!"

Nuriol had been sure that he was about to meet his end. Surprised and relieved at his chance to escape, he summoned his strength and descended the stairs, before leaving the refuge and disappearing into the night. None of the guards made a move to stop him. The domineering voice of their lord had intimated that the prisoner was to be let go, and his commands were always promptly obeyed.

The next day, the unit departed very early, as soon as the sun rose. They had benefited from a restorative night's sleep after the previous day's exertions. The worst part of the journey was behind them, and their plan now was to swiftly raft down the Sian Kanny River for Llymvranone. Before their departure, Duluin brought a cage containing five blackbirds to his lord. Curubor affixed to each of them a small scroll, bearing the royal seal that he had prepared overnight. Having performed a ritual, humming an exotic warble and making twittering sounds, he released them into the air. The birds took flight towards the west, their powerful, beating wings transporting them swiftly into the distance. Curubor turned to his loyal knight commander and said, with a wry smile.

"After this, I doubt we shall ever again enjoy the sympathy of King Norelin. It is a serious offence to misappropriate the royal seal and forge the stewards of Llymvranone's rune."

"The blackbirds shall deliver their messages to the cities of the Sian Kanny valley by nightfall. The gathering of the royal army will start tomorrow and, most probably, the first units will reach the battlements of Llymvranone in three days, shortly after us. The timing is perfect," Duluin assessed.

"As is the execution of our plan, so far," concluded Curubor, happy with how events had unfolded.

The clear voice of Duluin the Tall rolled like thunder across a clear sky.

"Hear me, guards of the Golden Arch! Fall in! We march southwards in haste!"

The unit set off immediately, maintaining a fast pace despite carrying their heavy equipment. The jangle of weapons, shields and steel reverberated across the landscape as they passed. They marched down a slight slope towards the south, towards Tios Lleny and the Sian Kanny River. The day was bright, the air pure and their mood joyous. They chanted songs, each melody succeeded by another rousing, rhythmic tune.

However, the unit did not get far. Their march was interrupted by the sudden presence of three Elves blocking their path. They were dressed like hunters, in green and brown garments. They did not carry weapons, not seeming to pose a threat. They were Morawenti; Nuriol led them. Waving his hand as a sign of welcome, he addressed the foremost guards of the column.

"I come in peace. Your master, lord Curubor, is invited to Menstoro."

No immediate response came, and no command was heard. During this brief hiatus, some of the guards encircled the three Night Elves, while others were sent to explore the surrounding area. The unit adopted a defensive formation, the form of a sun with long rays, expecting an imminent attack or treacherous ambush. For some time, Curubor was nowhere to be seen. Some thought he was giving instructions to his trusted lieutenant. Finally, he appeared, though the image of him seemed somewhat changed. His blue robes seemed gloomier, even fainter.

"I graciously accept your generous invitation, Nuriol," he announced, before turning to his unit.

"Guards of the Golden Arch, I shall not require your protection. You are to follow your Commander to the boat on the Sian Kanny and wait for me there, before we depart together. I shall most likely join you along the road. Duluin, I bid you farewell. We shall meet at nightfall. Remember my orders."

Curubor then turned to the Night Elves. "Nuriol, I am at your service. Let us make haste."

The two groups parted without another word. The smaller squad headed north-west to the hillsides of the Arob Nisty range, making swift progress through wild and difficult terrain. Curubor showed extraordinary endurance and agility, his thin silhouette moving swiftly in step with his companions. After a couple of hours, the small group came to an impassable tangle of bushes and brambles. The Night Elves quickly used long poles to remove the branches revealing a path through the area. Even a skilled ranger would never have detected such a hidden track. The path evolved to form steps which led down a long way through the scrubland, eventually arriving at a grove of trees that surrounded a naturally formed pit.

The chasm, about thirty feet in diameter, seemed bottomless. Curubor noticed that they were now at the lowest point of the plateau. The limestone earth, particularly crumbly in this area, had been carved into channels by the cascading run-off of heavy rains. The grove of trees had been planted to deliberately conceal the opening in the ground.

The Night Elves quickly reeled out long ropes that had been hidden in the foliage of the trees. Securely fastened to the trunks, the ropes were primed for a quick escape into the pit in the event of imminent danger. They prepared for their descent. One scout would remain stationed above ground to manage the ropes.

Curubor speculated to himself. 'It is an ancient cave. Long ago, the giants of Arob Nisty found shelter in these underground caverns to escape the Llewenti armies. These were true labyrinths, impregnable refuges.'

To the astonishment of his companions, Curubor refused the rope that he was offered, and instead uttered a quick incantation before jumping into the chasm. The Blue Mage landed softly forty feet below, after a slow, feather-like fall.

"So, this is Menstoro, the hidden refuge," he murmured as he looked around.

Fifty feet below, an underground river snaked through the abyss, disappearing into the darkness of two large galleries. The Night Elves retrieved torches, carefully stored in crevices in the cave walls. They formed a line with Curubor at its centre. In silence, they began to descend further underground. Only the rush of the river and the crackling of the torches could be heard, until the flow of a waterfall resounded and gradually became deafening. The river in front of them plunged into a large cavern, into a tumult of bubbling water beneath. The gallery's ceiling was particularly high in this stretch of the labyrinth.

The Morawenti directed their torches towards a hole in the wall high above them. They uttered a password in a strange, rasping language. Moments later, an Elf emerged from the hole in the half-light of their torches and threw down a rope ladder. The small party began climbing. At the top, Curubor found that the hole became a narrow tunnel, carved in stone and covered with soot, which they proceeded to crawl along in single file.

They eventually began to smell smoke, the air becoming warmer. They crawled for a long while until the passage widened and led into a huge cavern. Curubor could not help but exclaim in surprise. A vast underground room appeared before him, more than four hundred feet high and a hundred feet wide, its roof reached the height of a great oak tree. Fires were burning brightly around the edges of the cave, their light reflecting on the ceiling, illuminating the entire space.

Curubor counted a dozen Elves, each busy with their own tasks, but his gaze was soon attracted by a collection of furniture arranged at the centre of the great hall. Wardrobes, chairs and tables of the finest making were organized around a large floor tapestry. A singer and a musician were entertaining a solitary spectator, sprawled amongst the comfortable cushions. The entire hall was filled by notes which seemed to contain all the solemn beauty of some distant, mystical landscape.

The attentive listener was lounging carelessly on a comfortable armchair. The Elf wore a black tunic, with a wide, dark cloak. A silk scarf, the colour of leaves, was wrapped around his head, from which flowed his long black hair. His face was fair: almost as white as snow. His eyes, icy grey like a wolf, indicated his Morawenti origin.

A crystal vial was placed on the table next to a pair of skilfully crafted daggers. Their blades were coated with a viscous liquid. His bastard sword, flung down on the table, was propping up an unfurled scroll.

A sense of evil, sovereign power emanated from this Elf. His grin seemed to offer a glimpse into his depraved soul; he was no doubt capable of relishing cruelty. His domineering influence over the small community of Menstoro was immediately palpable. It seemed as if the smallest of his whims would be blindly obeyed.

Even so, he appeared to despise their devotion. A contemptuous smile crept across his face each time he spoke to one of them. An elemental power resided in his icy eyes, with a force like the all-consuming cold of the bitterest winter, which granted him a natural and ferocious dominion over his servants. A sudden malaise seized Curubor when he first observed the Elf's cold gaze, pervaded with intense aggression. The Blue Mage then looked to his host's right cheek, which was marked with the infamous rune of the outcasts. Troubled by the accursed sign, Curubor's eyes widened, glowing with a bluish light.

It was then that Curubor realized he was facing the fabled heir of House Dir Sana, a power who he had believed was long departed. This was a scholar of the shadows, capable of commanding the darkest forces, surrounded by myrmidons whose devotion was implacable. Curubor shivered. The Night Elf's gloved hand seized a glass. He swallowed the entire contents in a single gulp, before turning to his guest, who he had purposely ignored until then.

"Welcome to my home, lord Curubor Dol Etrond," the elegant Elf began. "It is a long time since we last met. What brings the Blue Mage of Tios Lluin so far from his stronghold? I hear you have been walking the dangerous passes of the Arob Nisty, like some bold, young adventurer." His voice was melodious, almost musical, but was also full of irony.

After a pause, which clearly betrayed his surprise, the Blue Mage replied hesitantly.

"I thank you for your hospitality... Master Saeröl. I am honoured... although you should not gratify me with the title of lord. As you know, my grandnephew, Almit, inherited the Blue Helm of Etrond..."

Curubor continued. "Last time I saw you, Master Saeröl, your body was strewn across jagged rocks, broken and mutilated after a great fall from the top of the cliff of Gwarystan. Several high mages of the Ruby College were gathered around your corpse to cremate it. You had been sentenced to death by King Norelin."

"I was sentenced wrongfully, to pay for the murderous crimes of others," replied Saeröl, distant.

"I know you were the victim of an injustice: used as a scapegoat by the new king to blindly avenge the murder of his father. An unforgivable wrong indeed was done to you, your bloodline and your guild," acknowledged Curubor.

"When it comes to spurring on the weak and the impulsive, injustice is perhaps the mightiest provocation imaginable. Bodies may fall, bones may break, corpses may burn, yet I am living proof that such a heinous ritual can be survived. The scions of House Dir Sana are resourceful, after all. We might hold suicide as the noblest of actions, but, until the day a lady is found to bear his heir, we still have a duty to perform. Such are our ways," Saeröl continued.

"So, for all these years, the Guild of Sana has survived in secret, concealing both its existence and the survival of its master. It still lives, despite the harshest repression and discrimination ever seen on the Islands," Curubor reflected, not without admiration.

"Such is the destiny of the Morawenti; we are respected and lavished with gold in times of peace and prosperity but persecuted and robbed without the slightest hesitation whenever it is deemed necessary for the kingdom. The Guild of Sana was rich, and the king was poor. War and defeat had depleted his treasury, and he needed gold for his overweening ambitions. It is never wise to retain the gold without wielding the sword! And Norelin has been rewarded for his treachery, for what he has now achieved is beyond even his own ferocious dreams. Have you been to Gwarystan recently? Have you looked upon those red towers climbing up into the clouds?" asked Saeröl.

"I reside in the Forest of Llymar. I prefer the calm and the beauty of the woods, and the company of the Llewenti clans," replied Curubor.

"So, I have heard. I recommend a visit to the royal city, so you may see with your own eyes what it is becoming: the jewel of the Islands, the greatest city ever built by Elves. It is a place of wonder, beauty and might. Multitudes of men work under the rule of the guild masters and their most skilled artisans. Slave Giants erect walls and towers, viaducts and theatres, as have never been seen before. Griffons and hippogriffs can be seen flying through the sky to transport the noble Dol to that night's feast or to the latest spectacle.

Everywhere, the high mages demonstrate their power. It is the Ruby College that commands the Flow of the Islands, using it to enchant the royal city beyond anything imaginable. Members of that great assembly wield incredible power; they are as respected and honoured as are the Dol lords. Each year, the Ruby Tower rises into the sky slightly higher still, after the most gifted apprentices have proven their dedication and are given the privilege to dwell in yet another of its numerous floors. Truly, lord Curubor, Gwarystan is a place of inbounding wonder," Saeröl concluded.

"And yet," Curubor could not help but ask, "You have chosen to leave that marvellous city, and take up residence in Menstoro?"

"You are right. This change is relatively recent: no more than a couple of months, I would say. Gwarystan was no longer safe for me. There was great turmoil last winter, when the tension between the king and the House of Dol Nos-Loscin escalated into what almost became open warfare."

"So, I have heard, Master Saeröl. The House of Dol Nos-Loscin now stands alone to contain the savage bands led by a renowned Dragon Warrior, Ka-Blowna. The king has denied support to his vassals who fight the barbarians in the south. This surely demonstrates a dangerous abandonment of his sovereign duty."

"I agree with you, lord Curubor. The House of Dol Nos-Loscin is the key to the south of the Islands, for it is they who control the most important cities and fortresses. But the king's latest gesture has a deeper significance, for the House of Dol

Nos-Loscin represents the old order, and the power of the Hawenti houses that is now constantly challenged by the rising influence of the men at Court."

Curubor nodded in agreement, adding, "I was told the king has closed the temples of the Llewenti deities, even the great shrine of Eïwal Lon that most of his subjects venerated. Many were those who prized the wise teachings of the Deity of Lore."

"This is true; only the cult of Eïwele Llya remains tolerated, and that is only because the Mother of the Islands is also worshipped by the human Druids. But priests of other cults are being persecuted. There are rumours of a secret exile. I hear that some of the noblest Dol have now fled. They were known for their devotion to the archipelago's deities. Worshippers of the Islands deities go to seek the Secret Vale of Llyoriane, where it is said they will find peace," explained Saeröl.

"So, have I also heard," Curubor stated.

"The rate of change upon these islands is accelerating; we find ourselves in a time that is more momentous than ever before. This is due to the influence of men. These days, events are happening at the pace of the short-lived.

The king refused Terela Dol Nos-Loscin's hand. He insulted her powerful family and chased that noble house from the court, banishing it to confront a most uncertain future. He chose to ally himself with men, to collaborate with the Westerners, and now he pretends to rule the masses of barbarians. He decided to arm their troops and give them red shields, glorifying them with the title of Soldiers of the Ruby. And though he still controls the remaining Hawenti houses for now, the grip of his new human allies tightens with every diplomatic step that he takes. It is the men who are pulling the strings, and the foolish young sovereign does not have the wit to notice.

Blinded by his loyalty to the Westerners, the young King Norelin has decided to throw away centuries of Hawenti domination to build a new realm for men and Elves, where all will have their place at his side.

What a vile joke this is!

What a fool is he!

His father, King Lormelin the Conqueror, would have sooner jumped from the top of the Gwarystan cliff than ever contemplate such foolishness."

Saeröl did not speak again before he had helped himself to another cup of wine. He did offer the fine nectar to his guest, but Curubor declined, staying well away from his host, not daring to sit down or touch anything.

Saeröl produced a thin dagger from a hidden pocket of his cloak and used it to draw a triangle around a rune. He gave a nod which was barely perceptible but indicated his considerable pride. He poured more wine into his cup, smiling grimly.

"I had to flee. I had to hide. I travelled the Islands and there is probably no hiding place on the entire archipelago that I have not tried. Only very few Elves willingly assisted me; even fewer still live to tell the tale of how I forced them to conceal me. I underwent absolute isolation and extreme poverty. It is remarkable how a single infamous marking on the cheek can change your life.

Elves want to enjoy love and nature. They want to create and share beauty. They turn a blind eye to injustice, evil deeds and perfidious lies. They will idly look away from you in your hour of need, heedlessly denying you justice. This is sad for left on his own, a Morawenti will invariably dedicate the remainder of his life to preparing just revenge."

Saeröl let his threatening words echo through the cavern before he went on.

"I have no knowledge of what noble design drives Curubor Dol Etrond away from the legendary ruins of his ancestral city, onto the dangerous tracks of the Arob Nisty pass. But I do know one thing. Despite the urgency of his errand, the Blue Mage did stop by and visit Menstoro, to pay his respects to an ancient Dir, the master of the Guild of Sana. For this, for the trades we have made in the past and for our future cooperation, I am grateful. I remain hopeful that the prospect of my friendship, and indeed my dreams of retaliation, will inspire your ambition. I hope too that next time you come across the Guild of Sana; you will consider the alliance I am offering. All rivers must meet at the sea, Lord Dol Etrond; it even appears that ours are cascading down one side of the same mountain."

Curubor was impressed by Saeröl's eloquence. His natural assurance imbued his words with a deep wisdom. But something in his manner undercut this eloquence with an undeniably sinister note; it was something far more profound than the strange accent colouring his voice. He was the sage of the infamous, the bard of discord, and the sorcerer of the cursed. His delicate features, dark braided hair and elegant garb all gave him a certain seductive power. His natural, cold grace could be interpreted as a kind of serenity, but at the same time he seemed to be filled with pride, disdain, and contempt.

In his reply, Curubor controlled his voice, consciously adding warmth that he did not feel.

"In that case, all is well, Master Saeröl, for we undoubtedly have enemies in common. I will therefore do all that I can to help you avenge your cruel fate. Consider me a friend. Though I cannot predict what lies before us, I do sense a great confrontation on the horizon, a fight between men and Elves, between monsters and heroes, and most of all between evil doctrines and noble ideals."

Curubor bowed and, without touching anything or anyone, he took his leave, anxious to continue his own task. Four scouts escorted him out of Menstoro through the maze of secret corridors and underground galleries.

The caves of Menstoro were ten leagues from the small city of Tios Lleny, but the distance, travelled along the paths through the hills, felt much longer. The track was defined by a row of golden flowers and was lined beyond with pines, lemon trees and wild vines. After the four scouts had escorted Curubor down through the wilderness for a few miles, they turned back to let him continue alone. He then reached the road and was relieved that his progress could now be much, much faster. Curubor's silhouette gradually disappeared from the twists and turns of the trail, even as he walked along them. The Blue Mage vanished slowly: first his arms, then his head, legs, and finally his torso. His azure robes seemed to hold within them a secret void, into which the wizard had simply dissolved.

★

"Are you well, my Lord?" inquired the familiar voice of Duluin concernedly.

"How long I have been?" Curubor replied hesitantly.

"You have been gone for many hours since you began those first incantations. You were in such a deep state of sleep that I was starting to fear for your life. It is dangerous to resort to such powerful Magic," the valiant knight protested.

"I did not want to take any risk with those Night Elves; indeed, what I discovered was beyond my imagination," replied Curubor.

"And what did you discover?"

The Blue Mage could not hide his self-content. "Let us say that, whereas we might have had a deadly foe on our back, we now have a powerful ally rallied to our cause..."

"Beware, my Lord, those Elves who swore the Oath of Shadows are not to be trusted. The Morawenti have wreaked many horrible acts of vengeance after the wrongs they endured. Their past has left them with stony hearts and warped, murderous minds. Their reputation shall be forever stained with suspicion and dread, and their savagery is feared by all. There are some who wonder if they have not become more steeped in evil than their enemies in the clan Myortilys," whispered Duluin.

"Indeed!" Curubor exclaimed, partly convinced by his faithful servant's warning. "Did you know, Duluin, that I saw a beautiful statue of Eïwele Llyi in the cave of Menstoro?" he asked vaguely, lost in thought.

"A looted work of art, no doubt," Duluin asserted.

"I disagree. I believe that this image of the Llewenti deity was placed in that small alcove on purpose, perhaps to be worshipped," the Blue Mage pondered.

"Eïwele Llyi," Duluin reminded him, "is revered by the Llewenti because she brings beauty and joy to the innocent: to those with pure hearts."

"Indeed, the matriarchs even say that the divinity of arts judges Elves by their intention and purpose, not by their deeds. I wonder if these ill-fated assassins, sworn to the Oath of Shadows, are not looking for redemption. Perhaps they seek forgiveness after committing such vengeful acts.

But where are we now?" Curubor asked, finally looking around him. "Is this the slipway leading down to the boat?"

Duluin was used to his liege's secretive ways, and he did not complain about his exclusion from the events of Menstoro. He replied concisely, with restraint, as was his duty.

"We are ten leagues southwest of Tios Lleny. The current of the Sian Kanny is strong. We are making good progress. You should now rest, my Lord. I will notify you when we are approaching the walls of Llymvranone."

Sian Kanny, 'Red River' in the Llewenti language, was given its colour by the purple clay it carried along its current. The river flew down westward into southern Nyn Llyvary, through Tios Lleny and other small cities built around it, towards Llymvranone, where it eventually opened out into the Sea of Llyoriane. Far upstream, twenty leagues from the sea, a bore-like wave would appear and disappear on the Sian Kanny, but it was far too inland to be the result of the tide. That stretch of the river, where the downward current met the mysterious upstream swell, was particularly treacherous for boats. No one knew the origin of the wave, but priests taught that it signalled Eïwele Llyo's passage, as she travelled through her underground halls deep below the Arob Nisty to wander the Islands, searching for the lost souls of dead Llewenti.

★

During the final three days of sailing down the Red River, Curubor was able to rest and recuperate his strength. He seldom relied on Sapphire Magic, and the powerful spell he had used to project his image into the Morawenti lair had drained him. Such a complete projection, at such a great distance and for such a long time was a complex and onerous exercise, and one that only a wizard of his experience could have successfully performed.

He spent his time alone, watching the banks of the Sian Kanny pass by from its cabin, and admiring the beauty of the hills beyond, covered with wild vines and vibrant fruit trees. He joyfully breathed in the river's sweet air, savouring the intense fragrances of spring. An accomplished drinker would have detected those very aromas in the faerie wines of the valley, which were known as the best in the island. But all too soon, this contemplation of the vast landscape struck a painful chord within his soul.

All of this land could have been his. The royal domain south of Nyn Llyvary, from Llymvranone to the strait of Nyn Llorely, might have been granted to the House of Dol Etrond after the last war: after the Pact was signed. It would have been just compensation for the losses of their fortresses, lands and capital city in the west, as well as for the death of their heroes and the slaughter of most of their army. When Curubor heard that the young king would maintain his iron grip on that rich province in order to nourish the growth of his capital, he felt deceived, and since then had harboured concealed anger.

'Am I so different from someone like Saeröl Dir Sana?' he wondered. 'Was my refusal to join the court in Gwarystan, and my decision to settle in an abandoned Tios Lluin, my natural reaction to an injustice? Even then was I sowing the seeds of rebellion?'

Curubor had convinced himself that the mockeries of the other noble houses did not affect him. They could laugh all they wanted about his love for ancient stones, for primitive knowledge and indeed for young Llewenti females in their prime. So be it, he had said to himself. He would sooner be esteemed by free Elves as a learned scholar and a good mentor than be obsequiously revered as a lord in his tower by lowly courtesans and servants.

'How could the scorn of my peers not have corrupted my mind, planting those seeds of revenge?'

But he knew that history had proven him right. After the disastrous last war, his grandnephew, Almit, had settled in Gwarystan, taking his place in the Golden Arch tower. For a while, he had performed his part as lord of the House of Dol Etrond at the Court. He played the role of a vassal always ready to bow and forever eager to praise a new royal enterprise or applaud the latest faerie spectacle.

Almit had ambition, he had a purpose. He had been promised entry to the Ruby College, that place of great knowledge and power. Almit had all the necessary qualities and had understood what such a position would demand. The expertise of the high mages drawn from the thousands of ancient tomes collected within the Tower of Crimson, gave them a unique insight into the Flow of the Islands: that high magical realm far beyond the grasp of other wizards. But Almit had been tricked and abused by false promises and lies.

The high mages seldom accepted noble Dol into their ranks, nor did they marry and produce heirs. They ensured the power they enjoyed through their command of High Magic remained firmly within their small caste; they left the burden of governance to the king and the dangers of warfare to the noble Dol. In fact, their oath forbade them from ever commanding armies. Instead, they dedicated their life to mastering the Islands' Flow, to studying all kinds of magic. The secrets of alteration, enchantment and conjuration had been known to them for centuries. They also controlled platinum, gold and silver; they were the coin masters and decided on the price of goods. This was perhaps their greatest source of power; as the Hawenti saying goes, everything and everyone has a price.

The high mages of the Ruby College were the greatest power on the Islands; they guarded the most sensitive secrets and influenced the fate of all. They had even overcome the Llewenti deities, who they now held prisoner far, out at sea, in the depths of volcanoes or in hidden mountain vales. The Ruby College had served and advised the line of Hawenti kings since the First Age. This had continued throughout the golden reign of Lormelin the Conqueror but, now, under the young king Norelin, their role had become less defined.

Almit had never stood a chance of being accepted into that prestigious assembly, a fact which he finally admitted when he joined his granduncle in Llymar. But his daughter, Loriele, had remained in the capital and this decision was proving a shrewd one, for her involvement in court affairs meant that the House of Dol Etrond had not entirely fallen out of royal favour. For the most part, however, over the past few decades, it had been overlooked; indeed, mostly ignored, for it was commonly known that Almit and Curubor had dedicated their lives to the restoration of old stones and the study of lost legends.

Curubor reflected. The disturbing encounter with the Master of Guild of Sana had left him feeling vulnerable and doubtful.

'I know in my soul that I belong on the archipelago. I love my homeland more and more with each day that passes, as truly as any scions of Queen Llyoriane, as religiously as any matriarch of the clans, and as passionately as any Protector of the Forest. My heart is filled with the archipelago's pervading sensuality when I walk in the shady paths of the hills and bays, when I breathe in the spirited oceanic air, when I hear the joyful melodies and behold the Islands' dancers. The noble truth is that, after a century of living in the forest, I have been transformed into an authentic Llewenti: a free Elf who would sooner give up the eternity promised to High Elves than ever abandon his desire for a joyful and chaotic life, however temporary that life might prove.'

★

The morning of their fourth day of navigating the Sian Kanny, the boat reached the edges of Llymvranone. Curubor's entourage had disembarked a few miles upstream, under the cover of the surrounding hills, leaving only Duluin to guide the small boat into port.

The port was built at the river's estuary around five small, rocky isles, a gateway to the open sea. Leaning on the ship's rail, Curubor looked at the city with nostalgic sadness. He contemplated the fallen towers and ruined domes that lined both banks of the Sian Kanny.

Llymvranone looked ruined, chaotic and fragmented. Two and a half thousand years of troubled history had inflicted many dark scars on the city. Though the baleful vista of decapitated towers, disembowelled houses and crumbling battlements had a certain attractive, historic grandeur.

Before the last war, few cities could have matched Llymvranone's size and wealth. Curubor vividly remembered the forest of masts: the incessant comings and goings of small boats along the curves of the river. It was in this very harbour that representatives of all Elvin trades upon the archipelago had gathered. One could find clothes from Arystan[58], carpets from Ystanondalen[59], wine from the hills surrounding the Sian Kanny, and jewellery crafted in Gwarystan. Manufactured goods were transported by merchant ships from the Islands to be exchanged for minerals and metals, fruits and wine, gold and coins. The Blue Mage could still picture the white smoke of the forges which used to rise in the clear morning air. Llymvranone was the home of Nisty steel, considered the strongest in the archipelago; save for a rare compound originating from the valley of Nargrond. The city had been so-named because of its strategic position, as it commanded all the trade routes of the archipelago. The peak of this once-glorious place was now nothing more than a distant memory.

Due to its location, Llymvranone had been ravaged throughout history by High Elves who had besieged the Llewenti; by barbarians who then drove out the Hawenti armies; by Men of the West who reclaimed the city and finally by King Norelin's troops who forced Westerners to surrender. All these invaders had left their mark. For centuries, the city had fallen victim to the disputes of different races. Each onslaught had forged its spirit into a volatile alloy of resignation and fierce resistance. Yet those who lived there, the old and the young, knew in their hearts that it would always remain Llymvranone, the city upon which the fate of the archipelago was written.

A few High Elves still lived within its walls. They were survivors of the sacking of Mentolewin[60] and refugees from Ystanetrond[61] who had migrated after that city's fall. These Elves held the most important positions within the city's army and guilds, where their talents and abilities could not be surpassed.

---

58 Arystan: 'City of silver fortifications' in lingua Llewenti
59 Ystanondalen: 'Fortified city of Rondalen' in lingua Llewenti
60 Mentolewin: 'The fortress of Lewin' in lingua Llewenti
61 Ystanetrond: 'Fortified city of Etrond' in lingua Llewenti

There were also some Morawenti whom unsurprisingly lived in a separate community. Due to their exceptional knowledge of alchemy, alteration magic and smithing, they were seen as essential to the city's prosperity, and were therefore rich and influential.

The vast majority of Llymvranone's surviving inhabitants, however, were Llewenti. Many had turned away from their clans and chosen to live under the protection of the High Elves, sharing in their wealth and comfort.

Whatever their origin or homeland, these Llewenti had submitted to the Dol noble houses and adopted their ways. Most of them held only subordinate positions. In addition to a yearly tribute, paid in gold or in kind, they were obliged to pay homage to the king, and in so doing they abandoned their sacred powers over the Flow of the Islands to their liege.

The boat passed under the city's only bridge, a bottleneck in the river where numerous vessels would have once made the passage difficult. But now it was all clear; no other ships could be seen on the river. As they docked on the southern bank of the Sian Kanny, a unit of royal guards, clad in red cloaks and plate mail, came to greet them. The Blue Mage only had to lift the curtain of his cabin to be immediately treated with the utmost respect. In Llymvranone, the arms of Dol Etrond were still as deeply revered as the royal rune.

Escorted by three soldiers with red cloaks, he embarked with Duluin aboard a barge. A final short crossing through the rushing waters allowed Curubor to contemplate the ancestral home of the Dol Etrond in Llymvranone. Somewhat curiously, the king's envoy had chosen the ruins of Curubor family's manor as their meeting place.

No one had yet made the time to organise its restoration. The place revealed much about Dol Etrond's history: a once rich and powerful House that had suffered severe defeat at the hands of the barbarians. They had been forced to flee and abandon their vast domains in the west of the archipelago.

Yet, amongst all their lost lands and possessions, this old mansion in Llymvranone remained. There had been a time when the family had dropped anchor there to rest when sailing between their stronghold in the west, Ystanetrond, and the capital city of Gwarystan.

The rock of Dol Etrond was one of five small isles at the mouth of the river, just upstream from the port. The mansion, an ancient building with classic Hawenti architecture, was built around a round tower a hundred feet high, the only unspoiled part of the structure. A vast garden, now overrun with wild plants and weeds, surrounded it.

Curubor walked slowly down the path to the steps of the mansion. His entourage respectfully waited behind him. His sharp gaze wandered from one bank of the river to the other, pondering the extensive work that would be needed to restore his property.

But Curubor's reflections were soon interrupted by the appearance of another luxuriously dressed High Elf, who was coming to meet him. He recognized Aplor, one of the city's royal stewards; a skilled wizard and renowned scholar who helped govern Llymvranone in King Norelin's name. Along with two of his peers, he ruled the vast domains south of Nyn Llyvary: the fishing port Llavrym[62] and the cities of Tios Vyar[63], Tios Gla[64], Tios Vyon and, far away in the east, Tios Lleny. Many Elves indeed lived under the protection of the royal rune in southern Nyn Llyvary.

Aplor bowed twice to Curubor, showing great respect. He then performed the offering of hands, a ritual salute to honour those of Dol bloodlines: revealing the royal Rune of the Ruby which was etched upon his palms, demonstrating that the king's magic protected him.

Curubor asked him to rise and greeted him with a few courteous words. Then, the steward guided the much-awaited guest to what had been the great hall of the manor. Only three walls remained, and the ceiling opened out onto the clear morning sky. Aplor then vanished under the pretext of informing the king's envoy of Curubor's arrival.

---

62 Llavrym: 'Harbour of Star Fish' in lingua Llewenti
63 Tios Vyar: 'City of Vines' in lingua Llewenti
64 Tios Gla: 'City of Flowers' in lingua Llewenti

Three white marble statues embellished the great hall. They represented the former lords of the House of Dol Etrond. Curubor's father and forebears were depicted, each pointing their swords towards heaven. In these effigies, the sculptor had captured their glorious deaths on the battlefield.

"I somehow doubt that statues of me will ever look like these," the Blue Mage thought with a wry smile. His ambition was certainly not to die fighting the wars of others.

There had been a time when the House of Dol Etrond had governed Nyn Avrony, one of the Sunset Islands off the Mainland. It was a time when their great city, standing proud above the green pastures bordering the Strait of Oymal, had been a powerful fortress of the kingdom, and its main defence against the barbarian hordes. But countless wars and invasions had eventually taken their toll the great fortification had one day been conquered. When Aplor returned, Curubor was standing motionless, a spider in the corner of his web, his gaze fixed upon the statues. He had known and loved each of these long-departed Dol lords.

The Blue Mage was invited to join his host in what appeared to be the only intact part of the mansion.

It was not a very large reception room, but its luxurious furnishings were fitting for a royal residence. At the back, a stage was covered by a vast canopy of purple velvet, dotted with white unicorns which were pinned down at the edges of the platform by heavy strips of silver. The four steps leading up to it were covered with a rich mauve fabric. The room was filled with sumptuous cushions, precious carpets from Ystanoalin and rich furs of the clan Llyandy, and its walls were draped with exquisite tapestries, woven in Gwarystan looms. The tapestries depicted scenes of the kin-slaying wars, where the Dol Lewin had earned incomparable glory fighting against the Llewenti clans.

The ceiling's frescoes were carved with the arms of the Hawenti households who were allies of the House of Dol Lewin's second branch. Light from the chandeliers illuminated the two bronze dragons of the House of Dol Oalin and the silver star of the House of Dol Rondalen, centred on the white unicorn against a purple field.

As was the case for all major Dol houses, a huge value had been placed on art and learning. The king's envoy always travelled with his library, a resplendent collection of precious books and manuscripts.

On a perch near the steps sat a hooded bird of prey, as motionless and impassive as the falconer who stood guard below. The centre of the platform was occupied by two wide and comfortable chairs which were covered in a purple silk studded with white stars.

On one sat lord Camatael Dol Lewin, Envoy of the King, a High Elf who, although slim and young, already was a majestic character. He had long black hair, a pale and austere face, and icy blue eyes that held both intelligence and learning.

As the new ambassador of King Norelin, Camatael Dol Lewin, the third lord in the history of the House's second branch, was a powerful and skilled Elf. His recent promotion to this influential position had been a reward for his commitment and talent.

He was known to be a subtle diplomat, extremely well versed in the ways of Hawenti nobility. He was the last Elf of his bloodline, and his inheritance had been taken from him when men had invaded the western islands; he therefore did not personally administer any lands, nor did he rule any communities or cities. He was dedicated exclusively to serving his sovereign.

Camatael had frequent dealings with guild masters, stewards, merchants, captains and sailors, as well as druids and priests of the six deities. He had precise knowledge of many fields; numerous subjects sought his help, on issues ranging from trade and diplomacy to architecture and religion.

When sent on an errand by the king, the envoy was also the depository of a unique and fearsome power, symbolised by the scarlet rod he wielded. The common Elves of these territories knew that Camatael's judgment could mean degradation, imprisonment or even exile.

The royal envoy could also command armies during wartime. He had the authority to muster units and warships under the King's banner.

Camatael's influence was important. His rugged features revealed his superiority.

Camatael was comfortably leaning back in his armchair when Curubor was shown into the room. The envoy's manner betrayed his tension; he expected this meeting to be something of an ordeal.

Below him, a beautiful and young Elvin lady stood in the middle of the reception room. She was dressed in the finest Gwarystan silk, and her bearing identified her as a noble High Elf of superior rank. Mixed azure tones combined exquisitely on her robes, and delicate jewellery adorned her neck and hands. The golden radiance of her rings, bracelets and necklace formed a stunning contrast with the silky black of her soft hair. Her gaze was as imperious as an eagle's. Her thin lips and delicate features showed a certain discontent; indeed, her lovely nose was slightly twitching, revealing her usual impatience. This was Lady Loriele Dol Etrond. It was often murmured in the court of Gwarystan that no other lady could make a finer queen, for she was venerated for her sovereign beauty and admired for her remarkable intelligence and education.

Once Curubor had been granted entry, Loriele turned to embrace her relative. So as to preserve his lordly composure, Curubor coolly stopped her warm greeting, avoiding her touch. Instead, he bowed before the lord of the House of Dol Lewin.

"Lord Curubor, welcome to Llymvranone," Camatael declared solemnly.
"I am glad to see you, Uncle. It's been such a long time," added the young lady genuinely.

Curubor smiled gently at his grandniece who he had always treated as his own daughter. Respecting convention, however, he addressed the king's envoy first.

"I thank you for travelling to Nyn Llyvary... lord Dol Lewin. I am honoured... but you should not gratify me with the title of Lord. As you know, my grandnephew, Almit, has inherited the Blue Helm of Etrond..."

After a pause, Curubor continued.

"I am glad that you have been appointed to such an important position, although, speaking truthfully, I had anticipated it. It shows that, despite your lack of lands, fortune and experience, your talents and merits are fully recognized by the King and the Ruby College. This is very reassuring. Although some think I am detached from the pulse of the archipelago, I remain interested in the events of our time, and I have keenly followed your rise. I offer my congratulations for such a rapid ascent. I have heard you are a high-ranking member of the Cult of Eïwal Lon and a reputed scholar in your own right, whose abilities may one day lead to admittance into the College of the High Mages."

"You are too kind. Thank you for your encouragement. I have indeed gained some experience, but my true education has not yet begun."

Curubor nodded, understanding what the young lord meant. "It takes decades, often centuries, of painstaking research and scrupulous study to even begin to discover the art of High Magic."

"One can only learn to control the Flow of the Islands in the Ruby Tower. For those who have mastered it, the shifting tides of the Flow are theirs to command," and, with this, Camatael's eye blinked, as though the very wind of ambition, that ceaselessly blew within his soul, had transformed from a gentle breeze into a raging tempest.

Curubor could not help but disagree. "Lord Dol Lewin, there are alternative paths that a promising young scholar can follow to master High Magic, if he commits himself to prayers and the ways of the deities, so that they may bless him. This path is far less dangerous, for the Flow has its source in the archipelago itself, and the Islands' deities are its cache.

Beware for the high mages have seized the Flow of the Islands at its source, disrupting the ancient balance."

Camatael disliked being lectured by his guest, believing that it was disrespectful. However, he regained his composure and gently added.

"You may call me Lord Dol Lewin, but rest assured that it is not necessary. You will pardon me if I address you in only the most respectful and conventional terms, Lord Curubor. I have read so many of your literary works and followed so much of your research that I can only treat you with the utmost respect."

"My dear Uncle," Loriele interjected. Eager to dispel the tension, she changed the subject. "Why do you not visit us more often in Gwarystan? We are currently enjoying spectacles and feasts like never before. The most accomplished artists, the most incredible wizards and the most talented bards are celebrating the glory of our king. Each day, the city grows, its towers reaching unparalleled heights. Indeed, our architects have rediscovered techniques which have not been used since the First Age. We have many men toiling for us, and they make efficient workers. Even giants are enslaved to do our bidding! Gold is available to those of our rank in greater abundance than ever before. Norelin is building nothing less than the greatest city in Elvin history. I cannot understand why you lurk with Father in that desolate place of yours, surrounded by wild Elves of... another time."

"But there is much to learn from the Llewenti of the clans," Curubor protested, "as one day you will see. They live according to ancient traditions; they approach life differently, as a matriarchy. I am sure that under King Norelin's rule, Hawenti females do not have nearly as much influence. Of course, you may find them irritating at first, owing to their idle chatter, superficial preoccupations, natural passivity and their love of leisure and pleasure. But, in time, you cannot help but realise the Llewenti are seizing all the good that life has to offer. They debate endlessly about the flavours of wines, the excellence of certain dishes, the beauty of sunsets, and it is not uncommon to hear them passionately extemporising on the rustling of the forest, the roaring of the ocean or the fragrance of flowers. This simply demonstrates what it is that truly enriches them: their love for the archipelago and their deep regard for their inheritance. Though often chaotic and blundering, there is much goodness in the Llewenti, Loriele," Curubor concluded sincerely.

His heir was far from convinced. "But Llymvranone is hardly a place to inspire excitement or happiness. It is a ruin," said Loriele.

"Unlike the Forest of Llymar, Llymvranone and its provinces belong to the King. For decades it has been bled of its resources under Norelin's orders. You cannot think that Gwarystan would thrive as it does if the kingdom's other provinces had not been so utterly drained and dispossessed. Minerals, steel, fruit, wines, indeed every valuable good is absorbed by the grand city, like a giant devouring its own children to feed its hunger. The destiny of Llymvranone and the region around it would have been very different if our sovereign had granted it to those Houses who had lost everything in the war, and in the Pact that followed," Curubor pointed out accusingly.

With a smile, he looked at the two young Elves before him.

"The Dol Lewin and the Dol Etrond could have ruled Llymvranone. The two of you might have sat upon the city's throne, as Prince and Princess of Nyn Llyvary. What an exciting thought! How different things would be now..." the Blue Mage speculated.

"Uncle, it is unwise... dangerous to be speaking as you are," Loriele protested, frightened by what Curubor was saying.

"Your naivety and sincerity warms my heart, my dear child. Though I may be somewhat biased, your beauty and spirit is overwhelming, although Lord Dol Lewin may be better placed to say so. It fills me with pride. I cannot deny I have heard rumour that you could become our next queen," Curubor pointedly suggested.

"The king's pleasure lays elsewhere," Loriele replied sharply, though her uncle could clearly read a certain disappointment in her expression.

It was incredible to behold the forceful self-confidence and intense ambition which was driving her. The Blue Mage worried for a moment that the future he was planning for her may not, in fact, be suitable; yet his quick mind, rapidly identified another option, a solution.

'Killing several birds with one stone,' Curubor thought enthusiastically.

He turned to his grandniece.

"Your coming to Llymar, Loriele, is a great event for the clans of the forest. Your reputation precedes you; you shall be honoured with attention and devotion that you cannot imagine. I do not doubt that you shall appreciate the opportunity to expand your horizons and complete your education."

The connotations of those last words did not escape Camatael who raised an eyebrow. There was more to Curubor's plan than he was letting on. The Blue Mage was an artist, a performer who could pluck upon the strings of his emotions with infinite dexterity. Camatael resolved to keep his wits about him, even more so than before, as Curubor dismissed his grand-niece.

"My darling, you remember Duluin the Tall, commander of my knights. He awaits you outside with a present that your father and I have picked out for you with care. I hope our gift will be to your liking. I hope it shall be a great companion, who will help you to discover all that Nyn Llyvary has to offer."

"It must be a stallion, Uncle! A white stallion! I am sure of it! Oh, Uncle, you have remembered how much I love horses. Thank you, I love you so much."

Overcome with joy at the generosity of her much missed grand-uncle, Loriele became almost child-like, charming her audience.

"Hold on! Hold on!" the ancient Elf cried, rising up his hands before Lady Loriele could embrace him. "You have no idea what the gift shall be, and perhaps Curubor's promises are not to be trusted at all," he said with a knowing smile. He knew that his young heir could charm with her exaggerated innocence.

"Now be on your way, darling, and enjoy yourself. Lord Dol Lewin and I have matters to discuss. After all, the king's envoy has not sailed to Llymvranone only to enjoy your company. His master has entrusted him with a mission of the upmost importance."

Camatael Dol Lewin stood up and, with all the elegance of a high-ranking courtly Elf. He escorted Loriele out of the room and took his leave of her with a graceful bow. For a split second, their eyes met and, in that moment, his desiring gaze showed how much he wanted her. This flash of fervour came as a surprise to the young lady, and she felt a flutter of pleasure.

Quickly regaining his composure, Camatael turned to his servant and gestured for him to leave and take the bird with him. He subtly ordered the falconer to gather his knights and have them bar all access to the reception room.

Camatael then summoned, with a few quick incantations, a gust of fresh air. An invisible force drew one of the heavy purple curtains aside, revealing a hidden alcove. The king's envoy gestured with his hand, and a large table slid out from the alcove into the centre of the room. A vast, colourful map of the archipelago covered the entire table top, upon which there stood hundreds of lead figures, painted in vivid colours. The statues symbolised cities and fortresses, mines and carriers, armies and fleets: all the key elements of a vast game. Curubor saw that what lord Dol Lewin had in his possession was an incomparable work of art. For the first time in many years, he felt envy.

"Lord Curubor, please take a seat. We have much to discuss. I must admit that the message you sent us did provoke particular emotion in Gwarystan. I trust that your influence in the Forest has helped resolve the tensions of which you spoke."

"Lord Camatael, I did not mention everything in my missive, for I feared that it might be intercepted. One can never be careful enough, and certain important tidings deserve to be delivered in person. I have much to tell."

Intrigued, the king's envoy sat up in his chair. He leant forward, preparing to digest each of Curubor's words, to measure their weight and to fathom out how much was fable and how much truth. Camatael Dol Lewin was focused. He knew that he was faced with a cunning orator.

For more than an hour, he listened without interrupting and, as the Curubor's story progressed, Camatael's amazement turned into incredulity, and his patience into a contained wrath. The Blue Mage's speech ended at the point when the nine matriarchs had appeared on the steps of the Temple of Fate, and it was announced that the Llymar's army would march to war.

Camatael leaned back in his armchair, like a commander regrouping his units before a decisive charge.

"You are telling me that castaways from Essawylor have settled on the northern coast of Nyn Llyvary. They are rebuilding the forbidden fortress of Mentollà. They have breached the Pact and defiled the king's glyph stone. And you tell me that the clans of Llymar are unaware? That the matriarchs do not know of events occurring fifty leagues from their sacred shrines? Do not take me for a fool, Lord Curubor," Camatael accused, his voice was marked with aggression although his composure remained intact.

"They were shipwrecked upon the deserted coast of a untamed territory, west of the peninsula of Gloren, at the heart of the land of wild Elves. It is a desolate place, haunted by renegades, all marked with the infamous rune by the very rod you carry. They are fierce fighters who were banished by your predecessor for refusing to agree to the Pact. The castaways from Essawylor are a long way from Llafal's sphere of influence," defended Curubor, with conviction.

"This I am unable to believe. Either you are wilfully attempting to deceive me or, worse, you yourself are in league with the matriarchs. This is grievous news you bring from Llymar. The Court of Gwarystan has long hoped your presence at the heart of the Llewenti clans' territory would be beneficial. I now wonder who you wish to help. The self-proclaimed Council of the Forest has declared war without consulting its suzerain, the rightful king of the archipelago. A usurper is calling himself Protector of the Forest, without even having the authority over a single grove. I am afraid that these developments constitute a severe offence."

"Barbarian aggression required an immediate response," Curubor countered.
Camatael was tense. "This puts me in a difficult position. I can already anticipate the taunts that will be heard at the court of Gwarystan. The king... the king will be furious. The Ruby College will seek to take immediate action."

Curubor had expected a severe response and was not caught off guard. He continued persuasively.

"The Llewenti clans do not pay homage to the king. True sovereignty lies with them alone. The Kingdom of Gwarystan has no reason to be offended. The clans are only defending what is theirs; they have no obligation to call upon the crown for protection."

Camatael was irritated. "If they have so decided, then the matriarchs are blinder and more reckless than I thought. The power of the archipelago's deities is diminishing as more and more Elves pay homage to the Dol houses. The old cults are declining, Curubor. Where will the matriarchs seek the power they need to weave High Magic?"

"The coming events are difficult to understand. It is like reading from an ancient stone; the message is complicated and difficult to decipher," said Curubor, doubt creeping into his voice.

"A foolish exercise," dismissed Camatael.

He decided to explain the position of the king.

"Our elite circles believe that the days of the Elves are numbered. The Kingdom of Gwarystan has now reached its age of twilight; long and bitter wars have ravaged our provinces, and our once-great race has begun to dwindle. The beautiful Elvin cities of the archipelago are becoming quieter each year, no longer bustling with life and wonder; shells of their former glory. The human multitude's time is upon us.

A huge wave is rising, and we are left with one sole choice: are we to be drowned by its flood, or do we ride it?

How can we possibly fight such a threat, with only few Dol lords who are worthy of their rank, a mere eight hundred units that are actually ready for battle, and less than a hundred warships considered seaworthy?

We are too few. We cannot resist the rising tide. The only way out is to take the lead, to ally ourselves with the rulers of men, and to strengthen our power by controlling the Islands' Flow."

Curubor immediately responded. "I do not doubt that the masters of the Ruby College have such irresponsible ideas. They poison King Norelin with their ill advice. They believe that we shall be able to convert the men to our way of life, by corrupting them with our gold and illusory pleasures. This is what we did with the majority of the Llewenti, by weakening them with new addictions.

But the reality will be the opposite. Our alliance with men will be like water mixing with lava. Which do you think will consume the other?"

"Facts do not cease to exist because they are ignored," Camatael declared.

"Indeed, they do not, in that you are right.

But how can you trust your masters so blindly? Did the priests of Eïwal Lon not teach you that doubt should be the foundation of all reflection and thought? The high mages of the Ruby College live cloistered in their towers; they are isolated, confined, and only see the future from their narrow viewpoint. Their pride is as immense as their blindness is incurable. They trample all history underfoot, gaining ever more influence with each new success. They have cast out and constrained the powers of the archipelago's deities. At the same time, they have alienated the ancient clans of the Llewenti. The masters of the Ruby College did all this to consolidate their control over the Flow of the Islands. The Elves who bow to the king have been deprived of the freedom and magic that is rightfully theirs, alienating them from the very world the Elves themselves created. The high mages have created a world of illusions in which all inhabitants are obsessed with comfort, corrupted by gold and ensnared by duty. Solidarity and compassion are seen as dangerous.

What the Ruby College has made is a world for weak Elves and simple men; they have laid the corner stone for the Kingdom of Half Elves, for everyone and that is to say for no one... but they have made one fatal mistake. They did not understand that the old world is not dead. You cannot erase the existence of thousands of years of history, legends and beliefs. The powers of the College can only banish the Islands' deities temporarily.

Also, the Cult of the Three Dragons is not dead; it is merely in hiding. You should know this, for it is what you were taught in your early years at the Temple of Eïwal Lon.

And now there has been a development of even more import. A ship has crossed the Austral Ocean, fleeing the perils of Essawylor: a vessel carrying hundreds of Elves.

If one ship can achieve this feat, what is there to stop many more following?

When last I walked along the shores of the Kingdom of the Five Rivers, I saw tens of thousands of Elves living there. What if something forces them to attempt the crossing? The fate of the archipelago would be altered once again. Do not dismiss the possibility, for it has already happened once in our history..."

Looking down at the miniature archipelago before him, Curubor added.

"Your colourful little map could appear to be missing a few figures."

A long tense moment of silence ensued.

"Lord Curubor," Camatael finally asked, "who do you truly serve?"

"I serve no one, and at the same time I serve all. I take no sides, my dear Camatael. I work for the greater good. That is my modest contribution to Elvin kind. These islands were given to us as our last refuge before the world falls apart," recalled the Blue Mage

Camatael was not impressed. "I hope you are not taking it upon yourself to challenge the sovereignty of King Norelin. It would not be wise. No one, no matter how powerful, could ever succeed in such a challenge."

"There are some who did succeed, and recently. It is not by following in the footsteps of he who walks in front that you shall ever find your destiny."

Curubor's eyes were hopeful.

"I know how the king consciously denied protecting the House of Dol Nos-Loscin and their lands. History has shown how dangerous it is to alienate that powerful family. The young Norelin is isolated; his position is weak, more so than you think, Camatael! Already, he cut the Llewenti clans off, going against the policies of his father.
Remember that Lormelin the Conqueror eventually resolved to forge an alliance with the matriarchs; that great king knew failing to gather the support of the Llewenti clans would

jeopardize his domination of men. Not only has his foolish son thrown away that, but he has even refused the support of the House of Dol Nos-Loscin. Instead, he sees them as rivals."

Seeing in the pallid face of his interlocutor an opportunity, Curubor carried on, more pressing than ever.

"How can you, Camatael, a former disciple of Eïwal Lon, tolerate such a suzerain? I cannot believe that you have sacrificed the wisdom and the moral strength you acquired in the Temple of Light for the sake of your ambition. King Norelin is now insulting the most powerful Dol House, a family who controls the south of the archipelago and, moreover, all trade with the clan Llyandy. His only purpose is to strengthen his unnatural alliance with the powerful Men of the West: to pursue his mad ambition. Each day he shows some new sign of that bond with the Westerners.

The king is childless and alone.

He is already isolated, Camatael! He shuns alliances with noble ladies of the finest bloodlines to experiment in perverse pleasures with mortal women. His half-Elvin bastard children will soon roam the street of the lower city. His penchant for extreme pleasures is obscuring his sight, as do the poisonous compliments and treacherous reassurances he receives from his enslaved courtesans.

Camatael! Be careful not to isolate yourself with him. A king without an heir is the greatest incertitude imaginable for any kingdom. When minds are pushed to predict the fate of a sovereign power, lines in the sand are necessarily drawn between allies and opponents, as everyone weighs up what they stand to win or lose by their trust or their betrayal. The question of who will stand and who will fall is everywhere. The time has come for auguries, divinations and plots. The time has come for everyone to risk everything, to let themselves be guided by invisible forces to uncertain futures."

Curubor's argument was becoming overwhelming. Camatael tried to fight back.

"The Ruby College believes there is nothing more perilous than trying to swing the balance of power within the Kingdom. He who attempts it shall have fierce enemies among all those who have benefited from Norelin; he shall only find weak allies from the very few who might think the change beneficial."

Curubor agreed. "War is always a deplorable last resort, and I always work to avoid it. But, when it is already at our doorstep, we must find ways to benefit from whatever the outcome may be."

"And I expect you claim to have the solution?" Camatael Dol Lewin asked irritably.

"I would rather say that I have different solutions to offer. Now, I always believe that a little impatience can ruin a great project, that, if necessary, we must postpone action and wait. Sometimes I have aborted my attempts to act as many times as there are days in a moon cycle until... the right moment arrived. That moment has now come, Camatael. You are the one who can help me. You talk of the King of Gwarystan... of the Ruby College... you always refer to a higher power when expressing the positions, you defend. I appreciate your distance, for it demonstrates that you are keeping your own beliefs and hopes hidden."

Camatael suddenly realized that he was being driven to betrayal by the cunning mage's speech. He decided to end the conversation abruptly. The king's envoy knew enough of Curubor's intentions. He stood tall and concluded the meeting in an imposing, solemn voice.

"Powerful Westerners at the Court will request that the guilty be punished for triggering a new war and breaking the Pact. King Norelin will follow their advice, for he has too much to lose. He may well gather the armies of his vassals and invade the Forest of Llymar to demonstrate his authority. No prince, no Dol lord, no guild master will dare oppose him. The traitors shall end up on the rocks below the Gwarystan cliff..."

"Please calm yourself, Lord Dol Lewin, and look at your map," Curubor offered.

The Blue Mage set his cold gaze upon the king's envoy and whispered to him, in a cold, deep voice.

"The Elves of Llymar did not light the fires of war; they are simply defending themselves against barbarian aggression. To cross the grassy hills of the Arob Salwy, in strength and in number, is their most fundamental right. Believe me, the king would find few allies to support any kind of retaliation against the clans of the Llymar Forest."

Then, half smiling, he continued, soft and ensnaring.

"Other factions will be eagerly looking for the slightest misstep on the part of King Norelin. The Dol Valra and the Dol Talas are among those Hawenti houses that are waiting for the first opportunity to challenge his legitimacy. They will not have taken the closing of Eïwal Lon Temple lightly. You studied the deity of wisdom's teachings with their children. You know them. They learnt from the clerics of the Temple of Light that there are lines that should never be crossed, not even by a King. If Norelin chooses to attack us, he will face the wrath of most of the Dol houses, and also of the majority of his own Llewenti subjects. They may have abandoned their clans' ancient customs but hear this: they have not forgotten their origins! For now, the northern forests of Nyn Llyvary are only home to four small cities, whose names echo like the many defeats of another age. Soon, history shall tell how the matriarchs of clan Llyvary walked alongside the survivors of Ystanetrond, the fabled archers of the clan Ernaly, and the last hero of the Avrony bloodline."

Curubor could feel Camatael hesitating. He smiled with all the grim humour of an ancient sage, which the king's envoy found more humiliating than the laughing jeers of a youngster. Camatael immediately reacted.

"I could call my guards. I could summon them to seize you. I could have you locked up in one of the city's deepest cells, where even your magic would be completely useless. And yet, the power of your voice must still be great, Lord Curubor, as great as when, long ago, your enlightened opinions influenced the decisions of the Dol Etrond lords. Now, as our meeting draws to a close, I almost feel gratitude. So, I thank you for your words. I shall consider each of them carefully and weigh up every piece of your advice...

But for now, you will honour me with your presence, as a... guest."

Curubor smiled at this. He could see a new dawn breaking in his interlocutor's mind; its contours were gradually becoming visible, like a landscape emerging from the fog. He replied, persisting with his persuasion attempt.

"In times of peace, there is little one can hope for. It is only in troubled periods that certain characters can demonstrate the virtues of which they are capable.
The clans of the forest shall begin a new era with this war, an era in which the great shall no longer devour the small, but where the quick shall annihilate the slow.
Camatael, I have been watching you for a long time. I have kept track of each step of your progression. You could become the heir I never had. It is up to you to forge your own destiny and, maybe one day, to forge that of all Elves of the archipelago. Gather the forces of the Sian Kanny valley, and sail towards the north. If you manage to conquer Kaar Corkel[65], our victory shall be complete. The barbarians shall fall inextricably into our deadly trap, for their only harbour is their sole means of escape. At this moment, it is almost defenceless. Seize Kaar Corkel and call upon the Druids; Restore their power, and then join us. This is the service the Council of the Forest demands before it welcomes the House of Dol Lewin into its ancient assembly."

Camatael violently raised his hand into the air, but a moment later he halted his attack: his prisoner had blurred before his eyes. The image of Curubor slowly began to vanish. Camatael did not move an inch; bark an order or curse in anger. The young lord had begun to understand.
Camatael allowed the image to disappear, observing each step of the process with a keen interest. He had read of such illusion magic; he remembered it was accessible only to wizards of great power, to wielders of Sapphire Magic.

Deeply lost in thought, Camatael stood alone long in the middle of the reception room

---

65 Kaar Corkel: 'Castle of the Well' in the barbarian tongue

What Curubor had just told could have major consequences for the future of the Realm. Closing his eyes, he focussed on every single word the Blue Mage had uttered, analysing both their explicit and implicit meanings. After decades of peace, the Elvin armies were on the move again. Camatael's mind evaluated the possibilities, weighing the odds and revisiting his many assumptions. His eyes changed to a white colour as he muttered mysterious incantations. Turning towards the table, he looked out across the vast map of the archipelago. More than two thirds of the figures denoting the Elvin armies were painted red: the colour of the Ruby and the colour of the King of Gwarystan. Their overwhelming presence commanded the heart of the Islands, controlling the shores of the Llyoriane Sea. Green, grey and dark figurines symbolised the scattered units of the remaining independent Llewenti clans.

Then, suddenly, as if influenced by the intensity of Camatael's gaze, some of the Ruby pieces started to move; they were shifting slowly away from Gwarystan, some of the red even changing to an unexpected yellow or blue. The young lord took in the spectacle with curiosity. He breathed in deeply and remained there for a moment, silent and focused.

★

Camatael finally resolved to open the door of the reception room. He moved calmly towards the royal knight on guard duty, showing no sign of the tempest of thoughts that raged within him.

"Where is Lady Loriele?" he asked laconically.

"She set out riding on her horse with a cavalier of the House of Dol Etrond," replied the knight.

"How long ago did she leave?"

"It must have been an hour ago... Should we fear for her safety? Shall we find her?"

"I doubt you could catch her," Camatael replied simply.

"Duluin the Tall was with her, my lord. I know him well. We fought side by side at the siege of Ystanetrond. The first knight of the Golden Arch has a strong reputation; he is a fierce and heroic fighter. You ought not to worry for the young lady's safety.

But has Lord Curubor already departed?" the royal knight inquired, looking behind Camatael.

"Not exactly... He was never really here in the first place," replied the king's envoy enigmatically. "Did you speak with this Duluin the Tall?

"I exchanged a few words, only briefly, my Lord. He was keen to show Lady Loriele a horse her uncle had bought her. He gave me a gold coin, in memory of the old days. I refused at first but he insisted, claiming that, where he lived, in the Forest of Llymar, money had no value. He even suggested you might be interested in the stamp. The coin is minted with the white unicorn of the House of Dol Lewin: surely a rare currency."

"May I see it?" asked Camatael, inquisitively.

"Here it is, my Lord... please keep it."

Camatael took the gold coin in his hand and started to examine it carefully. The white unicorn of the House of Dol Lewin was indeed minted on its two faces. This was most strange, for never in the history of the archipelago had a sovereign allowed anyone else the right to mint currency.

The king's envoy found the explanation soon enough. Upon closer inspection, he saw that it was a war unicorn that was depicted, not a racing unicorn. The gold coin came from Essawylor, from beyond the Austral Ocean. It came from the elder branch of the House of Dol Lewin.

Camatael frowned. He understood the message. Curubor's fantastical tale was true.

But a commotion in the corridor soon attracted his attention. The steward Aplor, escorted by several royal guards in red cloaks, approached in haste.

"Hear me, Lord Dol Lewin!"

"What is it, Aplor?"

"There are many ships, approaching from upstream, so many! It is as if all the boats from Tios Vyar to Tios Lleny have gathered to sail down the Sian Kanny and meet in Llymvranone. What can this mean? Nobody, to my knowledge, has sent any order to muster the royal army."

"It means, Master Aplor, war could well loom before us..." Camatael replied enigmatically.

CHAPTER 7: Rymsing

2709 of the Llewenti Calendar, Season of Eïwele Llyi, 6th day, Sognen Tausy woods

"Siw! Valy Vyrka! Valy keny! E nao fika ki!"[66]
"I cannot! I cannot Gelros! ... Gelros! Help me!"
"Ohos wal hega!"[67]

Gelros jumped from the tree that he was hiding in and agilely landed on the damp soil.

"Vyrka! Valy keny!"[68] he insisted.
"If I jump now, I'll be lost, Gelros," cried Vyrka, desperate.

The wild Elf was badly injured, a barbarian arrow embedded in his arm. He was confused and dizzy. He could no longer see clearly. He seemed to have difficulty breathing and beads of sweat sat upon his forehead. He moved as if to join his companion, who was eagerly awaiting him below on the forest floor.
Vyrka hesitated once more, but finally began his dangerous descent from the top of the tall pine tree. He did not get far. One of the first branches snapped. He slipped, unable to prevent his fall, and crashed onto the ground below. He was overwhelmed

---

66 E nao fika ki: 'I cannot stay here' in lingua Irawenti
67 Ohos wal hega: 'Others will return!' in lingua Irawenti
68 Valy keny: 'Jump quickly' in lingua Irawenti

with immense pain; his right leg was broken. The bone, cracked at the calf, was protruding through his skin. His now useless leg dangled like an unstrung puppet. In great distress, he could not stifle a scream. His cries tore through the silence of the forest.

Gelros, annoyed, turned back on his heels to assist Vyrka. He examined the wild Elf scout with little care.

'The arrow was poisoned,' Gelros thought. 'That is why his senses are confused. Now his leg is broken. The barbarians will come back in greater number and...'
     "Help me! Take me back to Mentollà, please..." Vyrka implored.
     "E nao llely ken a Mentollà..."[69]

Gelros did not complete his sentence. With one quick movement, he cut Vyrka's throat with his short sword. After a brief spurt of blood, the body fell motionless. The victim's lifeless eyes were frozen in shock.

Staying perfectly calm, Gelros methodically searched the body of his former companion. Disappointed with what he found, he took only three light arrows from Vyrka's quiver and a pair of daggers from his belt. He was then on his way, heading southeast towards the ruins of Mentollà. He sped up, reaching a consistently fast pace. Like a shadow among the trees, the scout progressed swiftly, leaving no trace of his passage behind him. His objective now was to join his other companions, Curwë and Nelwiri, who were waiting for him in a secret hideout by the boundaries of Mentollà. These surroundings were new to him, and very different from the tropical forests of Essawylor, but Gelros had a rare ability to always find his way, to blend into all sorts of natural environments; during the day, but most of all at night.

★

---

69   E nao llely ken a Mentollà: 'I cannot take you back to Mentollà' in lingua Irawenti

After an arduous, three-hour journey through the wild, rugged vegetation, Gelros finally reached the haven. It was a small cave, carved into the soft stone of a steep slope and protected by the sprawling forestry. The scout approached the cliff very cautiously. There was no telling how far the barbarian vanguard had advanced into their territory. Climbing the steep rocky wall, he reached an opening. The hole was small but wide enough to check who was inside. For the first time in several days, he could finally relax and breathe calmly.

Everything was normal inside. He saw Curwë; the bard was fully absorbed reading an old manuscript. Gelros recalled that the precious text had been a gift from Vyrka. The treasure was, no doubt, loot from one of the burglaries Vyrka had frequently committed in Llafal. Inside the cave, Curwë seemed unhappy; he let the book fall to the ground, complaining.

"How cruel life is! Here I am, reading the final page of this remarkable work of literature, knowing full well that I shall never read the subsequent volumes. I will be forever afflicted by the lack. What a sad feeling! It is rather like drinking that last glass of wine as you stare at the empty amphora. Those final few sips never taste the same... Nelwiri, you seem to care little for these matters I speak of. Am I right?"

"Siw! Indeed, I do care. You have my sympathy, my poet friend," replied the Irawenti sailor, but his ironic tone and strained voice showed that his mind was on other things.

"I suppose you aren't affected by life's little annoyances. Will you not stop that racket? Are you not concerned, anxious? Have these cursed feelings no hold upon you?"

Nelwiri responded suddenly by running across the room, leaping into the air, bounding off the northern wall to gain momentum and finally kicking against a second wall to perform a somersault. Landing gracefully on his feet, Nelwiri saluted an imaginary crowd.

"This is no racket! This is Essawylor dancing! You should know better, my artist friend. The following complicated and dangerous move will bring an end to my performance. Cil, Cim, Cir! I do intend..."

Nelwiri was interrupted by the echo of a bird cry. "I know that sound! There is no such tropical bird in these lands; Gelros must be back!" he exclaimed with excitement as he rushed towards the cave's entrance.

Gelros repeated his signal a second time; a traditional call used by Essawylor scouts and was admitted into the cave. Curwë stood up and warmly welcomed his companion, relieved at his return.

"Greetings Gelros, I am glad to see you. You were away for a long time."

"Greetings Curwë, and greetings to you also Nelwiri, we meet again!"

"Abriwa Gelros! We are eager to hear your news; there are tales of Blue Bards, spirits roaming the woods at night. The forest rustles with rumours of bloody battles and unspeakable horrors," added Nelwiri, as he hugged his companion with characteristic affection.

"Why do you come back alone? Where are the wild Elves?" Curwë interrupted suddenly.

"Dead."

"Siw, all ten of them?" inquired Nelwiri, astonished.

"All of them. Vyrka included."

"This is awful news," replied Curwë. "I had lately grown fond of Vyrka. I could not say that he was terribly smart, but he was generous... very generous. I loved his gifts. What could have happened to them?" he asked anxiously.

"The wild Elves chose to ambush the barbarian scouts. We killed over thirty of them. Those men are strong and fierce. Without iron armour, they are vulnerable at a distance, but they are deadly in close combat. They are full of fury. I killed eight... But then more came, many more."

"What do you mean? How many were they?" Curwë asked urgently.

"I saw their entire army: several thousand strong. The barbarians have crossed the pass of the Arob Tiude Mountains and entered the territory of the wild Elves, north of our location here. It is nothing less than an invasion," Gelros flatly declared.

"Ah! So when the highlanders' tribes crossed the peak of Nassy Gnanella[70] a few days ago to block our way to the southern road, it was no mere raid. It must have been part of a much wider plan," Nelwiri realised.

"Mentollà is now trapped between two fronts. We are at war," concluded Gelros.

The news froze Nelwiri and Curwë. Indifferent to their shock, Gelros began to busy himself replacing his equipment. He took the time to drink deeply, before he carefully selected new arrows for his two quivers and filled his pockets with food. He even picked up two black short swords to replace his bloody blades.

"The Morawenti have always made swords by the pair: one to tell you where to go, the other to remind you who you are," he added laconically, fully focused on his tasks.

When the three Elves left their hideout, the forest turned a deep, threatening green. The wind rushed furiously through the branches of the pine trees, as if pushing through the last stretch of a long race. Only the shrill cries of seabirds disturbed the silence of the dawn.

"I am going back to fight," announced Gelros.

"What do you mean you are going back? Alone?" Curwë exclaimed in disbelief.

"We must delay them. I will wound them badly, and so unsettle them. And, let me tell you, the wild Elves will not give up their fight. They have waited too long for this war. Though outnumbered fifty to one, they will plague their enemies and slow their advance. Those outcasts will fiercely defend their territory, believe me."

"If this invasion turns on Mentollà, we will be trapped with no means of escape. Someone needs to alert the clans of the Llewenti. They are our only hope.
Siw! Someone needs to go to the Forest of Llymar," Nelwiri urged.

"You are right, my friend. Time is of the essence. You are best placed for this mission. Use our small boat so you may reach the eastern shores of the bay more quickly," Curwë advised.

---

70 Nassy Gnanella: 'Yellow peak' in lingua Llewenti: It is known as the highest mountain of Nyn Llyvary.

"It is anchored just one league from here. I'll be there in less than an hour and, if the winds are favourable, I will reach the shores of the Gloren peninsula by nightfall."

"No doubt the matriarchs will pay more heed to an Irawenti envoy," added the bard, trying to convince himself that such a mission was the proper course of action, without reference to Mentollà's command. "Provided you do not get killed by their distrustful wardens before you get a chance to talk," Curwë added sarcastically.

Assessing the situation, he then declared.

"I will return to Mentollà. We will not regret our toil over the winter months, as we barricaded the ruins of the tower..."

"I have seen what is coming. I doubt Mentollà will be a safe place for you," warned Gelros.

Sensing that the three would soon have to part, Nelwiri grasped his two companions and invited them to join him in celebrating their friendship with an Irawenti ritual. The three Elves formed a triangle; each holding his companion's left shoulder with his right hand.

"Mywon tyn,"[71] they repeated three times.

Suppressing his emotion Curwë added melodramatically, with a smile, "I am not sure we will see each other again... But, rest assured, that if you do not survive what is coming, I will immortalise your glorious deeds in a wonderful song!"

Gelros had no more time to waste on the bard's black humour; he was already on his way, quickly disappearing from sight into the green foliage of the trees.

He was a true fighter but also a talented ranger. The Morawenti scout liked to travel light, dressed in dark green and brown clothes, hidden beneath a long cloak. For his armour, he favoured steel over chain mail. His cuirass, gauntlets and greaves were made of a rare metal that guaranteed protection without impeding movement. His war tactics were based on stealth, agility and intelligence rather than brute force. He owed his reputation to his archery skills. With enough strength to

71 Mywon tyn: 'Shining friendship' in lingua Irawenti

wield a great black yew bow, he could shoot many arrows over a great distance with deadly accuracy. Gelros called it his "Cruel Bow", and he worshipped it as a faithful companion.

It did not take long for the scout to decide a strategy.

"The wild Elves will harass the barbarian army on its flanks, slowing its progress. It would be too dangerous to join them, blinded as they are by their hatred. Instead of holding back, they deliberately choose direct confrontation. Massacring their enemies is their sole obsession. The barbarian chief has probably strengthened his vanguard after the blow our group inflicted. It is at the rear that I will strike now, among the wagons which carry the supplies. I will inflict terror upon the weakest point of our enemy. In doing this, I will strike their morale. And then, I will sneak towards the heart of the great army and... murder its commander."

Feeling reassured that he had now decided on a course of action, Gelros concentrated his efforts on finding a safe hideout. He finally chose a tall maritime pine tree. Hidden up in the air among the branches, with a view out over the woods, he would simply have to let the enemy pass by below, until he spied his prey at the tail of the column. Birds and butterflies were aplenty in these woods, so Gelros spent the first few hours of his watch befriending them. They would be useful spies to alert him of imminent dangers. He then dedicated his time to poisoning his arrowheads with great care and caution.

To his mind, war was not a contest of honour, but rather a hunt, in which there were winners and losers. Life was the stake of that great game and, so far, he had managed to stay alive. Once all his preparations and safety measures had been seen to, Gelros could finally enjoy a moment's rest. Alone in the wild, he listened to the sounds of the forest: the sweetest melody that no harp or voice could outshine. Above him, the clouds blown along by the ocean's breath, offered a changing but constantly beautiful spectacle. His senses, alert as ever, concentrated on capturing the beauty of his surroundings. He savoured this happy moment.

With a joyful heart, he started to hum his favourite tune, "Gelros' Complaint". It was a song in lingua Morawenti, which celebrated his numerous victories in a long litany that named the enemies he had killed and the battlefields he had graced. He dedicated it to his trusted companion, the Cruel Bow, which, like a single-stringed harp, emitted its own sweet music in response. Still muttering the lament, he set about carving an additional rune onto the bow at the tip of its lower limb, where many already figured. He endowed his companion with his first feat of arms on the archipelago: eight barbarians from the army of the Dragon Warrior.

Birds gathered around the tree, expressing their joy with melodious twittering. A squirrel soon joined them. Smiling, Gelros abandoned himself to this moment of communion and peace. He adjusted the leather mask on his face, covered his head with his hood and wrapped himself in his large cloak. The colours of his clothes camouflaged with the surroundings. His mind relaxed and his spirit roamed to the tropical forests of Essawylor, where it belonged. He could see the countless varieties of luxurious plants. He could feel the humidity of the air beneath the lower canopy, where the trees released water vapour from their large leaves. Visions of orchids, bromeliads and lianas filled his dreams.

But Gelros was not allowed to enjoy his reverie for long. He was soon awake: his senses fully alert. A shadow had crept across the sun. A rumour was running through the woods. The trees shook and made a deep, unknown sound, like some secret whisper of warning. The birds of the forests were suddenly seized with fright. All was chaos. Gelros noticed that some were seeking safe refuge, whereas the birds of prey were regrouping high in the sky in response to the forest's call. Gelros himself carefully climbed higher up the tree, until he could finally survey the entirety of the Sognen Tausy woods. Dozens, indeed hundreds of great birds were flocking together and moving east, towards the Llewenti cities. A power was summoning to its side the hawks and the falcons, the buzzards and the vultures.

7th day, Temple of Eïwal Ffeyn, Llafal

The nine matriarchs of the Forest of Llymar had gathered at the Temple of Eïwal Ffeyn, on top of the hill that overlooked Llafal. It was a place of power: a shrine dedicated to the storm deity. This was the sacred mount from which the high priestesses exerted their control over the Flow of the Islands.

"Hear me, Matriarch Lyrine! The birds of the forest have responded to our call. They have come in great numbers, such as we have not seen in over a century. They are gathering above the hills of the Arob Salwy and will protect the progress of our army," declared Matriarch Myryae. Her tone was humble and full of respect.

"This is good. You have done well, and you have my gratitude," thanked Lyrine, before she turned towards her daughter.

Nyriele was standing on the edge of the temple's terrace, contemplating the green waters of the Halwyfal below. The air was humid. The basin's banks, which formed the edges of the City of Llafal, were obscured by a mysterious haze. Not a breath of wind disturbed the atmosphere; the world seemed magically suspended. The dancing glimmer of the pale morning sun illuminated Nyriele's face. Lyrine contemplated her daughter with wonder. For one of the first times in her life, she admired her majesty, dignity and newfound strength. Knowing that times of trial would soon be upon them, Lyrine realised that Nyriele was indeed the worthy descendant of Queen Llyoriane. The maid's incredible beauty always made a vivid impression upon whoever beheld her. Her wisdom showed in her furrowed brow. Her chin, though delicately formed, expressed her strong will. A marine pearl tiara sparkled in her light hair. An assortment of colourful peacock feathers fell upon her bare shoulders. Wearing a long white dress of fine silk, she was standing tall, an ethereal being. The young matriarch embodied Eïwele Llyi's purity. The divinity of love and beauty had granted her high priestess with rare powers of insight; she could judge from afar the heart of any being.

Aware that her mother wanted information, Nyriele fixed her eyes on the waters of the Halwyfal and spoke slowly, her voice deep and measured, as though the events she described, occurring leagues away to the west, beyond the peninsula hills, were unfolding before her.

"Descending in great number from the mountains, the barbarians carry heavy equipment. They cross the paths of the Arob Tiude, following into battle the Dragon Warrior that they so idolise. Trails crawl with their convoys.

The horned heads of the H'Ocas and the red masks of the H'Ores have brought a large troop of archers from the coastal lands. The mountaineers of the H'Orunts lead the march brandishing their axes, and the riders of the H'Ontals protect their convoys at the rear. This army is almost ten thousand strong. We are outnumbered by at least four to one. These tribes form a long stream which becomes increasingly full as it approaches Mentollà. The barbarian power is gathering around the ruined fortress."

"We were too weak," interrupted Lyrine. "The refugees from Essawylor did not take the path I set out for them, which would have kept them away from Llymar Forest. We should never have let these castaways settle on the shores of the wild Elves' land. We should never have tolerated their presence in Mentollà. We ought to have handed them over to the King of Gwarystan. It would not have been a pledge of our vassalage to that... usurper, but merely a diplomatic gesture. We shall come to regret my lack of discernment, my weakness, in the face of my advisors. Think on this: it was Gal dyl who counselled me to simply keep them at arms' length."

"Do not blame Father! His advice was, to his mind, the best way to keep the peace," Nyriele protested innocently.

"How noble an aspiration that was, yet how poor a strategy it proved! Your father has always opted for passivity; he has always left it the future to decide his fate. See now what has happened: his protégés have triggered a war by openly violating the Pact," the Lady of Llafal countered. "Fortunately, their boldness will not be rewarded, for they will be facing the barbarian onslaught alone. I strongly doubt they will survive it. The black omens that accompanied their arrival were indeed fortuitous. The Halwyfal waters never lie. Eïwele Llyo sees all," she continued authoritatively.

"Mother, do you not see that we are on the verge of a global conflict, a conflict whose roots grow far deeper than the coming of one ship from Essawylor?"

Taken aback by the insolence of this last almost rebellious remark, Lyrine hesitated before answering. She finally whispered threateningly.

"No one shall tell me what to think. No one, Nyriele, not even you."

Regaining her composure, she turned to the seven other matriarchs within the temple, who were awaiting her command.

"Sisters of the Islands, come to me! The time has now come to address our prayers to the Master of the Ocean and to beg for his assistance!" she proclaimed. This would be a most perilous task.

Raising her voice, Lyrine commanded.

"Send the signal to the priests of Gweïwal Uleydon! Bid them take horses out along the pier. Let us sacrifice our steeds to the glory of the Greater God of the Waters.
O Gweïwal Uleydon, our offerings today shall be seven white stallions, for the matriarchs of the clan Llyvary, and two chestnut horses, for the matriarchs of the clan Ernaly. These are generous gifts, Gweïwal Uleydon, to haul your mighty coral chariot! So, hear what we call for in return! Matriarchs of Llymar, gather around me. All of you!"

Following Lyrine's command, the high priestesses joined hands on the edge of the temple's colonnades, their prayers and chants celebrating the sacrifice being made far below, by the shores of the Halwyfal. In perfect harmony, their melodious voices would rise a note higher each time the priests of Gweïwal Uleydon sent forth a horse, manic with terror, from the pier into the depths of the Halwyfal waters, where it would drown in cruel agony.

The horror of the scene was overwhelming. No matriarch underestimated the gravity of the sacrifice, for they could feel in their own bodies the energy of life escaping from the stallions' carcasses with each new loss. They also perceived how, as they deprived each animal of its life, their own powers grew, and their connection to Gweïwal Uleydon's realm became stronger. Moments after the last condemned horse was swallowed by the great basin's emerald waters. The chant of the nine matriarchs reached an unnatural intensity. Lyrine stepped forward and cried.

"The flow of Llymar Forest's streams, torrents and rivers must be reversed; the basin of the Halwyfal must gradually empty itself. The Halwyfal will draw to its heart the power of the ocean. It will absorb its strength, until the waves calm, the currents slow and all tumult ceases. The Lord of the Waters will give us his blessing, and the Austral Ocean will be as calm as a mountain lake."

"Hlan nois, Gweïwal Uleydon, Hlan nossa nalniy Gweïwal Uleydon!"[72]

As Nyriele heard these incantations and felt, as did all the matriarchs around her, her power draining away, she thought.

'This cannot be.'

The magical energy summoned by her mother was now entirely absorbed by the great spell that had been cast. Phosphorescent streams of azure flowed from the sea towards the temple's colonnades, circling around the eight lesser matriarchs. Nyriele observed the high priestesses, one after the other, seize the magical streams, hold and shape it in their hands, before offering it to Lyrine. It was Nyriele who stepped forward last, intuitively performing the High Magic ritual in all its detail, before finally kneeling in front of her mother and bestowing the Aquamarine Flow herself. In that moment, she saw Lyrine at the full height of her authority and might, capable of wielding divine power. Nyriele felt overcome.

---

72   Hlan nois, Gweïwal Uleydon, Hlan nossa nalniy Gweïwal Uleydon: 'Hear our call, Gweïwal Uleydon, Hear our prayers, Gweïwal Uleydon' in lingua Llewenti

The beautiful maid noticed that the nymph statues in the fountain behind her had ceased to pour out water. The flow of waters was gradually reversing. The nymphs were now sucking the pool's water up through their mouths. The pool was being filled by a small stream, flowing backwards, uphill into the temple. The tide of the Halwyfal had, too, been reversed. The ocean filled the wide basin with all its might.

★★

7th day, Mentollà

The evening was mild. The fog was rolling in a dense mass across the Arob Salwy Mountains. On the hilltops, large piles of rocks were gradually disappearing into the clouds. Dominating the ocean from its high position, the tower of Mentollà, a gigantic, mutilated peak of its own, reddened in the last rays of sunshine. The hunters had returned: some drinking beverages around the fires that were lit, others already hard at work. The ground was soggy; the air humid, the camp bristled with frenetic activity and yells rang all around.

After racing through the woods all day, Curwë had finally reached the walls of Mentollà. His coming had been eagerly anticipated, and there was great tumult in the courtyard as he progressed through the crowd towards the great keep. Gelros' warning had already reached the fortress compound and, despite the concerned look upon all the faces that Curwë passed, preparations seemed to be coming along well. The focus was now upon whatever might best bolster their defences.

Walking along the footpath which led down the immense rock to the harbour of Mentollà, Curwë noted that all the Irawenti had painted specific azure tattoos on the left side of their face, denoting each of their specific communities. The bard headed out towards a dangerous path along which the Irawenti held hands in a long line that led down to the waters of the creek where Arwela stood.

The seer remained in the water up to her waist, performing a heartfelt ceremony. One by one, the followers of Gweïwal Uleydon immersed themselves in the clear waters of the creek and carried out the ancient ritual that always preceded crucial battles. While underwater, the Irawenti cut their long hair and offered it to the Greater God of the Seas. Once the symbolic offering was complete, the seer of the clan of Filweni blessed them, so that they felt calm. No matter what may happen to their bodies during the coming battle, their souls would join the Almighty Lord of Waters, to dwell in the ocean's depths for eternity.

Curwë stopped awhile, touched by the poignant scene.

'Many of them will not survive the bloodshed that is to come," the weary bard could not help thinking. "The Irawenti are lively Elves, warm-hearted and generous. I greatly admire their passion for the arts. Like me, their favourite pastimes are singing and dancing. I appreciate the way they express their feelings with passion. I love the way they furnish their exotic language with expressive gestures. Indeed, in some ways, I have developed a special bond with their culture. They act so very differently from the High Elves.'

Curwë shivered when Feïwal came to greet him at the dungeon doors.
The Irawenti guide's skin remained tanned, despite the long, sunless winter they had experienced, but his appearance had somewhat changed. Feïwal's dark, wavy hair was covering the left side of his face, masking his eye and ear. Silvery feathers and natural vine leaves were woven into his dark locks, like a constellation of stars. There was a new tattoo upon his left cheek, the mark of a dolphin. Feïwal was finely dressed. His clothes, so light they were almost floating, gave him a mystical aura. His manners betrayed nothing but serenity and calm, oblivious to the dangerous situation at hand.

The two Elves were soon joined by Roquendagor and Aewöl. The small group decided to fall back to the tower chambers, which would offer greater privacy. Curwë soon spoke up.

"You already know that a strong detachment of several hundred barbarians was reported south of Mentollà. They must be experienced mountaineers to have crossed the Arob Tiude peaks. Until now, they have tried to keep their presence secret, but all the while they have been barring our exit towards the south: to Llymar Forest. Unfortunately, we have also received information from the Arob Tiude pass to the north, known by the Llewenti as the "Neck of the Hadon". Barbarian scouts have crossed the Arob Tiude and entered into the woods of Sognen Tausy. The wild Elves reacted, eventually engaging them in battle. Gelros had decided to escort them. He reported that the battle was brief. The fate of the human survivors was savage. Brutally mutilated, they were exposed to the wind, a bloody warning to other men. The wild Elves are ruthless; they are accustomed to torturing their victims according to their ancient rites. The magic they use during these cruel ceremonies enable them to extract their enemies' best kept secrets... This is how they came to know of the imminent, large-scale invasion."

There was a frozen silence as all considered the implication of these last words. Curwë continued.

"The signal for all wild Elves to gather was sent through the Sognen Tausy woods to the farthest corners of the Gloren peninsula. Vyrka decided to lead his own small unit and join his brethren on the path to war. Gelros accompanied him."

"Where are they now? Have they not returned with you?" asked Roquendagor.

"I will come to it soon enough, for I bear sad news and dark tidings."

"Ah!"

"I understand that Vyrka's unit, as it was travelling to join the rest of the wild Elves, encountered a strong vanguard of the barbarian army. They were most likely a group of scouts, sent ahead of the column to explore the field. Identifying well-worn paths is an important task for the invaders, as they carry considerable equipment: from siege weapons to chariots full of supplies. Vyrka decided to attack this party, even though he and the other wild Elves were clearly outnumbered. It is perilous to engage men in close combat, for they are tall and strong. Once cornered into a melee, it is difficult to escape the frenzy of their wrath."

"What are you saying?" Roquendagor asked impatiently.

"All were killed. The entire unit... Vyrka was among the dead. But Gelros escaped... He managed to report back to Nelwiri and me. The invading troops are several thousand strong. They are progressing extremely slowly and cautiously, hampered as they are by the inhospitable terrain and the constant attacks from wild Elves. They have enough arms and equipment to conduct a war campaign and are determined to besiege Mentollà. Given the hopeless situation we are now faced with, Nelwiri volunteered to alert the Llewenti clans and beg for their protection. He took our boat, anchored by the shores of the Sognen Tausy woods, to cross the bay of Gloren and reach the hills of the Arob Salwy," Curwë explained.

"This was most unwise. Nelwiri may well pay dearly for his thoughtless initiative. The matriarchs' minions will not hesitate in capturing him…or worse," said Feïwal, now worried.

"I have not yet received any news from him since," Curwë admitted before continuing. "Once Nelwiri departed, Gelros refused to safely retreat to Mentollà with me. He wished to return to the enemy. I trust by now he lurks close behind them, silent and alone, striking at them mercilessly in the dark, killing them one by one."

"Gelros will not return until he has spilled his ration of blood. He will make those men pay a dear price for the death of Vyrka," Roquendagor predicted, imagining his former hunt master as a jaguar on a savage hunt in the wilderness.

"That little Llewenti was our friend. Gelros will kill many men to avenge him. He will use arrows and… poison. He will strike terror into their ranks. They will never catch him. And, eventually, he shall make an attempt on the life of their leader," concluded Aewöl. There was a cruel inevitability in his words, for he was Gelros' true master, and knew that his orders would be blindly obeyed. The others could not help but shiver, looking at the pale Elf's cold, unfeeling eyes.

Moments later, after Luwir's horn had sounded, all the Elves of the community gathered in the main courtyard. Feïwal dyn Filweni soon appeared at the top of the tower steps. Arwela, the seer, and Luwir, commander of the clan of Filweni, were at his side. The Irawenti were joined by representatives of the High Elves: the defiant Roquendagor, the dreamer Aewöl, the flamboyant Curwë, and the fearless Maetor. Looking severe, Feïwal ordered the crowd to form a circle. This done, he stood in its centre, with a composure which announced the coming of a storm.

"Elves of Essawylor, you volunteered to serve under my command as sailors of the most perilous ocean voyage ever attempted. Furthermore, you swore your allegiance as soldiers of the clan of Filweni. The dyn of my family placed their lives into your hands.
Siw! These are profound and honourable pledges that you made."

Feïwal paused; the brief interval was filled by a soft murmur of assent.

"However, some of you, though you have survived the crossing of the Austral Ocean, may still not comprehend the full extent of the sacrifice demanded of you. Allow me to enlighten you."

Everyone became more attentive; it was clear that all were eager to know what would be expected of them.

"This tower or, I should say, these ruins, were called Mentollà by the Llewenti. At its summit now fly the azure colours of the clan of Filweni. This is now our land, for this is the shelter that Eïwal Ffeyn has granted us, in recompense for our faith.

A few leagues north of our border, beyond the Sian Tiude River, men are gathering in great number. What we will face is a multitude of bloodthirsty barbarians, determined to expel us from our new home. We could attempt to flee; we could try to escape the trap that is closing in around us. But, were we to run, where would we go?

What assistance would we seek?

For whose protection would we beg?

No, my companions, we are alone, and we shall remain alone."

Feïwal's body seemed somehow higher than before, as though he were rising above the ground. The wind swirled around him, sweeping up his long azure robes. With a tempestuous voice like prophetic thunder, Feïwal declared.

"Do you feel the gust flying through your hair? Do you feel the wind surrounding you? This is nothing less than the breeze of history; it is the ocean's breath, marking the first time we shall affect the fate of the Islands, on this storm-filled night of resistance."

Arwela stepped forward. With her clear voice that dominated the tumult of the elements, she proclaimed.

"I have looked up into the celestial vaults; Cil, Cim and Cir have set the stars of the heavens so that the future can be perceived in the night sky. Those three sacred lights know whether the arrows you shall loose will find their mark... or not. Such knowledge grants a power that should not be abused."

The seer of the clan of Filweni took her short bow and, with all her strength, drew back an arrow she had personally fletched, carved with intricate patterns and adorned with silver feathers. Aiming upwards towards the sky, she released the sacred arrow into the air. It flew upwards, and then seemed to hesitate as it lost momentum; in the next moment, it was carried forward by a sudden gust of wind, before plunging downward to immerse itself in the clear waters of the creek.

"We shall prevail!" she announced, her clear voice endowed with a mystic power, that resounded far beyond the compound. Curwë began to chant, "dyn! dyn! dyn!... dyn Filweni!!!"
And the assembled units cried back in unison, "dyn! dyn! dyn! dyn Filweni!!!"
The Irawenti rattled their weapons against their chainmail in ferocious challenge, as their battle cries echoed for miles around.
"We march to war! We march to war!"

Mentollà was ready to withstand a siege.

The two units of Unicorn guards began readying themselves for battle. Once fully equipped, they assembled in lines of six in the fortress compound, standing still as ancient statues covered in purple cloth and dark steel. Their commander, Maetor, inspected the ranks, examining every single detail of each of the soldiers' garb. The Unicorn Guard, now just fifty fighters strong, was still a formidable, ruthless force. Maetor checked that their weaponry and accoutrements were meticulously equipped and displayed. Their armour was beautifully fashioned from tiny plates of light metal, making it both flexible and extremely resistant, enabling the fighters to remain swift and agile. Their plate mail and weapons were decorated with interlaced runes, though the white unicorn was no longer anywhere to be seen. Each of their helmets was a work of art, intricately carved and encrusted with precious gems that glittered in the sunlight. The commander of the Unicorn Guard could be proud of his two remaining units. Resplendent in their purple robes and shining armour, he considered them peerless in their ability to crash through enemy walls with their sharp lances.

Meanwhile, Arwela was studying the movement of the waves at the bottom of the hill, beyond the cliffs which surrounded the fortress. She turned to Feïwal.

"Have you noticed? The sea has become as calm as a mountain lake. This is most unusual. How can it be possible?" Her brother replied, "I have indeed noticed. A great power is at work, bending the Islands' Flow to its will, even gaining control over Gweïwal Uleydon's domain."

★★

8th day, Strait of Tiude

The Elves of Mentollà were not the only ones to notice that change in the ocean. At the same time, thirty leagues west of the ruined fortress, on the northern shore of Nyn Llyvary, the fleet of Llymar progressed cautiously along the rugged coastline. They were opening the way for the great vessel of Cumberae, its mainmast dominating the rest of the fleet with its incomparable height.

Most of the fleet's swanships came from Penlla. While other Llewenti cities had mustered units of archers, scouts and sentinels to join the combined army of the clans, it had been Penlla, the 'cliff port', which had provided most sailors. Their role in Llymar's overall campaign was to crew its many warships before securing strategic beaches, enabling the rest of the units to come ashore. To pursue this perilous mission, for which they had to debark, swim and then reach land, they needed to be able to move as quickly as possible. They were therefore poorly protected, clad only in leather armour and wielding light weapons, mainly short swords and bows.

The sailors of Penlla and their captain, Leyen dyl Llyvary, had been entrusted with a task of the utmost importance by the Council of the Forest. Their ships were responsible for transporting the entire army of the clan Ernaly to enemy shores. They were a fierce force, comprised of twenty units, whose mission was to breach the barbarian rear guard and cut off its supply line. Mynar dyl was the commander of the clan Ernaly's dangerous expedition.
The warlord of Tios Halabron, who was standing vigilant on the aftcastle of the main swanship, suddenly grasped the arm of his brother, Voryn dyl.

"Call upon Leyen dyl! It has begun! This is the moment we've been waiting for. Gweïwal Uleydon is abandoning his power over these waters. It is time to enter the Strait."

A few moments later, the swanships were alive with frantic activity. Sailors and oarsmen were busy coordinating instructions from their captains. All the warships now headed at full speed towards the Strait of Tiude, the most treacherous sea of the archipelago, where the Austral Ocean's powerful currents rushed towards the Sea of Isyl. It was known as a highly difficult route to navigate, owing to the unpredictable winds and currents that prevailed along the narrow passage.

Joining the two dyl of the clan Ernaly, Leyen, captain of the fleet, confided.

"I never thought such a thing as this would be possible: sailing along the Strait of Tiude as if we were gently fishing upon the Halwyfal. Gweïwal Uleydon honours us greatly indeed. We will reach our destination in only a few hours. I must say, I am curious to see how our allies from Cumberae will manage."

Mynar dyl concurred. "I have crossed this strait once before, when I had to flee Nyn Ernaly. I had never seen anything as wild and desolate as those dark rocks jutting forth from the raging waves. Those craggy cliffs were a frightening sight indeed. By the dim light of the horizon, we could see gigantic waves crashing down with such force. And yet today... all is so quiet."

Forming a long line, the fleet progressed swiftly along the western coast of Nyn Llyvary. The power of the swanships' oars compensated for the lack of wind. After hours of effort, they finally reached their destination, at the narrowest point of the strait, where the ocean tides connected with other sheltered waterways. It was in this area that a breeding ground for whales could be found. The fleet regrouped in an orderly manner, indifferent to the groans and grunts of the leviathans.

One by one, the swanships transferred their soldiers to the merchant vessel from Nyn Llyandy, solidly anchored at a safe distance from the rugged coastline. The large cog was built of oak, an abundant timber in the southern regions of the archipelago. The vessel was fitted with a single towering mast and one square-rigged sail. The Principalty of Cumberae would use these heavy boats for trading across the Sea of Isyl, mostly along the shores of Nyn Llyandy. It stretched fifty feet in length with a beam of sixteen feet. It could carry up to some two hundred tons.

The clan Ernaly's troops were the first to be transferred, along with their equipment and supplies. It took more than an hour for each of the swanships to complete the operation. Then, with absolute discipline, the fighters queued aboard the great deck, awaiting their turn to climb the mast. Once they reached its top, they were securely harnessed to a long rope and, one by one, they slid down and along the cord for a hundred yards until they reached the cliffs of the coastline. Like pearls sliding along a silver thread, the clan Ernaly's fighters, each in turn, stole towards the wild shores.

Leyen dyl and Mynar dyl joined Aertelyr, captain of the cog, on the main deck, watching the fighters disembark. The southern navigator looked relaxed, sitting nonchalantly in a large armchair. Until now, he had not been particularly involved in the steering of the vessel, relying on his officers to perform the manoeuvres. He spent most of the time contemplating with relish.

"Your assistance, Master Aertelyr, is of great value to our cause. I would never have believed that it could be possible to land an entire army in waters such as the Strait of Tiude," Leyen dyl thanked the captain.

"We have gained at least two days. Our attack will be totally unexpected by the barbarians," Mynar dyl added.

"These are the kind of stratagems," Master Aertelyr replied, "that one develops when one wishes to continue trading despite King Norelin's blockade. When ports and harbours are no longer safe, alternatives must be found. The clans of Llymar are not alone in their struggle against such tyranny. To the south of the Islands, the Principalty of Cumberae also suffers. We are allies, Leyen dyl, and allies freely aid one another."

"This will be remembered. Let it be known that Master Aertelyr is a trusted friend of the clans of Llymar."

The southern Elf nodded distantly, unemotionally accepting the offer of friendship. His conspicuous attitude marked a kind of disdain towards others. Mynar dyl preferred to ignore him.

"I wonder how far the enemy has progressed into the woods of Sognen Tausy," said the warlord of Tios Halabron. "I trust they are now a mere few days from Mentollà's walls."

★★

10ᵗʰ day, Mentollà

The morning was clear, and the ocean breeze was fierce, sweeping away the storm clouds above the tower of Mentollà. Thunder rumbled tempestuously. Multiple ranks of barbarian archers stepped out from the edge of the forest and mustered down the hill, three hundred yards from the fortress walls. The compound and keep had been erected at the foot of a cliff on a small rocky peninsula. The natural formation of the site provided a significant defensive advantage against attackers from the forest, as well as strategic control of any passage between the bay and the creek. The silhouette of the ancient tower seemed to look out upon the threatening progression of the many men as if they were mere ants, encircling some giant tree.

Without a single war cry, without the sound of a single horn, the battle for Mentollà was beginning.

"Siw! The wild Elves claim that there are no barbarian archers on the entire archipelago who could compare to the ones in the service of the Dragon Warrior Ka-Bloozayar. It would be wise to raise the canopy and bulwarks to protect us from their arrows," Luwir advised.

"Let them come," came the calm reply of Maetor, commander of the Unicorn Guard. "And do not doubt Roquendagor, Oars Master. He saw his fighters through many sieges as a Dol, and always put the safety of his troops first before any glory of his own. He knows full well that it shall not be his sword that will decide the outcome of this battle; only a rational strategy will get us out of our desperate situation.

We must concentrate on managing your light archers and my heavy spear fighters so that each group can support the other. Roquendagor will keep our reserves safe and order them to engage when he knows they might tip the balance of the day. He has keen eyes that can see how best to use the arrangement of the fortress. Doubt it not: he will choose the perfect moment to order the charge and break the siege."

"Cil, Cim, Cir! Break the siege?' the oars master could not help thinking. 'These Dol Lewin guards are either arrogant or mad. Reports are telling us that there are thousands of barbarians roaming the woods of Sognen Tausy. There are barely two hundred of us to defend these ruins... and they intend to break the siege!'

Luwir looked out at his troops. He had organized his small army into six units of archers. There was a total of around a hundred and fifty fighters. As the potential defenders of Essawylor, their armour was fine, and their appearance was most noble. They wore silver feathers on their small helmets, and their chainmail was covered in a fine azure cloth. They had been expertly built as fighters; under Queen Aranaele, there was a conscription whereby all Elves of the Kingdom of Five Rivers had to be given specialised training. They had been educated in the rudiments of warfare, and were skilled at the broad sword, but most of all they were renowned as deadly archers. The short bows of the Irawenti sailors were made from overlapping layers of exotic wood, taken from the tropical forests of Essawylor, which endowed them with great flexibility and speed. Although the range of these weapons was limited, the archers could unleash accurate volleys of arrows down upon their foes with remarkable frequency.

Luwir admired the way the High Elves were organised. Each of the fifty Unicorn guards had proven his worth. They had fought as part of the same unit for decades, if not centuries. They favoured long spears, which required coordination and discipline to wield. Each member always knew what his companions were thinking; the whole unit would fight as a unique body. Each fighter played his part: either providing protection to his fellows or opening the defensive lines of their enemies. Turning to Maetor, Luwir said.

"The two units you command, with their hard-won experience and utmost courage in battle, will give my archers much heart, instilling confidence among our ranks.
But will some mere Irawenti sailors be resolved in the midst of battle?
I cannot tell for, until now, they have only ever faced the perils of the sea."
"Rest assured that the Unicorn guards will hold the gate and take the worst of what the enemy has to throw at us," Maetor reassured him. He continued with a note of regret in

his voice. "See how, according to the orders of our lord, we have erased the white unicorn from our shields." He steeled himself before continuing. "Each of the guards maintains his own weapons and armour with a great deal of pride and care. Each is attired in the finest purple robes above his magnificent Elvin plate mail, for this is the colour of our house, and it symbolises our determination to fight to the very end. Purple is red and blue combined: a mix of courage and virtue. This display shall be rightly feared by our foes."

"The Unicorn guards' equipment certainly marks their superiority," admitted Luwir, appreciatively. "Those strong shields, tall helmets, fine hauberks and, most of all, the long spears would strike fear into the hearts of the bravest enemy."

"You shall see, Luwir, how the Unicorn guards will form an impregnable bastion of resistance at the main gate. The doors of the fortress are our weakest point despite all efforts we made to reinforce them. Therefore, they will be the enemy's strategic goal. This is where I will stand until the end. Our wall of spears will impale any men brave enough to charge at us. With only a dozen of my guards, I will make it impossible for the barbarians to battle their way into the fortress. They shall behold us standing our ground resolutely, amid scores of their fallen warrior companions."

But Maetor was interrupted by a noise coming from the enemy ranks. In a great clatter of arms, the barbarian archers were kneeling down. Men bowed their heads and opened their hands as an offering to their evil Dragon Gods, as they listened to their shamans' prayers. Many of them took out small amulets from their tunics. Those who held the sanctified treasure soon passed it on to their companions; each man brought it to his lips and kissed it, in the hope of retaining the strength of the dragons.

A whisper was heard among the troops. Behind the multiple ranks of archers, the tribes' chief, Ka-Bloozayar, appeared. Seated upon his throne, carried by no less than eight servants, he was dressed in a red cloak the colour of blood. There was no doubt that this man commanded profound respect, for his appearance provoked a great show of devotion. He was an authentic Dragon Warrior, judging by the cut of his armour, which comprised of a full plate mail of rare quality, enhanced with dark engravings.

His face was hidden behind a copper mask, a magnificently sculpted work of art in tribute to the power of the mightiest Dragon God, Fyranar the Red. The mask's dreadful features inspired fear and obedience in all around. Ka-Bloozayar raised his right arm and there followed bustling activity. Men were hurrying around their small, improvised camp, hauling tools, long pieces of oak and works of steel.

The barbarians began to assemble the multiple pieces of a gigantic trebuchet. Judging by its many constituent parts, the siege engine towered above the pines' top and weighed many tones. The trebuchet needed nearly a hundred workers to be assembled. The process involved men running inside wheels, themselves twelve feet high, in order to lift the enormous counterweight into the air. This catapult was designed to hurl heavy projectiles at a great distance. The siege engine looked as if it could cause severe damage to the main gates.

To protect the craftsmen and their great construction as it was built; the barbarian archers advanced and started climbing the steep slope up to the fortress walls.

"Wuinca!" [73] yelled Luwir.

The Irawenti archers opened the shutters and raised the bulwarks in a silent readiness. They formed small groups, sheltering behind wooden panels from which they could safely fire their arrows and bolts. In the meantime, others were carefully watching what was being built beyond the ramparts. Pouches filled with water, designed to extinguish any flaming arrows that found their way to the barracks, were brought forward.

"Taon nari!" [74] Maetor ordered.

The Unicorn guards immediately placed themselves in front of each weak point of the wall, ready to strike back at any incursion.

---

73 Wuinca: 'Archers' in lingua Irawenti
74 Taon nari: 'Form ranks' in lingua Hawenti

A moment later, projectiles flew in on every side. The attackers were bombarding them with all manner of sharp missiles to cover their approach. Arrows were falling upon Elves who had not taken cover in time but were invariably bouncing off plate mail. The initial ranged attack had been harmless. The response of Mentollà's archers came hard and fast.

A continuous line of barbarians walked to the edge of the fortress' moat, each soldier bearing an armful of branches that they would throw into the waters below. Many fell under Elvin arrows. But, before long, a wide ford of branches had been formed, leading across the moat to the door. This had cost the lives of over a hundred barbarians. The gate was now vulnerable to a barbarian ram. With a loud cry, some of the most powerful human warriors rushed at the door with a pine trunk, whose pike-shaped end crashed into the wood. The first assault was not enough to break through, and the gate remained solid.

Elvin archers were shooting blindly at the crowd of humans below, however they failed to stop them. More men were already seizing the battle ram again, taking it back to create the distance for another assault. Two new assailants fell but the others, protected by the shields of their companions, proceeded to run screaming at the fortress. They crossed the ford of branches and collided against the door, which cracked from top to bottom. Swinging their powerful weapon back, the barbarians continued to pound at the door, moving the ram slightly with each hit. Each strike caused a little more damage as the doorframe was bent and distorted. Sensing the danger, Luwir and Maetor headed towards the gate near the door that was threatened, encouraging their archers to resist.

When the two commanders reached the stronghold's entrance, the panels broke in a deafening noise of splintering wood.
The destruction of the door did not lessen the determination of the Unicorn Guard, who would rely on their excellent discipline to snatch victory from the barbarians, however brutal and savage their foes may prove. Their formation was only three ranks deep. The barbarian attackers had never before witnessed the Unicorn Guard on the field of battle, and they could not fully comprehend the power that confronted them. The highly

trained guards were motionless, and utterly silent. The very air shimmered around them, as if to pay homage to the stoic sentries of an ancient Elvin temple.

"Puca ecco!" [75] ordered Maetor, his voice deep and warlike.

The first rank of the Unicorn guards lowered their long spears and thrust forward. They exchanged no words, yet each knew his place instinctively. Without flinching, proving their brave resolve, they raised their shields and soon felt the distinctive crunch of metal cleaving flesh as their powerful weapons pierced the bodies of their enemies. Watching the progress of his unit, the commander of the Unicorn Guard insisted.

"Puca ecco atta nar!" [76]

The second rank of High Elves rammed their spears forward; many more barbarians were slain.

"Etya ecco nelde nar!" [77] Maetor finally instructed to complete the manoeuvre.

More screams were heard as the third rank of the Unicorn fighters thrust their long spears at the oncoming barbarians. There was no fear upon the faces of the High Elves, only calm and ruthless determination. The fate of the melee had soon turned: to the favour of the Elvin army.

When Maetor finally ordered them to retreat, the damage they had caused to the enemy was so great that their nerves of steel had shocked their enemy, horrifying their opponents. Two battalions of men had been destroyed by the fiery intensity of the assault, the fiercest ever seen by the inexperienced human warriors. Any able to stand were fleeing, overcome with dread. Their eyes still blazing from the slaughter, the two units, silent, grim and resolute, withdrew back into Mentollà, carrying their wounded with honour. Their ornate armour, tall helmets and long spears were splattered with the blood of their victims.

★★

---

75 Puca ecco: 'Lances forward' in lingua Hawenti

76 Puca ecco atta nar: 'Second rank, Lances forward' in lingua Hawenti

77 Etya ecco nelde nar: 'Third rank, Lances forward' in lingua Hawenti

10th day, the Pass of the Hadon

While on the eastern side of the Arob Tiude there were wild orchards and lush gorges, to the west of the mountain range there was only a desolate, arid plateau of endless brown soil, interspersed by large outcrops of granite. Weaving through this wild territory were dangerous torrents, which surged in foaming cascades as they crashed across the landscape. Only the roar of the water, the cry of the buzzards and the howling of the wolves would ever break the silence. It was through this inhospitable region that the units of the clan Ernaly were now progressing: across vast plains, in the shadows between great mountains, and along the edges of the steepest precipices. They had now been battling through the Arob Tiude range for two days, overcoming narrow paths, steep slopes and treacherous summit passes. Finally, the horizon widened in front of them, and they could see the vast Sognen Tausy woods emerging beyond, stretching from between the Arob Tiude down to the ocean. They could finally see the dense, blooming vegetation to the east of the Arob Tiude foothills. It was the land of the brown bear, the fox and the deer, of thick woods and brimming streams.

Five hundred fighters of the clan Ernaly marched behind their two dyl. Night had not yet fallen when their units began to take up their positions on the slopes above the Hadon, the Llewenti name for the strategic pass through the mountains: a narrow parade, strewn with rubble, two hundred feet wide and some four hundred yards in length. They set up on the slopes in total silence; this army of scouts was accustomed to approaching its prey undetected. Many of them were surprised to find that this arid gorge, the only path through the Arob Tiude, was not already guarded by the barbarians.

"So, chance really does favour the bold. Who could have guessed that our units would take control of this strategic pass without shooting a single arrow?" declared Mynar dyl with a certain delight.

"There were many in Llafal who regarded this part of Curubor's plan to be madness. Some even declared that we should not risk the survival of an entire army for the sake of one improbable victory. I can still see their faces when you volunteered to lead the clan Ernaly's army to the Hadon," Voryn dyl dryly recalled.

"Indeed, I think some of those faces were relieved..." the warlord of Tios Halabron smiled. "But I did not put myself forward out of pure generosity, or for the sake of glory against the odds. I swore to defend this pass, and to deny the Dragon Warrior's army any chance of escape, because of the simple fact that the clan Ernaly's troops are the only Elves capable of succeeding."

Thus, the two brothers had condemned their troops to fight beyond the reach and assistance of the rest of the Llymar army. The clan Ernaly now risked being attacked on both sides, by reinforcements from the west, and by the main force should it retreat from the east.

The next day at dawn, reddish light illuminated the tops of the Arob Tiude peaks, while the valleys remained in shadow. But the morning calm was suddenly disrupted. Barbarian horns resounded from the east. The noise came from a hamlet, abandoned long ago by the wild Elves, which led to the passage of the Hadon.

An elite unit of the barbarian army, the Jackal Raiders, so named because of the tamed beasts they fought with, was returning from the wild Elves' territory. Despite the Llewenti's precautions, word had reached the barbarians that their supply route was cut. Their reaction had been immediate; the Raiders had been sent to secure back control of the road. A shaman of the Three Dragons' Cult, armed for combat with a heavy mace in hand, rode his warhorse at the head of the three companies, which marched behind him in a haphazard formation. The evil cleric was probably a noble among his people, for he was wearing a copper mask with red dragon features, a privilege reserved for higher-ranking officials of the cult. When he entered the apparently deserted Hadon pass, he raised his formidable mace and the first ranks of his warriors moved off, just as the emerging sunrise lit the whole sky purple. The Jackals Raiders were a strong but light infantry unit, composed of three hundred experienced warriors. They were animal tamers and trained all manner of wild beasts for combat. Sure of their strength, they boldly entered the neck of the Hadon, along the single breach into the mountain range, as one long column.

Within a few moments, the clan Ernaly's scouts had warned the other units of the enemy's movements. The lookouts stationed upstream relayed the alert, using hawks to dispatch instructions to prepare an ambush. All of the clan Ernaly's fighters were formidable hunters, accustomed to staying hidden for long periods, masters in the art of making themselves invisible on rugged terrain. Sheltered behind rocks and crevices, there was no way to detect their presence above the strategic pass. The two brothers commanding the Elvin army were hidden behind bushes on top of a ridge downstream, towards the end of the route, so as to embrace fully the battlefield.

Mynar dyl wielded just two javelins, which he could use at short range. He was thus preparing himself to assist Voryn dyl, a formidable expert with the longbow. Voryn dyl could hit a target with accuracy from up to two hundred feet away. Mynar dyl would supply him with flaming arrows during the battle. With their combined efforts, they planned to rain a deluge of iron and fire upon the attackers.

Soon, the Raiders, cursing and shouting, set their trained jackals loose upon the slopes of the pass. The howling wild beasts tore through the silence as they searched for prey.

"Let the scavenger dogs come. They will soon have plenty of human meat to feed upon," Voryn dyl declared raging.

They now had a direct view of the advancing enemy. One of the barbarian troops had already passed the first Elvin units without any of the jackals detecting their presence. Their sense of smell was being disrupted by animal scents that the Llewenti had taken care to spread overnight. Turning in circles, sniffing frantically in confusion, the beasts looked fatigued, provoking significant concern in their human masters. The second company of men passed, then the third. The barbarians were now almost at the other side of the bottleneck, just in front of the two Ernaly brothers, and almost within reach of Voryn dyl's arrows.

The men were completely surrounded by almost twice as many Elves hidden above them, completely unaware of their enemies' presence. But fear and doubt began to seize them. They stopped.

"They will give up any idea of progressing further," whispered Mynar dyl, who was waiting impatiently for the perfect moment to call the ambush. The whistle of a javelin through the air stopped Voryn dyl before he could respond. Thirty feet below, a barbarian fell, crying out in a scream of pain.

Immediately, the battle cry of the clan Ernaly's fighters roared all around the narrow pass of the Hadon, as if hundreds of hawks were calling out to signal a kill. The sky above the ridge was suddenly covered by a cloud of javelins, spears and arrows. A deluge of Elvin projectiles rained down upon the three barbarian units, trapped in the gorge. Archers were stationed along the entire length of the pass, on both sides, preventing the barbarians from taking any shelter as they tried to retreat. Men, like their jackal pets, fell one after the other, as the roars of the beasts mingled with the last of the human curses, in a vast, gory spectacle of death. If light arrows caused mere injuries to the barbarians, the javelins spared none. The clan Ernaly's fighters handled those formidable weapons with great skill. They targeted the wounded with no mercy.
Each new volley of arrows was ripping further holes in the barbarian ranks. In the merciless crossfire, barbarians were surging backwards in confusion, abandoning their wounded to the javelin-throwers. The survivors of the first attack could no longer see any way out. They all joined in a desperate attempt to flee. The path was strewn with the corpses of humans and beasts. Jackals sprinted in all directions, seized with terror, attacking their own masters, driven mad by the stench of their blood-stained fur.

Mynar dyl was by his brother's side, setting arrowheads alight and handing them over with great speed, so that Voryn dyl's fire was much faster and deadlier than any other archer. Feeling that victory was close at hand, the warlord of Tios Halabron turned to his loyal brother.

"They are disbanding. All will perish in this ravine."

An evil grin twitched into being upon Voryn dyl's lips. His eyes shone with unusual light: a reflection of the murderous madness that inhabited him.

"Let them all die there. War is now upon them."

Sixty paces below them, a lone, terrified barbarian had foregone his helmet, spear and shield in a supreme effort to reach the cover of some small trees. Voryn dyl drew back his longbow and released. The arrow pierced the temple of the unfortunate man, who fell immediately before rolling down the slope. His body came crashing onto the rocks at the bottom of the ravine.

"Miserable worm: may your soul return to your dragons' lair and burn there for eternity!" Voryn dyl screamed, overwhelmed with hatred.

For a long while still, Elvin projectiles continued to rain on the slopes of the Hadon. Of the three hundred barbarian warriors who had advanced into the pass, most were now lying on the rocks of the ravine, drenched in their own blood. Survivors had managed to flee and return to the shelter of their camp, under the protection of their rear guard. But, among the fleeing barbarians, many were terribly injured, and would pass from life to death before the day had ended. The victims of the Elvin arrows were now harassed by the hawks, which inflicted their own cruel wounds, piercing eyes and cutting ears. Few of those men would survive the dreadful pain their wounds would cause. The Elves of the clan Ernaly, now masters of the battlefield and galvanised by the magnitude of their victory, capped their success by finishing off the casualties who had been left behind, savagely mutilating them by removing their tongues. They also seized from the corpses everything that might have some value in the fights to come: weapons, armour, and most of all arrows.

Mynar dyl could not help regretting that the fame of this victory would be tarnished by such useless slaughter and mutilation. Voryn dyl answered him with a cold, sinister tone.

"I ordered this. These practices are the customs of the wild Elves. It is a way to strike fear into the hearts of our foes. These gullible barbarians have been made to believe by their evil shamans that a man without a tongue will not be allowed to enter the Dragons' lair after his death, and thus that his soul will be doomed to endlessly wander the underworld."

Mynar dyl was not convinced by this explanation, but he did not insist. His brother was a reliable servant and, just like a faithful hawk, he deserved to be rewarded from time to time with savage pleasures, which his complex nature sometimes demanded. There was no harm in that.

The warlord of Tios Halabron observed that the commanders of his units were giving instructions to regroup; everywhere his Elves were leaving their shelters on the slopes of the Hadon and heading to the edge of the Sognen Tausy woods. Arrow reserves had been replenished and, now that their position was revealed, they would no longer have the same advantage, were they to stay put. Mynar dyl thought it wise to use the opportunity that the quick victory had given them to disperse his archers around the foothills in the woods. His strategy was shrewd and unexpected. Speed, stealth and surprise: these were the clan Ernaly's best assets, and the warlord would use them to lead his army to victory. His strategy was always to be one step ahead. He felt confident, as he always did.

Before entering into the thickness of the woods, Mynar dyl looked up at the sky. High in the air, beyond the white clouds, flew three great eagles, moving east towards Mentollà and Llymar. They came from beyond the Strait of Tiude, from another island of the archipelago, probably from the peaks of Nyn Ernaly's mountains. The Llewenti considered these birds to be Eïwal Ffeyn's most trusted servants.

'The powers that the storm deity confers to the matriarchs are even greater than I expected. Omens are certainly favourable,' the warlord of Tios Halabron thought.

★★

11ᵗʰ day, Mentollà

Warm gusts were colliding with the cooler air, leaving the atmosphere polarised and volatile. The weather around Mentollà was stormy, though there was no rain. Dark clouds were racing towards the tower high above, as though in a hurry to watch the grim spectacle of the siege.

Feïwal was standing alone at the top of Mentollà's keep. From this high point, the Irawenti guide could see the barbarian army gathering around the fortress. Its number seemed to endlessly grow, as if that big trebuchet threatening their defences were some rallying point of for the immense masses of men. Lost in his thoughts, Feïwal obsessively replayed what Curwë had told him of Gelros' report.

"Our best scout is not one to exaggerate perils. The magnitude of this threat is indeed frightening. There are thousands of them. If we let them put their powerful trebuchet to work, our frail ramparts will not last long."

Turning towards the ocean, Feïwal addressed his prayers to the almighty deity of storms, who he knew would be their only salvation.

"Ô Eïwal Ffeyn, Ô mighty storm-bringer,
We are ever your faithful servants.
In your hands, I place our destiny,
To your will, I submit our lives.
May your wrath punish the defilers
Who have come to profane your shrine!
May your wrath bring about their ruin!"

The potential for High Magic was extremely high in the region of Mentollà, rich as it was in natural sources of energy: the ocean tide, the strong winds, the plentiful streams and the whispering woods. Unlike the western part of Nyn Llyvary, which was weakened by the desecrating presence of men, Mentollà was a wild region; its inherent strength was unspoiled, and its air was filled with the invisible influence of the deities, just as in the days of old.

The Flow of the Islands flooded through Feïwal and into his soul; his faith was growing stronger. It was a raw, chaotic magic that was difficult to control. He could sense the energy which emanated from the winds. Day by day, he had been forming a mystical connection with the land, weaving his own soul into that unseen web of living energy. His abilities now far surpassed the powers of other priests or wizards, who lacked the inherent skill necessary to command genuine High Magic.

Now, closing his eyes and calling upon Eïwal Ffeyn's support, Feïwal could see how the Islands' Flow was permeating the land before him, interacting with the elements and influencing all beings. He started performing rituals of immersion, channelling the gusts of wind to harness its energy. Bound to the sky was a mystical energy, the unsteady winds of the Islands' Flow, which was drifting towards Mentollà. From the top of the ruined tower, Feïwal acted as a focal point for those powerful gusts of magic that blew across the peninsula from the Austral Ocean. The drifting energies were being drawn to him, like water in a whirlpool: a vortex of High Magic. The Irawenti guide was draining the Islands' Flow: chaotic and inexperienced though his control over it was.

"Ô Eïwal Ffeyn, Ô mighty storm-bringer,
You do your servant much honour,
You bestow your follower with such trust,
Ô Eïwal Ffeyn! I praise you from the depths of my soul!"

Far to the west, flashes of lightning illuminated the silhouettes of three great birds, progressing high across the dark blue sky.

Feïwal was standing still on the edge of the parapet, as if frozen by the favour he had been blessed with. Storm Eagles were unknown in Essawylor, thought to exist only in tales, as the legendary birds praised by Llewenti priests. The Irawenti guide knew that the pact binding Storm Eagles to Eïwal Ffeyn was ancient, originating in the time of deities, when even the Elves had yet not appeared. Legends told that the mighty birds were known to be proud, haughty creatures that did not willingly obey command. The deity of winds showed extraordinary favour by letting his prized children come forth and rescue Feïwal and his community.

The three Storm Eagles were closing the distance that separated them from Mentollà with phenomenal speed. Soon they were circling around the tower. Raising his arms as though imploring the heavens, Feïwal saluted them, calling upon Eïwal Ffeyn to protect their coming.

The winged creatures whirled around the top of the keep, cautiously approaching it ever closer. Feïwal could now appreciate them in all their might, for their size was prodigious. The Irawenti guide and the legendary birds beheld each other in palpable mutual wonder. A form of communication was being initiated by the Storm Eagles; fragments of an unknown language reached Feïwal's mind without a single word being uttered.

"I am Feïwal dyn Filweni, Lord of Mentollà" he responded, caught off guard.

"You are not... You are Eïwal Ffeyn's servant, his envoy," the Irawenti guide understood, as the eagles responded in their telepathic tongue.

The great birds beat their wings, and their cry was heard from afar.

"IIIRWAA!"

And Feïwal echoed.

"IIIRWAA!"

His voice was altered and amplified, in the solemnity of that moment in which his destiny was being revealed to him.

The Storm Eagles spiralled upwards, high into the sky.

Feïwal breathed in deeply, his mind communing with the elements, avid to master the new force with which he had been bestowed. He began to mutter incantations, and the winds began to circle violently around him. In response, the rumbling thunder was heard from afar. Like one possessed, Feïwal began a frenzied dance.

The battle for control of the fortress walls was raging below. Elves were dying as they held their ground, while hundreds of barbarians were assembling on the field to maintain the assault. Feïwal continued his wild dance along the keep's highest parapet. He diced with death as his feet kicked out chaotically into the void. Light began to flash across the stormy clouds. A bolt of lightning suddenly came crashing down from the sky, striking the ground in front of the fortress walls. A roar of thunder tore through the air. The bolt killed many men, set fire to the clothes of others, and damaged barbarian equipment, provoking panic and chaos. The momentum of their attack seemed to falter for a moment, disrupted by this heavenly intervention.

Feïwal's face was illuminated by the lightning. His wild eyes betrayed the formidable wrath that now consumed him.

★

Roquendagor had not yet been seen among his troops at the heart of the battle. He had delegated command of his units to Maetor, who he trusted as his faithful lieutenant.

The knight stood high above the battle, on the upper platform of the keep, with his councillor Aewöl, behind a large, grey canvas, the colour of stone, which was concealing the war machine that the two Elves had designed and built. They were not hiding; they were calculating. And they were also arguing, apparently not in complete agreement about which firing angle they ought to begin with. The numerous tests they had run during the winter firing Ganol wallen, their ingenious war machine, had enabled them to set out a specific compass. They knew that their instrument should be able to hit any target within range with a high degree of accuracy.

"We should not allow the wind to affect our calculations, Aewöl. This is my final plea. The weight and speed of the projectiles are such that nothing will alter their trajectory."

"Very well, I concede; you have always showed prowess operating ranged weapons such as this. But you ought to have listened to me. My opinion is that we will be a few yards short our target. But time is of the essence. The enemy trebuchet will come into action any moment now; we need to stop it," urged Aewöl.

Made out of composite layers of wood from the Alwïryan, and from the remains of the ship's catapults and ballistae, Ganol wallen, or 'far-reaching death' as Roquendagor had named it, worked with a torsion spring and counterweight system. It could hurl large boulders with incredible force and precision: targeting from afar charging enemy soldiers, large ships, or, indeed, big siege engines.

Ganol wallen was clinging onto the keep's battlement in waiting, like an eagle with its claw dug into a high-up branch. It was manned by guards of the Unicorn. The crew was responsible for reloading the deadly war machine with boulders as well as specially made bolts, for it could also fire clutches of four missiles, the length of spears, at almost the same time.

Four hundred yards away, at the edge of the woods, the barbarian's gigantic trebuchet, the most dreaded war machine of the besiegers, was itself being loaded with heavy boulders by a large crew of men.

"Unveil Ganol wallen," ordered Roquendagor. His voice was strong, and his eye was proud. The four guards pulled back the large protective canvas, and 'far-reaching death' was revealed to all. "Prepare to fire," he instructed.

As Aewöl muttered powerful incantations, the large boulder loaded into the machine rapidly acquired a reddish colour, as if some hellish lava consumed it from the inside.

"Fire!" shouted Roquendagor.

His cry was so loud that it was heard all along the walls of Mentollà, and many were those who could not help but watch the fiery projectile as it completed its course: climbing high into the heavens before falling back down towards the ground. The red boulder came crashing down a few yards in front of its target, crushing several men who were standing in ranks operating their gigantic siege weapon. The boulder then bounced, severely wounding other barbarians, before finally striking the base of the trebuchet and coming to a halt. The big structure shook violently with the impact, and its component parts rattled together loudly. It swayed but did not go down.

"Fire the bolts," Roquendagor shouted anew.

Ganol wallen spat out bolts of fire at the enemy. Four spears, glowing red with Aewöl's magic, were released in rapid succession, crossing the battlefield with speed. With tremendous force, the long projectiles struck the barbarian crew manning the trebuchet. More warriors fell, impaled, their armour torn to shreds by the missiles.

"Reload! Reload while we adjust the angle," cried Aewöl. The crew, swiftly and skilfully, set about reloading another deadly volley.

Meanwhile, a wild cry resounded throughout the barbarian camp. The trebuchet was fired in response. The counterweight was released, and, as it fell, force of gravity pulled the attached throwing arm around the axle with significant rotational acceleration. But when the sling sent forth the projectiles with all the force of the swinging throwing arm, the boulders' trajectory was not as intended. The impact of the Elvin missile had set the siege engine off balance. Once released from the sling, the boulders did not travel at the angle required to crush Mentollà's gate, but rather they flew straight into the walls on the northern side of the fortress. With a loud noise, a section of the outer wall, recently mended rather hastily, now completely collapsed, opening up a large breach in Elvin defences.

From the top of the keep, a wild cry was heard.

"IIIRWA!"

The three Storm Eagles, who until now had been circling high above, watching as the battle developed and steering clear of the lightning strikes, now suddenly plunged down from the sky. As the barbarians approached the breach in the wall, the noble birds joined the throng. With their powerful talons, the great eagles swept down upon the attackers and tore them apart. Some who resisted were swiftly carried away with the power of the eagles' wings before being cast down upon rocks at the bottom of the cliffs. The winged creatures' destructive power was unleashed upon the enemy with great savagery, but the men were numerous. Hurling spears and firing arrows, the barbarians managed to chase the great eagles away. Yet, the Elves had gained some crucial respite, during which Luwir had rushed to the breached wall with a full unit of archers. Once his fighters had taken their positions, he ran to the northern flanking tower of the fortress wall in order to command their defence of the breach.

Roquendagor's cry was heard once more from the top of the keep's battlements.

"Fire again!"

Another fiery boulder flew high into the air above the heads of the barbarian warriors, who collectively flinched at its approach. This time, the heavy missile came crashing straight into the heart of the trebuchet. The gigantic construction shook, tilted and finally fell to the ground, utterly destroyed. Its fall whipped up a large cloud of dust, which added to the confusion among the ranks of the barbarian army; none could tell how many more had been killed. Some did not have time to ponder this question for long, for a volley of fiery spears soon shot out at them through the billowing dust to take their lives too.

Hope soon returned to the defending Elves; for hours, Ganol wallen, now sole master of the battlefield, continued its reign of terror with regular devastating bombardments. From time to time, lightning would also strike the battlefield, causing ever more barbarian casualties. The waves of the assault had soon retreated back into the protection of the woods, like an afternoon tide withdrawing into the ocean.

"Black arrow!" suddenly cried one of the Unicorn guards operating the siege engine, as he loaded more long spears into the war machine. "Look! A black arrow is shooting straight up, extremely high into the sky. Oh! See it bursts into a shadowy rain!"

"It is Gelros," exclaimed Aewöl. He could not see the spectacle, positioned as he was in the machine's innards, adjusting its angle.

"A second black arrow has just been shot from the woods."

"Gelros warns us of immediate danger," said Roquendagor.

"From the sea," Aewöl added. "A second arrow signifies the danger is coming from the sea," he insisted; all turned towards the azure surface of the Bay of Gloren.

"A third!" the Unicorn guard suddenly exclaimed.

All stood motionless for a moment, watching the third dark arrow climb in the air to an impossible altitude, before bursting into shards of black pieces. 'What can this mean?' all wondered, without uttering a single word.

"The threat will come from the air," was Aewöl's answer to the unspoken question.

Indeed, a moment later, all watched in horror as dark form emerged from the barbarian army's camp. It was heading straight for Mentollà. A reptilian monster with large wings, two legs and a very long tail was now flying above the treetops. It gained speed as it approached the keep from the west. The creature, the colour of red fire, was twenty feet long. It had the head of a dragon.

"How is this possible..." exclaimed one of the Unicorn guards, struck with incredulity.

"Run! It is a wyvern! Run for cover!" yelled Aewöl and he rushed into the keep's stairs to find protection.

Two of the elite fighters found shelter behind their war machine, holding their spears firm. But Roquendagor had other instructions for the two guards that stood by his side. Grasping a heavy lance, and moving along the parapet to meet his opponent, the tall knight cried out his order.

"We fight!"

The red wyvern narrowly skimmed the tops of the fortress walls, impervious to the flimsy arrows being shot up from the battlements. It beat its huge wings, rapidly gaining altitude, and soon it was by the walkway at the top of a tower, flying straight at the small group of three Elves. The impact was extremely violent. The spears of the High Elves broke against the creature's skin, failing to pierce its scales, which proved as resistant as steel armour. One of the two guards was immediately knocked off the parapet, silently falling to his death a hundred feet below. His armour, along with his body, was torn into pieces.

The second fighter was caught by the Wyvern's tail. The long reptilian limb wrapped around him; a moment later, he could only utter a horrible, muffled cry of pain as the deadly sting at the end of the tail drilled itself into his mouth, injecting its poisonous liquid. Soon afterwards, he was being burnt from the inside out, his entrails consumed by fire. Dying in horrendous pain, he turned back to his lord, imploring assistance that could never be given.

Roquendagor was trying to get back to his feet. The impact had propelled him against the wall of the tower. He watched the wyvern leap out into the void before it regained altitude and turned back to attack once more.

Suddenly, a bolt of lightning tore through the sky with a deafening crack, its flash illuminating the stormy landscape. The lightning almost struck the monstrous creature as if flew, causing it to divert its course away from the danger.
Roquendagor, emboldened by this heavenly intervention, ran to grab his two-handed sword that he had left close to the war machine.
The wyvern was coming back. Its attack was aimed directly at Ganol wallen, which appeared to be its real target. Roquendagor rushed forward, his sword high in the air, yelling his war cry.

"Roq Laorn!"[78]

The tall knight brought down his long blade with unbelievable strength. The impact was tremendous. The metal cut through scale, flesh and bone. The creature's right leg was severed. The wyvern landed heavily on the tower's walkway, its formidable momentum sending it crashing straight into the war machine. The catapult was knocked clean off the battlements; it came crashing to the ground at the foot of the tower, taking its two unfortunate operators down with it. With a shrill howl, the wyvern managed to take off again. The wounded creature was flying with difficulty over Mentollà's creek in an effort to

---

78 Roq Laorn: 'Charge Unicorn' in lingua Hawenti

escape, when suddenly a second bolt of lightning struck it: this time directly. The wyvern fell from the sky onto the rocks of the shore.

Roquendagor was gradually catching his breath. Stolid as ever, he looked up the wall of the keep and saw, on the highest platform, the azure silhouette of Feïwal. The Irawenti guide, dancing dangerously close to the void, was paying tribute to the elements.

Relieved but still shocked by the confrontation, Roquendagor looked towards the Bay of Gloren with scrutiny. There was neither sail nor boat on the horizon.

"Where are you, Nelwiri?" he grumbled.

★★

12th day, Hills of the Arob Salwy

The army of Llymar had set up camp on the tops of the Arob Salwy hills. It was a great force, almost two thousand strong, made up of sixty units of light infantry from the clans Llyvary and Avrony. All were entrenched behind a line of wooden fortifications and natural trenches. Six days had passed since it had reached its position, and so far, the Elvin army had not left the protection of its base, even though the siege of Mentollà was now well under way. The lethargy which reigned in the camp cruelly contrasted with the savage fighting taking place at the same time below the walls of the fortress.

Standing boulders, carved with runes, marked the borders of the army's camp. Wardens marched along the perimeter upon great stilts, which provided them with unnatural agility. They evolved like living trees. The vegetation around them, with its leaves and branches moving slowly in the wind, seemed to be assisting the sentries and watch stones as they guarded the camp. Loam and mist spread throughout the forest's hollows and glades. The place was filled with an ethereal music. It was as though the macabre events taking place a dozen leagues away had no bearing whatsoever upon the army and its commanders here.

The war council had been called. Sixteen noble dyl of the clan Llyvary were gathered around their natural leader, the 'Old Bird' Tyar dyl, warlord of Llafal. As discussions were being held in the command tent, it was clear that Gal dyl and Dyoren, the two dignitaries of the lesser clans, were being paid little attention, despite their reputation and status.
These handfuls of dyl were the commanders of the clan Llyvary's army. Their authority came from their bloodline, as their mothers were matriarchs and the blood of Eïwal Vars, the deity of war, flowed in their veins. Each dyl had inherited a rank, along with the command of a certain number of units, according to the station of his birth. A dyl answered to the warlord of his city and ultimately to the Protector of the Forest, but his true allegiance always lay with his clan. Thus, the highborn of the principal Llewenti clan favoured their most seasoned warrior to defend them against the enemy.

Tyar dyl, the 'Old Bird', appeared as serene as a peaceful lake, as he reminded the dyl of their instructions.

"The Council of the Matriarchs has entrusted us to guard the western glades of Llymar. We must be vigilant and ensure that all who try to cross the Arob Salwy shall meet their end. The plight of others is not our concern. Our duty is to protect our cities from those who seek to invade them. We must wage battle against any despoilers trying to corrupt the Forest of Llymar."

In the defence of their woodland realm, the Llewenti were known to be deadly and unforgiving. They were wilfully cruel in their efforts to preserve the borders of their territories. During their long history on the archipelago, they had been forced to surrender two whole islands, and countless territories, forests and grasslands to their enemies. Llymar Forest was their most sacred realm. Anyone threatening its sanctity provoked the Llewenti clans' wrath. Over time, they had developed an intrinsic bond with the legendary forest, and they believed that their fates were entwined.

"And what if, this time, we ought to join a fight beyond our borders to save us from a future threat?" questioned Dyoren, the Lonely Seeker. His tone was respectful; He was mindful that eighteen of the twenty commanders present were dyl of the clan Llyvary.

"We should not interfere with events taking place beyond our own land," Tyar dyl firmly replied. "We must only ever engage in combat at home, where the powerful High Magic of our matriarchs protects us, and where the spirits of the Forest can be awakened to confront the invaders."

The old warlord spoke with assurance, for Lyrine herself had entrusted him with this mission.

"Let us pursue the strategy we have agreed upon," Nerin dyl Llyvary concurred. "So far it has proven deadly to those who wish us harm. Those men we killed barely even saw us before they were struck down. I did not lose a single archer from my units. From here, we can leap from the trees to cut down the barbarians with stealth and speed, before vanishing back into the woods."

All Llewenti were highly skilled archers, and masters of the sudden ambush in woodland surroundings. The clan Llyvary's fighters were determined combatants with unparalleled stealth.

"And how many have you killed, Nerin dyl, in the past three days? Twenty, perhaps thirty? Can you not see that there are thousands of barbarians surrounding Mentollà? I do not doubt your courage, my young companion, I simply question our strategy," insisted Dyoren.

As he spoke, his hand caressed the blade of his fabled broad sword, Rymsing, reminding all these young Elves who he was. The Lonely Seeker continued.

"What I saw yesterday deserves your attention. Almit Dol Etrond has achieved what we do not dare even attempt. He has fulfilled his vow and completed his part of Curubor's plan."

"Tell us what has happened!" demanded Nerin dyl, suddenly curious.

"I joined the troops of House Dol Etrond when they positioned themselves on the western flank of the barbarian army," explained Dyoren. "They were relatively few, only a dozen units, but all were prepared to fight from horseback. The high helm of Etrond was their rallying point. Despite his usual reluctance to wear the great helm, Almit Dol Etrond had decided to make an exception. The warlord of Tios Lluin positioned his knights close to the banks of the river Sian Tiude, where a vast clearing allowed for a promising charge. They circled the human army and found a ford upstream to gain access to their final position. Once hidden by the foliage of the trees at the edge of the glade, they waited calmly, letting the barbarian army pass by."

"I imagine they were waiting patiently for the most promising opportunity to earn glory. Those arrogant High Elves always believe they will prevail in the end, whoever the opponents," one of the youngest dyl Llyvary sarcastically commented.

But Dyoren disagreed, "Almit knows the character of his proud cavaliers; his role was to protect them from their own folly. He waited, for a long time, holding his magnificent stallion with a firm hand, until his prey was finally within range. In the late afternoon, battalions of barbarian warriors protecting the shamans of the Dragons' Cult reached the main ford on the Sian Tiude River. These elite troops were looking after the most important dignitaries of that accursed religion. Their mules carried precious supplies.

Without so much as a spoken command, Almit moved his steed forward. Immediately, House Dol Etrond units followed, ready to finally unleash themselves upon their foes.

The barbarian battalions were still struggling through the deep waters of the ford when a rain of fire started to pour down upon the men, setting their clothes aflame, burning their flesh and terrifying their mules. Flaming arrows unerringly found their targets. Enormous confusion already reigned among the barbarian ranks when the cavalry charge hit them.

No man can equal the prowess of the knights of the Blue Helm, nor their incredible horsemanship. They rode unflinchingly into the heart of the battle. They threw themselves against the disordered human ranks, reckless and unforgiving. They tore through the enemy, driving deep into their lines: trampling scores of barbarians beneath their horses' hooves and pushing others off the ford and into the river... Let it be recognised that, yesterday, Almit Dol Etrond won an important victory."

"Then we must rejoice, and honour those victorious knights," concluded Tyar dyl, but his tone was ironic, and he did not hesitate to make his position clear. "But we are not High Elves. How many defeats during the kin-slaying wars of old taught us this lesson? We do not possess their might in battle, and we never will ...Furthermore..."

But Gal dyl, unable to contain his impatience and disagreement with the current strategy, suddenly interrupted this litany of well-rehearsed arguments. Until then, he had remained in the shadows within the tent, like one waiting for an opportunity to spring. The warlord of the clan Avrony turned towards Tyar dyl and violently addressed him.

"How can you think that the Protector of the Forest will remain at the rear and watch, while other Elves fight and give their blood for our cause?" he intervened. "No, the rear guard is no place for one who wields the Spear of Aonyn. I will lead the clan Avrony to the walls of Mentollà. I will lead the assault. The time has come."

"Your clan's fighters are barely three hundred, Gal dyl. What do you think you can achieve?" Tyar dyl replied coolly, with all the confidence of a commander who had direct authority over fifty units.

The clan Avrony's fighters were brave, relentless hunters, experts at harassing their enemies from the trees, and they could also call upon the help of the spirits and creatures of the woods. But charging an enemy head-on during a pitched battle was an altogether different matter.

Nevertheless, Dyoren, who until now had remained calm, now spoke up. "These are noble words, worthy of a High Warlord of the Llewenti, Gal dyl. Rymsing, the Blade of the West will march at your side. Let our enemies confront the Protector and the Seeker... together," he added. The legendary bard stepped forward, his noble face appearing in the light.

This resounding support had come at the right time for Gal dyl, who now decided to pursue his advantage.

"We are not fighting an army of thousands... Our enemy is much weaker than you think Tyar dyl. Its power is in fact very limited. What we are facing is a small group of fanatics: a Dragon Warrior, a dozen shamans of his cursed Cult, and a few battalions of elite warriors who serve them. The rest of their army is composed of peasants, farmers, and craftsmen, terrorized and driven into war by tyranny and fear. Those people would much prefer to bow before the Druids, their former rulers. I can affirm that with certainty."

The Protector of the Forest looked around to observe the impact of his words before continuing.

"The tactics we have pursued until now have been inefficient and counterproductive. By harassing them but keeping our distance, we have only been hitting the weakest and most useless men of the barbarian army. We are not inflicting any damage whatsoever upon the core troops who reside at the heart of the army, well protected by their slave companions. We are letting them preserve their genuine soldiers for their attack on the walls of Mentollà: their real objective. The castaways have already successfully fought off two assaults, displaying extraordinary courage. But their capacity to resist is not infinite; if they at all falter, they will be immediately destroyed. Mentollà will eventually fall. Do you understand?"

"Then what are we to do?" asked Nerin dyl dubiously. The young captain of Llafal was showing more agitation than he wanted to demonstrate.

Suddenly the council was interrupted by the unexpected arrival of a sentry. Admitted by the Protector of the Forest's guards, he immediately regretted his interruption.

"Noble Tyar dyl, I apologise for disturbing your debates."

"What is it? Why are you so agitated?"

"It is the prisoner... He is gone," announced the sentry.

"What do you mean he is gone?" asked the 'Old bird', angry and surprised.

"He has fled. He broke free from his bonds. Somehow, he untangled the ropes that we tied and must have climbed down the pine tree... he has gone," admitted the sentry, helpless.

"No one saw him escape?" questioned Nerin dyl furiously.

"Yes and no... He stole some equipment: a bow, daggers, arrows, rope and some clothes. He was seen heading towards the sea, to the cliffs."

"You shall pay for this!" threatened Nerin dyl with the contempt of a Llewenti high-born towards an Elf of lesser lineage.

Gal dyl intervened once again, anxious to show his authority. "It was stupid enough to imprison the Irawenti messenger in the first place. To have let him escape is idiocy. You are a fool... Now return to your duties."

"The fate of this acrobat is the least of our concerns. I fear he will have difficulty reaching his brethren in Mentollà, for several battalions of barbarian warriors lie in his way. Let him roam the coastline freely; we have other priorities," concluded Tyar dyl calmly.

★★

12th day, Mentollà

The Elves in the fortress compound were anxious, for they feared that they could not hold out much longer. Thick clouds were obscuring the moon intermittently, and the trees of the forest were creaking in the wind, providing an ominous underscore to the prevailing darkness. They had been watching the glade in front of Mentollà's walls all night, until the golden rays of dawn began to shine through the foliage. All could see no sign of their enemies' preparations; their vigilance soon waned as their thoughts became suffused with concern.

As morning broke, the barbarians started building great pyres to burn their dead. Pillars of smoke stained the sky with the mingled ashes of human corpses and wood. As the army of men prepared for a third day of battle, none could ignore the signs that the forest was suffering.

There came the haunting sound of a horn, accompanied by the baying of hounds and the war cries of the Dragon Cult's followers. Tall and strong in his blood-red armour, Ka-Bloozayar brandished his powerful lance before his assembled battalions and bellowed his challenges to the Elves of Mentollà. A fierce, evil energy swelled from the Dragon Warrior, and all the barbarian soldiers who looked upon him were filled with a burning hatred and a furious temerity.

The smoke from the smouldering dead flooded the battlefield.

The barbarians charged forward, their eyes afire with their Dragon Gods' furious power, like rabid hounds ready to tear their enemy apart with fang and claw. Hundreds upon hundreds of men ran forward, determined to storm the walls of Mentollà. The violence of the assault was such that all Elves within the compound were summoned to answer the challenge. Soon, the weak gates were once again broken down, and the bloody melee began.

Roquendagor had led armies through conflict many times. He prided himself on his mastery of the art of war. He could demonstrate prowess while commanding large numbers of units from a distance, and he was also capable of fighting blade to blade in the heat of combat. His sharp, incisive mind enabled him to read the ebb and flow of any battle before it unfolded.

Roquendagor stood on top of the tower's steps. From this high position, he saw that the flow of the barbarians would soon overwhelm the troops holding the gate.

"The time for me to join the battle has come. Let them face the knight of the Unicorn," he decided.

Roquendagor felt no fear. He was inhabited only by certainty. He had studied and practised warfare and personal combat for such a long time that he believed his skill was unmatched. The knight felt that he could wield his weapon with such speed and precision that opponents did not stand a chance.

Roquendagor moved towards the gate with determination. Despite being clad in his black full plate armour and hindered by a tall purple helm, he moved gracefully and swiftly. His closest companions were on his heels, fully armed for battle. Reaching the walls, they proclaimed loudly the coming of their lord.

"Hail to Roquendagor! Hail to our champion!" Curwë yelled frantically, powerfully beating his drums to accompany his cries. "The White Unicorn enters the fight! Hail to Roquendagor! Hail to our commander!" he repeated like one possessed. His drums resounded obsessively.

The archers ceased firing to watch the knight's coming. Their faces expressed dread but, such was the reverential respect and wonder they felt in that moment, they all cried in awe. The voice of Maetor was heard, shouting orders. The two units of Unicorn guards opened their ranks to let their lord join them in the fray.

A few moments later, Roquendagor was at the centre of the deadly melee. Wherever he sent his blows, the knight was so agile and dangerous that he struck down all his foes with a frequency that few, even among his guards, could match. Soon, he had felled a full line of barbarian warriors.

Although he lacked the Blade of the Unicorn, that Dol Lewin heirloom fashioned in Ystanlewin's forge and held by his family for hundreds of years before being irremediably lost, Roquendagor was an expert wielder of a myriad of weapons: equally deadly with a lance, spear or sword.

He possessed courage that was second to none, and an unshakable sense of duty towards his elite guards. Much was expected of his coming and, indeed, his charge invigorated his troops and caused considerable damage to the barbarians' ranks. Roquendagor fought with great sweeps of his blade, the air itself was humming as his weapon weaved a web of death that only the very best barbarian warriors managed to survive. Fighting knee-deep among the corpses of those who had fallen at the gate, the tall knight inflicted grievous wounds upon any man that dared confront him.

After an hour of ceaseless combat, the entrance to the compound had become so choked with the bodies of the dead barbarians that the access was completely denied.

Roquendagor decided to retreat, fatigued with the chaos of the battle. He needed to distance himself from the bloody melee to understand the way the fight for the gate was progressing. He joined Aewöl, safely positioned in the shadows of the stronghold. Dressed in a long, dark green cloak which masked his black chain mail, his councillor could survey the entire battle without being seen.

Breathing deeply, Roquendagor threw away his heavy helmet. Unexpectedly, a strong gust of wind disturbed his movements. The air moved persistently around him, altered by an unnatural force.

"What is this sorcery?" he muttered to himself.

But then his eye was caught by the bright, flamboyant figure of Feïwal, up in the air, perched on the edge of the keep's highest parapet like an ethereal vision. Roquendagor turned back towards the small air spirit, now attentive to its convulsions. It suddenly vanished in a small explosion, the air penetrating deep into the High Elf's ears, nose and throat.

Roquendagor heard like a whisper in the wind. "The northern wall is about to fall."

Looking up towards Feïwal, he noticed that the Irawenti guide was pointing towards the other battlefield, where Luwir was in command.

Standing beside Roquendagor, Aewöl immediately captured the essence of the warning. Indeed, his anxious gaze had often turned towards the north, where the wall had been breached by the initial trebuchet attack, and where the defenders now had to fight among the rubble. Aewöl decided to oversee the situation himself. Calling upon Curwë for assistance, he moved quickly along the compound walls towards the second battlefield.

The fortress walls facing Gloren Bay were strengthened by a vast, round flanking tower which overlooked the defences of the northern part of the compound. It provided additional support to the central keep. Built at the edge of the primitive fortification and at its highest point, the rock at the foot of the round tower had been carved into a slope in order to make scaling difficult. It was now their best defence against an intrusion into the compound's courtyard now that the wall had been irremediably breached. Aewöl and Curwë could see that the narrow opening in the tower facing the slope was, for the time being, enabling the defenders to repel their enemies. Arrow slits, loopholes and battlements enabled the Irawenti units to halt the progress of the assailants while they remained protected.

From this position, Luwir, who commanded these troops, was well protected behind a large stone overlooking the bulwark. He handled with skill a crossbow made of composite exotic wood, tendon and horn bow. The advantage of the weapon lay in its range and force, as its bolts could be shot at great speed and cause considerable damage. It was much more effective defending a wall than for use on the battlefield, for it was heavy and took time to reload.

But bolts and arrows soon became inefficient, as the assailants finally succeeded in approaching the breach. Aewöl rushed to the Irawenti commander's hideout.

"Luwir, switch to your heavy, short-range projectiles."

"Hear me, Elves of Filweni!" Luwir immediately called out with a warlike gesture. "Throw down stones and quicklime, over the ramparts and through the trap-doors!"

"We must prevent them getting through what is left of the walls! They have brought ladders. They will attempt to climb!" shouted Aewöl in the confusion.

Moments later, several battalions of elite barbarian warriors, Ka-Bloozayar's personal soldiers judging by the cut of their red armour, launched a decisive assault on the weakest point of the fortress' defences. Overwhelmed, Luwir's units were inundated by the flow of attackers, and were about to lose the control of the damaged battlements. Quickly, Aewöl could understand the situation with lucidity.

He ran towards the ruined wall, jumped and then climbed up the stones like a spider in its web. As Aewöl clung onto the wall, he cried powerful utterances in a dark tongue.

His hands clutched the dirt and the clay between the stones. His loud incantations began to create a seismic disturbance in the wall; the vibrations were concentrated on a specific point a few feet above where he hung. The vibrations soon became intense tremor, cracking stones apart and forcing the entire wall to shake dangerously. Larger cracks appeared, before a weak part of the wall started to collapse. A huge chunk of it broke away and tumbled towards the assailants, killing a score of them. Some barbarians were crushed directly, while others were buried under the rubble.

The lower part of the wall was completely fractured, but the large central stones still held. The defenders, while completely exhausted, regained some hope.

Aewöl uttered another potent incantation. Thin, wispy flames began to surround his body, shedding a pale light around him. They had soon enveloped him, and an unnatural force emanated from his fiery being. Aewöl unexpectedly leapt from the wall towards the dry moat. He landed safely ten feet below, upon the branches that had been built up by the barbarians into a makeshift bridge. The fire around him had already begun to spread when he ignited an incandescent explosion beneath his feet. The entire improvised structure had now caught fire. The pine branches that it was largely made of were burning fast. The clothes and hair of the men were also set alight in the blaze. The barbarians on the bridge were leaping to their left or right, down to the floor of the dry moat, rolling on the ground in the hope of extinguishing the flames.

Their chiefs, sheltered by their armour, did their best to extinguish the flames that had caught those wearing only leather coats for protection. Bolts and stones hailed down upon them continuously. Flayed, tired and burned, the survivors climbed as best they could to the top of the slope and out of the moat, clinging to every hand held out to them. They fell back amid the shouts, screams and challenges of the Elves. A pile of ashes and charred human carcasses was all that remained of their improvised bridge.

As he walked further along the edge of the moat, Aewöl caught sight of the enemy chief, Ka-Bloozayar, positioned at a safe distance but close enough to have witnessed the destruction of his battalions. Aewöl drew his two black swords. He saw the groups of men who were scurrying around, trying to soothe their burns or wounds. All cursed the Elvin silhouettes dancing on top of the fortress' ramparts. The victory was complete and, carried away by the success, and impervious to his magical fire, Aewöl progressed into the burning trench, sowing death with his two dark blades. But, to his astonishment, the Dragon Warrior jumped down to join him, ignoring the danger and burning flames. His formidable blood armour glowed, uninflected by the burning flames.

Caught off-guard, Aewöl quickly made up his mind. He decided to flee to the breach of the fortress' wall. He quickly passed over the corpses, swift and agile thanks to his light chain mail. He reached the gap. He turned back one last time to check how much distance he had put between him and his opponent. A long, heavy spear hit him on the left of his helmet, knocking it clean off. Incredible pain seared through him; it felt as if half of his head had been blown away. Relying on his ferocious will and the last of his strength, he managed to climb the stones that led out of the burning ditch and into the compound. A hand grabbed him.

"Ah! Your left eye! You need assistance immediately!" screamed Curwë, horrified, as he pulled him aside to find cover.

"I cannot see!" cried Aewöl. As he touched the left side of his face, he realised that his eye was punctured, and the socket had been broken. Aewöl fainted.

"Help! Help! Aewöl is dying! Can we not get some help? Aewöl is dying!" Curwë yelled frantically.

Archers rushed to rescue Aewöl, whose condition looked desperate. Obeying Curwë's instructions, they carried him back to the keep, where Arwela and the ladies were inside arranging care for the wounded.

Meanwhile, the ocean wind began to rise, blowing from the coast towards the forest, from Mentollà to the barbarian camp. It soon became extraordinarily strong, and, in the whistling of the squall, many men heard incantations in an unknown language. Already some of the burning branches were being swept down the slope which separated the fortress from the forest. The foliage was dry. The heather began to ignite first, and it was soon followed by the ferns. Finally, the fire spread to the huge pine trees, whose cones were soon exploding in the heat.

The men initially reacted feverishly, their leaders still reeling from their defeat at the fortress walls. They sought to extinguish the many fires that had now begun on the edge of the woods. All wondered where this sudden, forceful breeze might have come from. But soon order and discipline gave way, and many fled in panic, for the wind was still coming in hard and was now blowing at different angles, reviving the smouldering blaze in the dry moat. Countless glowing embers were now flying through the air, carried by the breath of the fire that was now unstoppable. The retreat was ordered, as some of the barbarian tents had already caught fire. Horns began to blow as the shamans, with some difficulty, restored order among the ranks and arranged the evacuation of their base camp.

★★

12th day, shores of the Gloren peninsula

'What I am doing here is very, very, very stupid! I cannot believe I am doing it at all. Siw! I was known as the happiest Irawenti in Essawylor because of how carefree and reckless I was. And yet here I am, attempting this desperately dangerous journey to join my clan, who themselves are locked in what promises to be the most hopeless siege in the history of warfare! How have I come to this? I curse my suicidal loyalty to my kin!'

Despite this torment, Nelwiri kept himself busy with intensive preparations. He was making the best of the equipment he had stolen from the Llewenti army during his escape. Still frantic, like an Elf possessed, he continued to mutter in his dialect.

'The clan Llyvary's guards were easy to trick. No doubt they underestimated my abilities. I have spent my entire life high up in the masts of Essawylor ships, playing with nodes and pulleys. They should have known I would break free from my bonds, even though I was suspended from the top of a tree, twenty yards above the ground...'

Taking a small axe, he set about carving a rough log. He skilfully cut the pinewood, shaping what appeared to be a wide plank. He grasped an arrow plumed with green feathers, selecting the longest and most solid he could find in the quiver. He tied a thin rope to the shaft. Using knots of his own invention, he added further ropes and string to extend it. Happy with his achievement, he tested the solidity of his improvised harpoon. Nelwiri's features suddenly stiffened when he realised that the cordage was not long enough for his purpose. After pondering for a while, he smiled. He had found an alternative solution.

"Siw! If I'm going to do something mad, there's no point being half-hearted about it," he thought.

He pressed the arrowhead against the freshly cut piece of wood and began a long, guttural incantation.

"I have not used this spell for some time, and I'm not quite sure what the last words are. But no matter; the rune I am using on both objects is the most important part of it anyway," Nelwiri optimistically concluded.

He carefully engraved a complicated inscription onto both the arrow shaft and the plank.

"I suppose this is it," he concluded before taking several deep breaths. "I will miss the ocean's scents! If I die today, it's this I will miss the most. O Gweïwal Uleydon! You are the only witness of this exploit! May you grant me a little more life, if only so I can recount this madness to the next generations of Filweni!"

Nelwiri boldly strode up the cliff's edge and threw the plank out at the sea below with all his strength. The piece of wood fell from a height of more than sixty feet before hitting the surface of the water. It did not take long for it to surface above the foam. Meanwhile, Nelwiri notched the unusual harpoon he had so carefully prepared. He securely tied the end of the rope to his belt. Though his new bow had a fairly long range, he would rely on the support of the strong sea winds to reach his target. Nelwiri breathed in the wind and began his loud incantations.

He fired his arrow directly upwards, towards the clouds. The rope began to unroll rapidly, as though the arrow were being pulled up by some unnatural force. The arrow continued to climb in the sky until it paused. It did not fall back to where it had come from as one might expect, but rather it was taken by the ocean breeze towards the sea. Nelwiri did not bother to track his arrow's course; he stepped back, began his run-up and, before the rope had fully unwound, dived into the sea from the top of the cliff.
It was a great plunge that only the most desperate of Elves would have attempted. The Irawenti sailor came crashing down onto the sea like a meteorite hitting solid ground. For a long moment, only the rippling circles of water caused by the impact could be seen on the surface. There was a long silence, disturbed only by the sound of the sea.

Suddenly, the arrow, still being carried through the air by the winds, flew down, and struck the bottom corner of the floating plank, making a loud noise of shattering wood. The cord attached to the arrow began to tighten. Nelwiri emerged violently to the surface of the water, gasping desperately for air, like a prisoner who had escaped a deadly oubliette. It took him some time to realise that he had, in fact, survived.

"Cil, Cim, Cir! No one will believe this. I am sure no one will believe it," he kept repeating, laughing out loud. He swam and pulled on his rope until he reached the improvised long board a hundred yards away. The current in the bay was strong, and he had already moved a long way from the shore.

"Now, let us see if I can reach Mentollà on this makeshift boat," he thought. "Gloren Bay must be around twenty leagues across. I cannot even see the outline of the Sognen Tausy coastline to the west. It could take me more than a day, depending on how the currents evolve."

★★

13th day, Mentollà

In the west, one league southeast of Mentollà, a barbarian sentry looked up, his senses alert, like a wild dog sniffing the air. He was worrying about a distant, repetitive echo which was odd considering how early it was. He cautiously approached the old road that connected Mentollà to Tios Halabron, taking care to hide behind the many tree trunks that lined the abandoned path. As the noise got closer, it became more distinct and grew in intensity. The man decided to hide, consumed by fear.

A flock of night birds swept along the trail, twisting and turning through the trees, searching for hiding places. The man lay down, frozen by shock. He did not sound his horn to warn the other barbarian sentinels carefully positioned by Ka-Bloozayar at the rear of the camp.

The man was soon found by a flock of birds that then set upon him. He got up, batting away his attackers with the flat of his axe, trying to reach his horn. Suddenly, a wild animal cry interrupted the ferocious struggle. The man gasped in disbelief while the birds disappeared into the night. Incredulous, he stood still and alert for a moment. He glimpsed an arrow flying into a nearby tree on his right, its pale glow illuminating the undergrowth. An Elvin war cry sounded, and a javelin whistled through the air. The man fell. A warrior of the clan Avrony, resplendent in the clan's distinctive peacock feathers, emerged from the shadows. He approached the dead body, retrieved his javelin and took care to extinguish the glowing arrow. Behind him on the abandoned trail, other Llewenti fighters passed as swiftly as spectres between the shadows of the tall trees. They too were searching for prey.

Dawn was breaking when the clan Avrony's scouts gathered within a league of Mentollà. In under an hour, they had managed to dispose of every barbarian sentinel. A few horns had been sounded, but they had been weak and soon muffled, so no general alarm had been triggered. The brave Llewenti fighters were paving the way for the remainder of Llymar's units to assault the rear guard of the barbarian army.

Suddenly, a great noise was heard at the edge of the forest, south of Mentollà's walls.

Cries of "Avrony! Avrony! Llymar! Llymar!" resounded on the flanks of the barbarian battalions, and a great shock ran through the entire barbarian army as Gal dyl led the charge.

The cries were those of his fiercest fighters. Ten units of the clan Avrony, some two hundred and fifty Elves, lightly armed with spears and short swords, suddenly set upon the barbarians. Each attacker, overwhelmed by hatred, had the death of a relative or a household to avenge. They did not coordinate their attack, rushing in murderously, choosing their opponents at random, like vultures tearing into their prey.

Urging his fighters into battle with his cries, Gal dyl was at the forefront of the charge. Reaching full speed, he raised his fist and hurled the Spear of Aonyn. The formidable weapon flew a long distance; emitting a high-pitched whistle before it eventually struck its target. The first victim fell, causing confusion among the enemy ranks... It was the beginning of a long and bloody trail of human corpses; each time the Spear of Aonyn found its mark, it would disappear from its victim's corpse and reappear in Gal dyl's hand.

The clan Avrony's attackers followed their warlord to the fight in a collective frenzy, galvanised by the incredible power of the holy weapon. None but Gal dyl could wield the long Spear of Aonyn, and each time he launched it at the enemy, another skull would crack, or another torso would be pierced. The first battalion of barbarians had been scattered by Gal dyl's charge, like a flock of sparrows by an eagle. The clan Avrony's fighters were masters of woodland warfare. They swiftly struck the head of the barbarian ranks with fatally accurate volleys of arrows and javelins, before charging forth to slay the survivors with a flurry of blades. Buoyed by their success, they pushed forward, without discernible strategy.

At first, they stayed in a line, as they tried to overwhelm their opponents by circumventing their flanks. The Avrony fighters enclosed the disconcerted barbarians in a circle of arrows. Light arrows and heavy javelins tore into the men; many were soon laying face-down in the mud. Gal dyl's troops handled their heavy spears with horrific accuracy. The tips of their lances had been forged in Tios Lluin and were covered with magical runes of war. Each time these deadly weapons were thrown, a new victim would fall, some were killed quickly, and others suffered a long and painful death. None of the defenders were adequately protected against such an assault, even those who believed themselves invulnerable behind their thick wooden shields. As the clan Avrony's units continued to push forward and gain ground, the barbarians began falling back to their camp. A hundred corpses now littered the ground. Many were dying. The wounded groaned, pleading in vain that their conquerors spare them their lives.

Ka-Bloozayar's minions contained the fugitives, urging them to fight. Now enveloped by bands of Elves, the surviving barbarians struggled hard in close combat to prevent a complete routing of their army. The barbarian chief had sent instructions to his personal henchmen to protect his rear guard. Despite being exhausted already, the elite warriors managed to rally the barbarian battalions to contain the rush of the Elves. They succeeded in halting the clan Avrony's momentum for a time.

But soon the voice of Dyoren the Lonely Seeker was heard in the heart of the battle. His war ode was chanted by all Llewenti fighters, who were in dire need of a second push. The sword of Dyoren, Rymsing, swirled through the air, steamrollering men. The frail, solitary bard weaved his legendary sword with all the fantastical power of an ancient clan warlord. All the clan Avrony's fighters who heard his chant above the uproar of the battlefield soon regained courage. Seeing that the Blade of the West was paving the way, they understood that their survival depended upon the success of this initial charge. They summoned all their remaining strength and returned to the battle.

The Elves of Mentollà had first seen the fire to the rear flank of the barbarian army as a distant, flickering glow. They heard the sentinels' cries without suspecting anything other than an isolated skirmish, probably provoked by the last-ditch attempts of the wild Elves. They expected the fortress to be overrun at any moment, given the heavy casualties they had suffered.

When the defenders were alerted to the clan Avrony's attack, their sentries, with a gleam of incredulity in their eyes, brought reports that more than five hundred Llewenti were attacking the human army. Many other Elvin horns were blowing from the west, from the depths of the forest, announcing the arrival of additional reinforcements. They were overwhelmed with relief. They knew that the westward access to the forest was of critical importance to the Dragon Warrior's army and its supply lines. Their evil leader could not afford to be cut off from his troops that were based beyond the path of the Hadon. His battalions had suffered greatly from their multiple assaults on Mentollà; they were not in a position to fight this new army. Ka-Bloozayar needed to retreat. The castaways, elated with renewed hope, suddenly expected him to withdraw his troops at any moment.

There was then a great noise in the courtyard, where all fighting had ceased since the attack of the Llewenti army. Roquendagor made one of his impulsive decisions that characterised his genius so well. The fire of anger burned within him; the knight was thinking no more of his own mental anguish or the regrets gnawing at his heart. He was now carried only by immeasurable rage.

"Guards of the Unicorn, will you follow me?" he yelled.

"WAAAARRRRR!" his remaining loyal followers replied unanimously.

"Then throw open the doors! We charge!" roared Roquendagor. "Sword!" the knight shouted as he stormed towards the gate.

Maetor had expected this request, and immediately handed Roquendagor a two-handed sword as he was procuring another for himself. Though there was nothing unique about the blade, its size was impressive and, when Roquendagor seized it with a single hand, his fighters could not help but look upon their commander with awe. This very heavy weapon, which weighed at least ten pounds, required a considerable amount of strength to wield at all. Though it lacked speed, its reach and the power of its blows made it a devastating weapon.

Roquendagor was followed by a full unit of his guards: heavily armed but without emblem or standard. The remains of the gates were burst open in a crash. They rushed out, screaming their war cry. The unit rushed onto the main path, which was littered with dozens of human corpses. The guards of the Unicorn formed a large, compact square. Roquendagor and Maetor, following a highly disciplined routine, positioned themselves with their great swords at each corner, so as to stop any potential enemy from breaking into the square. Curwë joined them, safely positioned at the centre of the formation.

The squad had no difficulty in driving the last of the barbarians off of the enclosure's edge. All men were now disbanding, focussed only on the absolute need to flee since the horns of their army began to sound the retreat.

Roquendagor beheaded a barbarian chieftain who was trying to gather his warriors to block the path. All fled at the sight of his wrath. Three hundred yards down the hill, the guards of the Unicorn regrouped at the edge of the forest. Curwë was singing the Lewin song of war as they formed a compact squad, protected from projectiles by a wall of long shields. Benefitting from the seaward-facing slope, they charged into the woods at full speed. Sweeping aside all that lay in their path, the unit soon found itself at the heart of the barbarian camp, where there was so much confusion that no one had taken care to organise the defence of the eastern front. The bloody melee began between Unicorn guards and barbarian warriors. Meanwhile the two Hawenti leaders regrouped.

"Move on, we move on!" urged Roquendagor.

"The barbarian command has turned its attention to the southern front, where the fight rages against the Llewenti units," replied Maetor.

"The Dragon Warrior must be surprised by this sudden reversal of fortune. He will not be able to withdraw and admit defeat. We must use this opportunity," insisted Roquendagor before continuing, with relish, "Perhaps he will be left behind, cut off from his guards."

The two saw that the waves of the clan Avrony's assaults were being contained by the efforts of Ka-Bloozayar best warriors. Elvin horns continued to resonate in the depths of the forest to the west, but no reinforcements had yet surged to support the efforts of the first attackers. They realised that less than five hundred Elves were trying to push back an army that numbered in the thousands who was about to abandon victory.

"Move on, we move on!" Roquendagor shouted again in anguish, as he realised that command of the Llewenti clans had set a trap for the enemy.

This assault would be decisive. Its success was crucial. He started to run, towards the heart of the barbarian camp, madly yelling,

"Roq Laorn! Roq Laorn! Form ranks! Now is the time to inflict the final blow! Form ranks! Roq Laorn! Roq Laorn!"

Roquendagor's intuition soon proved well-founded. A few yards away, barbarian horns sounded the retreat. It was as though a dam had broken, and that the long river of the barbarian army was streaming away, in a chaotic flow, towards an invisible waterfall.

Ka-Bloozayar, still escorted by a few faithful soldiers, approached his throne of command. Storming through the labyrinth of the camp's tents, his small retinue came across the Unicorn guards.

Roquendagor immediately recognized the dragon armour and red mask.

"Kill the Dragon Warrior! Kill the Dragon Warrior!" Roquendagor cried his heart full of hatred. Raising his sword with both hands, he rushed forwards, followed by his guards.

Two barbarians attempted to intervene and were quickly struck down. Their sacrifice gave Ka-Bloozayar just enough time to rid himself of his cumbersome cloak and draw his sword out of his scabbard.
Roquendagor was already upon him.

The barbarian leader managed to counter a flood of heavy, murderous blows that Roquendagor inflicted on him. The last stroke of the frenzy was so powerful that it knocked his long shield out of his hands, landing far away from him. Ka-Bloozayar was now isolated from the last of his defenders, who could no longer be of any help to him, struggling as they were under the might of Maetor and the Unicorn guards.

Ka-Bloozayar found it difficult to breathe. Desperate, the Dragon Warrior lashed out at Roquendagor with all the fury of a wild beast. The blows of his sword, more incisive and faster than his opponent's, found their mark several times. His Dragon-skin armour protected him just as well as the full Elvin plate of his opponent, but it also allowed him to move around with agility. He could have fled. But, unexpectedly, a barbarian arrow flew into the back of Roquendagor, piercing a gap between the layers of his plate mail. It caused a severe wound. The tall Elf screamed out in pain and stumbled forward. The barbarian archer did not get the chance to display his expertise again: one of Curwë's crossbow bolts had pierced his temple, cracking his skull.

Ka-Bloozayar hesitated for a split second, and then ran towards the knight in the hope of striking a fatal blow.

At this point, Maetor intervened. Throwing his sword at his previous opponent's face, he rushed to block the barbarian chief's attack. They collided as the chief's sword was in the air, and Maetor, who had escaped his enemy's blade, fell to the ground, losing several parts of his plate mail armour. Now unarmed, he quickly rolled to one side to seize a large shield that had been abandoned on the battlefield. Raising it above his head, Maetor parried the first assault from Ka-Bloozayar. Other formidable blows were successfully repelled, and the commander of the Unicorn guards started to regain ground. An expert handler of the Hawenti shield, he used its sharp edges to attack. The shield's design made it a weapon that could pierce the enemy as surely as any blade.

Faced with such fury, Ka-Bloozayar began to retreat. But the Dragon Warrior was a deadly fighter, and he finally saw an opening in his opponent's defences. He swung at the High Elf, using all his strength, in one powerful blow. His blade slashed between the plates of Maetor's armour, cutting through chain mail and tearing through flesh. Maetor's attacks ceased as blood spurted from his torso. The commander of the Unicorn Guard retreated, leaning on a tree trunk, desperate for support.

Meanwhile, Roquendagor had managed to recover. He straightened to his full height. The pain he endured seemed only to increase his strength. He mercilessly charged at the barbarian chief. The first strokes were parried with great difficulty. Those that followed broke the sword of Ka-Bloozayar. The final blow severed his leg at the thigh, bringing him to the ground. Roquendagor cut the straps of the barbarian chief's mask and pulled it off. Victorious, he brandished his trophy above Ka-Bloozayar, whose eyes were glowing with terror. Roquendagor uttered a muffled roar and raised his two-handed sword. He brought the long blade down.
The barbarian chief was beheaded.

Roquendagor threw his sword away. Though the air was still thick with deadly flying arrows, the tall knight, impervious to the battle that raged all around him, screamed out, possessed by fury, his hands held up towards the sky.

"Is this all? Is this really all I must face?"

Roquendagor slowly turned back and retraced his path towards the fortress. He did not take any further interest in the fight; he was simply walking away from the battlefield, an arrow still sticking out of his back.
The severely wounded Maetor noticed his lord's movement. Summoning the last of his strength, he ordered his troops to retreat.

"Let us withdraw," he bellowed. "We take our dead and our wounded with us!"
"Form ranks! Form ranks!"
"Protect our Lord!"

Only a dozen Unicorn guards were still able-bodied; though they were completely exhausted, they helped their many wounded, and carried their dead back to the fortress. They adopted a defensive line, circling around their lord. Slowly, they walked backwards, climbing the slope back to the gate.

None noticed a lone Elf, soaking wet, emerge from the water and stumble up onto the beach, for their view of the creek was obstructed by the remnants of the barbarians' siege engine.
It was an Irawenti, haggard and exhausted, almost naked, rising from the emerald waters of Mentollà's creek like a spirit from the ocean depths.

Meanwhile, still standing tall and upright, with his purple helm now underneath his arm, the fiery Maetor coordinated the retreat of his unit, protecting his lord and liege. Without a single complaint, nor any display of pain, he managed to lead his surviving fighters back to the protection of Mentollà's walls. Maetor tried to give one final instruction, but this proved to be one effort too many.

"Clo...Cl...C...the gates!"

Maetor fell, heavily, face-first onto the ground. The nearest guard rushed to assist him. But, after a few moments, he announced, incredulous.

"My Lord, our commander is dead. Maetor is dead."

*

Curwë was not among those who had safely returned to Mentollà. In the midst of all the hazardous fighting in the woods, he had been pushed beyond the main battlefield and isolated from the Unicorn guards. Indeed, he was not even aware that his companions were withdrawing behind the fortress walls. As he tried to find them, a dramatic scene caught his attention for a moment.

Deep in the woods, beyond the reach of his crossbow, he could see a small number of Llewenti fighters being cornered by a group of barbarian warriors, who were commanded by shamans of the Cult of the Dragons. A magnificent voice sang out above the cries of the melee, and a vivid shining glaive was engaged in a deadly dance, barely avoiding inevitable defeat. The vision did not last, the gleaming blade fell, and the song ceased amid war cries.

Struck by what he witnessed, Curwë progressed into the woods as other Llewenti units reached the bloody battlefield. The army of Llymar were organised haphazardly, each group followed its captain, and each of them determined his own course of action separately from his warlord. Such confusion led to overlapping lines of battle, with individual fighters advancing and withdrawing like leaves in a storm. Whenever the barbarians turned to face the Elves' charge, the Llewenti would slip away into the trees, circling back around their foes to attack them from a different side. Many men had been slaughtered, and their battalions variously moved forwards and backwards as their running battle within the woods continued. It was chaos.

Drawn deeper into the enemy's camp by his vision, Curwë remained concealed from his enemies' view. The battle had moved further west when he jumped out of a trench and walked toward the barbarian chief's tent. It was no longer being guarded.
He rushed inside.
A long table was littered with bottles and glasses. At the end of the table, a man was bending down, his head bowed. He was busy stuffing a bag full of precious items. But the noise of Curwë's entrance made him stand up straight and turn around. He stared at the intruder with hatred. The man had a strange head: big, tanned and hairy, like that of a bear. His broad face seemed etched in sin.

When he saw the newcomer, he began to scream. His heavy long sword sprang from its scabbard. But Curwë, who was much faster, jumped on him and seized hold of his arms. Both of them rolled under the table. Beast-like Curwë grabbed the throat of his prey and maintained his hold until the man's final spasms had ceased. The fight ended in one last agonizing scream.

Curwë rose. He seized the barbarian's bag and put away his own bloodied sword. But a glistening object deep within the bag caught his eye. The bard removed other precious objects and discovered a beautiful broad sword, the same one he had glimpsed through the woods, adorned with emeralds. Paralyzed by the purity of the shining blade, for some time his gaze lingered on the extraordinary masterpiece in his hands, which he knew must have remained unchanged over the course of many years.

"Cil, Cim, Cir!" he exclaimed aloud, with an incredulity more typical of Nelwiri. "I have never beheld such a weapon. It's a sword like those mentioned in the book Vyrka gave to me. A deity must have forged it."

He remained there for a long while, hypnotized by the blade's power.

But the cries and clattering of the combat outside brought him back to reality. Seized again by the rage of battle, he rushed outside in search of his companions, with new sword in hand. But the fight had moved away, and Curwë was now alone. Aware of the danger that this isolation posed, he quickly slipped back into a trench and retraced his steps, seeking to flee the combat zone. He was now desperate to return to Mentollà and protect his precious plunder.

Despite his agility and caution, his movements did not escape the notice of everyone. A shaman of the Cult of Dragons, who was leading a battalion of barbarians back to battle, noticed him running in the same direction as them. The cold grey eyes of this barbarian cleric and the way that he harangued his warriors frightened Curwë. The man was small and stocky with a powerful chest. He pushed his way through the foliage. Dressed in coarse wool, he wore a piece of scarlet cloth through his black curly hair. He wielded a double-edged axe, and his brown arms were stained with blood, like two large branches of gnarled oak. His tanned face was wild, proud and sullen, and split by a long white scar from his chin to his temple. In an instant, the shaman and his retainers were upon Curwë, surrounding him.

"Help! Help!" the bard yelled frantically, trying to attract the attention of the Llewenti fighters who he knew must have been nearby.

The fight began. Like wild game cornered by a pack of hounds, Curwë was facing six opponents.

"I cannot die like this! This destiny is not worthy of me!" laughed the bard.

Seized by a surge of panic, he unleashed a formidable tempest of blows. His movements were quick, and his strikes came fast. The magical blade in his hand was so light that he wielded it like a mere dagger. Swinging at his enemies, he attacked them one by one with a speed and skill they hardly expected from one in such a desperate situation. Two opponents quickly fell; a third was dangerously wounded, his eye incurably split. A kind of frenzy obscured Curwë's mind. He jumped, swirled and lashed out, in a wild uncontrollable dance. A fourth opponent fell, but still more enemies surrounded him. Blinded by his wrath, Curwë plunged his sword into the heart of the wounded man. Blood spurted forth from the dead body.

But all of a sudden, without warning, a hammer struck Curwë on the back of his neck. Severely wounded, he fell to the ground. The barbarian shaman came closer, lit a torch and drank a potion. He looked around, feeling at ease as the glade was still controlled by a dozen of his warriors. All of a sudden, he spat out the red liquid, which immediately ignited into long, vicious flames. Trying to regain control of his senses, Curwë was finding it difficult to stand. He did not see what was coming. The evil cleric, like a terrifying red dragon, unleashed a powerful jet of fire.
The bard was set alight as quickly as a primed torch. His cloak ignited and became an inferno. His body fell and convulsed terribly before it finally lay still.

Above the men's cruel cries of victory, a loud whistle resounded through the glade.
A long arrow pierced the shaman's throat, and blood spurted from it. A second deadly missile hit his head, bursting his right eye. The evil cleric fell, dying in horrible pain.

The silhouette of a tall dark Elf emerged from the thick bushes. It was Gelros. The Morawenti scout had a tremendous rate of fire with his 'Cruel Bow'. Standing on the edge of the glade, he unleashed an unceasing and unerring stream of black-shafted arrows. Four barbarians were cut down. By the time Gelros had emptied his quiver, there were no more men to be seen in the glade. All the survivors had fled.

Like a silent sentinel, the master of concealment had remained unnoticed for several days in the heart of the barbarian camp, waiting for the moment to murder the enemy's commander. Knowing that the end was near, he had sprung into action when he heard Curwë's calls for help.

Gelros rushed towards the corpse of his companion, which was still burning, face-down. Already anticipating the horror that he was about to witness, he overturned the body. To his astonishment, Curwë's face was unscathed, as was the rest of his body. The bard still held his new sword in both hands, like a priest in solemn prayer to the gods. The fire that had fully consumed his cloak had not burned him at all. Gelros felt Curwë's heart beating and realised that his companion was still alive, albeit shocked and terribly wounded.

Birds of prey circled above the surrounding trees. Fighters from the clan Avrony marched past the two Elves in the glade. The Llewenti seemed to be regrouping in small units. Llymar's horns blasted out a poignant call. There was some sad event to which all Llewenti were rushing, eager to perform their duty. No Elf stopped as they passed through the glade, ignoring Gelros, who remained alone in his attempts to save Curwë.

Gelros set about carrying his wounded companion back to Mentollà, when the most unlikely newcomer suddenly stepped out from the trees. Such was his surprise that he remained stock still.
It was Nelwiri. Half-naked and soaking wet, the Irawenti sailor was armed with a barbarian axe and a small wooden shield, bearing the arms of the green peacock. Seeing Gelros struggling, Nelwiri threw down his equipment and immediately came to his aid.

"Oh, Gelros! You will never imagine what has happened to me. You will never..." he started, as he helped to move Curwë into the cloak they would use as a makeshift stretch.

"I know," Gelros replied sharply. It was clear he would not hear a word of Nelwiri's tale.

⋆⋆

14th day, Mentollà

The following day, the war ships from Penlla sailed into the creek of Mentollà at dawn. News of the victory had been sent, and the fleet had rallied the rest of the army to bring them support and food supplies. The sailors disembarked from their swanships as the keel brushed against the creek's shore. They progressed through the churning foam, bows at the ready.

The captain of the fleet, Leyen dyl Llyvary, was enthusiastically carrying out his duties, and even a certain air of self-satisfaction. Determined to prevent the barbarian raiders from returning to Mentollà, the warlord of Penlla oversaw violent, punitive work on the creek's shores. His sailors were obliterating the entire barbarian settlement, killing the helpless and the wounded, finishing off all those who could not flee. As the battle continued deep into the Sognen Tausy woods, the Penlla units culled those that tried to flee with volleys of arrows and shots of bolts. Any barbarian who had survived the clan Avrony's charge the day before now had to battle the grim-faced sailors in their scattered ranks, with their short swords lowered. The onslaught continued and, as the defeated men fled, their settlement was razed to the ground.

In complete disorder, the battalions of men retreated to the north and to the west, towards what they thought was their escape route: the path of the Hadon. They were unaware of the threatening presence of Mynar dyl and his army. This mass of men, still several thousand strong, much bigger in size than its aggressors, had only one thing in mind: to return to Kaar Corkel and to the protection of its high walls. The human army had failed, they had been defeated, and, in the absence of its tyrannous chief, its very unity was at stake, for each tribe now cared only for its own survival. The initial doubt that had filled their minds after multiple failed assaults on Mentollà had now become fear, and this fear was close to panic. Escape was now their only objective. But the fatal trap was set. Victory belonged to the Elves.

★

Meanwhile, within the fortress compound, a very different spectacle was underway. The courtyard of Mentollà had become a camp for the wounded and the mutilated, the ill-fated. Many Elves had died during the battle for the control of the fortress, but many more were still grievously wounded. Irawenti of the Filweni, Hawenti of the Unicorn Guard and Llewenti of Llymar clans had all found refuge within the compound, seeking assistance and care from priests and healers. Neither discussion between leaders nor diplomacy between envoys had been necessary to organise this spontaneous act of solidarity. After their collective trauma, all the Elves felt deeply wounded, in their flesh and in their souls, and it was natural for them to help each other and share whatever they had left.

Arwela was in the midst of the dreadful scene, incessantly coming and going, bringing assistance and providing comfort. Her eyes were streaming, the tears rolling down her cheeks. Her body was shaking, unable to contain her pain. She was not ashamed, for the Irawenti did not hide their emotions but she was on the brink of exhaustion after several days without rest. Nevertheless, her frail silhouette continued to roam the courtyard, running from one building to the next. Hundreds of Elves suffered around her. She tended to all, regardless of their origin or allegiance.

As she headed towards the keep's steps, her attention was caught by a peculiar character. That Elf was of Llewenti origin, and from the cut of his light armour and his fine cloth, she knew immediately that he was of noble blood. Walking with the assistance of a crutch, he progressed slowly, like a spectre among the living. His gaze was frightening and incommensurably pained. Ignoring her suspicions, the seer of the Filweni approached him and addressed him with benignity.

"What is your name, noble Elf? How can I help you?"

The Llewenti looked at her strangely but was unable to reply. Arwela could see that his grievance was not caused by his wounds. This Elf had been struck by an awful loss.

"Come with me. You need immediate assistance. I will take you to my brother... he will know what to do," she decided.

"This loss will have consequences, unimaginable consequences..." the Elf muttered, and Arwela could see his grief was making him mad, penetrating his mind like poison flooding through his veins.

Their tentative conversation was interrupted by a group of fighters surrounding a stretcher. They had just entered the courtyard and looked around at the desolation that they found with sadness. They carried Gal dyl Avrony back from the battlefield. The Protector of the Forest's legs had been wounded during a particularly bloody assault upon fleeing barbarians. Many of the Llewenti who were still able to walk gathered around their leader as he was brought into the halls of the keep. All wanted to pay homage to his bravery and honour him for their historic victory.

But there were also voices of discord because, in truth, Gal dyl had only escaped death at the cost of many other Elvin lives. Isolated deep within the enemy ranks, his rage had led many of his fighters to a frightful end. Gal dyl had behaved bravely, his legendary spear had caused terror among his opponents, but when his arm had become weak and his breath short, he had found himself in great danger, besieged by many barbarians, eager for revenge. The heroic intervention of his guards had saved him. More than one had fallen to save his life.

Entering the halls, Arwela asked a wounded archer where she might find Feïwal. But the clan Llyvary fighter did not completely understand her question and instead addressed the wounded Elf that she was supporting.

"Even you, the Lonely Seeker, fell in battle. I was there. I was one of those who pulled you from the conflict. We saved you from the clutches of the barbarians..."

But Dyoren could not even find the strength to thank the brave Elf. The Lonely Seeker had failed to keep his oath. He had lost his legendary blade during the fight; it had been taken by the enemy. For him, no Elvin victory could compensate for that loss.

Arwela, still holding Dyoren's arm, continued to climb the tower's steps until she reached the room that had been dedicated to the most seriously wounded. They were told that Feïwal was at the bedside of one of his companions, who had been miraculously saved from fire.

A beautiful Irawenti lady, named Fendrya, showed them to Feïwal. The guide of the clan Filweni was tending the wounds of his friend, Curwë, worry set into his face.

Dyoren froze in front of the wounded Elf who rested on a makeshift bed. The Lonely Seeker's gaze turned from the sword that Curwë still held to his exceptionally glowing eyes. Dyoren muttered to himself several times, as if experiencing a revelation.

"You have green eyes."

Curwë, who was struggling between life and death, could not find the strength to reply, but he did notice that the noble Llewenti fighter was crying. With a simple look, he indicated that Dyoren could come closer.
To the surprise of the two Filweni, the Lonely Seeker took in his hand the fabled sword and caressed its shining blade. His lips trembled into a smile of relief and new-found faith.

"It is like in the manuscript given to me by Vyrka," Curwë muttered, finding new strength. "One of the Nargrond blades..." He pointed with his finger towards the end of the bed. The effort was too great, and the bard fainted.

Dyoren looked to where an old book was lying open. It included a collection of poems. The poetry celebrated the ancient deeds of the Elves from Nargrond valley. The book's binding was threadbare, but its illustrious cover indicated its value and origins.

Looking at Curwë, who now lay still, Dyoren expressed his immense gratitude, his voice trembling with emotion.

"You have brought Rymsing back to me.

May you be blessed and protected by the deities of the Islands, for it is a blade of great worth, so named because it was made of the iron that fell with the Star.

There are very few swords on the archipelago like it. It is the most precious relic that we possess."

★★

EPILOGUE

"It is time, my Lord. The banners of the House of Dol Etrond have been spotted south of the Hadon. Lord Curubor and his knights are approaching," Aplor advised.

"We certainly cannot let Lord Curubor wait. He deserves better," Camatael replied in typically laconic fashion.

The young lord of the House of Dol Lewin remained very still and calm, breathing in deeply the fresh air coming from the mountains. Their snowy peaks were melting away in the morning mist. He was enjoying this moment. The landscape that surrounded him was magnificent. He was standing at the centre of the remains of what had once been a temple to Eïwal Lon. Located on the top of a steep hill, these ruins dedicated to the deity of knowledge and wisdom looked out over a vast, arid region west of the Arob Tiude. The place was peaceful and had a meditative effect.

Around Camatael, three units of Elvin fighters, their purple shields emblazoned with racing unicorns had gathered to pray and make offerings. All came from Llymvranone, and all had demonstrated extraordinary devotion during the celebration that had been overseen by the Dol Lewin lord.

"Eïwal Lon is proud of us, Aplor. We have done well," Camatael acknowledged simply.

"My Lord, all credit goes to you. You proved your worth at the battle of Kaar Corkel. Your triumph was complete; the capture of that port will be remembered. There are many who owe a lot to you; the Druids' circles and even the people they will rule. You have freed them from the grip of the Cult of the Three Dragons. You gave them their freedom, along with a chance to build a peaceful future for the province of Kaar Corkel," Aplor lauded.

Content, Camatael concluded, "And that they will build. We have renounced the favour of King Norelin and chosen the path of exile. But this sacrifice is small compared to the glory of following Eïwal Lon's teachings."

Turning to his followers, Camatael examined them with pride and fondness. For the first time in his life, his personal guards were serving him freely, with infallible devotion and loyalty because of who he was and what he had achieved. Only very few royal soldiers volunteered to follow him once they understood he had led them into battle without King Norelin's leave. But those Elves around him had a pure heart, and this was a comforting thought. They had willingly chosen to embrace the teachings of Eïwal Lon and abandon their past existence without fear.

Camatael took the gold coin from his pocket. He looked at its engraving one last time: a white war unicorn, the unicorn from Essawylor. For a moment he rubbed it between his fingers, weighing it in his hand, feeling its edges and appreciating its softness. Eventually, he threw it down onto the surface of the ancient temple's altar, like dice in a childish game. Satisfied, Camatael turned towards his troops.

"Follow me, servants of Eïwal Lon! Unfurl the banner of the House of Dol Lewin! The White Unicorn rides east. It rides towards the dawn."

ANNEXES

Elvin nations

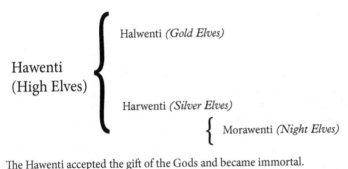

Hawenti
(High Elves)

Halwenti *(Gold Elves)*

Harwenti *(Silver Elves)*

Morawenti *(Night Elves)*

The Hawenti accepted the gift of the Gods and became immortal.

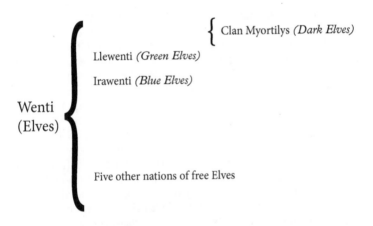

Wenti
(Elves)

Clan Myortilys *(Dark Elves)*

Llewenti *(Green Elves)*

Irawenti *(Blue Elves)*

Five other nations of free Elves

The Wenti refused the gift of the Gods and remained free and mortal.

The Llewenti

One of the seven nations of 'free' Elves, they are called 'Llewenti' in their language, 'Llew' meaning 'Green' and 'Wenti' meaning 'Elves'. They were so named, because their first Patriarch's attire was green. They are counted among the nations of Elves who refused the gift of immortality offered by the Gods. Llewenti enjoy much longer life than Men, living for five to six centuries depending on their bloodline. Their race is similar in appearance to humans, but they are fairer and wiser, with greater spiritual powers, keener senses, and a deeper empathy with nature. They are for the most part a simple, peaceful, and reclusive people, famous for their singing skills. With sharper senses, they are highly skilled at crafts especially when using natural resources. The Green Elves are wise in the ways of the forest and the natural world.

The Irawenti

One of the seven nations of the 'free' Elves, they are called 'Irawenti' in the language of the Llewenti, 'Ira' meaning 'Blue' and 'Wenti' meaning 'Elves'. They were so named, because their first Guide's eyes had the colour of the tropical seas and azure reflections emanated from his black hair. They are counted among the nations of Elves who refused the gift of immortality offered by the Gods. Irawenti enjoy much longer life than men, living for four to five centuries depending on their bloodline. Their race is similar in appearance to the Green Elves but darker and wilder, with greater physical powers and a closer empathy with water. They are for the most part a free, joyful and adventurous people, famous for their navigation skills.
Having sharper connection with rivers and oceans, they are at their strongest and most knowledgeable when aboard their ships. The Blue Elves are wise in the ways of the sea.

The Hawenti

The High Elves are called 'Hawenti' in the language of the Llewenti, as opposed to the 'Wenti' who identify as 'free' Elves. The Hawenti accepted the gift of immortality offered by the Gods. They are immortal in the sense that they are not vulnerable to disease or the effects of old age although they can be killed in battle. They are divided into two main nations: The Gold Elves (the most prominent) and the Silver Elves. The Hawenti have a greater depth of knowledge than other Elvin nations, due to their natural inclination for learning as well as their extreme age. Their power and wisdom know no comparison and within their eyes the fire of eternity can be seen. This kindred of the Elves were ever distinguished both by their knowledge of things and by their desire to know more.

The Morawenti

The Night Elves are called 'Morawenti' in the language of the Llewenti. The Morawenti are a subdivision of the Silver Elves, the second of the Hawenti nations. They are therefore counted among the High Elves as they accepted the gift of immortality offered by the Gods. Morawenti are immortal in the sense that they are not vulnerable to disease or the effects of old age although they too can be killed in battle. Morawenti tend to be thinner and taller in size than other Elves. Their very pale skin, almost livid, characterises them while their gaze is deep and mysterious. They all have dark hair while their eye colour varies between grey and black. They favour wearing dark coloured tunics with grey or green shades and robes of fine linens, cotton or silk.

MAIN ELF FACTIONS AND CHARACTERS

KINGDOM OF ESSAWYLOR

The Royal House of Dor Tircanil
The Hawenti ruling House of the Kingdom of Five Rivers in Essawylor

• **Aranaele Dor Tircanil**: Queen of Essawylor

The Clan of Filweni
One of the twenty-nine Irawenti clans of the Kingdom of Essawylor

• **Feïwal dyn Filweni**: Guide of the clan of Filweni, Captain of the Alwïryan
• **Nelwiri dyn Filweni**: Pilot of the Alwïryan
• **Luwir dyn Filweni**: Commander of the clan of Filweni, Oars master onboard the Alwïryan
• **Arwela dyn Filweni**: Seer of the clan of Filweni

The House of Dol Lewin – Elder branch
One of the five Hawenti Houses of the Kingdom of Five Rivers, banished from Essawylor by the Queen

• **Roquen Dol Lewin**: Lord of the House of Dol Lewin elder branch
• **Curwë**: Herald of the House of Dol Lewin
• **Aewöl**: Counsellor of the House of Dol Lewin
• **Gelros**: Hunt Master of the House of Dol Lewin

KINGDOM OF GWARYSTAN

The Royal House of Dor Ilorm
The Hawenti ruling House of the Kingdom of Gwarystan, principal realm in the Llewenti Islands

• **Norelin Dor Ilorm**: King of Gwarystan

House of Dol Lewin- Second branch
One of the twelve Hawenti Houses of the Kingdom of Gwarystan, originating from Mentolewin

• **Camatael Dol Lewin**: Lord of the House of Dol Lewin, Envoy of the King in Nyn Llyvary

The Guild of Sana
Secret Guild in the Llewenti Islands

• **Saeröl Dir Sana**: Master of the Guild of Sana

FOREST OF LLYMAR

The clan Llyvary
Llewenti clan, principal and historical members of the Council of Llymar Forest

- **Lyrine dyl Llyvary, 'the Lady of Llafal':** Elder Matriarch of the clan Llyvary
- **Nyriele dyl Llyvary, 'Llyoriane's Heir':** Matriarch, High Priestess of Eïwele Llyi in Llafal
- **Tyar dyl Llyvary, 'the Old Bird':** Warlord of Llafal

The clan Ernaly
Llewenti clan or iginating from Nyn Ernaly, members of the Council of Llymar Forest

- **Mynar dyl Ernaly, 'the Fair':** Warlord of Tios Halabron
- **Voryn dyl Ernaly, 'the Ugly':** Captain of Tios Halabron

- **Lore, 'the Daughter of the Islands':** Envoy of Eïwele Llya
- **Dyoren, 'the Lonely Seeker':** Knight of the Secret Vale

The clan Avrony
Llewenti clan originating from Nyn Avrony, members of the Council of Llymar Forest

- **Gal dyl Avrony:** Warlord of clan Avrony

House of Dol Etrond
Rebel Hawenti House originating from Ystanetrond, members of the Council of Llymar Forest

- **Curubor Dol Etrond, 'the Blue Mage':** Guardian of Tios Lluin
- **Loriele Dol Etrond:** Lady at the court in Gwarystan

Anroch
Desert

Essawylor

Nen

Austral Ocean

Atolls Fadaluÿ

Sea of Cyclones

Llewenti
Islands

Sea of Isyl

ANTIPODES

200 Leagues

Sea of Cyclones

Nyn Llyvary

Nyn Llorely

Nyn Ernaly

Sea
of
Llyoriane

Gwarystan

Nyn Avrony

Gwa Nyn

Sea of Isyl

Nyn Llyandy

LLEWENTI ISLANDS

50 Leagues

Austral Ocean

Isle
of Pyenty

Peninsula
of Gloren

Bay of Penlla

Bay
of
Gloren
• Mentollà

• Llafal
Halwyfal

Penlla •

Forest of Llymar

Kaar
Corkel

• Tios
Halabron

• Tios
Lluin

Sian Llewa

A r o b

Tios Lleny •

Sian Kanny

• Tios
Vyon

• Tios
Gla

• Tios
Vyar

Sea of Llyoriane

Llymvranone

• Llavrym

NYN LLYVARY

20 Leagues

MENTOLLÀ

Strait of Tiude

Peninsula of Gloren

Pass of
the Hadon

Bay of Gloren

Sognen Tausy

 Mentollà

Nassy
Gnanella

Sian Tiude

A rob Tiude

A rob

Kaar
Corkel

40 Yards

4 Leagues

GENEALOGY HAWENTI
ROYAL BLOODLINES

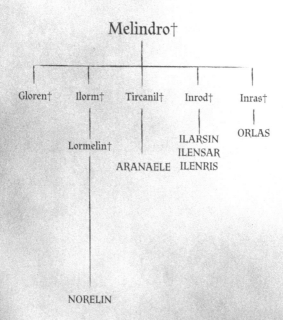

1st Age

0 —

2nd Age

2700 —

Melindro†

Gloren†   Ilorm†   Tircanil†   Inrod†   Inras†

Lormelin†

ILARSIN   ORLAS
ILENSAR
ARANAELE   ILENRIS

NORELIN

† Dead

GENEALOGY HAWENTI
DOL NOBLE HOUSES

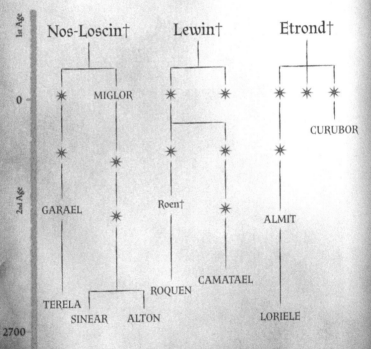

1st Age	Nos-Loscin†	Lewin†	Etrond†

† Dead
✳ Father

GENEALOGY
LLEWENTI CLANS

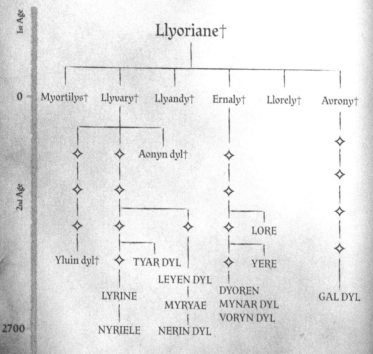

GENEALOGY IRAWENTI
FILWENI CLAN

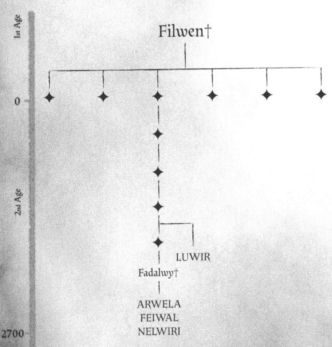

Filwen†

LUWIR

Fadalwy†

ARWELA
FEIWAL
NELWIRI

1st Age

0

2nd Age

2700

† Dead
◆ Father

CPSIA information can be obtained
at www.ICGtesting.com
Printed in the USA
FSHW010505140819
61033FS